VANISHED IN VALLARTA

Also by Kimila Kay

MEXICO MAYHEM SERIES

Peril in Paradise (2019)

Malice in Mazatlán (2022)

STONEYBROOK MYSTERIES

Redneck Ranch (2023)

Five Golden Rings (2023)

ANTHOLOGIES

"Whispering Willows" Whispers (2023)

"Happy Birthday" Harbinger (2023)

"Table Talk" Guests (2022)

"Hates Kids" A Cup of Comfort for Mothers (2010)

"Burying Bea" A Cup of Comfort for the Grieving Heart (2010)

"The Apology" A Cup of Comfort for Single Mothers (2008)

ADVANCED REVIEWS

The beautiful backdrop of Mexico along with suspense, drama, and a little bit of spice, the third installment in the **Mexico Mayhem** series will keep you riveted. **Kimila Kay** does a wonderful job of weaving a story that is interesting and makes you want to keep coming back for more. Loved the complexity of the characters and the storyline in **Vanished in Vallarta**. *~ Stacy Robinson*

Kimila Kay continues to write a captivating series and **Vanished in Vallarta** doesn't disappoint! Not only to you feel as if you're actually in Puerto Vallarta, but her characters also draw you in as well. The anticipation of knowing who Jade might fall in love with created a spicy thread and had me vacillating between a handsome *Federale* and a sensual Lieutenant. *~ Sharon North*

VANISHED IN VALLARTA

MÉXICO MAYHEM – BOOK THREE

KIMILA KAY

www.KimilaKay.com
author@kimilakay.com

Windtree Press
http://windtreepress.com
info@windtreepress.com

Cover Art by *James McCracken*
The cover picture is a photo the author took while on vacation in Puerto Vallarta of a pirate ship sailing beautiful Banderas Bay at sunset. The ship and bay also have small roles in the novel!

Vanished in Vallarta - México Mayhem, Book 3
Published in the United States of America – History:
ISBN 978-1-962065-18-4
1st Release: 11/5/2023

DEDICATION

To the women in my life! Whether you're an aunt, sister, daughter-in-law, adopted daughter, niece, or girlfriend—I hope you see a trait I may have borrowed from you in the fabulous female characters in **Vanished in Vallarta**.

While, I have a vivid imagination, infusing my characters with characteristics from the people I love helps to bring the fictional person to life.

Consider yourselves all toasted with a shot of Hornitos!!!

This beautiful rendering is compliments of my talented granddaughter, Sloan E. Henson. I wish you could see the vivid greens she used for the palm fronds and island, or the warm brown of the tree's trunk, and finally the bright blue hues for the ocean and message. Her simple "Thank You" encompasses how I feel about my readers whom I'm grateful to for taking the leap and reading my third novel. Enjoy!!!

VANISHED IN VALLARTA

PROLOGUE

The ocean had claimed its prize. The body creating a morbid marionette, turning and spinning as it sank farther into the dark depths of the sea. A few inquisitive fish swam close enough to surmise the form was not a threat to them before continuing their aquatic journey.

The salty water began an Ekman spiral, the powerful swirling water intent on eradicating any signs of a human being. But this specimen became gassy before the ocean could wreak its havoc, and it slowly ascended to the surface. Various members of the underwater society fed upon the corpse along the way before the floating smorgasbord was claimed by a crocodile. The beast attacked swiftly and viciously, conquering his underwater battlefield. After all, the briny seawater of Banderas Bay belonged to these ferocious reptiles. They came in hordes to snag such a prize, fighting other amphibious predators, and members of their own species. The victor would drag the sustenance to a den for future dining.

Such would be the fate of this once-vital person: death by drowning before being deposited in a ravenous crocodile's larder. The immense male trapped his reward in powerful jaws, swimming his spoils across the top of the aqua water toward his lair.

Then a surprise spring storm rolled in on strong, howling April winds, whipping the usually calm waters of the bay into turmoil. The crocodile adjusted his bite, battling the strong waves.

But the massive reptile was no match for the undulating waters of Banderas Bay. To survive, the crocodile let go of his prey and headed for the beach.

CHAPTER ONE

She slept as if she had no worries. As if she had no fear. As if she hadn't been abducted. For a moment, Novio wondered if he'd given her too much valium.

Tracing the curve of her luscious lips with his eyes, he imagined they would taste as sweet as fresh mango. He let his gaze caress her breasts, the silver sequin top she wore rising and falling with each breath. He thought about how soft her skin would feel beneath his hands. His eyes followed the length of the turquoise mini skirt, and he sucked in air at the thought of exploring her barely covered *V*.

Ezmé stirred and called out for her sister, Jade, and shame from his impure thoughts burned Novio's cheeks. Despite his platonic friendship with Ezmé, he couldn't control his intense desire for her. Or the fact he'd fallen in love with her over the past few months. And he thought she had feelings for him too. Novio believed Ezmé, like him, was a virgin; and he dreamed of how beautiful their first time together would be.

He hadn't restrained Ezmé; and when her eyes fluttered, he crossed to the bed. She flailed her arms as if she was fighting someone. Her floundering sent a floral aroma flowing through the air. Hoping she wouldn't be frightened and try to flee, Novio had prepared a speech. He would explain to her his boss wanted Novio to bring her to his boss's compound. But he would tell Ezmé that he wanted her to run away with him. Novio wouldn't tell her that escaping Raptor's reach would be difficult.

Novio had guessed Raptor was in love with Ezmé, or at least thought he was. But regardless of his boss's attempts to change, Novio still saw Raptor as a human trafficker and worried what he might do to Ezmé. Raptor had encountered Ezmé at a café and without knowing his true identity, she'd flirted with him.

His boss didn't know Novio was in love with Ezmé too, and he prayed Raptor would lose interest in her. Novio had pointed out her flaws, even though he felt she had none, but Raptor dismissed Novio's comments, saying, "One man's perceived imperfections are another man's fantasy. Bring her to me and I will decide."

The unfortunate incident that led him to work for the human trafficker happened before Raptor had killed their old boss and taken over the operation. But Novio still blamed Raptor for his fate. Novio glanced at Ezmé as the memory seeped into his mind.

It was a beautiful day in Puerto Vallarta and Novio had taken his eighteen-year-old sister, Valéria, on a rare outing without their protective parents. They'd enjoyed a day of shopping, then dinner. It was early enough in the evening, so he thought their parents wouldn't disapprove if they had a drink at his favorite club, *Bebe y sé Feliz*. At twenty-one, Novio was a regular at the hip bar and anxious to show his little sister how popular he was with all the *chicas*.

They had ordered a second round of drinks—*Modelo* for him, a Paloma for Valéria—when they were joined by an *hombre* Novio didn't know. Valéria laughed and flirted with the slick Hispanic, probably not much older than Novio, as he told an elaborate tale. Something about the man bothered Novio, but when the DJ played a popular song, he forgot his concerns and asked a pretty girl to dance.

When he returned to the table, Valéria and the Mexican were gone. That day four years ago was the last time Novio remembered being happy.

CHAPTER TWO

Jade Mendoza leaned against the headrest. She and Sandrine had left Mazatlán in a whirlwind and her mind was still trying to put the puzzle pieces of the last few days together. Their attempt to arrest Sarita García had ended when García escaped with her *sicario*, Hector Ramos. Not even Jade telling the drug queen that she was her daughter kept her bio-mom from pointing a gun at her. And news of Ezmé's abduction had caused Jade to leave before she could resolve her relationship with Christopher.

Now all Jade wanted to do was close her eyes. But every time she did images of her little sister, Ezmé, being tortured by a faceless monster flooded her brain.

Sandrine offered to drive, and her aggressiveness made Jade cringe. Too tired, though, to drive and think at the same time, Jade was thankful Sandrine sat behind the wheel. They'd arrived last night at ten-thirty and had stayed with Juan Vega's pilot, Felipe, who had an apartment near the Puerto Vallarta airport. Jade and Sandrine had both slept briefly on the three-and-a-half-hour flight from Mazatlán, but sleep evaded Jade after they settled into Felipe's place.

This morning, after a breakfast of black coffee, they'd jumped into the bright yellow Kia Sol, compliments of Vega, and begun their hunt for Ezmé. It amazed Jade that the kindness of their friends Humberto Álvarez and Juan Vega reached across the miles from Mazatlán.

Sandrine cut into her thoughts. "Joy hasn't been able to find anyone who's talked to Ezmé since she went missing?"

"Not yet." Jade stared at the passing residential scenery: a sea of cream-colored stucco houses, dotted here and there with small *mercados*. She knew Joy Beck, her sister's modeling coach, felt responsible for Ezmé and was as worried as Jade.

"What's your plan?" Sandrine braked for stopping traffic.

"Start at the last place she was seen," Jade said. *"Pub de Nopal."*

When Sandrine swung wide of a taxi, Jade palmed the dash.

"In English, please." Sandrine said.

"Prickly Pear Pub."

"You think they're open this early?"

"I'm not interested in what's inside," Jade said. "I want to walk the perimeter and look for cameras."

"Got it." Sandrine nodded. "You don't think the police already checked?"

Shrugging, Jade glanced at Sandrine, who held up a finger. "Right, right." Sandrine nodded. "We need to see everything through our own investigative lens."

"That," Jade began, "and we don't know who we can trust."

"Me." Sandrine looked at Jade. "You can trust me."

A swell of tears burned Jade's eyes and she fingered them away.

"Has anyone told your folks your sister is missing?" Sandrine asked.

Jade couldn't control her emotions this time, and sobs shook her shoulders. Her crying fit stole her breath, and for a moment, she could only gasp. Sandrine angled into a curb and slammed the car into park. Jade turned her tear-stained face to her friend who was crying too. Jade and Sandrine had been partners on a drug investigation in Columbia a couple of years ago. When the assignment was over, they stayed in touch, strengthening their budding friendship.

After a few minutes, Sandrine handed Jade half of a napkin she found in the center console. "It looks clean." She blew her nose.

"Let's go." Jade dried her face. "I told Joy we'd be at her hotel by noon."

"Yep." Sandrine pulled into traffic behind a city bus.

"I haven't called my parents yet." Jade gazed out her window at the calm waters of Banderas Bay. How was she going to tell her mom that Ezmé had been missing for almost forty-eight hours? Jade knew the first twenty-four hours were crucial in the investigative process. She also knew each passing hour Ezmé was missing didn't bode well for her baby sister.

After whipping a U-turn, Sandrine slipped into a parking spot on the street in front of the *Pub de Nopal*. "Want to walk together or separate?"

"Together." Jade stepped from the Kia and turned in a circle as Sandrine joined her on the sidewalk.

"Bloody hell, it's already hot!" Sweat beads dotted her dark skin and she lowered sunglasses from the top of her head.

The Prickly Pear Pub sat in the middle of the block. A tequila tasting room was to their left with an upscale restaurant at the other end. They spotted an employee at *Perla del Pacífico* placing a sign for the special of the day, *Cóctel de Camarones*, on the sidewalk. Jade headed his way.

"Are we eating?" Sandrine asked as she caught up to Jade. "I'm hungry."

Glancing at his name tag, Jade said, *"Buenos días, Rico,"*

"Buenos días, señorita," he replied. "Would you like a table?"

Sandrine's *yes* competed with Jade's, *"No, gracias."*

Jade cut her eyes to Sandrine, then smiled at Rico. Pointing to the uppermost corner of the building, she asked, "Does your camera work?"

Rico followed her line of sight. *"Sí."* His eyebrows pinched together. "If you have questions, you will need to speak to the owner."

"The owner of the building or of the restaurant?" Jade asked.

"Same person." As he headed inside, Rico motioned for them to follow. "Come."

"Seriously," Sandrine whispered into Jade's ear. "We don't have time to eat?"

"Get the special to go." Jade followed Rico.

They wound their way past a bar that allowed patrons to enjoy a cocktail while taking in the view of the bustling *malecón* under an endless blue sky. Banderas Bay served as the perfect backdrop. A bartender adding garnish to a couple of Bloody Marys, smiled at Jade as she passed by. Jade looked over her shoulder and saw Sandrine speaking to a waitress, then stopped when Rico ducked into a serving station.

He rummaged through a couple of drawers, then handed Jade a business card. "Call *Señor* Costa. He can tell you about the cameras."

"*Gracias*, Rico." She shook his hand and headed for the exit.

Jade found Sandrine sitting at the bar noshing on a shrimp cocktail and sat on the stool next to her.

"I'm eating as fast as I can." Sandrine double-dipped a shrimp the size of a small lobster into cocktail sauce. The spicy scent of horseradish made Jade's nose tingle.

"You're fine." Jade signaled the bartender.

"Perfect," Sandrine added. "I'll have a Bloody Mary, too."

"We're not drinking," Jade grumbled, then flashed a flirty grin at the handsome barkeep.

"What can I get you?" he asked.

Jade held her phone up to him. "Have you seen this young woman?"

He looked at Ezmé's picture, then raised his dark eyes to Jade. "*Sí.* She has been here with friends."

"Was she here two nights ago?"

"Maybe." He shrugged. "Why?"

"She's missing." Jade thought she saw a flicker of concern cross his face.

The bartender broke eye contact. "Sorry." He picked up a tumbler and began to polish it with a bar towel.

Jade flipped over Sandrine's lunch bill and scribbled their phone numbers on the back. She slid the slip of paper toward him and said, "This is our contact information."

He looked at her note, but didn't pick it up. When he met her gaze again, she sensed he knew more than he was saying.

"Thanks." Jade climbed off her stool and headed for the exit as Sandrine placed a twenty-dollar bill next to her water glass.

Sandrine unlocked the car doors with the key fob. "He knows something."

"Agreed." Jade reached for the handle.

Before they could settle into the car, a blood-curdling scream filled the air. Jade looked at Sandrine as another chorus of shrieks came from the beach.

"Bloody hell!"

"Come on!" Jade called and hustled across the *malecón*.

The two agents cut their way through the gathering crowd and stopped at the three foot sea wall. On the beach below, another mob was forming.

Someone yelled, "Call an ambulance!"

A different voice said, "Dude, she's dead."

The cluster of people parted slightly, and Jade could see a young woman lying in the sand.

"Jade!" Sandrine called after her as she hurtled over the wall and dropped down onto the soft beach.

Racing toward the throng hovering around the motionless figure, Jade felt as if she was running in quicksand. Sandrine caught up to her and tried to keep her from kneeling next to the body. But Jade had to know. *Was this her sister? Would her biggest fear be realized? Was Ezmé dead?*

"It's not her." Sandrine tugged Jade's arm. "Come on."

But Jade couldn't take her eyes off the girl. She had long dark hair, like Ezmé. She was about the same age. And she was dead.

Jade couldn't tell exactly what had happened, but the body was missing the right arm and the lower half of the left leg. Her death had been horrific. The putrid smell of decaying flesh drew bile up the back of Jade's throat. Rising to her feet, she swallowed the urge to vomit as she imagined Ezmé suffering the same fate.

CHAPTER THREE

Eladio Ortiz stared at the thin file taunting him from the middle of his desk. The limited details within told him Ezmé had been adopted as a baby by Arturo and Leta Mendoza from Phoenix, Arizona. If his math was correct, Jade had been two when she gained a baby sister.

Eladio knew that no matter how long he looked at the folder, it would not magically fill with tips, leads, or answers regarding the disappearance of Ezmérelda Mendoza. Or the vanishing of eleven other young women.

He'd been able to glean little information since arriving in Puerto Vallarta, but it seemed the missing females were mostly prostitutes. He'd uncovered a few missing persons reports, in which the woman had been in an abusive relationship, then suddenly disappeared. Despite investigations into their abusers, there had been no indication the women had been murdered.

Ezmérelda Mendoza's disappearing act was different. It seemed to be the first abduction in a few years that didn't involve a working girl or female in distress.

Lacing his fingers together, he cradled the back of his head. His assignment to this task force was better than being fired. After all, he had allowed Sarita García to escape and disappear. But the lack of progress in finding any of the missing women made him feel as if he were being punished for letting the drug queen get away.

Eladio closed his eyes and allowed an image of Sarita to fill his mind. Her dark eyes were probing his—waiting for him to apologize for deceiving her for sixteen months. And as always, his attention focused on her lips, painted bloodred and slightly parted—as if she were about to say something. He could almost smell her Scandal perfume. Eladio knew he should open his eyes and forget Sarita's goodbye kiss, but he didn't. Instead, he savored the memory almost as much as he'd enjoyed the actual moment her lips touched his.

"*¿Qué pasa?*"

Eladio jerked out of his reverie and opened his eyes to see Lieutenant Amado Peña standing in the open doorway.

"*¿Necesita una siesta?*" Peña looked at his phone. "It is only ten AM."

"You are early." Eladio opened the investigation file and shuffled the papers within.

"*Sí.*" Peña plopped down into a chair in front of Eladio's desk. "Now that I have been assigned to this task force, I have no other cases."

Eladio frowned at Peña, who looked more like a cartel leader than a policeman. "What can you tell me about Valéria Carrizo?" Eladio asked.

Peña shrugged, then leaned forward. "Not much. She is FBI, *¿sí?*"

"*Sí.*" Eladio held up a single sheet of paper, which held scant specifications on the young agent.

"And you are wondering why FBI and not *Federale*?" Peña stated.

The only useful intel on Valéria was she'd enrolled at Arizona State University when she was eighteen, then entered the academy after graduation.

"*¿Qué dice?*" Peña prodded.

"She's Mexican-American with dual citizenship and grew up in Arizona. Graduated from ASU with a master's in criminology and criminal justice and was top of her class at the academy, graduating with honors.”

He passed the paper to Peña, who studied the one-page dossier, then slid it across the desk toward Eladio. *“Impresionante.”*

“I would like to know more about her.” Eladio drilled Peña with a dark stare.

Peña plucked a *concha* roll from the box on Eladio’s desk. “And you want me to see what I can find out.”

Eladio nodded. His phone buzzed and he looked at the text from Jade Mendoza.

Jade: *We’ll be at your office this afternoon.*

“We do not need any more help,” Peña grumbled as if he could read the text upside down, then popped the last of the *concha* into his mouth.

“Need it or not.” Eladio set his phone down. “Jade Mendoza is the missing girl’s *hermana.*”

“¡Mierda!” Peña swore. “Too many people will be *complicado.*”

Before Eladio could respond, his phone vibrated with an incoming call. As he looked at the number, Peña’s phone dinged.

“Bueno,” he answered the call and met Peña’s questioning gaze when he raised his eyes to Eladio. *“Sí.”* He disconnected.

“Tenemos un cuerpo en la playa.” Peña stood.

Without responding, Eladio opened a drawer, retrieved his Sig Sauer, and replayed the call in his mind. *“Agent Ortiz, we have a dead girl on the beach. You should come before she is moved.”*

Peña, already on his way out the door, called over his shoulder, “I will drive.”

CHAPTER FOUR

He hated being locked down at his compound *La Pedrera* but recent news that a hit had been ordered on his life made being sequestered a necessity. Raptor lifted his protein shake and took a large drink, the taste of peanut butter dancing on his tongue. He looked out his office window at the mountains standing tall at the edge of the dark green forest. His corporate president, Edgar Dimas, had sent a list of wares he hoped to purchase for *Sol Ardiente Galería*, Raptor's legitimate business. He knew Edgar had made his usual excellent choices, so he barely perused the list before approving the invoice with his initials.

Raptor had been working diligently for three years to change the human trafficking business he'd inherited after killing his boss. He hoped being isolated wouldn't delay his progress. Changing how his men practiced their trade had been a long and difficult process. Now, he could see they too preferred to not capture women and sell them like they were chattel. Of course, there were always holdouts. Raptor had been forced to order the death of the men who'd broken his three rules. Don't take or touch a girl without approval. Don't leave the organization without permission. Don't cross Raptor.

Raptor had been part of the last deal with his original boss. A fat, rich American had contracted them to find him a companion. Raptor had been disgusted by the *bastardo's* requirements: She must be a young, voluptuous virgin, and speak English.

Raptor had lost sleep after the young woman had begged to be set free, and then was dragged away in tears. He'd decided he no longer wanted to be party to ruining women's lives. Unfortunately, he had made his decision to change too late, because that girl was the daughter of an accountant who worked for a mid-level cartel. It had taken the *Cartel de Cocos Pequeña* four years to locate the girl. A week ago, she was rescued from the man who had bought her, and he'd been tortured and executed. Then a hit was ordered on Raptor since his boss was dead and he'd participated in the sale of the young woman. The cartel would use Raptor's execution to send a message.

Over the past few years, Raptor had shown his men they could still make money by helping women—instead of ripping them away from their families and forcing them into a life of hell. He'd convinced his lieutenant, Milo Rios, to solicit prostitutes, then offer them an opportunity to trade the street life for a relationship with one of Raptor's many buyers. It sounded easy enough, but to ensure the working girls weren't trading one hell for another, he hired a private investigator to vet would-be buyers. Word spread. Soon women from Mexico and other countries, were reaching out to Milo hoping to find a better life.

The first assignment Raptor had given the PI was to find Belen. The slick gringo had reported he'd been unable to locate Belen and assumed she was dead. At first Raptor had rejected the idea. Surely he would've felt something if the woman he loved had died. Although he'd paid the PI a bonus to find her, the report was always the same.

So now Raptor, too, dreamed of finding a better life. He wanted to become the man he used to be. Find someone he could love almost as much as he'd loved Belen. Leave the past behind.

He would start over somewhere far away from Puerto Vallarta. Raptor stared out the window again as the events that had changed his life forever played in his mind.

Eight years ago, he and Belen had fled the economic collapse in Guatemala with a small bag of clothes and all the money they'd saved. After months of careful planning, they knew it could take them up to four weeks to work their way through México to Nogales. Once there, they would cross the border into Arizona. In love and filled with the dream of making it to America, the young couple had set off on a beautiful January morning. Belen's cousin had a spare room in his apartment they could stay in and had secured them jobs at a trendy Mexican restaurant. He and Belen couldn't wait to meet their bright future together.

What they hadn't known—and couldn't have planned for—was the nightmare that began after Belen broke her ankle. They'd hopped into a boxcar outside of México City, and she'd fallen when the train jerked around a corner.

At the time, he'd been grateful for the simple fracture in her fibula bone, just above the ankle. For the sympathetic doctor who'd tended to Belen and took only half their money. For the kind young man who'd offered them a ride to the border.

He touched his lips remembering their last kiss and how, at the time, he was thankful she was alive. It had been the last time he was thankful.

"*¿Patrón?*" one of his men called from the open door of his office, bringing him back to the present.

Raptor shifted his gaze to the man. "*Sí.*"

"*Un cuerpo ha aparecido en la playa cerca del malecón.*"

"In English," Raptor growled. How many times did he have to tell his soldiers to learn and speak English?

"*Sí.* Yes. A body is on the beach near the *malecón*," the man repeated. "The boardwalk."

"Did one of the men try to capture this girl?"

"I do not know."

"Do we have someone at the scene?"

"*Sí.*"

"Keep me apprised." He waved the man from his office.

Raptor prayed one of his men hadn't gone rogue and caused the girl's death. But since the *policía* had been notified, he needed to be sure.

He also doubted she was Ezmérelda Mendoza. The young beauty had captured his attention six months ago when she passed by his table at the outdoor *Café del Mar*. The café was his favorite lunch spot when he was at his office at *Ardiente Sol Galería*. He couldn't take his eyes off her. The fresh plumeria bloom she wore tucked into her long dark hair had enveloped him in a fragrant cloud of citrus.

He'd eventually managed to engage her in conversation, and that led to having coffee with her a few times. Raptor had planned to ask her to dinner, then found himself locked away at his compound. He couldn't understand his fascination with the lovely Ezmé, but knew he wanted to get to know her better. *Could it be she reminded him of when he was a better man? Or was it because she looked so much like his beloved Belen?*

CHAPTER FIVE

Jade worried if she closed her eyes, she'd fall into a deep sleep. She also feared images of the dead girl on the beach would morph into Ezmé. But even with her eyes open, Jade could imagine her sister suffering the same fate—or worse.

Eladio argued his point that the recently-discovered body could be one of Raptor's captives, but Lieutenant Peña had a different theory.

"It was a *cocodrilo*." Peña crossed his arms.

"I think we should wait for the coroner's report before we jump to conclusions," Eladio countered.

"It rained last night, which draws the crocs into the ocean." Now Peña leaned forward, his hands held palms up to punctuate his declaration.

"But where would the reptile find someone to attack?" Eladio's question echoed with impatience.

"We should check with the hotels along that section of beach," Peña said. "The beast could have snatched her during a walk in the surf last night."

"Jade." Eladio tapped his desk with a pen.

It took her a beat to realize he was speaking to her. The two cops' verbal volley had almost lulled her to sleep.

"Yes? What?" She blinked to bring the *Federale* into focus.

"Does Ezmé ever walk on the beach at night?" Eladio asked.

"No." She wished she knew the agent better because Eladio's handsome face revealed nothing. "I mean," she began, stifling a yawn with the back of her hand. "I don't think so."

Amado Peña kicked a chair toward her. "Sit—before you fall down."

If she wasn't so damn tired, she would've told the arrogant lieutenant where he could shove the chair. "I'm good."

Peña smirked at her, then spoke to Eladio, "Did you hear back from the bookstore where Ezmé worked?"

"I have left a message for—" Eladio checked a notepad in front of him. "Kyla." He looked at Jade. "But no return call."

Tears pooled in Jade's eyes, and she ran her hands over her face to stem their flow. "What can you tell me about Raptor?"

"Us." Sandrine stood next to Jade. "What can you tell us?"

Jade cocked an eyebrow. "I thought you were going to the hotel?"

"I did." Sandrine handed her a cup. "All checked in." She pointed at the drink. "Mexican latte."

"What about *Señora* Beck and her daughter?" Peña asked. "They were supposed to come here and give a statement."

Sandrine narrowed her eyes at him. "I said we'd talk with them tomorrow."

"Ah, I see." Peña threw his hands in the air. "You are in charge now!"

"Tomorrow will be better," Eladio interjected.

Sandrine looked at Eladio. "What information do you have on Raptor."

The scent of cinnamon wafted over Jade when she took a sip of coffee. Eladio, whose face was a mask of calm, made her question whether he was the right person to head the task force. For a fleeting second, she missed Christopher. But she knew Special Agent Temple had his hands full in Washington DC wrapping up their joint investigation into the now-missing Sarita García.

Instead of waiting for Eladio, Peña said, "I believe this *cabrón* is not a Mexican National."

Eladio set his jaw. Jade thought he wanted to punch Peña as much as she did. But Eladio maintained his professional demeanor and flipped through his notepad.

Stopping on a page, he said, "I agree." He raised his eyes to Jade. "We do not have much information compiled yet, but I can share what we do know."

Sandrine sat down and pulled another chair close. She rolled her eyes at Jade. "Bloody hell! Sit your ass down!"

Despite fearing she'd pass out, Jade slumped into her seat.

Eladio's phone buzzed, and he glanced at the screen. Before he could answer, a young Hispanic woman strode into his office.

"Agent Ortiz." She extended her hand. "Special Agent Valéria Carrizo."

Standing, Eladio shook her hand. "Welcome."

Valéria looked around the office, her blue eyes settling on Jade. "Agent Mendoza." Valéria tilted her head, causing her long blonde hair to swing to the side. "I'm to tell you *all is good* from Agent Temple," she said, her accent barely noticeable. She smiled and handed Jade an envelope.

Jade looked at her name scrawled across the front in Christopher's bold handwriting. She slid a single sheet of paper from inside and read his note.

Jade ~ Valéria told me there are no updates on Ezmé. I know you're worried, but your sister is smart, and she'll lead you to her if she can. Ortiz came through on the García investigation, so be nice. Still no sign of your "mom." I'm taking a few days to recharge but call me if you need anything. Hang in there, C

"What's surfer boy say?" Sandrine reached for the note.

Jade pulled it away and glared at her friend.

"*¡Perdona!*" Peña snapped his fingers. "Can you save your love letter for later so we can get back to work?"

Ignoring her exhaustion, Jade jumped to her feet. She was ready to slap the condescending look from Peña's face. Sandrine grabbed her wrist as both men stood.

Jade shook off Sandrine's grip and stepped toward the lieutenant. "What the fuck is your problem?"

"*¡Tú!* You should not be involved in this investigation." Peña's hands were balled into fists.

"Enough!" Eladio pounded his desk and silence filled the office.

Touching Jade on the shoulder, Sandrine said. "Let's call it a day."

Jade didn't respond, still intent on punching Peña in the mouth. She'd had enough of being told what to do. Enough of feeling helpless. Enough of playing by the rules.

If Agent Ortiz and Lieutenant Peña couldn't help find her sister, then she might have to take matters into her own hands. And Jade didn't plan to let anyone stand in her way.

CHAPTER SIX

Eladio sipped tequila from the partially-salted tumbler. The large square ice cube tilted, then settled when he placed the glass down onto the bar top.

As soon as he'd locked his office door, he'd headed for Captain Jack's, a popular tourist bar famous for their Drunk Pirate drink. Eladio had never sampled the rum concoction since he preferred tequila. Besides, the idea of drinking the sweet swill made him cringe.

Jesús appeared with the bottle of *Kah* tequila. *"¿Uno mas?"*

Eladio nodded. He'd tried all three types of Sarita's favorite tequila, deciding the *reposado* suited him best. The yellow sugar skull staring back at him from the label conjured the memory of the night when they'd bonded over too much alcohol and their shared hatred for her *Padrino*, Agustín Castro. When Sarita's face flashed in his mind, he found himself comparing her features with that of her daughter. They both had the same eyes, dark and alluring, but Jade had a stronger jawline. He wondered if her lips were as luscious as her mother's.

He took another sip and thought about the beautiful Jade Mendoza. Though she was young, she seemed more mature than her twenty-three years. The argument between her and Peña replayed in his head, and he found himself wondering if the young DEA agent carried her passion into all things.

"*¡Mierda!*" Eladio swore under his breath. "She's a child." He drained his glass, waved at Jesús, and reached for a menu. Clearly lack of food was affecting his logic.

He perused the menu even though he knew he'd order his usual, Pirate's Pizza. His favorite pizza came on a large tortilla with pepperoni as coins, red sauce as blood, cheese as sand, and pineapple as gold. He looked toward Jesús, who gave him the thumbs-up indicating he'd already placed Eladio's order.

Eladio sipped from the tumbler and contemplated the day's events. He had a dead girl on the beach with possible *cocodrilo* injuries. Ezmé Mendoza had been missing for forty-eight hours. And they had absolutely no leads as to what had happened to her.

Maybe now that the investigative team included Valéria, they'd have more resources through her FBI affiliation. Valéria's presence had improved Peña's mood, but Jade's anger caused him to worry that she was about to go rogue. Maybe, if she'd let him, Eladio could provide the same partner-like balance she'd had with Temple.

Eladio massaged the scar from the flesh wound he'd acquired in the shootout with Sarita García's men. He thought about how he might feel if it was his little sister who was missing. Thankfully, Isla was safe at home with their parents in Monterrey. A year younger than Ezmé, Isla worked at a café while finishing college. He admired his little sister's determination to find a job in the states after she graduated as a bilingual pharmacy technician.

Jesús delivered the pizza and asked, "A *Pacifico* now?"

Eladio nodded, color tinting his cheeks. *God I am predictable*, he thought to himself. He munched a slice of pizza and glanced at an incoming text.

Peña: *With Valéria. Come to Marriot. Croc attack two nights ago.*

Eladio finished his slice, took a long pull from the *Pacifico* bottle, then reached for his wallet. Jesús headed toward him with a to-go box and the bill. As Eladio placed eight hundred *pesos* next to the empty pizza tray, his phone buzzed again.

Peña: *Dead beach girl not from two nights ago.*

Ortiz: *On my way.*

Eladio slid another slice of pizza from the box as he navigated the Friday night traffic. A mental image of Puerto Vallarta formed in his mind as he savored a bite. *The El Cora Cocodrilo Sanctuary* sat inland between Nuevo Vallarta and Bucerías. He scanned his mental map and recalled *Estero El Salado*, a natural habitat for crocodiles. The reserve was located east of the Puerto Vallarta Marina on a channel flowing into *Bahía de Banderas*.

If their dead girl wasn't from the attack two nights ago, possibly she'd fallen into the water from one of the marina docks. Or maybe she'd been on one of the many boats frequenting the bay and had gone overboard.

Eladio turned into the hotel's long, sweeping driveway and stopped in front of the main entrance. A valet appeared and Eladio handed him the keys to his black Jeep Renegade, then flashed his credentials. The valet gave a thumbs-up and Eladio knew his SUV would be parked close by.

Peña met him at the double glass doors and motioned for him to follow. Cold air blasted Eladio when he stepped inside.

"¿Tomaste la ruta escénica?" Peña grumbled.

Eladio ignored the Lieutenant's remark about taking a scenic route and followed him across the lobby. He wanted to tell the *pendejo arrogante* if he'd taken a scenic route, he would have kept going.

Valéria sat on the orange cushion of a wicker armchair speaking with a young woman who twisted a tissue around a finger. She looked at them with tear-filled gray eyes, and Eladio thought he saw the desire to flee cross the girl's face.

Valéria touched the young woman's arm and spoke softly to her, then she stood and approached the men. Noticing a tear track down the FBI agent's cheek, Eladio wondered what past trauma could cause her to relate to this *turista's* tragedy.

"I believe I have all the information she can recall." Valéria waved at the young woman who was heading for the elevators.

"Are you going to share?" Peña barked. "Or do we guess?"

Eladio braced himself for Valéria to unleash a barrage of swear words like Jade's earlier rant, but she surprised him by flashing Peña a dazzling smile.

Valéria touched Peña's arm and Eladio almost laughed at the goofy grin curving the lieutenant's lips.

"Of course I'm going to share." She turned her bright smile to Eladio. "Do you think we could move this meeting to the hotel bar?" Valéria didn't wait for a reply. She strutted away, leaving the scent of lemongrass hanging in the air and the men gawking at her perfect backside.

Peña shrugged and followed the pretty FBI agent with a little swagger in his step. By the time Eladio arrived at the small table, Peña had taken the chair next to Valéria. A waiter hurried over and took their order; *cervezas* for the men, tequila neat for Valéria.

"The young woman I interviewed, Gwen, is here with two friends. They are not affiliated with the girl who was attacked by a crocodile two nights ago while sitting in the surf."

The waiter delivered their drinks and asked, "Anything else?"

"*Sí.*" Peña pointed to another table. "A bowl of *chiflado.*"

The waiter did a head bob before heading off to fetch mixed nuts for them.

"What else did she tell you?" Peña asked, then took a long swig from his *Modelo*.

"Gwen went to the hospital and visited the girl who'd been attacked on the beach." Valéria reached for her drink. "Her injuries aren't life threatening since she hasn't developed an infection from the bites. But the crocodile severely mangled her legs."

"If she doesn't know the girl attacked in the surf," Eladio said, "then why did she visit her? And why is she so upset?"

Valéria sipped some tequila and Eladio saw a whisp of sorrow flutter in her eyes. "Because her friends, Lexi and Blake, are missing." She tossed down the rest of her shot. "And she thinks one of them is the dead girl found on the beach."

CHAPTER SEVEN

As dawn lit the sky, Raptor yawned and rubbed his eyes. He was exhausted and frustrated, and he hated waiting. One of his *halcones*, men he had placed throughout the city to act as scouts, had sent word. The body found on the beach yesterday was connected to his operation. His *policía* contact was also earning his money. He reported a guest on the pirate ship thought he saw the girl go overboard. She'd been fighting with an unknow man during the fireworks display.

So now he waited in his office, watching a squall move across the mountains. He inhaled the fresh, earthy smell of the passing rain as air seeped through a slightly open window.

His soldiers had had a busy night. They'd also found Novio and Ezmérelda Mendoza. When Raptor got the call at one AM, he'd instructed Toro Aguilar to place Novio in an empty room with a guard at the door. Toro informed his boss Ezmé was hysterical. He requested permission to sedate her, which Raptor granted.

He trusted Toro, a *sicario* who'd joined the crew after Raptor killed his boss. Though Raptor had begun paying his men a wage instead of making them compete for a percentage of the spoils, there were still soldiers among the ranks who preferred their previous way of life. Toro became Raptor's enforcer, offering protection and meting out punishment when warranted. Toro had been the one to deliver the news that a hit had been ordered—with Raptor's head as the desired prize.

"Patrón." Milo Rios stood in the open doorway.

Raptor waved him into his office. "What do you know?"

"The girl from the beach jumped overboard from the *Perla del Océano* when one of our men tried to grab her during the pirate cruise."

"¡Maldita sea!" Raptor pounded his desk. "Who?"

"Ferdo brought the newest girl in last night." Milo rubbed his chin. "It was her friend who jumped."

"Has the new girl been touched?"

"No." His lieutenant shook his head. "She was drugged but seems fine."

Raptor shifted his gaze out the open window, taking in the pre-dawn sky as he contemplated Milo's news. Since he wanted time to get to know Ezmé, the last thing he needed was the *policía* questioning his men. Or God forbid, discovering his well-hidden complex here in *La Pedrera.*

"¿Patrón?" Milo waited for instructions.

"See to it she is comfortable for now." Raptor shifted his gaze to Toro who now stood behind Milo. "Ask her if she can identify the men on the ship." He waved Toro into his office. "Talk to Ferdo as well."

Milo nodded. *"Sí, Patrón."* He skirted around Toro, who looked more Aztec Indian than Mexican.

Raptor motioned his *sicario* forward and Toro dropped into a chair.

"Has Novio said anything?" Raptor asked.

"No, Patrón." Toro crossed a knee with his ankle. "Not a word since he tried to talk his way out of the hotel room."

"Did he offer an excuse?"

Toro shook his head. "He claimed he had just texted with you and was leaving to deliver the girl."

Raptor tried to suppress a slight smile, since the kid was so like him. "Bring him to my office," Raptor said. "And the girl?"

"She is still sleeping." Toro consulted his watch. "Do you want me to wake her for breakfast?"

"Sí." Raptor looked at the time on his phone. "Have the girl, and breakfast, delivered to my suite at seven."

Toro stood and turned to go, adding, "I will have Milo bring Novio."

Raptor moved to a well-stocked bar. It was early for a shot of tequila, but after the night he'd had, plus what was still to come, he didn't care. He filled the shot glass to the rim and tossed down the *Patrón*. Closing his eyes, he savored the citrusy taste, and the burn that followed. For a beat, he considered tipping the bottle to his lips and drinking half the contents, but he had work to do. He poured another shot and returned to his desk just as Milo arrived with Novio. Milo pushed the young man toward Raptor, and Novio spun around. If not for his zip-tied wrists, he probably would have taken a swing at Milo.

Milo stepped back and crossed his arms. Raptor knew his men did not like being responsible for another soldier's discipline, but the rules were clear. And Novio had broken all three.

"Cut his restraints and leave us," Raptor said.

Milo did as instructed, closing the office door as he left.

Raptor locked eyes with Novio. "Does it hurt?" He pointed to Novio's blackened, swollen eye.

Novio shrugged.

Motioning to a chair in front of his desk, Raptor said, *"Sentarse."*

Novio rubbed his wrists and sat as instructed.

When Raptor slid the *Patrón* shot toward the young man, Novio narrowed his good eye.

"Drink," Raptor said. "I have already had mine."

Novio picked up the glass and tilted it to his cut lips. He winced slightly as he downed the shot.

"Almost sixty hours." Raptor resisted the urge to smile at the young soldier's impressive accomplishment. "What am I to do with you now?"

Novio glared at him. His clothes were torn and dirty and he had a patch of dried blood under his nose. Raptor admired the fight Novio had put up in his attempt to escape with Ezmé.

Novio squared his shoulders. "You can let us go."

This time, Raptor allowed a slight smile at the young man's brazenness. "You know I cannot grant your request."

"Por favor, Patrón—"

"English, Novio."

Novio pursed his lips and raised his chin. "I would very much like for you to release me from service." The young soldier hesitated, and a flicker of fear shone in his eyes. "And allow me to leave with Ezmé."

"Bravo!" Raptor clapped his hands. "How long have you practiced that speech?"

Novio's bravado wilted slightly but he countered with a curt reply. "From day one."

Once again, Raptor admired the young man's courage. A trait he'd kept hidden in the four years he'd been indebted first to the original *Jefe*, and now to Raptor. Of course, to sacrifice yourself to save another was the definition of courage.

"I know your name means *boyfriend*, but I do not think Ezmé is destined to be your girlfriend."

"And you believe because your name means *gift of God* that Ezmé will see you as a *regalo* instead of the monster you are?"

Raptor shot to his feet and Novio stood as well. He had worked hard to remove the anger that had hardened his heart. But Novio's insolence had cracked the precarious control Raptor had on his rage.

"For now." Raptor crossed to the bar, grabbed the bottle of *Patrón* and another glass. "I will let you live." He returned to his desk and poured two shots.

Novio lifted his glass in toast. "And I will keep trying to escape with Ezmé until you kill me." He tossed down the tequila.

Raptor tipped his glass toward Novio, then drank his shot. The boy of twenty-one had become a confident, probably dangerous, young man. Raptor had no doubt Novio would try to make good on his promise.

CHAPTER EIGHT

She had slept for ten hours, so why did she still feel tired? Probably her tequila-fueled slumber was the answer.

"Yep." Jade scrunched her eyes closed. "I always have to have one more shot even though I know better." She cracked an eyelid and listened for any indication Sandrine was up, but silence filled their suite.

Jade cringed at the memory of her friend guiding her to the large king-size bed, placing the trash can close by and leaving bottles of water on the nightstand. Jade had mumbled something about Peña being a bastard and Eladio being a handsome gentleman.

"Sure, sweetie." Sandrine's parting words bounced around Jade's brain. "Peña's an ass and Eladio's a prince." She'd brushed Jade's bangs from her forehead and whispered, "You're going to be sorry in the morning, Love."

Jade sat up, and other than a dull thudding in her head, didn't feel too hungover. "Good Mexican genes," she declared, her cheeks instantly coloring.

The phrase belonged to her dad, Arturo. She loved pretending she had the same DNA as her adoptive parents. But now that she knew who her biological mother was, Jade had to concede the saying probably applied to all Mexicans.

She began to reassess her initial evaluation of how she felt, slumping back into the pillows. Eyes closed, she let the memory of discovering her true heritage boil up from her emotional lockbox.

"Your next DEA assignment is in Mazatlán," Ellice Benson had said as she slid a folder toward Jade. "You'll be working with a Fed in a joint effort to apprehend Sarita García."

Jade had opened the file and almost spit coffee onto the desk. The face of a beautiful woman stared back at Jade with her own eyes. She held the photo closer and studied every detail.

"I noticed the resemblance too," Benson said.

Lowering the picture, she stared at her boss.

"Since you haven't kept your adoption a secret." Benson leaned forward and handed Jade a document. "I decided to look into the history."

Tears blurred Jade's vision, but she could see the names Alarico and Estrella García at the top of the page. Picking out her date of birth and key words, Jade understood the form was her official adoption agreement. Sarita was listed as her mother, with a doctor's notation stating Sarita was mentally incapacitated.

Both women were silent for a moment, then Jade raised her gaze to Benson.

"There's no father listed," her boss said.

Afraid her voice would crack if she spoke, Jade nodded.

"If you'd like," Benson said, holding Jade's stare. "I can keep searching for information regarding your bio-dad."

She punched her pillow sending the recollection slithering back to the corner of her mind where she kept difficult memories. Jade hadn't responded to Benson's offer. She and Ezmé had known from an early age they were adopted. But did Jade want to know more than she'd just learned? That her maternal grandparents had taken her from her mother and given her up for adoption. That her bio-mom was a drug queen on the run. What if her real father was more notorious than Sarita García?

Jade propped herself up and sipped some water. The suite still seemed quiet, so she decided there was no need to jump out of bed. Coffee would probably help her hangover, though. She checked her phone but had no texts or voicemails. A fuzzy recollection of threatening Ortiz that she'd be in his office at the crack of dawn flitted through her mind. Jade knew working an investigation was filled with chasing down leads, trying to get inside criminals' minds, and working to make sense of every piece of information. But nothing they'd done so far had brought them any closer to finding Ezmé.

Today they were meeting with Joy and Erica. She hoped they would fill in some of the blanks surrounding the hours before Ezmé's disappeared. Slipping her feet free of the covers, she shuffled across the tile floor of her bedroom to the kitchenette. A half pot of coffee sat warming on the burner, the strong brew permeating the air. Jade poured a cup, leaving space for a splash of Baileys. A breeze blew through the open patio slider, ruffling the curtains, and crashing waves called to her from the beach below. Padding across the living room, Jade stepped onto the deck into the warm tropical air. She stretched out on a lounge chair and sighed at the breath-taking sight of Banderas Bay.

The chocolatey Baileys danced on her tongue after a sip of coffee, and she thought about what Sandrine had asked her when they'd been in Mazatlán. "Are you sure you're not related to Marco Torres?"

Jade took a bigger drink and thought about Captain Marco Torres. He seemed about the same age as Sarita, but Jade had a hard time imagining the buttoned-down captain being involved with a drug queen. Then again, they would have been teenagers at the time of her conception. Perhaps their paths crossed, and they had a romantic encounter before going their separate ways.

Closing her eyes, she matched her breathing to the drumming waves and conjured up the handsome captain's face behind her eyelids. She mentally studied his features trying to superimpose her face over his, but nothing appeared to match up. Eyes open, she took another sip, then compared one physical attribute at a time to Torres. When her list reached his mouth, she licked her lips. Did they share this characteristic? The same grim set to their lips when frowning? And was it possible they had the same jawline?

"Does it really effing matter?" she asked the sparkling sea. "I'll probably never see him or Sarita again."

A sequence of chimes echoed from the bedroom. Jade hustled to retrieve her phone, which continued to sound alerts as a string of texts filled the screen.

Sandrine: *You up?*

Sandrine: *Joy wants to take us to breakfast.*

Jade: *Yes. When?*

Sandrine: *Now!*

Jade rolled her eyes, then texted: *Fine. Down in 15.*

Sandrine: *We'll be in the lobby.*

Jade sent the thumbs-up emoji.

She returned to the kitchen and added hot coffee to her cup as she opened the next text.

Ortiz: *Buenos días. Sandrine said you will be meeting with Joy this morning. Peña will be joining you. Appreciate you conducting this interview.*

"Seriously!" Dealing with the egotistical lieutenant while she walked Joy through her last contact with Ezmé was the last thing she wanted.

Jade: *Peña?*

Ortiz: *Neither you nor Sandrine have official status. He needs to oversee the meeting.*

Jade wanted to text something inappropriate and unprofessional, but refrained.

Jade: *Fine. Does he know where to meet us?*

Ortiz: *Sí*

Jade sent another thumbs-up emoji, added more Baileys to her cup and headed for a shower. She turned on the water, stripped and stood under the hot spray, wishing she hadn't over imbibed last night. Then she could have met Joy earlier and avoided being babysat by Peña.

"God, I hate being told what to do!"

CHAPTER NINE

Eladio wondered how many swear words Jade had said before she texted her reply: *Peña?*

While he understood her annoyance, he knew every aspect of this investigation had to be properly conducted. If—not if—when they captured Raptor, he did not want anything to allow the human trafficker to escape prosecution. Not only that, but his superiors had informed him they did not see any reason to involve the DEA. Eladio had lobbied for both Jade and Sandrine to be included on the task force and was granted permission. Unfortunately, for now, the approval came with parameters, hence why Amado Peña would be overseeing Jade's interview with Joy.

When he thought about it, he and Jade shared the same frustration when it came to this case and the task force. He would've preferred to handle the investigation alone as he had when he built his case against Sarita García. And despite Sarita's disappearing act, Eladio's undercover work had helped bring down Agustín Castro's drug empire.

Maybe, he thought again, he and Jade would make a good team. She knew her sister well and he had the ability to blend in. Together, he believed they would already have proof Raptor held Ezmé captive. His intuition told him they'd also know the real identity of the man they hunted. And, if it was just the two of them, he'd have an opportunity to get to know Jade Mendoza beyond the fact that she was Sarita García's daughter.

A buzz emanated from his phone, and he checked the screen.

Peña: *Llegan tarde.*

Ortiz: *Paciencia.*

Peña: *Me voy en 10.*

Eladio didn't respond. He doubted the lieutenant would leave in ten minutes if Jade and the others hadn't arrived. He knew how much Peña liked exerting his authority and that he wouldn't want to miss an opportunity to do so with Jade.

Valéria knocked on his open door, then stepped into his office. "Ready?"

She looked stunning in a tan skirt, white cotton tank and red sandals. Eladio envied her simple outfit and wished he could ditch his trousers for shorts and hang up his jacket until cooler weather returned.

"*Sí.*" Eladio stood, retrieving his gun from the desk drawer. "My car is in the back parking lot." He motioned for her to exit ahead of him.

They navigated the hallway to a back door, which he held open as she stepped outside. The cool morning air had given way to a mugginess suggesting the day would be sultry and hot. Eladio released the locks of his Jeep with his key fob. He laid his jacket onto the backseat, then joined Valéria in the stuffy car. The air conditioning sputtered to life when he cranked the engine and he lowered the windows for fresh, albeit hot air.

"Sorry for the heat." Eladio retrieved his sunglasses from the dash.

"No worries." Valéria lifted her long honey blonde hair, twisted it into a knot and magically secured the mop to the top of her head. "We *are* in Puerto Vallarta after all."

Eladio merged into traffic, and they rode in silence for a few minutes. He hated attending autopsy review, but he needed to have a face-to-face with the coroner regarding the young woman from the beach. Did she die from *cocodrilo* wounds? Or did she drown first, making her an easy snack for the predatory reptile? Or could both scenarios be true?

"So." Valéria cleared her throat. "Do I need to be in the same room with the, uh, body?"

Eladio suppressed a smile. "First autopsy review?"

"Yes." She looked out the window, then back at Eladio. "I'm not sure how I'll react. I would hate to embarrass you by vomiting all over the victim."

A chuckle escaped Eladio. "It is fine if you would like to remain outside the exam room, but I think you will find the process more clinical than gory." He looked at her. "Besides, you have Gwen's picture with her friends on your phone, *¿sí?*"

"Yes, but couldn't you have the coroner check the photo against the victim?" Valéria asked. "And why see the body instead of just reading the report?"

Eladio shrugged. "I need to see things with my own eyes to get a complete picture." Flipping the blinker, he changed lanes. "I find I do not like to rely on information from other sources."

Turning toward him in her seat, Valéria said, "Right? In case there's an *odd sock*."

He glanced at her. "Odd sock?"

"A clue someone might have missed." Facing forward, she continued, "Like what if the girl has restraint marks on her remaining limbs?" Her face grew animated. "Or did the police overlook a puncture mark indicating she'd been drugged?" She frowned. "Before whatever else happened to her occurred."

Eladio pulled into a parking lot next to a white stucco building with red trim. There was no sign indicating the Coroner's Office or that a morgue was located within. Eladio's first visit here had been soon after he'd arrived in Puerto Vallarta. He parked and they both exited the vehicle.

When the oppressive heat slammed into him, Eladio was thankful he'd worn a short-sleeved linen shirt. He glanced at his jacket in the backseat, then clicked the locks. They crossed to the building and Eladio held the door open for Valéria. The inside air's bouquet of antiseptic cleaning products and death was overwhelming. Eladio resisted the urge to cover his nose and mouth with his hand, remaining stoic alongside his FBI partner. Her lightened pallor and twitching nose indicated she too was struggling to maintain her poise against the aromatic onslaught.

A woman dressed in lilac scrubs, her dark hair twisted into a bun at the nape of her neck, approached them. When she removed a mask, her smile was revealed. "Agent Ortiz, good to see you again."

Eladio didn't bother to extend his hand. On his prior visit, he'd been informed that Dr. Carmentis Cabello would not shake hands. Something to do with striving to always maintain a sterile field.

"Good to see you as well," Eladio said. "This is Special Agent Valéria Carrizo with the FBI. She is part of our task force."

"*Bueno.*" Dr. Cabello turned and led them down a hallway. "I am ready to discuss the autopsy results on your victim from the beach," she said over her shoulder. She pushed through a glass door and stepped into a brightly lit room.

Valéria entered ahead of Eladio. Along the back wall mortuary cabinets were stacked three high and six across. The room itself was cool, but not as cold as the cabinets, which showed 1°C to 5°C on each temperature regulator.

The body lay on a cold steel table, covered with a white sheet. Dr. Cabello handed Eladio a small jar of camphor cream. He unscrewed the lid and dabbed the menthol salve under his nose before handing the jar to Valéria. After repeating the process, Valéria set the container on the counter.

"Ready?" Dr. Cabello asked.

Eladio nodded and Valéria blew out a breath.

Pulling the white sheet from the body, Dr. Cabello whispered, "*Lo siento, mija.* This will not take long."

The coroner's apology to the corpse reminded Eladio this victim had once been a vital young woman. And she deserved the best he and his task force had to offer. He glanced at Valéria, her pale cheeks the only sign the sight of the dead girl made her uncomfortable. He noticed she had opened the record app on her phone, which was more efficient than taking notes by hand.

"Sea water in your victim's lungs indicates she was alive when she went into the ocean." Dr. Cabello pointed at a bruise on the girl's left bicep. "This, along with broken fingernails, tells me she struggled with someone." Lifting the left hand, she continued, "She also has a club stamp."

Eladio leaned closer but could not discern any markings on top of the hand.

"Invisible ink," Dr. Cabello said. "The blue spider monkey glowed when I scanned the body with a UV light."

"Was she in the water too long for nail scrapings?" Valéria asked.

Dr. Cabello nodded. "Yes, approximately forty-eight hours, but I was able to recover a small piece of skin from her teeth."

Eladio exchanged a look with Valéria who flashed a grin. This evidence could be her *odd sock*.

"Is the sample big enough for DNA testing?" Eladio asked.

Dr. Cabello frowned. "It is very small, but I did send the specimen to the lab." She moved to the girl's severed left leg. "I believe," she continued, motioning to the mangled arm, "these wounds are from a *cocodrilo*, and they occurred after she drowned."

Eladio's stomach lurched, and bile burned the back of his throat when he looked closely at the jagged, discolored flesh.

"Thank God," Valéria mumbled.

"It is surprising she washed up on the beach," Dr. Cabello continued. "Because most *cocodrilos* stash their prey in a den, for later feeding."

Valéria gagged and covered her mouth.

"Vomit in the sink if you must," Dr. Cabello ordered.

Valéria held up a finger. "I'm good."

Nodding, Dr. Cabello continued, "I started a SA kit and determined she is a virgin with no signs of an attempted rape."

"But died to escape her attacker," Valéria added.

"I took prints and made dental impressions—in case you identify her at some point." Dr. Cabello handed him an envelope.

"We actually have a photo for possible identification." Eladio looked at Valéria who handed her phone to the coroner.

Dr. Cabello held the phone's screen close to the bloated face of the dead girl. "She has the same hair and eye color, but her features are too distorted to make a positive ID."

"I will request her dental records for comparison," Eladio said as Dr. Cabello handed the phone back to Valéria.

"Is one, or both, of the other girls in the picture going to end up on my table?" Dr. Cabello asked as she covered the young woman.

"We know the woman with the short blonde hair is missing," Eladio answered. "How long can you keep this victim?"

"I embalmed the body, so thirty days. Unless I get a full house." She tucked the girl's hand under the sheet.

"*Entiendo.*" Eladio looked at Valéria, who shook her head indicating she didn't have any additional questions. "*Gracias*, Dr. Cabello." He smiled. "I will return once I have the dental records."

Carmentis Cabello returned his smile, then wheeled her charge toward a refrigerated locker. "*Bueno,* she is in good hands for now."

Eladio headed for the door, Valéria close on his heels. He picked up his pace and pushed through the exit, inhaling deeply.

Valéria bent at the waist and gulped in air too. She righted herself and pulled a tissue from her purse. "Glad that's over." She rubbed the camphor away from her nose.

As they approached the car, Eladio clicked the locks open, then climbed in. He started the engine as Valéria settled into the passenger seat.

"I think this girl is Lexi, which means Raptor has Blake?" Valéria looked at him. "Right?"

Eladio nodded but didn't reply. Anger boiled up from his core. He knew they needed to act fast to save Ezmé and Blake, and arrest whoever had sent Lexi into the waters of Banderas Bay.

CHAPTER TEN

The table looked nice. *Acogedor*, Raptor thought. Of course, he doubted Ezmérelda Mendoza would welcome being his captive. He hoped she'd tolerate breakfast and give him a chance to explain why she was here. He'd tell her he wanted to get to know her better. *Eres un tonto*, he thought to himself. But the fool in him struggled with the urge to discover more about the exquisite Ezmé.

I could try telling her the truth. The thought conjured the haunting memory of the day Belen left him standing next to his would-be executioner as Raptor begged her to stay. When these memories played in his mind, Raptor could usually distract himself with work or tequila or some willing lovely young thing in his bed. The anticipation of spending time with Ezmé, so like his beloved Belen, had resurrected his pain from that day.

He knew Belen had chosen to leave with the *cabrón* who had bought her in order to save him, but Raptor had never recovered from losing her. In the months following, a darkness had enveloped him, and he'd spent many nights sampling the sweetness of the women captured by his new boss. Eventually, he'd even been accepted by the other men who now worked for him.

His original boss encouraged his soldiers to have vasectomies. Though most of the men passed on the offer, Raptor jumped at the opportunity. He had accepted the fact that his life would now be an endless stable of *hembras* meant to satisfy his dark desires. The last thing he wanted was to leave his seed in a female who would be sold and taken away with his child growing in her belly.

Looking in the mirror, he realized he hadn't thought about his appearance for a long time. Not since the day long ago that had stolen his youth. Losing Belen had left him with hatred in his heart, masking the handsomeness she'd fallen in love with.

After a quick shower, Raptor didn't put much effort into his morning attire, choosing a black T-shirt and jeans. To control his unruly curls, he pulled his long dark hair into a ponytail. He trimmed his beard and wondered if there was a magic cream that would erase the crow's feet fanning out from the corners of his eyes. The wrinkles made him look older than his twenty-eight years.

He crossed to the open windows of the small dining area and eased them closed. He'd requested plumeria-scented candles and now he brought their wicks to life with a lighter. Hopefully, the citrusy scent would mask the stuffiness of his suite.

When a knock sounded, Raptor blew out a breath, then said, *"Entrar."*

Toro pushed the door open and stepped aside. The entry was empty for a beat, then Ezmé appeared in the doorway.

"Please," Raptor smiled, "come in."

Ezmé took a couple of tentative steps, her dark eyes wide and wary.

"Gracias, Toro," Raptor said. "We will need nothing further."

The *sicario* nodded and pulled the door closed.

Ezmé startled and swung around—as if she intended to yank the door open and run.

"Let me introduce myself," he said and waited.

She turned around. "You are the man from the café." Glaring at him, she asked, "Why am I here?"

"I am Mateo and—"

"That's not the translation for *kidnapper*." Ezmé narrowed her eyes.

Raptor laughed, moved to the dining table, and pulled out a chair. His jaw muscles flexed but he mentally coached himself to remain calm.

A frown drew Ezmé's dark eyebrows together. She smoothed her turquoise miniskirt; the silver sequin top she wore shimmering with the action. Raptor noticed the top was missing sequins here and there. His cheeks burned at the thought that Novio had already discovered what lay beneath.

Ezmé strode toward him, the rhinestones on her sandals reflecting the overhead lights. She sat without a word and folded her shaking hands in her lap. Her eyes darted around the room as if looking for an escape route.

Raptor noticed her eyes grew round when her gaze landed on the slightly open door to his bedroom. He poured champagne into flutes already partially filled with hibiscus juice. He set a glass in front of his guest before taking his seat.

"I also have coffee, if you would prefer." He sipped his mimosa.

Ezmé frowned at him. "Why am I here?"

Without responding, he peeled a linen towel from a basket of *pan dulce*. He selected a *cuernos* roll and placed it on the small plate in front of her. She continued to drill him with her eyes. During their coffee dates, she'd always been flirtatious and uninhibited, so he hadn't expected her to be defiant.

"I wanted to get to know you better so—"

"So you thought having Novio abduct me was a good idea?" Nostrils flaring, she continued, "Did it occur to you to simply ask me on a date?"

"The idea did occur to me, but I am needed here for an extended period of time. I hoped you wouldn't mind being my guest." Raptor raised his glass in toast.

"Guest?" Ezmé took a small sip. "Where are we?"

"My compound." Raptor plucked an *orejas* from the basket and took a bite, the caramel pastry melting on his tongue. "And you are friends with Novio?"

Ezmé picked up her flute and slurped a large drink. An image of Novio and Ezmé being intimate flashed in Raptor's mind and his cheeks flushed.

"I know him from the bookstore where I work part-time." She pinched off a piece of *cuernos* and popped the morsel into her mouth. "I would like to see Novio to make sure he is okay after your goons beat him."

"Novio is fine." Raptor sipped some mimosa. "I will tell him you have asked after his well-being."

"If I have dinner with you, then I can leave?" Ezmé crossed her arms.

Raptor smiled and leaned back into his chair. "You are different than what I expected."

"If you think I'm going to beg you to not—" Her narrowed eyes were back. "I won't."

"I do not want to hurt you."

"What about the girl I saw in the hallway?" Anger punctuated her words. "She has a black eye and a cut lip."

"You do not need to concern yourself with her."

"And how do you explain the scratches on the arm of one of your thugs?"

He hoped shock at the revelation of the scratches did not show on his face.

"I am not interested in getting to know you or what you do here!" Ezmé jumped to her feet. "I demand you let me go! Now!"

Raptor's chair toppled over when he abruptly stood. "You, *Cariño*, are in no position to demand anything!"

Ezmé ran to the door and wrenched it open. Toro looked at her, then past her at Raptor. A small whimper escaped her lips when Toro pulled the door closed. She turned toward Raptor, tears streaming down her cheeks. His heart skipped a beat. He did not want to harm her and admonished himself for losing his temper.

"If you return to your seat." Raptor righted his chair and sat down. "I will tell you why I would like to spend time with you."

Ezmé swiped away her tears, then returned to her chair and sat.

Raptor spooned a mixture of cantaloupe, pineapple, strawberries, and mango onto a larger plate in front of her before serving himself. He used tongs to lift pastry cups filled with chorizo, egg, and cheese from a warming tray, adding the savory treats to their plates.

As Ezmé stared at her food, Raptor forked in a couple of bites. He wanted to give her a few minutes to calm down. He sipped some mimosa and watched her over the rim of the flute. She'd stopped crying and looked defeated. There was something about her helplessness that caused him a moment of reflection. *Did he really want her to be afraid of him? To worry what might happen next? To hate him for having her brought to his compound?*

"You remind me," Raptor cleared his throat and Ezmé looked at him, "of someone I lost long ago."

Ezmé tilted her head. "What happened to her?"

"She—she chose to leave me for someone else."

Ezmé narrowed her eyes. "Did you hurt her?"

Raptor shook his head. "We were taken by an evil man." He ran his hand over his face, then met her questioning stare. "She …" he reached for his mimosa and drained the flute, refilled the glass with champagne, then drank half the contents, "she had to choose whether to go with another man who bought her—or stay and watch me die."

Ezmé picked up her flute and took a long sip. "And now *you're* the evil man?"

His jaw muscle jumped again. "I believe I am simply a survivor."

"I am not—"

"Belen."

"I am not Belen." Ezmé's tone had softened. "I am not the woman you loved."

"True." Raptor pushed his food around his plate. "But after our coffee dates, I am intrigued by you. I want to know you better."

"Here is what you need to know." Ezmé sat tall in her chair and hoisted her glass in a toast. "I don't appreciate you having Novio bring me here." She drained her glass. "And, though I enjoyed our coffee dates, I have no intention of letting you get to know me better!"

Her shift from vulnerable creature to defiant warrior princess brought a smile to his lips. After a sip, Raptor refilled their flutes. He smiled at his beautiful guest, then raised his glass.

"Challenge accepted."

CHAPTER ELEVEN

When they arrived at *Bistró del Tucán*, Peña waited for them at the entrance, arms crossed, scowl in place. Jade ignored him, following Joy to a table the hostess had prepared for them.

Joy looked stunning in a sleeveless leopard print Boho romper. Jade wished she'd worn something nicer than her simple scoop neck tank and black chino shorts. Maybe she could have even added a little flare to her makeup, which had become minimal since Ezmé's disappearance.

Though Joy and her daughter, Erica, had moved from Canada to Puerto Vallarta, neither of them spoke with an accent. Mother and daughter were almost carbon copies. Joy's golden blonde hair a contrast to her dark skin and Erica's darker hair was a nice compliment to her slightly lighter skin tone.

Joy sat at the head of a table with an amazing view of the marina and motioned for everyone to take a seat. A waiter appeared and she ordered her favorite dishes, then she said, "You must be Lieutenant Peña."

He'd sat next to Jade, and she scooched her chair away.

Peña attempted a charming smile, but all Jade could see was his arrogance. "*Sí*, it is a pleasure to finally meet you." He turned a stupid grin to Erica. "And your beautiful daughter."

Erica, stunning in a yellow sundress, gave Peña a slight smile that morphed into thin, tight lips. "Do you know anything about Ezmé's disappearance?"

The question hung in the air like an unexpected storm cloud as the waiter delivered grapefruit and tequila mimosas to the table.

Peña wrinkled his nose. *"Pacífico, por favor."*

Jade reached for a glass and drained half the contents, the citrusy drink causing her to cough.

Peña cut his eyes to her, then looked back at Erica.

"Era-K." Joy looked at her daughter. "Maybe we give everyone a minute, yes?"

"No, she's right." Sandrine finished her mimosa and waggled her empty glass at a waiter. "We need to find out about the time right before Ezmé went missing. The sooner we do, the quicker we might find her." A waiter replaced Sandrine's glass. "Be a love"—She made a circle motion with her finger—"bring a pitcher of this deliciousness for the table."

"Sí, sí." He sat a beer in front of Peña, then made his exit.

Jade thumbed the record app alive on her phone as Peña opened a small notebook.

"I'll start." Jade took another sip from her glass. "Joy, you were with Ezmé on a modeling assignment the day she went missing, correct?"

Joy nodded. "Yes. We met with a photographer and a few other models by the beach pier." She looked at Erica. "When we finished the shoot, Ezmé left to meet some people for dinner—"

"She was meeting me and my friends." Erica took up the conversation. "We ate at *Perla del Pacífico*, then had drinks at *Pub de Nopal*." She looked at her mom, tears budding in her eyes.

Joy touched her arm. "It's not your fault, Baby."

"But, but—" Tears streamed down Erica's cheeks.

"Your mum's right." Sandrine exchanged a look with Jade. They'd been right about the bartender at *Perla del Pacífico*; he knew Ezmé.

"None of this is on you. Someone had probably been watching Ezmé, and took her when the opportunity presented itself."

"Do either of you know if Ezmé had her phone with her?" Jade asked, even though she knew her little sister was rarely without her electronic appendage.

"She had it with her at the pub." Erica wiped tears from her cheeks with a napkin.

"And what about social media?" Jade asked as waiters approached the table.

Conversation was paused as platters of fresh fruit, sliced meats and cheeses, and a basket of delectable rolls were placed on the table. They were followed by individual plates of black bean *huevos rancheros* covered with avocado.

"She had profiles on Instagram and Snapchat," Erica replied.

"Facebook?" Sandrine tilted her head, sunlight bouncing off her hair product, creating the illusion of diamonds nestled in her tight curls.

"We don't spend much time on Facebook," Erica said. "I've checked all of her accounts and she hasn't posted anything new." Another round of tears shook her shoulders.

"Oh, Era-K." Joy reached for her daughter's hand. "It's going to be okay."

"Erica." Jade waited for Erica to look at her. "You're not to blame for my sister's disappearance."

"Joy, the food looks delicious. Can we eat and continue to talk?" Sandrine asked, fork halfway to her mouth. "Erica, where did you go after the pub?"

Peña's phone dinged and he stood. *"Perdón."* He thumbed the screen, then put the phone to his ear as he walked away.

Jade was watching him and wondering why he was dressed in street clothes instead of his uniform. When he turned back to look at her, he held her stare while he talked to someone on the other end.

"Ortiz?" Sandrine asked Jade.

"Maybe." Jade refocused on Erica.

"I went home, but some of them went to the Zoo to dance." Erica blew her nose on the napkin. "She was with friends; she should've been fine."

Peña took his seat and slid his notepad close to Jade. As she chewed a savory bite, she glanced at his barely legible handwriting. The word *Zoo* jumped off the page. But the next words almost made her choke on her food: silver sequins.

"Joy." Jade heard excitement in her tone. "What was Ezmé wearing?"

Before her mom could answer, Erica blurted, "After the shoot, she changed into a silver sequin, sleeveless top, a turquoise skirt, and sparkly sandals."

Peña had eaten half the food on his plate and grabbed a roll. "Agent Mortieau," Peña said, his professional tone taking Jade by surprise. "Agent Mendoza and I are needed elsewhere." He glanced at Jade, then continued, "Would you mind finishing the interview?"

"Joy, it was nice to finally meet you and Erica." Jade came to her feet. "And thank you for brunch."

Peña stood also. "We need a list of names and numbers of the friends who were the last to see Ezmé."

"Go." Sandrine smoothed a wrinkle from her romper as she stood. "We'll meet up later and compare notes."

Jade gave her friend a thumbs-up and headed toward the restaurant's exit, the lieutenant on her heels.

Peña popped the locks on an older Nissan Rogue, which Jade guessed was his personal vehicle. He climbed behind the wheel and Jade slid into the passenger seat. Gunning the engine, he jumped into traffic before Jade could buckle her seatbelt.

"Where are we headed?" she asked as he careened around a corner.

"Casa de Bahía." Peña accelerated around a taxi parked in the road.

"Where the sequins were found?"

"*Sí.*" His skeptical glance dashed her hopes that the silver spangles belonged to Ezmé. "It is a popular hotel for *prostitutas*."

Jade nodded. Sensing Peña was withholding information, she didn't respond. Well, she'd know soon enough if the sequins were a lead. She kept her eyes on the road so he wouldn't see the emotions marching across her face. *Fear. Dread. Hope.*

"Ortiz met with the coroner. Beach girl drowned before *cocodrilos* got to her." Honking at a cluster of *turistas* in a crosswalk, he slammed on the brakes.

"Jesus!" Jade braced herself on the dashboard. "Try to get us there alive, okay?"

Peña flashed a grin and punched the gas pedal. "Almost there."

Casa de Bahía, a sprawling hacienda-style hotel, took up a whole block at the beginning of the *malecón*. It was tucked into a seedy section of town near a small beach access road.

Peña found a spot on the street and parked. Jade stepped onto the sidewalk in front of the hotel and scanned the area, spotting the Zoo across the street at the other end of the block.

"*Sí.*" Peña headed for the entrance. "It will be our next stop."

Noticing the dilapidated state of the hotel, Jade followed him into the red-tiled entry.

A buxom redhead with a bad dye job rushed up to Peña and lip-locked him.

Peña freed his lips and held the woman at arm's length. "*¡Detente, Cayena! ¡Estoy trabajando!*"

"All work and no play." Cayena set her bright pink lips in a pout. "*¡Aburrido!*"

"Enough, Cayena," an older woman chastised. "Leave the Lieutenant alone."

"You come see me later." Cayena blew Peña a kiss. "And I do all the work." She departed with an exaggerated sashay, her ample ass swinging from side to side.

"Basilia Casas." The older woman offered her hand, which Peña shook. "You are here about the girl, *¿sí?*"

"Sí." Peña looked at Jade. "This is my partner, Jade Mendoza."

The word *partner* took Jade by surprise. She shook Basilia's hand and asked, "Did you see this young woman?" She showed a picture of Ezmé on her phone.

Basilia shook her head. "I did not see her or the young man who rented the room." She headed toward the lobby bar. "Can I get you something to drink?"

"No, gracias," Peña answered. "We would like to see the room and the sequins that were found."

"Paco," Basilia said to the bartender. "Is this the woman you saw Wednesday night?" She pointed to Jade's phone.

Paco leaned close and Jade fought the urge to take a step back when he leered at her.

Peña placed a hand on the bar. *"¿La viste?"* he asked, an edge to his tone.

Narrowing his eyes at Peña, Paco shrugged. *"Sí.* She was passed out, but I think it is her."

A twinge of fear tightened Jade's shoulders. "What can you tell us about the man she was with?"

"He wanted a room for a week." Paco reached under the bar top, and Jade watched Peña's hand drift close to the Glock tucked into the waistband of his jeans. "I took this when they arrived," Paco said and turned his phone to show a photo. "When he was helping the girl to a chair."

The shot only showed the man's profile, but it had also captured a young woman with long dark hair covering her face, dressed in a silver sequin top. Peña snapped a picture of the image on the bartender's phone.

"Paco and I were not here when the men came and took them away." Basilia motioned to a counter behind the bartender. "Bring the little bag."

Paco scooped up the baggie and placed it on the bar, the small spangles winking at them through the plastic. "They were found wrapped in tissue and tucked under the phone on a nightstand."

In her heart, Jade knew Ezmé had left the sequins for her to find. She leaned closer and squinted at the small bag, as if her sister had managed to write a note on the tiny silver dots.

"What about the *pendejos* who came for them?" Peña glanced at Jade and handed her the baggie. "Can you describe them?"

"I think the young man in Paco's photo has been here before. Always polite when he meets with one of my girls. But he never has sex with them, just talks." Basilia exchanged a look with Paco, then looked at Peña. "The other *bastardos* terrorized my girls. Threatened to take them to a real *casa de putas* and told them if they were not good at *chupan pollas*, they would be fed to the *cocodrilos*."

"How did they treat the woman in the photo?" Jade asked.

"Cayena said one *bruto*, Julio, who's been here a few times, was rough with the *chica*." Basilia shook her head. " The other *hombres* beat the young man."

"You did not have any security that night?" Peña asked.

"Our guard is a *borracho*." Paco shook his head. "His girlfriend said he has been missing since Wednesday."

"What is his name? Girlfriend's name?" Pulling his notebook from a pocket, Peña searched for a pen.

Paco handed him one. "Fonsie Cano and his *chica* is Adora."

Peña added Adora's phone number to his notes, then looked at Jade. "Anything else?"

"Can we see the room they were in?"

Basilia glanced at Paco, who gave a nod. Jade assumed that meant the room wasn't currently occupied.

"Come." Basilia led them toward a hallway. "The room was cleaned after they left and has been used since."

Jade didn't expect to find anything useful in the room, but she needed to see the space for herself.

A bundle of keys jangled as Basilia unlocked the door. "If you decide to use the room," she winked at Peña. "I will give you and your partner a *tarifa con descuento*."

Heat warmed Jade's cheeks, but before she could utter a cutting retort, Basilia pulled the door closed.

"Do not worry." Peña laughed. "You are not my type."

"Yeah, well not if you were the last man on earth …" She moved toward a window and observed working girls sunning themselves around the pool. Jade added, "Besides, you only have eyes for Cayena."

Peña slammed the drawer of a nightstand shut. "I do not screw *prostitutas*."

Jade stepped from the small bathroom. "Does Cayena know that?"

"I helped her little brother out of a jam, so she thinks she owes me for the favor."

"You." Jade sat on the edge of the bed, then opened the other nightstand drawer. "Lieutenant, are an anomaly." Lifting the Bible, she placed it next to her on the bed.

"You do not have *honesto policía* in America?"

"Yes." Jade flipped through a few pages. "Just didn't expect *you* to be an honest cop."

Two pages were stuck together. Jade held the Bible close to see if she could tell what was between the thin pages.

"What did you find?" Peña crossed the room and sat next to her.

As the bed shifted from his weight, Jade found herself leaning toward him, a warm spicy scent wafting over her.

"The pages have something between them."

"Not surprising considering the *biológicos* that flow in these rooms."

"I think it's a powdery substance."

Peña's knee touched hers when he scooted closer to get a better look. "Be careful, it could be fentanyl."

Jade raised her eyes above the pages to meet his. "Open the baggie with the sequins."

She slowly tore the pages from the Bible and Peña opened the clear bag. Jade folded the thin paper into a small square, then tucked it inside the baggie.

"I don't think it's fentanyl, but better safe than sorry," Jade said as Peña closed the seal and returned the small bag to his pocket.

"Estoy de acuerdo."

He still held her stare, and Jade broke eye contact first. "We should go." She tucked the Bible back into the drawer as she stood.

"Again, I agree." Peña came to his feet. *"Vamos,* I will buy you dinner at the Zoo."

Jade looked at the time on her phone. 3:00 PM. It was a little early for dinner, but her grumbling stomach thought food sounded good. She also had a text from Sandrine, which she read as she followed Peña back through the hotel.

Sandrine: *How's it going with Peña?*

Jade: *Good. Think Ezmé was at Casa de Bahía and left sequins for me to find. Headed to Zoo next.*

The lobby was empty except for the bartender. He watched as they left through the hotel entrance. Peña opened the passenger door of the Nissan and placed the baggie into the storage compartment of the middle console.

A thumping base boomed from the Zoo as they headed toward the bar. Peña was texting on his phone and Jade's chimed with a new notification.

Sandrine: *With Eladio and Valéria running down the names on the list of Ezmé's friends. Nothing new.*

Jade: *Don't wait for me to have dinner. Don't know how long we'll be at the Zoo.*

Sandrine: *Copy. I'll eat with Ortiz and Carrizo and update them. Enjoy the angry LT!*

Jade sent a raised-eye emoji, slid her phone into her back pocket and glanced at Peña. Her annoyance at the smug cop had kept her from noticing his handsome, albeit rugged face, athletic build, and assured swagger.

"Beach girl." Peña stopped and glanced at Jade.

Her cheeks warmed as if she'd been caught ogling. "And?"

"Had the Zoo's club stamp on her remaining hand."

CHAPTER TWELVE

"Sí, gracias," **Eladio** said. *"Qué tengas una buena noche."* He set his phone down. "That was my last name to call."

"I'm done with my list too." Valéria laid a pen on top of a notepad.

"Ortiz." Sandrine didn't look up from the laptop screen. "Did Anita have anything new to add to our list?"

"Sí." He looked at his notes. "She recalls a young man talking to Ezmé."

Sandrine raised her gaze to meet his. "Description?"

Eladio nodded. "Mexican, about twenty-five, slight build."

Sandrine's fingers banged the keyboard. "That's not much."

"I had a similar comment from Luna," Valéria added, "she said the guy seemed *enamorado* with Ezmé. Also, he has a tattoo on his left wrist."

"Oh, great!" Sandrine glanced at Valéria. "Did she describe the ink?"

Valéria handed the pad to Sandrine. "The words *God Goes Before* in the shape of a cross."

"Might be something." Sandrine's fingers flew across the keys. "Scratch that." She leaned back into her chair. "There's too many parlors to check."

"I asked Luna about social media accounts. Ezmé's friends have been scouring the platforms for any new posts." Valéria looked at her notes. "Luna said the last post on Ezmé's Instagram account was a tease about a new man in her life, but no picture."

Eladio looked at his phone. "Peña texted. Ezmé had dinner at *Perla del Pacífico*." He raised his gaze and continued, "Can I treat you *señoritas* to dinner?"

Sandrine stood. "Good idea, I'm starving."

"Valéria." Eladio smiled at her. "Peña thinks you should be the one to question the bartender."

"Brilliant!" Sandrine grinned at Valéria. "He knows something, so it's a great idea to have someone he hasn't met quiz him."

"Perfecto. " Eladio grabbed his keys. "We can take my car."

Sandrine led the way from his office toward the back of the building. Though Valéria was only a year younger than Jade, Eladio thought Peña's suggestion was probably due to the blonde Mexican's beauty and flirtatious manner.

They piled into Eladio's Jeep, and he headed for the busy *malecón*. The temperature had begun a slow descent toward the projected low of sixty-six degrees. He missed the dry heat of Mazatlán and had found Puerto Vallarta's humidity a difficult adjustment.

"Do you think we need a reservation?" Sandrine asked from the passenger seat.

Eladio shook his head. "I reserved a table outside on the sidewalk, thinking we would send Valéria to the bar."

Sandrine cocked an eyebrow. "Good plan, except she doesn't know which bartender to talk to."

"Sí. " Eladio nodded. "But you will be able to see the bar staff. The sliding wall of windows will be open, and you can point him out."

"Ah, got it!" Sandrine said as Valéria leaned forward from the backseat.

"Okay, I'll know who to talk to, but about what?"

Eladio exchanged a look with Sandrine. "I am thinking keep the conversation general. See if he asks specific questions or suggests any activities or places to visit."

"Yes," Sandrine agreed. "If he's part of Raptor's crew, he'll want to know if you're here alone. And will probably recommend you go to bars like the Zoo."

Eladio nodded. "Or say he can get you a discount on tickets for cruises like the *Perla del Oceano* pirate ship sunset excursion."

Valéria scooted back into the seat and Eladio thought he saw trepidation in her reflection in the rearview mirror, so he added, "Valéria, you handled the *hosco* Lieutenant Peña with a light touch and a warm smile."

"I hope *hosco* means sullen," Sandrine added.

"Close." Eladio changed lanes, turned, and headed toward *Bahía de Banderas*. "Surly."

"I'll say." Sandrine laughed. "What's his deal?"

"We have not always had good experiences with American officials."

"I get it." Sandrine shrugged. "But some of your fellow lawmen are batshit crazy."

Braking for a delivery truck, Eladio asked, "Martínez?"

"Exactly!" Sandrine said.

Valéria leaned forward again. "What did Martínez do?"

"Bastard tried to kill Katelyn when we were in Mazatlán," Sandrine replied.

"It's a long story, and we are here." Eladio slipped into a parking spot at the curb a block from *Perla del Pacífico*. Rounding his vehicle, he joined the women on the sidewalk and offered an arm to each of them. "We should make an entrance, *¿sí?*"

"Lets!" Sandrine looped her arm through his, but Valéria hesitated. "Come on Rook, join the charade."

Valéria took Eladio's other arm, and he smiled at her. "Your first undercover assignment, but do not worry." He glanced at Sandrine. "We have your back."

"¡Sí!" Sandrine gave her a thumbs-up. "You'll be great!"

A light breeze rolled off the bay and filled the air with a myriad of scents: tobacco from a smoke shop across the street that advertised free tequila shots with any purchase, the aroma of chicken *fajitas* wafted from *Polla Sabroso* as they waited at the crosswalk, and one of Eladio's companions wore perfume with a hint of mango.

For a moment, he wished he was on a date with one of these beautiful women. Then the hostess greeted them, and he shifted his focus back to the task at hand.

"*Ortiz para tres.*"

"*Sí, bueno.*" The young woman plucked menus from a rack. "*Sígame, por favor.*"

Eladio indicated Sandrine should go first, then Valéria followed him, bringing up the rear. When they reached the table, Eladio pulled out a chair for Sandrine. This seated her with her back to the open-air bar.

"Lucky us." Sandrine nodded at Valéria. "The right bartender is working tonight."

Valéria took her cue, stepped to the bar, and claimed a barstool close to the table. Sitting across from Sandrine gave Eladio a perfect line of sight to the bar.

One waiter delivered water, chips, and salsa, and another asked, "Something to drink?"

"*Margarita con hielo y sal.*" Sandrine smiled at Eladio. "Practicing my Spanish."

"*Pacifico,*" Eladio said, and the waiter headed for the bar. "Valéria just ordered from the bartender."

"She's got this." Sandrine dipped a chip into the salsa, then popped the bite into her mouth.

Eladio looked at his phone. "Nothing new from Peña."

"I think it's a good sign no one has reported a brawl at the Zoo."

A laugh escaped Eladio at the thought of Jade and Peña rolling around on the dance floor trading punches and verbal jabs.

Sandrine stifled a giggle too as the waiter delivered their drinks.

"¡Salud!" Eladio hoisted his beer in toast.

"Cheers!" Sandrine touched her glass to his, then took a long slurp.

The waiter was back. "Ready to order?"

"Queso fundido con chorizo y guacamole." Eladio looked at Sandrine. "Anything else?"

She raised her almost-empty glass. *"Otro de estos por favor."*

"Mismo," Eladio called after the departing waiter. Smiling at Sandrine he added, "Your Spanish is good."

"It's a seriously hard language."

"As is English."

"Agreed." Draining her glass, she cocked an eyebrow. "What?"

Eladio glanced at her, then focused on the young woman now sitting next to Valéria. "I think Erica Beck just joined Valéria."

Sandrine pulled her phone from a small purse. "Give me a sec." She studied her screen, lowered the phone, and placed it on the table. "It's her." Eladio began to stand, but Sandrine motioned him to sit. "Wait."

Nodding, he said, "Valéria just smoothed the back of her hair and gave me a thumbs-up."

"Nice move."

Their second round of drinks was delivered, and the waiter promised their food was coming.

After a sip of beer, Eladio reported, "Valéria is agreeing with something Erica is saying."

"Is she smiling?" Sandrine asked.

"Sí, and now they are coming this way." Eladio pushed his chair back and stood.

Valéria rounded the table and took a seat. Erica sat across from her, and they both placed their drinks onto the table.

The appetizers arrived and they sat in silence while the waiter added small plates and napkins.

As soon as he departed, Sandrine asked, "You two figured out who each other is?"

"Yes." Valéria nodded. "After Erica asked the bartender if he knew where Ezmé might be, I introduced myself."

"Well?" Sandrine tilted her head.

"The bartender, Goyo, knows Ezmé," Valéria began.

"But he had nothing to do with her disappearance." Erica sipped her white wine.

"And," The two young women exchanged a smile before Valéria continued, "He's in love with Ezmé."

"Bloody hell." Sandrine smiled. "That's what he was hiding."

"Did he have anything useful to share?" Eladio asked as Erica spooned guacamole onto a plate.

"The only new tidbit is he tried to talk Ezmé out of going to the Zoo the night she disappeared." Valéria reached for a napkin.

"Goyo wanted her to meet him after his shift ended." Erica looked at Valéria.

"But she never showed." Valéria held up a finger. "And he thought he saw the same guy one of Ezmé's other friends mentioned seeing." She added salsa to a spoonful of guacamole.

"I don't remember ever seeing that guy talk to Ezmé." Erica frowned.

Eladio's phone buzzed, and he checked the screen.

"Peña?" Sandrine asked, then her phone signaled an incoming text.

Nodding, Eladio countered, "Jade?"

"She says they've been at the Zoo for over two hours with nothing to report," Sandrine shared.

Signaling the waiter, Eladio looked at Sandrine. "Peña said Jade's bored. I think I should relieve them." He handed the waiter a credit card. "I want you ladies to stay and enjoy dinner as my treat."

Coming to her feet, Sandrine said, "I'll come with you."

"Por favor, quédate." He held up a hand. "Stay."

Smiling, Sandrine resumed her seat. "If you insist."

"Make sure you travel home together." Eladio pushed in his chair.

"Good plan," Sandrine agreed. "Valéria, where are you staying?"

"The Hilton by the marina," Valéria replied.

"No, that won't do." Erica waved a hand. "We have room for you at *El Mar Llama*, so we'll cab over and pick up your things from the Hilton."

"Oh, that looks like such a quaint hotel." Valéria smiled. "Thanks for including me."

"Perfecto." Eladio looked at Sandrine. "You will text when you arrive at the hotel?"

Sandrine smiled and nodded. *"Sí."*

Eladio gave a slight bow before departing. As he headed for his Jeep, he thought about what Sandrine had said about it being a good thing no one had reported a fight at the Zoo. He didn't know what he'd find when he arrived, but as head of the task force it was his responsibility to check in. Besides, the idea of seeing Jade again put a little bounce in his step.

CHAPTER THIRTEEN

After his busy night and then breakfast with Ezmé, Raptor had slept most of the day. When he woke, he showered, ate a light meal of *flautas de pollo*, and then was brought up-to-date regarding the body that had been found on the beach. He didn't believe the girl's death would be connected to his operation. But the fact that one of his men had captured her friend, with another friend still at large in Puerto Vallarta, could pose a problem.

Now a young man stood in front of Raptor's desk, and he hoped the look of dread on the soldier's face wouldn't result in him losing control of his bowels.

"Why were you on the pirate ship trying to abduct women?" Raptor asked.

"I was told we were meeting two *prostitutas* who wanted to come talk to you." The man touched a bandage on his wrist.

Raptor drilled him with a narrowed stare. "Who were you with?"

He shook his head and looked down.

"Look at me!" Raptor barked.

"Lo siento, Patrón." He met Raptor's glare, his palms raised. "I did not know the targets were *turistas*."

"Who were you with?" Raptor asked again.

"Julio."

This information took Raptor by surprise. While he knew his soldier, Julio, liked to bend the rules, he hadn't done so since he'd been caught raping a captive. That was before Raptor issued the mandate. Now his organization was no longer kidnapping women to be trafficked. But he'd also heard several of his soldiers were unhappy, regardless of being paid a significant wage, and wanted to return to their past ways.

"Tell me what happened," Raptor said.

"Julio had Devil's Breath and tried to blow the drug into both women's faces."

He hesitated, and Raptor waited.

"One girl slapped Julio and when he hit her, she lost her balance." He met Raptor's gaze. "I tried to grab her, but she bit my arm before falling into the ocean."

Raptor recalled being trained in using Devil's Breath—both the liquid drops and the fine powder. He'd learned the hard way how Devil's Breath, the street name for scopolamine, could be used to render a person into a zombielike shell. It made the individual compliant and susceptible to any manner of suggestion, usually with evil intent. The odorless, tasteless drug was derived from nightshade plants in Columbia, and had become a favorite weapon of criminals.

His experience with the powerful drug had been when his previous boss dosed him. He was then ordered to fight a fellow soldier his boss felt had betrayed him. The battle was also how he'd acquired the scar on his chest, which had earned him the moniker Raptor. The soldier before him sniffed, chasing the memory back to a corner of Raptor's mind.

He stood and motioned for the man to come closer. "What is your name?"

"Fernando Munoz." He squared his shoulders. *"Novio me reclutó."*

"You are the one they call Ferdo?"

"Sí, Patrón." He gave a slight smile.

"Ferdo." Raptor pointed to a chair in front of his desk. *"Sentarse."*

Ferdo nodded and sat. He no longer wore a mask of trepidation, but Raptor still saw fear in his eyes.

"You and Novio are friends?"

"Sí." Wariness flashed in Ferdo's eyes. "He rescued me from the *policía*. He is a good friend."

"What was your trouble with the police?"

"A neighbor raped my sister, and I killed him."

The admission took Raptor by surprise. Pointing to the bandage, he asked, "Is the injury bad?"

Ferdo looked at his wrist, then raised his eyes to Raptor. "It is nothing."

A knock on his office door announced that Toro and Milo were ready to meet with him. Ferdo's fate would need to wait until Julio had been questioned, but Raptor had no doubt the abduction had been Julio's idea.

Raptor stood again and Ferdo came to his feet, another look of dread crawling across his face.

"Ask Vito to see to your wound." Raptor offered a smile.

A whisper of relief reflected in Ferdo's eyes as he nodded. *"Gracias, Patrón."* Ferdo gave a slight bow, then headed for the door.

Before Ferdo could reach for the knob, the door swung open and Toro filled the opening. He stepped into Raptor's office, and Ferdo edged past the large *sicario*.

"Where is Julio?" Raptor asked as Toro sat in a chair.

"Gone." Toro frowned. "I have *halcones* looking for him. *Sin suerte.*"

Milo stepped into the office and sat next to Toro.

Raptor narrowed his eyes at his lieutenant. *"Llegas tarde."*

Scrubbing his face with a hand, Milo nodded. "It is Ezmé." He held his hands palms up. "She is asking about Novio and wants to see him. Also say she hear *mujeres* crying and asking what is going on."

Toro shook his head. *"Ella va a ser una problema."*

Frowning at the *sicario*, Raptor knew Toro was right about Ezmé being a problem. "Are all of the women crying?"

"It is always the newest *hembra*." Milo looked at Toro, then back at Raptor. "The one Ferdo took from the pirate ship."

"And what about a female with a black eye?" Raptor narrowed his eyes at his men. "Does one of the men have scratches on his face and neck?"

Milo scrubbed his face with a hand, then met Raptor's stare. *"Sí."*

"Tell me what happened." Raptor stood and crossed to the bar. He poured three shots of *Patrón*, the familiar sweet scent of agave drifting toward him. Returning to his desk, he handed a glass to each of his men and resumed his seat.

"Julio snatched a female from the *malecón* late one night." Milo drank half his shot. "Instead of bringing her here, he kept her in his car overnight."

"And?" Raptor sipped some tequila.

"He raped her." Milo finished his shot. "And when she tried to escape the next morning, Julio kicked her in the face, knocking her out." He shook his head. "Julio handed the girl off at the checkpoint and she attacked one of the men before the other soldier could subdue her."

"Why was this not reported to me sooner?" Raptor looked from Toro to Milo. "Never mind. Find Julio. Make sure he is dealt with, so the other soldiers are reminded of his failure."

"I will take care of Julio," Toro said.

Raptor took another sip. "Milo, did the girl receive medical care from Vito?"

Milo nodded. *"Sí, Patrón."*

"Do you think it would be possible to release her without repercussions?" Raptor asked.

"Possibly." Toro looked at Milo. "But we should wait until her injuries have healed."

"I agree," Milo said.

"Now, do we know the location of the remaining friend of the pirate ship captive?"

"As far as we know, she is still at her hotel," Milo replied.

"Find out if she's talked to the *policía*," Raptor instructed.

"What do you want us to do with Ezmé?" Toro asked, his tone suggesting he wanted to dispense with the young troublemaker.

Raptor leaned back in his chair, cradled his head in his hands, and contemplated his next move.

"Ezmé will join me for dinner." Raptor sat straighter in his chair and looked at his watch. "Milo, bring Novio here at seven and make sure he is cleaned up." He shifted his gaze to Toro. "You will bring Ezmé at seven-thirty."

Toro, who was built like a bull, but had a stare as intent as an eagle, squinted at Raptor. "*Patrón*, this is a good idea?"

Raptor nodded. "I expect the two of you to be in the hallway at the ready."

Milo stood. "*Sí, Patrón.*" He headed for the office door. "I will return in an hour."

Toro rose from his chair. "The *cabrito* threatened to kill you and rescue the *doncella justa*." He held Raptor's stare. "At least have Milo bind Novio's hands."

Smiling at his *sicario*, Raptor said, "I am not worried about Novio, but the fair maiden could be a problem."

CHAPTER FOURTEEN

While watching the nearly empty bar for over two hours, they'd initially occupied themselves with chicken nachos and a few *cervezas*. Now Jade was bored out of her mind. She sent a text to Sandrine complaining about her sore ass, then placed her phone face down on the table.

"Explain your," she said, looking around the bar, "plan to me again."

"You are not very patient." Peña finished typing on his phone and grinned at her.

Jade frowned, drained the last drops from her *Corona*, and signaled the waiter for another.

"It's Saturday night and nothing has happened since we've been sitting here." The waiter placed a *Corona* in front of her. "So, I don't understand the point of waiting any longer."

"It is early." Peña watched a young man circulating inside the Zoo. "Have you noticed the boys flitting in and out of the bar?"

Jade nodded. "Trying to sell their wares."

"*Sí.*" Peña continued to watch the young man as he moved from table to table hawking beaded bracelets. "They are *halcones* in training."

It took Jade's brain a second to do the translation. "Falcons?"

"*Sí.*" Peña took a sip from his *Pacifico*. "They work for the cartels, low level drug dealers, and probably some for this *cabrón*, Raptor."

"Is there a way to know who works for who?" Jade scanned the small crowd in the bar.

Peña shook his head. "They use bird calls to communicate, but each group has their own sound." He grinned. "It is eerie, but some of the calls actually sound like the *Halcones de la Pradera* that live in Puerto Vallarta."

"Damn!" Jade chugged some beer. "It would help if we could capture one of Raptor's guys and ask them about kidnapping women."

"No." Another head shake from Peña. "If we managed to catch one of the young *halcones* or a *halcón* who is now a *secuestrador*, they would not talk."

A large group of twenty-somethings barged into the bar, their boisterous laughter competing with the music blaring from overhead speakers. Every now and then, Jade envied young people her age and their carefree approach to life. Though she was proud to have been handpicked by Benson to work with FBI Special Agent Christopher Temple in their agencies' joint pursuit of Sarita García, the responsibility and undercover work in Mazatlán seemed to have aged her. Not to mention, learning the drug queen was her mother became an added burden to her job as a DEA Agent.

"Mendoza?" Peña snapped his fingers at her. "We should order dinner."

"I'm good." Jade took another sip of beer.

"We will be here for a few more hours." Peña waved over a waiter.

"*Sí.*" The waiter waited, pen and pad in hand.

"*Plato de tacos con pollo, bistec, cerdo. Ceviche de marlín. Dos cócteles de camarones.*" Peña looked at Jade and she gave him a shoulder shrug. "Pitcher of margaritas."

"Hope you're hungry." Jade finished her beer.

"We are on a date." Peña glanced around the bar. "Need to look the part."

"Seriously?" Jade laughed. "We are not on—"

"Hola, señor." A scrawny boy about ten years old with a colorful gecko on his shoulder, stood next to their table.

"Gecko!" Peña grinned at the boy. *"¿Cómo estás?"*

"Bien, Señor Peña." He cradled the gecko in his hand and offered the bright green lizard to Jade who gently plucked the small reptile from his palm. *"Tu novia es muy bonita."*

A glint of mischief danced in Peña's dark eyes. "Gecko says you are very beautiful."

"Gracias, Gecko." Jade smiled and handed back the lizard.

"Señor." Gecko's face morphed into a frown. *"He oído hablar de hombres que usan el Aliento de Diablos para secuestrar chicas."*

Peña's face mirrored Gecko's seriousness as he repeated the boy's news in English. "You probably translated most of what he said. He has heard of men using Devil's Breath to abduct girls."

Jade felt the color drain from her face. Devil's Breath, aka scopolamine, was a very dangerous drug. It was capable of incapacitating someone. In the wrong hands, it could kill a person.

Jade glanced at Gecko, then returned her gaze to the lieutenant. "Can he identify any of these men?"

Peña shook his head, then pulled one hundred pesos from his wallet and handed it to Gecko. *"Gracias, Gecko. Tendrás cuidado, ¿sí?"*

Gecko's eyes grew wide. *"Sí, sí. ¡Gracias, Señor Peña!"* Flashing a grin at Jade, he hurried from the bar, his lizard clinging to his shoulder.

"Very brave of your cute informant to tell you about Devil's Breath." Jade drilled Peña with her eyes. "How do you keep him safe?"

Peña held her stare and she didn't see any concern on his face. "I cannot keep him safe. All I can do is pay him well for information, even when it is not useful, so he and his family have a little extra income."

"Are you afraid he'll become a falcon otherwise?"

A waiter arrived with a pitcher of margaritas and two salt-rimmed glasses filled with ice. Another waiter delivered two shrimp cocktails and they both departed without a word.

Peña poured the lime concoction into a glass and handed it to Jade before filling one for himself. He slurped some margarita, flakes of salt sticking to the corners of his mouth. For a moment, Jade couldn't take her eyes off his sensuous lips. From the fishbowl glass in front of her, she plucked a large shrimp, dripping with cocktail sauce, and took a bite.

"It is very difficult to keep young people from working for the cartels or other criminal organizations." Peña followed her lead and munched a shrimp.

"Similar to the problem we have in the states." Jade sipped from her glass. "Every year approximately a half-million teens join one of the thirty-three thousand gangs we have throughout the US."

Peña nodded. "Crime pays, and gangs offer a sense of *familia*."

"Exactly." Jade agreed. "Do you think the white powder we found in the Bible could be Devil's Breath?"

"Possibly." Peña nodded as their waiter set a large platter of taco fixings onto the table, and another added a container with corn tortillas.

"*¿Algo más?*" The waiter asked.

"*No, gracias,*" Peña replied.

"Good call on the taco platter. It smells delicious," Jade said. "But after I eat, I'm going back to the hotel."

"It is still early." Without looking at her, he fixed a chicken taco. "And I wanted to talk to you about a possible undercover operation to infiltrate Raptor's stash house."

Jade piled pork into a tortilla and added onion, cilantro, and salsa. She took a bite and chewed as she processed Peña's suggestion. Surely he didn't think he could blend in with young men and flirt with women long enough to drug them?

"Do you have some male officers in mind?"

Peña raised an eyebrow and swallowed a mouthful of taco. "Not *hombres, mujeres*."

"Women?" Jade knew her surprise showed on her face. "You mean as captives?"

"*Sí.*"

"And you have female officers who would be up to the task?"

"I am thinking Valéria Carrizo."

Jade wiped away a dribble of taco juice from her lips. "She's too green to go undercover alone." She reached for her glass and took a long drink. "I can go under too."

Peña laughed and Jade's cheeks burned hot. "What's so funny?" she growled.

"You are too *mal ventilado* to attract attention."

God, she wished he'd stop dotting his conversation with Spanish. "What did you just say?" Jade heard anger in her tone.

"You are stuffy." Peña poured each of them more margarita. "Closed off. If you cannot flirt or at least look like fun, no man will approach you."

Jade picked up her glass and drank half the contents. She felt certain Eladio would never let Valéria go undercover alone, but Peña's smug assessment of her made her blood boil.

The group of twenty-somethings hit the dance floor when Demi Lovato's "Cool for the Summer" blasted from the speakers. Jade finished her drink, slid off her barstool, and held out her hand to Peña.

"Dance with me, Baby." She swayed her hips to the music.

Peña stood and grabbed her hand, spinning her into the middle of the dance floor. He matched her moves, keeping rhythm with the beat. Jade tried to put some distance between herself and the lieutenant, but he placed his hands at her waist and drew her closer.

"You are trying to prove a point, *¿sí?*" he whispered into her ear.

Damn straight! Jade thought. She turned her face toward him and captured his lips with her own, his mustache tickling her upper lip. What she'd planned to be a quick kiss became a consuming embrace as Peña raised his hands and twined them into her hair. She knew she should break free, but desire flooded her senses and she leaned into him.

When another dancer bumped into them, Jade recovered her composure. She placed her hands on Peña's chest and pushed away, turning into the gyrating crowd. He stood still and watched her for a minute, then closed the distance between them in long strides. When he took her hands and placed them on his shoulders, Jade didn't resist. She let him hold her close as the song changed to Ed Sheeran's "Perfect".

Peña nuzzled her neck, lowered the neckline of her tank with a fingertip, his lips leaving a trail of fire. He kissed her tattoo, then met her eyes with a lusty stare. *"Libélula."* He kissed the dragonfly again, then covered her lips with his, grinding his hips against hers as they moved about the dance floor.

To control her own lust, Jade played the lyrics in her head and was surprised when Peña sang a phrase in her ear in Spanish. It took her a beat to loosely translate the lyric: *a woman, stronger than anyone I know.*

She lifted her eyes to his and he kissed her, a long slow kiss that warmed dormant parts of her anatomy. She wanted this moment to last long enough to morph into something more satisfying, but Peña abruptly released her and headed for their table.

The song played on, and couples continued to move with the music as Jade made her way from the dance floor. Once again, her cheeks warmed, and she focused on erasing embarrassment from her face. Peña stood with his back to her, and she could tell someone had taken his seat.

"Buenas noches, Agent Mendoza," Eladio Ortiz said when she reached the table, his tone cold and professional. "Would you two like to tell me what is going on?"

Jade cut her eyes to Peña, then looked at Eladio. "We were testing a theory before we proposed an undercover operation to you."

"What are you doing here?" Peña reached for his glass.

"It is not important." Eladio stood. "I will leave you to your evening and we can discuss your proposal in the morning."

Before Eladio could make his exit, Jade grabbed her phone and bolted toward the exit.

"Jade!" Peña called after her.

She heard her colleagues' footsteps behind her. But she pressed on, racing down the sidewalk into the dark night—chasing after Sarita García.

CHAPTER FIFTEEN

Captain Jack's was crowded with tourists, which annoyed Eladio. He'd come here to avoid the loud atmosphere of Monkey Business bar.

As he sipped his double *Kah reposado*, the image of Jade and Peña dirty dancing at the Zoo burned through his mind like wildfire. Eladio wished Jesús had left the bottle of tequila so he could refill his tumbler when he wanted.

After he and Peña had caught up to Jade, they'd persuaded her to give up the chase. But she was convinced the woman she had followed was her mother. The three of them had popped into Monkey Business and Eladio had ordered *cervezas* and *Hornitos* shots for their table. Under the angry gaze of a lifelike bronze gorilla statue in a corner of the bar, he and Peña waited until Jade was ready to talk.

"It was her," Jade finally said before drinking half of her shot.

Since Eladio hadn't seen the woman Jade had chased, he held his tongue. He had no idea where the drug queen had disappeared to, but doubted Sarita García would risk being caught just to see her daughter.

"I did not see who you chased." Peña stared at Jade. "Why do you think it was García?"

Jade looked at Eladio, then Peña, then pointed to her eyes. "We have the same eyes." She finished her shot.

"I do not know what that means." Peña shrugged.

Eladio touched Jade's arm. "You have not told him?"

Shaking her head, Jade reached for her beer.

"Told me what?" Peña leaned toward Jade.

"Sarita García is my birth mother." Jade sipped some beer.

Eladio noticed Peña's eyes soften. He continued to look at Jade as she studied her glass. He wondered what Sarita, if it *was* Sarita who'd watched them at the Zoo, thought of seeing her daughter in the arms of Amado Peña. Eladio also asked himself if he would have given chase if he'd been the one to see Sarita.

He sipped some tequila. "Jade." He cleared his throat. "I think you, like me," he continued despite her wary look, "are haunted by Sarita's escape." Her brow creased as he pressed on. "But I believe you." His admission surprised him, and he reached for his beer.

"*¿Qué?*" Peña looked at Jade. "Regardless of you being here, I would think she would be far from anywhere she might be captured."

Jade glared at the lieutenant. "I know what I saw!"

Peña held up his hands as defense from her anger, then stood. He finished his shot and drained the remaining beer in his glass. He looked at Jade with a glimmer of lust, and for a second, Eladio wanted to punch Peña in the face.

Heading from the bar, Peña called over his shoulder, "I will see you in the morning."

"He's right." Jade tipped her glass to her lips, then looked at Eladio. "Why would Sarita risk being close to us when we still need to arrest her?"

"I am guessing she wants to get to know you." Eladio smiled at her, but Jade's attention was focused on her beer.

"But how would she know I'm here?" She sipped some beer.

"My office issued a statement about the task force, which included your name." She finally met his eyes and he smiled again. "Sarita must have seen the article online."

"Which means she knows about Ezmé's disappearance too." Jade finished her beer. "I don't want to be distracted by my *mom* while I'm trying to get my sister back."

"Agreed," Eladio said, though he still wasn't sure the woman Jade had chased was Sarita. "We will stay focused on our current assignment." He covered her hand with his, and she gave him a wan smile. "And not Sarita García."

Eladio waited until Jade left in a taxi to join the others at Joy's hotel. Watching the rent-a-wreck cab drive away with her, Eladio had wondered once again if his budding attraction to Jade was due to her uncanny resemblance to Sarita.

A chorus of "shots, shots, shots" boomed through Captain Jack's, dragging Eladio back to the present. He reached for his own shot and contemplated going home, but he hadn't eaten since his few bites at *Perla del Pacífico*. If he intended to keep drinking, which was likely, he knew he'd need something in his stomach. He mentally searched his fridge and cupboards, conjuring up images of cold cuts, crackers, and a stale loaf of *Telera* bread.

"Pizza?" Jesús asked.

Eladio shook his head. "The ribeye, medium rare, salad with salsa ranch, no rice. And another of these." He lifted his glass and drained the tequila, then handed the empty tumbler to Jesús.

The bartender cocked an eyebrow. *"¿Estás bien?"*

"Sí." Eladio grinned. *"¡Perfecto!"*

He had become friends with the bartender, who also owned Captain Jack's, when Eladio had frequented the bar on a previous stay in Puerto Vallarta.

A group of giggling women stumbled inside, drawing Eladio's attention. Their leader claimed space at the bar and waved at Jesús. Eladio wondered if her height and coppery red hair, combined with a toned physique, nominated her to be in charge. He normally didn't pay attention to women like her, assuming they were all pretense and no substance, but he enjoyed watching her command Jesús to do her bidding.

The harried bartender delivered his double shot and rolled his eyes. The woman leaned across Eladio, her firm breasts brushing his arm, to grab a stack of napkins.

"Food is coming," Jesús said. "You want a table?"

The woman touched Eladio's arm. "Don't be silly." She flashed a bright smile that reached her piercing blue eyes. "He wants to party with us!" She picked up his tumbler and took a long sip. "I'll share mine when it arrives." She cut her eyes to Jesús who threw a bar towel over his shoulder and stalked off.

Eladio returned her smile. "Thank you for the offer, but after my meal, I must call it a night."

She took another sip and studied him over the rim of the tumbler. "I have already eaten but would be interested in sharing dessert."

"Sienna!" one of her friends shouted. "We want to finish our drinks, then go to Monkey Business bar."

She extended her hand. "Sienna, obviously." She laughed, the sound almost musical.

He shook her hand, allowing her to hold his in her soft palm. "Eladio Or—"

Sienna put a finger to his lips. "Let us be strangers enjoying a delightful encounter—without our boring lives tagging along."

Jesús delivered a tray of shots to Sienna's friends at the other end of the bar, then placed her glass in front of her. She picked up the tumbler and offered it to Eladio. He took a large sip.

"I believe we are now even." Eladio handed back her drink. "Where are you from?"

"South Beach." Sienna tipped the glass to her coral colored lips.

"As in Miami?" Eladio asked.

"Yes, and you are from?"

"Monterrey."

"As in California?"

Eladio laughed. "No, Monterrey, México."

"Ah." Sienna nodded. Her friends were summoning her. "I must see if I can persuade them to stay, so I can get to know you better, Eladio."

Sienna clinked his glass, raised hers, then drained the contents. Eladio took a sip of his tequila. She flashed another thousand-watt smile before rejoining her friends.

Jesús delivered Eladio's steak. "Another double?"

Eladio cast a glance at Sienna, who was leading her friends in a toast, then shifted his attention back to Jesús.

His friend grinned and nodded toward Sienna. "You should skip dinner and accept her offer to share dessert."

"A glass of cabernet—" Eladio began as Sienna returned to his side.

"Dinner smells delicious." She placed a hand on his shoulder. "Alas handsome stranger, I must depart with my *amigas* and conquer Monkey's Bar." She looked at Jesús. "We have settled our bill with you?"

"*Sí.*" Jesús turned his attention to another group stepping to the bar.

"Goodbye, Eladio." Sienna leaned down and kissed his cheek.

He grasped her arm as she turned to go. "Would you like to join me for dessert?"

Sienna captured his lips in a promising kiss, then said, "I thought you'd never ask."

Jesús was back with a bottle of cabernet. "I will put your dinner in the cooler for you." He picked up Eladio's dinner plate. "The wine is on the house."

Eladio paid his bill and Sienna went to tell her girlfriends she'd made other plans. "I'll see you in the morning for our trip to Punta Mita," she called over her shoulder as she returned to Eladio.

Once they left the bar, Sienna said, "I'd offer to take you back to my place, but I'm sharing a hotel room with Fran, so we won't have much time before she stumbles in for the night."

"My apartment is not far, if you are comfortable with the idea of being alone with me in a strange place."

She looped her arm through his. "I'd say comfortable is an understatement as to how I feel."

They settled into Eladio's Jeep, and he headed for home. His voice of reason kept asking if this was a good idea, but he ignored the thought. It had been a long time since he'd enjoyed the company of a beautiful woman.

"I love visiting here." Sienna smiled. "There's a fun, energetic vibe to Puerto Vallarta."

"*Sí.*" Eladio flicked his blinker, then made a right hand turn. "It is a very busy city."

A flash of guilt washed over Eladio as he remembered his reason for being in Puerto Vallarta. But would a few hours of pleasure make a difference in the task force's progress toward capturing Raptor? Besides, if Peña and Jade could enjoy a date night, then so could he.

Sienna caressed his back as he unlocked the door to his apartment. When she touched his weapon, she held up her hands.

"Cop or crook?" she asked, her tone husky with longing.

"Cop." He turned and kissed her as they stumbled inside. Eladio preferred a slower pace, but his body responded to Sienna's touch with an urgency he hadn't felt in a long time.

"Give me a minute." Eladio ducked into a small bedroom, removed his gun and credentials, then locked them in a safe.

Sienna met him when he stepped from the room. She tugged at his linen shirt until the buttons popped off, and then freed him of the garment. She stroked his chest, looking into his eyes before kissing him again. Sienna took a step back and lowered the straps of her violet sundress. She let the dress float to the floor, exposing her glorious nakedness. Clad now in only a purple lacy thong and strappy black sandals, she glided toward his bedroom.

"Bring the bottle of wine." Sienna blew him a kiss before disappearing from the hallway.

Eladio stepped into the kitchen, opened the wine, and grabbed two glasses. The sight from his bedroom door took his breath away. Sienna now lay on her stomach across his bed. She'd opened the sliding glass door to the small deck, letting in a salty ocean breeze and night sounds of the city. Eladio placed the wine and glasses on his dresser, then stood admiring the view.

"Can I pour you a glass?"

"Dessert first." Sienna came to her knees. "I think in order to fully enjoy my share though, you're going to need to lose your clothes."

She moved to the edge of the bed and sat, spreading her legs for him to step between. As Eladio kicked off his shoes, she worked to free him from his trousers, then stood and melded her body into his. He twined his hands into her luxurious locks, easing her head backward until her throat was exposed.

Eladio liked that their pace had slowed, and he took his time leaving a trail of kisses from her neck to her breasts. Sienna moaned and turned in his arms, pushing her ass into his groin. Then she climbed onto the bed, crawled to the pillows, and flipped onto her back.

"Por favor, señor," she said in a husky whisper. "Come taste your dessert."

Eladio laid on the bed next to her, caressing her body, his hand finding her sweet spot. Sienna arched against his touch, then pulled him on top of her.

She matched his rhythm, touching his chin so he'd look at her. "This is just our first serving." She kissed him. "Because we have all night."

An explosion of ecstasy enveloped Eladio. Though he knew he'd be tired tomorrow, he planned to enjoy Sienna as much as possible in the next few hours.

Maybe, since tomorrow was Sunday, he could forget about the task force, Raptor, and Jade. Then he could persuade the lovely Sienna to spend the day with him in bed—resting.

CHAPTER SIXTEEN

The kitchen staff was busy preparing the dining area of his suite for his dinner with Ezmé, and Raptor waited to meet with Novio in his office. Knowing he'd need to command respect from the young soldier, Raptor had dressed in a short sleeved, white button-down and black chinos. He was also hoping to enjoy a romantic dinner with Ezmé, so he wanted to look nice.

Despite Toro's concerns, Raptor didn't fear Novio. He wouldn't be surprised if the young Romeo tried to rescue Ezmé once again, though. Raptor probably should have Novio executed for breaking the rules, but he admired the young man's resolve. So like his own determination, many years ago. And he could not blame Novio for falling in love with Ezmé—as he himself had done.

"He lives for now," Raptor said as a knock thudded against the door. *"Entras."*

Novio stood in the entryway. He wore clean clothes and his wounds had been tended to, his black eye now various shades of dark purple and blue. Milo gave Novio a push and then followed him into Raptor's office. Novio whipped around, red-faced, fists balled at his sides.

"That will be all, Milo," Raptor said.

Milo squared off against Novio, and said, "I will be in the hall." He glared at Novio as he pulled the door closed.

Raptor sat in the chair behind his desk and motioned for Novio to sit.

He sat tall and held Raptor's stare. "You have decided to let me leave with Ezmé." A slight smile curved his lips. "Wise choice."

"I am allowing two things. For you to live," Raptor grinned, "for now." He leaned forward. "And for you to spend some time with Ezmé."

Novio's good eye grew wide. "So we can plot our escape."

"How?" Raptor threw his arms wide. "Do you think you can run from here?"

Novio shrugged. "I cannot reveal my secrets."

Raptor studied Novio, the young man's face a mask of determination. *Maybe,* Raptor thought, *if Ezmé allows me to taste her sweetness, then I should let her leave with Novio.* But Raptor suspected once he sampled Ezmé's treasures, he would not be able to let her go.

His office door opened after a knuckle rap, and Toro stepped inside. He glowered at Novio, then turned and reached past the doorjamb.

"Let go of me!" Ezmé protested when Toro dragged her forward. She looked stunning. Even in the drab clothing she'd been given to wear. The simple white tank was too big for her, and he could imagine her alluring body beneath the thin material. It appeared she'd had to roll the waistband of the pink jersey shorts.

Toro shook his head. *"Ella es una problema."*

"Novio!" Ezmé raced to the young man, who had come to his feet. "You're alive!" She touched his bruised eye.

He held her hand in his. "I am glad you are okay too."

Raptor stood and Ezmé shot him an angry look. "*Señorita* Mendoza, you look lovely."

She faced him, hands jammed onto her hips. "I hope this meeting is so you can tell us goodbye before you let us go."

"I will give the two of you some time alone." Raptor stepped around his desk and joined Toro at the door. "You have fifteen minutes to catch up."

Toro stepped from the office and Raptor followed him, pulling the door closed behind him. Toro cocked an eyebrow. Raptor put a finger to his lips. He then thumbed his phone awake, tapped an app, and turned the screen to the *sicario*. Looking over Toro's shoulder, Milo smiled as the young couple appeared on the screen.

In anticipation of this meeting, Raptor had had one of his men install a hidden camera, complete with a microphone, at the top of his bookcase. The result was a bird's-eye view of his office.

"Ezmé." Novio grasped her by the shoulders. Her back was to the camera. "I am so sorry I took you and you are now his captive." He kissed her forehead. "We need to find a way to escape from here."

She touched his cheek with her hand and her response was muffled, but Raptor thought she said we should have run. Ezmé walked to the large picture window and looked out onto the view of the dark green forest bleeding into the mountains beyond.

Facing Novio, she said, "I wish we'd been able to run away somewhere far from here."

"I tried, but Raptor thinks he's in love with you." Novio brushed hair from her eyes.

Ezmé stood on tiptoes and kissed Novio. Raptor knew the camera was necessary but wasn't sure he could watch the intimacy between the young couple.

Wrapping his arms around Ezmé, Novio drew her close, and returned her kiss. He held her away from him. "I love you, Ezmé," he rasped.

"I've longed to hear you say those words." She smiled. "I love you too, Novio."

Raptor's stomach roiled at this revelation, and he felt ill.

"That is why we need to escape." Novio kissed her again. "So we can be together."

She took his hand and led him to the chairs in front of Raptor's desk. "You know he has men waiting to see if we try to leave." She pointed to the unlocked window. "I can't bear the idea that he would kill you if we were caught."

Novio pulled her chair closer and gazed out the window too. "I am sure you are right." Longing reflected in his dark brown eyes when he looked at Ezmé. "But what I cannot bear is what he would do to you."

Raptor's cheeks warmed with a combination of jealousy and anger. He looked at his watch. Five more minutes.

"Why do you work for him if you think he is a bad man?"

"It is a long story," Novio answered. "But working for Raptor saved my sister, Valéria."

"Did he hurt her?" Ezmé leaned closer to Novio.

"No." He shook his head. "She is safe now, and I believe living a good life."

"How long have you worked for Raptor?"

"Four years."

"That's forever." Ezmé ran her hands through her hair. "Maybe we should ask—beg if we have to—for Raptor to let us go."

"I have asked, but I do not believe he will ever let either of us go." Novio kissed her again, then added, "It is why we need to escape."

Ezmé stood and faced the door, creating the illusion she was looking directly into the camera. "I will give him what he wants from me." Raptor was surprised by her declaration. "If he agrees to let us go."

Novio had moved to stand behind her and he put his arms around her again. When she turned to face him, he consumed her lips. Raptor closed the screen on his phone and knocked on the door of his office.

"Do not offer yourself to him to protect me." Raptor heard Novio tell Ezmé before he marched into the office.

The lovers stood, hand-in-hand, and faced Raptor with rebellious stares.

"Novio." Raptor sat in his chair. "For now, you will remain under lockdown."

"Por favor, Patrón." Novio stepped toward the desk. "I have repaid my debt to you. And Ezmé has done nothing to warrant being your captive." Ezmé moved next to Novio. *"Por favor, déjanos ir."*

Jealousy brought heat to Raptor's cheeks, and he glared at Novio. "You should be careful about suggesting you are no longer useful to me."

"Let Ezmé go, then—" Novio jabbed an index finger into his chest. "You can soothe your anger and frustrations by torturing me."

"Your offer is tempting, Novio." Raptor waved for Milo to come forward.

Milo grabbed Novio by the arm, propelling him toward the door.

Ezmé held onto his other arm and wailed. "No!"

Stepping between them, Toro pried her hand free. Milo ushered Novio from the office. She spun around and stomped toward Raptor.

"I will sleep with you if you let Novio go." Sobs punctuated her words. "Please, don't hurt him."

Raptor stood and took Ezmé's hand, leading her from the office. "Toro, please let the cook know we will be ready for dinner in thirty minutes."

When they reached his suite, Raptor stood aside and motioned for Ezmé to enter. Flickering candlelight bathed the front room in a warm light and the sweet scent of magnolia drifted through the air. Raptor walked straight to the bar and poured a shot of *Patrón*. He downed the tequila, then refilled the glass and poured a second shot.

Ezmé stood before him, hands on hips. He offered her the shot. She narrowed her eyes, then crossed her arms instead of taking the small glass.

"Will you not need liquid courage to make good on your offer to join me in my bedroom?"

She extended her hand for the tequila, downed the fiery liquid, then coughed as she wiped her lips with the back of her hand.

Raptor stepped close to her and caressed her cheek, a whisper of anger blooming in him when she stiffened. He wanted to make love to Ezmé, not force himself on her. More importantly, he wanted her to choose to be with him.

"I am not Belen," Ezmé said.

"I think we should plan on dinner another night." Raptor poured a shot. "Toro will take you back to your room." He pushed a button under the bar and the door to his suite opened revealing the *sicario*.

"Toro." Raptor didn't look at Ezmé. "Please take *Señorita* Mendoza back to her room and see to it she has everything she needs."

"Sí, Patrón." Toro held the door open.

"And, Toro, please ask the girl from the pirate ship if she'd like to join me for dinner," Raptor began, causing both the *sicario* and Ezmé to gawk at him. "Maybe she will be interested in helping me relieve some tension."

"No!" Ezmé struggled against the *sicario's* grip. "Do not punish someone else because you are angry with me!"

"This may come as a shock to you, *mi dulce Ezmé,*" Raptor downed the shot, "but some women enjoy being in my company."

Ezmé glared at him. He nodded at Toro, who escorted her from the suite. Raptor had planned to meet with the newest captive to assess whether he could let her go without any repercussions. But now that his date with Ezme had ended before it started, he hoped the girl from the pirate ship would be willing to enjoy dinner … and whatever else the night might bring.

CHAPTER SEVENTEEN

Jade stared across the dark ocean, watching as the waters grew light with the arrival of dawn. She sipped some tea, wishing snippets of memories from last night would scuttle away like rats on a sinking ship.

"Can't sleep?" Sandrine asked from the open slider.

Jade responded with another sip of tea. She didn't want to verbally recount the events of last night. Suffer again the embarrassment of her actions with Peña at the Zoo. Relive her breathless chase after Sarita. Endure the memory of Eladio's condescending demeanor.

"I know you came in last night and went straight to bed." Sandrine sat on the edge of the other lounge chair. "And ignored my knock on your door."

Jade blew out a sigh. "There's nothing to talk about."

"Come on, Love," Sandrine prodded. "You know you'll feel better if we hash out whatever happened."

Setting her cup on the small table between them, Jade looked at her friend. "I saw Sarita watching me from the entry of the Zoo."

"Bloody hell!" Sandrine was on her feet. "We're going to need coffee," she called to Jade as she hustled inside to the small kitchenette.

Since it was Sunday morning, Jade wondered if Eladio would be in his office today. She wanted him to see if Ezmé's phone had pinged since her abduction. And he could have someone in the police department scour Ezmé's social media, even though Erica had said she and her friends were monitoring the platforms. *What if they'd missed something?*

Sandrine resumed her seat. "Okay, coffee's brewing." She swung her long legs onto the chaise and leaned back. "Tell me everything."

Jade reluctantly shared her evening, from dancing with Peña at the Zoo to Eladio's silent disapproval of their behavior to chasing her mother down a sidewalk crowded with evening tourists.

Sandrine had fetched them coffee halfway through Jade's narration, but otherwise didn't interrupt. Jade took a long drink of the dark Mexican roast, contemplating the addition of a splash of Baileys.

"First of all," Sandrine said, switching back to sitting on the side of the lounger. "No judgement. But Peña?"

Leaning back and closing her eyes, Jade said, "I was trying to prove a point."

"About?"

Jade heard confusion in Sandrine's tone.

"Being the right person to go undercover with Valéria." Jade opened her eyes when the memory of the lieutenant's lips covering hers loomed behind her eyelids.

"Undercover?" Sandrine tilted her head, then said, "As captives?"

"Yes, but the arrogant lieutenant doesn't think I'm sexy enough to draw the attention of Raptor's crew."

Sandrine laughed, then covered her mouth with her hands. "Sorry, Love. But I wished I'd been there to see how you convinced him otherwise."

"I'm not sure I did anything except make Ortiz angry with us."

"Do you think Eladio's displeasure stems from his interest in you?"

"Interest?" Jade narrowed her eyes at Sandrine. "Ortiz is *not* interested in me."

"Obviously you haven't noticed how he looks at you." Sandrine headed back inside, returning with the coffee carafe. "Look." She splashed coffee into Jade's cup, then filled hers, placing the glass pot on the small table between them. "I know it's been a long time since you and surfer boy hit the sheets, so it's no surprise you're ready for a little stress relief."

Jade sat up abruptly, sloshing hot coffee, which luckily missed her lap. "Shit!"

Sandrine grabbed a beach towel from a basket next to the door and tossed it to Jade. Her cheeks burned and she took her time mopping up the mess. *Was Sandrine right? Could Jade's poor judgement be a by-product of needing to get laid? Or was the need to find Ezmé causing her to grasp any available lifeline?*

"Did you burn yourself?" Sandrine asked.

"No, I'm fine." She looked at her friend and saw concern reflected in her dark brown eyes. "I'm not interested in Amado Peña or Eladio Ortiz." Jade picked up her cup and sipped what was left of her coffee. "I just want to find Ezmé, and I feel very inadequate about what I bring to the investigation."

"I know it's no consolation." Sandrine reached out and touched Jade's arm. "But we've only been at this for two days."

"Jesus!" Jade marched into the suite. "You know the longer Ezmé is missing, the more unlikely it is we'll find her alive!"

"Of course I know that." Sandrine followed her inside with the empty carafe. "I also know if your sister was taken by this trafficker, Raptor, she's worth more alive than dead."

Tears sprang from Jade's eyes, and she doubled over with sobs. Sandrine was right about Ezmé's value, but Jade worried her sister was being tortured by her captor. Jade took her crying fit to the bathroom adjacent to her room and jumped into the shower. She let the hot water pummel her skin until it glowed red, then she stepped from the stall and toweled off.

In an attempt to shift her dark mood, Jade dressed for the day in a pink spaghetti strap tank, paired with a fuchsia and white floral skirt. Her efforts were wasted, though, because it simply looked like she'd dressed up a dour-looking doll. When she emerged from the bedroom, a new pot of coffee sent a warm, nutty aroma, tinged with cinnamon and orange, wafting through the room. Sandrine sat at the small dining table.

"Come." She pointed to a tall mug. "I made *café de olla*." Sandrine had changed into tan boho shorts, and a short-sleeved, brown and blue paisley print blouse.

Jade padded bare foot to the empty chair and sat. She held the Mexican coffee concoction to her nose, inhaled the comforting scent, then took a sip.

"Thanks." Jade smiled at Sandrine over the top of her mug.

"Tell me about seeing your mum." Sandrine sipped from her cup.

Shaking her head, Jade blinked to stem another round of tears. "I believe it was her, but it happened so fast, and I wasn't able to catch the woman to know for sure."

"I know Sarita just found out about you, but why would she risk being caught?" Sandrine's full eyebrows drew together as she continued, "Especially if it's you that brings her in?"

"I have no idea."

"What about calling Captain Torres?" Sandrine asked.

"I thought about it." Jade shrugged. "But what can he do from Mazatlán?"

"Well," Sandrine began, shifting in her chair. "If he's your bio-dad, then maybe he's in contact with her."

Jade wanted to shout at her friend that the idea of Marco Torres being her biological father was ridiculous, but how could she—when the same thought had crossed her mind?

"It might be better to ask Ortiz to make the call," Jade said.

"I know he's not tall, blond, and dreamy, but Agent Ortiz has a certain *je ne sais quoi*." Sandrine smiled. "An alluring, mysterious air about him."

"Maybe *you* should take Agent Ortiz for a spin between the sheets." Jade smiled.

"Don't be absurd," Sandrine laughed. "You know I have my own hot agent waiting for me at home in San Deigo."

"Right." Jade raised an eyebrow. "Mr. Commitment Avoidance expects you to be a good girl while you wait for him to marry you."

"Hey, now." Sandrine narrowed her eyes. "Oliver isn't the only one avoiding marriage."

Jade wished she'd held her tongue. She knew Sandrine's longtime boyfriend, Oliver. and marriage were a sore subject. And she was one to talk, since no one waited anxiously for her to return to Phoenix.

"I'm sorry." Jade touched Sandrine's arm.

"Don't be." Sandrine covered Jade's hand with her own. "You know you and I are probably never getting married."

"I'm not planning to." Jade took a long sip of coffee.

"But you could have a little fun every now and then." Sandrine smiled. "Ortiz is very handsome—with those dark, sultry eyes and full lips."

Jade grinned. "Quite a contrast to Lieutenant Peña's drug dealer persona?"

"You forgot arrogant." Sandrine laughed. "It's his best quality."

"Thanks for the *café de olla*." Jade lifted her mug in toast. "And for letting me vent."

"It's hardly venting, Love." Sandrine clinked Jade's mug. "When I have to drag every bloody word out of you."

CHAPTER EIGHTEEN

Sienna had awakened Eladio in the predawn with kisses that led to more amorous sex. He'd tried to persuade her to stay with him in bed all day, but her friends were texting her regarding their trip to Punta Mita. She'd finally escorted him to the shower for a last orgasmic ride.

As Sienna dressed, Eladio made coffee and rummaged through his cupboards for a package of *concha* rolls he knew he'd just bought. By the time his lovely guest stepped from his bathroom, the coffee was ready, and he'd plated the pastries.

"You look stunning," he said, handing her a cup.

She kissed him, then took a sip. "Not like I was ravished all night by a handsome stranger?"

Eladio leaned in for another kiss. "Even ravished, you look beautiful."

Her phone chimed and she frowned at the screen. "As much as I'd love to stay, I must go." She set her cup on the counter and stepped into his arms. "I had an amazing time."

He drew her close. "As did I."

Eladio tucked a strand of coppery hair behind her ear, then kissed her. She wound her fingers into his hair and held his lips to hers. Despite a night that had left him exhausted, desire flooded Eladio's loins, and he swept Sienna up into his arms.

She freed her lips and mumbled, "I really need to go."

"*Sí,*" he whispered in her ear. "As soon as I have said a proper *adiós.*"

After Sienna left, Eladio donned a blue short-sleeved pullover and jeans, then headed for the police station. On the way, he stopped at *Taza de Joe* for a large black coffee and a small box of pastries to accompany the *concha* rolls. He'd discovered the coffee shop, owned by an American from Oregon, during a previous visit to Puerto Vallarta.

Now sitting at his desk, sipping coffee, and enjoying an old-fashioned donut, he smiled as he replayed Sienna's goodbye. She'd left his apartment, then knocked on the door five minutes later. Her bright smile greeted him when he opened the door.

"I'm truly going, but we didn't decide if we're doing this—again."

"When are you back from Punta Mita?"

"In a week."

"Meet me for dinner next Sunday night at Captain Jack's." As soon as he made the statement, Eladio immediately wished he'd suggested somewhere more elegant.

Sienna placed a hand on his chest, then kissed him. "I'll see you in a week." She gave a finger wave and strode off, turning once to see if he watched her depart.

The memory of her touch rekindled his desire, and he mentally calculated the time until their dinner date in a week—only one hundred sixty-eight hours to go.

Since this was his first Sunday in the office, Eladio didn't know if anyone else would show. Wondering about the others conjured the image of Jade and Peña embracing on the dance floor last night at the Zoo. The thought of them continuing their lusty moves between the sheets caused his cheeks to warm. But they were consenting adults and free to do as they pleased, as he and Sienna had done last night. Still, the idea of Jade with Peña didn't set well. He needed something other than the smug lieutenant and sullen agent to occupy his mind. He rolled an old whiteboard into his office and started his criminal tree with the name RAPTOR written in all caps at the top. After drawing a square next to the name, he added the word *Jefe*.

As he worked on the chart, which included lines without names, Eladio noted questions on the side.

1) Is Gwen safe at the Marriot? Are Joy and Erica in danger too?
2) If Gwen's friend Lexi was the girl on the beach, was her other friend captured by Raptor?

On the opposite side of the board, he made notes:

1) Review data gleaned from Ezmé's friends from night she disappeared.
2) Ask Peña and Jade about visit to *Casa de Bahia*.

Regardless of his efforts to focus on his task, Eladio's mind returned to the image of Jade wrapped in Peña's arms. "What could she possibly see in him?" Eladio asked the whiteboard.

"Buenos días," Peña said from the doorway of Eladio's office. He didn't wait for an invitation to enter, and the scowl on his face suggested he'd heard Eladio's question.

"You are early for a Sunday," Eladio said as Peña lifted the lid on the pastry box.

Peña selected a chocolate glazed donut. "You too." He licked frosting from his fingers and crossed to the coffee maker.

Eladio didn't respond, turning his attention back to the whiteboard as Peña yawned and plopped into a chair.

Peña mumbled, "I did not get much sleep."

Neither did I, Eladio thought, but still had to shake the idea that Jade had actually gone to Peña's place instead of back to her hotel. He added another box to his chart and placed a question mark inside.

Peña stepped to the board and tapped the square. "The *hombre* who took Ezmé?"

Eladio nodded. *"Sí."*

After a loud slurp of coffee, Peña set his mug on Eladio's desk and pulled his phone from a pocket. "I think this is him." He handed his phone to Eladio.

Eladio studied the photo. It showed a young man and a young woman whose face was partially covered with long, dark hair. He handed the phone back to Peña.

"And you think the female is Ezmé?" Eladio crossed to his desk and sat down.

"Sí." Returning to his chair, Peña continued, "I think the male was ordered to grab her, but for some reason took her to the hotel."

Eladio raised his eyebrows.

"Sí, sí." Peña nodded. "The reason seems obvious, but if he raped this girl before bringing her to his boss, he would have been killed."

"Probably," Eladio agreed.

"The hotel manager said the *pendejos* who came for Ezmé took her and a young man."

Eladio made a note on a legal pad to ask the coroner about any recently—discovered bodies.

As if he could read upside down, Peña pointed at the page. "Have someone check the name Fonsie Cano, the security guard at the hotel." He leaned back and added, "I will have officers talk to his girlfriend, Adora."

After adding the names to his notes, Eladio looked at Peña.

"Also, a street kid told me someone is using Devil's Breath to subdue women," Peña added.

Eladio leaned back in his chair. "That is a dangerous drug."

"Sí." Peña nodded. "He does not know who is abducting the *mujeres.*"

"I will ask Agent Mendoza to see who might be dealing Devil's Breath in Puerto Vallarta."

Pointing to the board, Peña said, "I agree we should have an officer check on the remaining friend, Gwen."

Eladio scribbled on his pad, then looked at Peña. "Do you think the *policía* can provide protection?"

Peña shrugged. "Maybe she would be safe at *El Mar Llama* where Jade and Sandrine are staying?"

"Valéria is staying there now also, so that is a possibility," Eladio agreed.

"Bueno," Peña said. "I can have a rotating shift of officers keep an eye on Gwen at the Marriott for now."

"Erica Beck showed up last night at *Perla del Pacifico* and was questioning the bartender."

"¡Maldita sea!" Peña swore. "You need to set some boundaries for these *loco* women!"

Eladio didn't disagree with the lieutenant, but he doubted anyone could control these strong-willed females. "Tell me about your undercover plan," Eladio said.

Peña shrugged and sipped some coffee. "I do not think Jade should be involved in any way."

After what he'd witnessed last night, the comment took Eladio by surprise. Before he could ask why, Peña continued.

"She is too *emocional.* And not thinking clearly."

Obviously, Eladio thought. Jade couldn't be clear-headed. Otherwise, why would she fall into Peña's arms?

"We have discussed this before," Eladio said. "Ezmé is her sister, so she needs to be part of the task force."

"¡Bien!" Peña jumped to his feet. "But no undercover op." He strode to the coffee pot and refilled his cup, then returned to his seat.

"Who do you think should go undercover?" Eladio sipped some coffee.

"Valéria." Peña plucked another donut from the box.

Pen hovering over his pad, Eladio leaned forward. "As a captive?"

"*Sí.*" Peña squared his shoulders. "It is the only way to know if Raptor has Ezmé."

Eladio laid the pen onto the pad. "We do not know Raptor's identity, so how can we be sure Valéria would be captured by his crew?"

Voices echoing in the hallway halted Peña's response. Sandrine, Valéria, and Jade stepped into the office.

"Morning," Sandrine said, heading for the coffee pot. "You two got here early. New leads?" She filled three cups and handed one to Valéria.

Jade picked up a cup and took a sip, but didn't make eye contact.

"*Buenos días.*" Eladio stood in welcome. "We are just getting started." Resuming his seat, he motioned to the vacant chairs close to his desk. "Please, sit."

Sandrine nodded as she perused the remaining pastries. She selected a raspberry-filled donut, then offered the box to Valéria.

"No thanks," Valéria said.

Sandrine looked at Jade, who held up a hand and said, "Just coffee."

"I delivered a white substance we found at the hotel to the lab and asked for a rush on the results," Peña reported. His gazed locked on Jade, who studied her cup.

"Lieutenant," Sandrine began. "Jade said you have a picture of the young woman who could be Ezmé?"

"*Sí.*" Peña thumbed his phone open, tapped the screen, then handed the phone to Sandrine.

She studied the photo, then swiped to the next picture. "And is this the guy we think took Ezmé?"

"Probably." Peña looked at Jade again and this time she met his gaze. "Hotel manager said he was beaten by the men who took both of them away," Peña said.

Sandrine used her thumbs to enlarge the picture of the young woman. "You're right Jade." Sandrine passed the phone to Valéria. "She could definitely be Ez—"

"Oh my God!" Valéria shouted and sprang to her feet.

Sandrine stood, followed by the men.

"Agent Carrizo?" Eladio waited for her to look at him.

With tears streaming down her cheeks, Valéria stuttered, "It-it's—" She turned the phone screen toward them. "This is my brother, Novio."

CHAPTER NINETEEN

Brushing his scar with his fingertips, Raptor watched her sleep.

Initially, the blonde had taken his mind off his failed romantic attempt with Ezmé. He'd actually lost himself in the pirate girl's enthusiasm and was spent after a couple of rounds of sexual gymnastics.

He'd left her sleeping in his bed and sat at the dining table, sipping tequila and eating part of the now-cold filet mignon that had been prepared for his dinner with Ezmé. Once he'd emptied the tequila bottle, Raptor returned to the bedroom and the willing nymph in his bed. He'd tried to drain himself of any remaining sexual desire.

Now, as sunlight streamed across the bed, the girl stirred. She rolled toward him. He smiled when she opened her eyes and threw the sheet from her voluptuous body, inviting him back to bed.

Raptor laid next to her, and she caressed the scar on his chest, three ragged cuts that looked like he'd been clawed by the extinct Velociraptor dinosaur. She moved her lips to the old wound, then kissed his nipples and cupped his package in her hand. Once he rose to attention, she straddled his hips and lowered herself to cover him. He raised his hands to her breasts, and she moaned, moving her hips with more urgency.

His hatred for women stemmed from Belen's choice to leave with the man who'd bought her. And though her decision had saved his life,

Raptor never let himself get close to other women. But he found the blonde's unique style intriguing, admiring the impressive tattooed sleeve on her left arm. Her platinum hair sported a single black color strip and was cut in a funky, short style. She'd tucked her long bangs behind an ear. He liked her edgy flair and wondered if there was a story behind her artwork and distinctive hairstyle.

When they were finished, she'd taken a shower, and Raptor had the remains of last night's dinner removed. It was replaced by fruit, rolls, and coffee.

The woman now sat across from him at the dining table, wearing one of his cotton shirts, a single button secured to cover her nudity.

"What is your name?" he asked, lifting a pitcher to fill a flute with hibiscus mimosa.

"Blake." She sipped from her glass. "Are you going to tell me your name?"

Raptor smiled, but didn't answer. "Why are you not afraid of me?"

"You haven't hurt me." She drained half of her glass. "And you don't seem like a bad man."

Tilting his head, he said, "My men tell me you are always crying."

Her lips curved, but did not create a smile. "My theory is men don't want to deal with a hysterical female."

"But your lack of fear is different from your pretending to be hysterical."

The slight curve to her lips was back. "What good will it do me?"

"Your friend was afraid, and jumped from the pirate ship." Raptor watched her over the rim of his glass.

A whisper of dread fluttered across her face. "Do you know if she's dead?"

"*Sí.*" Raptor nodded. "I believe so." He saw no need to share that the mutilated body discovered on the beach was probably her friend.

Tears flowed from her eyes, and she dabbed them away with a napkin. After draining her flute, she reached for a croissant. Raptor watched as she pulled the roll apart, placing pieces onto her plate. She picked up the small container of raspberry jam and drizzled the sticky jelly across the chunks. After popping a piece into her mouth, she raised her eyes to his, then licked jam from her lips.

"You and your friends are here on vacation?" Raptor asked, ignoring a thread of desire snaking through his loins.

"Yes." She nodded as he refilled her glass.

"Where are you from?" Raptor took a sip.

"Lexi and I are from Portland, Oregon." She popped a bite into her mouth. "Gwen's from Bend. Did your men abduct her also?"

"No," Raptor replied. "Would she be afraid like—"

"Lexi." Blake placed another morsel dripping with jam into her mouth. "Yes," She paused, then looked at him. "I'm the wild friend. Not much scares me."

Raptor grinned. "That is not always wise."

"Would you rather I act afraid of you and beg?" Blake sipped from her glass. "I've been kidnapped before." Sitting straighter in her chair, she continued, "I was terrified. I begged. I endured three days of rape and torture." She drained her glass again.

Raptor looked into her green eyes and saw a survivor. "And?"

"After he broke my arm, shattered a kneecap, and slit my throat. He dumped me in a ditch and left me for dead. But I crawled onto a road, where I was rescued by a passing car."

"Was your kidnapper ever caught?"

"No." A flicker of anger flashed in her eyes. "I found him, though."

"And?" Raptor asked again to continue the game.

"I got my revenge." Blake spooned fruit onto his plate, then left her seat and sat in his lap, facing him.

When his hands cradled Blake's bare ass, lust coursed through Raptor, and he wanted to sweep everything from the table and take his captive amongst the breakfast debris. Blake held the dish of fruit and offered him a strawberry. He took the sweet bite from her fingers, sucking on them until she pulled them free. Next was a succulent grape, followed by a slice of orange she held between her teeth.

Raptor covered the slice with his mouth, then kissed her deeply. When Blake lifted her ass high enough for Raptor to push down his sweats, the woody scent of his body wash wafted off her skin. She lowered onto him, and he had to control his need for release. He flicked open the button on the shirt she wore and latched onto a nipple as the two of them found the perfect rhythm.

Blake freed his hair from a rubber band and ran her hands through his shoulder-length curls, then tossed her head back and moaned. With a finger, Raptor traced a tattoo that partially hid the scar on her throat. The ink depicted two linked pinkies, one of them a skeleton.

He brought her lips to his and kissed her, then whispered into her ear, "I do not know what game you are playing, but you should be afraid."

Blake lifted her head, her eyes now a darker shade of green, and slowed the movement of her hips. "Afraid of you?" She hovered on the tip of his cock, her lips curved in a malicious grin.

Raptor grabbed her waist and thrust deep inside of her. Blake moved with him, leaned down, and kissed him. She moaned with bliss and stared into his eyes.

As he reached his crescendo, she said against his lips, "Maybe it is *you* who should be afraid."

CHAPTER TWENTY

Valéria held Peña's phone tight to her chest, bunching the sunflower embossed onto her yellow tank top. She turned her tear-filled eyes to Jade. "You think Novio took Ezmé?"

Jade held her hand out for the phone. "Yes."

"Oh, sorry." Valéria handed Peña his phone. "If he did, it's because he was forced."

"Everyone take a seat." Eladio sat in his chair.

Peña joined Jade where she stood near the door. She could smell his musky cologne. It reminded her of his closeness when he'd kissed her on the dance floor at the Zoo, and she fought to keep from blushing.

"Valéria," Eladio said. "Start at the beginning."

Sandrine handed Valéria a box of tissues, and Jade pushed the record app on her phone. Eladio sat at the ready, pen hovering over his legal pad. Peña crossed his arms and leaned against the counter, jostling the coffee pot.

"I had just turned eighteen," Valéria began, "and Novio wanted to celebrate at his favorite bar, *Bebe y sé Feliz*." She looked at Eladio, who was noting the name. "It's closed now."

Nodding, Eladio set his pen down.

"We were drinking and dancing." Valéria looked at them, and Jade's heart stuttered at the terror she saw in the young woman's eyes. "A man joined our table and bought me a Paloma."

"Do you need a minute?" Sandrine asked.

Shaking her head, Valéria continued, "He was handsome, flirting with me, and I didn't feel afraid."

"It is his job to make you feel comfortable," Peña interjected.

"Lieutenant Peña's right," Jade said. "These men are trained to be charming, and they know how to gain your trust."

"And now my brother is one of them." Sobs shook Valéria's shoulders. "I-I'm so sorry he took Ezmé."

"Agent Carrizo." Eladio's tone was commanding. Jade assumed he intended to help Valéria refocus and remember her FBI training. "Tell us how Novio came to work for a trafficker."

She blew her nose. "Novio tracked down the man who took me, and beat him until he told my brother where I was being held."

"You were held here, in Puerto Vallarta?" Peña asked.

Nodding, Valéria blew out a breath. "Yes, but I was blindfolded, drugged, and kept in a dark room."

"Did you meet the man in charge?" Jade asked, even though she knew the answer.

"No." Valéria had recovered her composure. "I only saw the man who took me, but I heard him call another man Raptor." She sat taller in her chair.

"Can you describe him?" Peña had thumbed his phone alive. "I can request a sketch artist."

"He's dead." Valéria looked at Peña. "Novio killed him."

"How do you know?" Sandrine asked.

"Before I was put in a car and driven back to the *malecón*, I got to see Novio." Valéria twisted a tissue around her fingers. "He told me he killed the man who took me." A new round of tears glistened in her eyes.

"Novio said he volunteered to take the man's place as a soldier and work for Raptor if I was set free."

A fresh wave of tears overcame Valéria for a few minutes, then she continued, "It was the last time I saw Novio." She fingered tears from her cheeks. "My parents moved me to the states, and we never spoke of my brother again."

"Is Raptor the reason you volunteered for the task force?" Eladio asked. The background search Peña had done on the young agent had not revealed any of this information. Eladio assumed that if her superiors had known her history, they wouldn't have approved her participation in the task force.

Valéria's eyes narrowed, and she gave a slight nod. "As soon as I heard you were looking for a human trafficker named Raptor, I wanted to be part of the team who takes him down."

CHAPTER TWENTY-ONE

Valéria's story describing her capture by one of Raptor's soldiers helped explain Novio's involvement in abducting Ezmé. But Eladio knew they were still a long way from rescuing Jade's sister. Now, as the task force sat around his office, he could see additional questions on the faces of his team.

"Why wasn't a task force created four years ago, after Valéria was taken?" Jade asked, an edge to her tone.

"Because she is not the sister of a DEA agent." Peña's tone was as sharp as Jade's.

Jade cut her eyes to Peña. "Ezmé isn't the only missing woman—"

"My abduction was never reported to the police," Valéria interjected. "My theory is Raptor focuses on taking women who won't be missed— or at least not reported missing."

"*Sí*. There was a previous group assigned to find the missing women, but it was disbanded due to lack of leads," Eladio added. "This task force was formed when the third woman, from Costa Rica, was reported missing by her boyfriend." He reached for a folder on the edge of his desk and flipped it open. "He reported his girlfriend missing after they'd had a fight." Eladio frowned at notes in the margin of the report made by the officer who'd talked to the boyfriend. BF HAS CUTS AND SCRAPES. MAY HAVE BEEN ABUSING GIRLFRIEND.

"According to the *policía*," Eladio continued. "The only reports filed were for non-Mexican nationals."

"So, if a Mexican female disappears, no one files a report?" Sandrine asked. "Why not?"

"Corruption," Peña answered. "The women are probably reported missing, but if their family cannot pay to encourage the *policia* to look for their loved one, the report is never filed."

"When Ezmé was abducted," Eladio began, "the FBI's involvement accelerated the forming of the task force."

"Were the previous missing women Americans?" Sandrine finished her donut, wiping away powder residue from her lips with a napkin.

"No." Eladio looked at Jade. "We think the first missing girl is from Canada and the second woman is from Ireland. Both went missing from México City." The note about the boyfriend possibly abusing his girlfriend was still bothering him, so he made a mental note to check the background of the other missing women.

"We believe the fourth woman was abducted from the pirate ship," Peña said. "And that it was her friend who jumped."

"Lexi, the girl from the beach." Valéria added.

"*Sí.*" Eladio closed the file. "Raptor's crew has probably captured more than these four, but we will not know until we find him." He leaned back in his chair.

"Which is why we need someone to go undercover—" Peña looked at Jade.

"And I volunteer." Jade cut him off. She began pacing Eladio's office, as if preparing for battle, leaving the citrusy scent of verbena in her wake.

"It needs to be someone who can draw attention to themselves," Peña stated.

"What about me?" Sandrine said. "I have an exotic look different from most female tourists."

Peña shrugged and Jade rolled her eyes. "The lieutenant doesn't think we're"—Jade pointed to herself then Sandrine—"sexy enough to attract the attention of the kidnappers."

Glaring at Jade, Peña took a step toward her. "That is not what I said!"

Jade crossed to Peña and thumped him in the chest with her palm. "But that's what you think!"

Sparks flew between the lieutenant and Agent Mendoza. Eladio wondered if Sandrine and Valéria felt the sexual tension between the two as he did.

Eladio pounded his desk with a fist. "Enough!"

Valéria jumped in her seat and Sandrine pinched the bridge of her nose with her fingers. Jade stepped away from Peña. His face was still mottled with anger.

Sandrine raised her hand. "Can I suggest all three of us women go undercover?"

"This is what is going to happen." Eladio looked at Valéria. "If you are willing, I would like to place you undercover, since you know Novio. Assuming he's a captive too, you could ask for his help in rescuing the other women."

The same look of trepidation Valéria had shown when she'd been asked to question the bartender at *Perla del Pacífico* crossed her face, but she nodded, then took a sip from her cup.

"Bueno." Eladio turned his attention to Jade. "And I would like for you to be Valéria's partner on this assignment."

Peña muttered an expletive and stomped from Eladio's office.

Jade watched the lieutenant leave, then gave her attention to Eladio. "Works for me."

Rapping Eladio's desk with a knuckle, Sandrine asked, "And?"

Eladio looked at the three agents and exhaled a breath. "Sandrine, I need you as standby in case we need someone else to go undercover."

"All right," Sandrine said. "What are our next steps?"

Before Eladio could respond, Peña burst back into the room.

"Gwen, the friend at the Marriott is missing," Peña said. "The officers I sent to check on her said she has not been seen since last night."

Jade's phone buzzed with an incoming call, and she answered on speaker. "Hey, Jo—"

"Jade!" Joy's voice boomed from the phone. "Erica's missing!"

CHAPTER TWEWNTY-TWO

After their breakfast, Raptor had arranged for Blake to be placed in one of the compound's nicer rooms. He found her interesting. Since she didn't seem to be concerned that she was his captive, he'd changed his mind about offering to set her free. Dressed in chinos and a tan short-sleeved shirt, he headed to his office. Toro had texted; he wanted to meet and discuss various issues that had come up.

Now, sipping coffee, he looked out his office window at the sun-kissed mountains beyond his complex and replayed his night with Blake. While she'd managed to soothe his need for Ezmé, Raptor still yearned for the young, dark-haired beauty. For a moment he imagined spending the day on the beach with Blake. clad in a barely-there bikini, enjoying an ice cold *cerveza* and watching as she romped in the waves. The fictitious image morphed into Ezmé—running from him—into Novio's arms.

A rap on his door cleared his mind and he barked, *"Entrar."*

"Patrón." Toro, dressed in his usual black on black uniform, stepped inside.

"¿Café?" Raptor asked as he moved to the bar and poured another cup.

Toro waved off the offer. *"No, gracias."*

Returning to his seat, Raptor thought about how his *sicario* was the first one up each day, overseeing their operation. Raptor wondered if on his days off, which were few and far between, the *sicario* managed to satisfy his own carnal needs.

"Where would you like to start?" Toro asked.

"Have you found Julio?" Raptor sipped some coffee, the dark roast dancing on his tongue.

"No." Toro cast a glance through the window at the mountain range. "He knows we are looking for him, so he will be hard to find."

"Why were two girls taken last night?" Raptor set his cup down and picked up a sheet of paper. "You know I no longer want to traffic in kidnapped women."

"*Sí.*" Toro nodded. "I have learned from Ferdo that Julio, along with Pablo and Cisco, have decided not to honor your wishes."

"You are worried about something else?" Raptor tilted his head.

"I think the trio has been hired to complete the hit on you for the *Cartel de Cocos Pequeña.*"

"Are the cousins missing too?" Raptor asked, knowing that Pablo and Cisco were thick as thieves. If one was gone, they were both gone.

"*Sí.*" Toro met Raptor's stare. "I have added guards to our access roads and at the compound entrance."

"Did you get word to our *halcones* to alert you if they see any of the three?"

Toro gave another head nod.

Raptor studied the notes from Milo regarding the kidnapped women. "How did these two find themselves on Cisco and Pablo's radar?"

"Erica Beck." Toro ran a hand over his chin. "Ezmé was staying with her and her mother." Toro's dark eyes narrowed. "She was asking Nacho too many questions and he alerted one of the cousins. They snatched her from the Zoo."

Milo had always given Nacho, a bartender at the Zoo, high praise. He said the transplant from Guadalajara had natural instincts when it came to selecting females for abduction. Raptor had made it clear that no more women were to be kidnapped, but Nacho was encouraged to put the word out that Raptor's crew could help relocate a female if she requested assistance.

"And Gwen, Blake's friend?" Raptor asked.

Toro cocked an eyebrow.

"Blake and I had a productive evening." Raptor grinned. "She told me about her friends. Lexi is the dead girl from the beach. And her other friend is Gwen, who I really wish we did not have here at the compound."

"Gwen was also asking questions," Toro said. "Once the cousins took them, they drove them to the access road and handed them off."

"Why take the women, but not bring them to your own fortress and begin trafficking them?" Raptor stared out the office window. "I think the cousins and Julio are trying to set us up to get caught with kidnapped women."

Toro nodded again. "Do you want them returned to Puerto Vallarta?" he asked, and Raptor could tell the *sicario* wasn't in favor of the idea.

"Can you check with our *policía* contact to see if they've connected the two women to us?" Raptor finished his coffee.

"*Sí, Patrón.*" Toro thumbed the keyboard on his phone. "Milo says the new girl, Gwen, is asking if we have her friends."

"Place Gwen and Erica in the same room for now and make sure they are comfortable." Raptor said. He stood, crossed to the bar, and poured two shots of *Patrón*. "Tell me how Ezmé and Novio are this morning." He sat and handed Toro a shot glass.

"*Novio es tranquilo.*" Toro took a sip of tequila. "He is not asking about Ezmé or talking much to anyone."

"And the fair Ezmérelda?" Raptor held the tequila to his nose, then savored a drink.

"She only asks to see you." Toro finished his shot. "We need to talk about the threat on your life."

"Do you think paying off the young woman's dad would deter the cartel from seeking revenge on his behalf?" Raptor took another sip, the sweet agave smell blending with the spicy taste of the tequila.

Toro shrugged. "We could make the offer."

"We are going to need to close down sooner than I had hoped," Raptor said. "How much time do you need to put things in motion?"

"Things are ready now."

"*Bueno*. Have the kitchen prepare food and drink for a party in my suite this evening." He finished his shot. "I will be entertaining the four lovely ladies."

Toro's narrowed eyes suggested he didn't like Raptor's idea of a party, but maybe if Ezmé saw him as a charming host, she'd allow him to get to know her better. And since he planned to let the other women go, it might bode well for him if they didn't think of him as a monster either.

Raptor raised an eyebrow and held Toro's stare, until the *sicario* nodded.

"*Sí, Patrón.*" Toro stood and exited the office.

Raptor kicked back in his chair and crossed his ankles on top of his desk. He knew he'd have to leave here, and with any luck, he wouldn't be leaving alone.

CHAPTER TWENTY-THREE

Controlled chaos ensued in Eladio's office after the news of Gwen and Erica's abductions. Jade was on the phone with Joy, telling her that two police officers were on their way to pick her up. Peña talked to one of his men in the hallway about the missing friend, Gwen, and Jade could hear anger in his tone. Eladio received a call from Marco Torres, and left his office.

"Joy," Jade said. "I know you're scared, but we think we have a lead on who may have taken Erica."

Sandrine's eyes grew wide at Jade's lie, but Jade felt lying to Joy at this point was the only way to calm her down.

"Yes." Jade cast a glance at the hallway and, as if he knew she was looking at him, Peña met her concerned stare. "You need to let the officers bring you to the station."

As Jade ended her call, Valéria stepped back into the office with a young man. Jade and Sandrine exchanged a look and waited for the young agent to fill them in.

"This is Geovany Herrera," Valéria said. "He has information about a bartender at the Zoo."

"Please," Sandrine said and pointed to a chair in front of Eladio's desk. "Have a seat."

The officer gave Sandrine a hesitant look. "I am here to speak with Agent Ortiz."

"Right, right." Sandrine offered her hand. "He had to take a call. I'm Agent Mortieau and this is Agent Mendoza."

"You are the DEA agents?" Geovany shook Sandrine's hand.

"Yes." Jade extended her hand too. "Agent Ortiz will be back shortly, and you've already met FBI Agent Carrizo."

"Officer Herrera," Peña said as he joined the group. "Sorry I missed your call but am glad you got the message to report here."

"*Teniente.*" Officer Herrera didn't salute, but straightened his posture even though he was out of uniform, dressed in blue board shorts and white T-shirt.

Peña, who Jade had noticed seemed to have taken extra care with his appearance wearing snug jeans and a gray short-sleeved Henley, took charge in Eladio's absence. "Agent Mendoza, would you please record Officer Herrera's report?"

Jade looked at Peña, tapped her phone alive, and opened the voice memo app. She nodded at Geovany, and he took a seat. He had kind eyes set in a handsome face, and Jade guessed he hadn't been a policeman for very long.

"I was having drinks at the Zoo with a group of friends last Friday night." He glanced around the office, taking in each face. "One of the females in our group became sick."

"What was she drinking?" Jade asked.

"That is the problem." Geovany did a head shake. "She was drinking water from a bottle she brought with her."

"What the eff?" Sandrine looked at Jade. "How would someone drug a bottle of water?"

Jade still held Geovany's stare. "Did she put something in the water?"

"*Lima,*" Peña said before Geovany could answer. "It is common to squeeze lime juice into water."

"The lime was dosed?" Sandrine said. "Jesus."

"Why do you suspect—" Echoed from both Peña and Jade, with Jade finishing the question. "The bartender?"

"Because I asked him for a bowl of fresh limes." Geovany scrubbed his face with his hand. "I turned away when another friend shouted at me to bring more beer."

"So you didn't see him cut up a lime?" Jade asked.

"No. I was also surprised to suddenly see another man behind the bar." He tilted his head in response. "He is the one who handed me the limes, because the bartender was talking to someone else."

"And no one else puts lime in their beer?" Sandrine added.

"*Lima* in beer is an American thing." Peña wrinkled his nose. "It makes the beer taste and smell funky."

"The other females at the table were drinking margaritas and seemed fine," Geovany continued. "Only Neva was drinking water."

"Where is she now?" Jade asked.

"I took her to the hospital as soon as I noticed she had been drugged," Geovany answered. "She was given fluids and is now home."

"She's lucky to have you as a friend." Sandrine blew out a breath. "Bloody hell."

"Lieutenant," Jade said to Peña. "Should we bring in the bartender?"

"*Sí.*" Peña nodded. "He will be our connection to put Valéria undercover."

Jade ignored the lieutenant's slight as Geovany came to his feet.

"I would like to go under also," the young man said.

"It's a good idea," Sandrine agreed. "We need someone who can get us information once our girls are captives."

"What is a good idea?" Eladio asked from the doorway of his office.

"We have a plan to place Valéria undercover," Peña said, pointing to Geovany, "along with Officer Herrera."

Jade glared at Peña. "And me."

"Sandrine." Eladio looked at her, then at Jade. "Would you and Valéria see if Officer Herrera can help fill in any of the blanks on our board?"

"Sure." Sandrine walked to the board and picked up the marker.

"*Señor* Costa, the owner of *Perla del Pacífico* called. Add he checked his cameras and saw nothing unusual." Jade instructed.

"*Gracias*, Sandrine," Eladio said. "Agent Mendoza, will you join Lieutenant Peña and me in the conference room?" He left without waiting for a response.

Peña locked eyes with Jade, then shrugged. "I have no idea."

Jade cast a glance at Sandrine, then followed Peña. Jade had no idea either. But she planned to make it clear to the lieutenant that she would be part of the undercover operation, despite any objections he might raise.

As she followed Peña down the hall toward the conference room, another thought jumped into her head. *What if they were about to be reprimanded by Eladio Ortiz for their unprofessional behavior last night at the Zoo?*

CHAPTER TWENTY-FOUR

"Please, have a seat." Eladio sat in a chair at the head of the gleaming Mexican pine conference table. Peña sat three chairs down, and Jade selected a chair across from him. Eladio assumed their somber demeanors meant they expected to be lectured about their dirty dancing at the Zoo.

"I just spoke with Captain Torres," Eladio looked at Jade, "and I have an update regarding Sarita García."

Jade leaned toward him, hands placed flat on the table. "Does he know if she's in Puerto Vallarta?"

Eladio looked at his notepad. "Marco said there have been several sightings of your mother along the west coast of México and the east coast of the Baja peninsula."

Jade nodded. "What about Puerto Vallarta?"

"No one has reported seeing Sarita here, but she was spotted in Sayulita a few days ago."

"How far is Sayulita from here?"

"Twenty-five miles," Peña answered. "Any description?"

"Short dark hair, slim figure, about five-five." Eladio smiled. "And always in sunglasses."

"Not at night!" Jade leaned back and crossed her arms. "I saw her eyes, which as you well know, are the same as mine."

"Jade," Eladio continued. "Here is something else Marco had to share. Sarita's BMW was found at the bottom of a canyon in the *Sierra Madre Occidental* mountains, just under the *Baluarte Bridge*."

"Body?" Peña asked.

"Yes." Eladio grinned. "But the coroner said the dental records of the burnt remains are not a match to Sarita's."

"So, she could be here in PV." Jade flashed a smug look before a slight smile curved her lips.

"Yes." Eladio nodded. "I will ask Agent Carrizo to have the FBI issue a BOLO for Sarita."

"And I will also notify our officers to be on the lookout for *Señorita* García." Peña jotted something in his small notebook. "What else can you tell me about her?"

Eladio exchanged a look with Jade, then said, "She likes expensive tequila, preferably *Kah*." He could almost taste the subtle vanilla notes of the *reposado* tequila. And he wanted to add: she's exceptionally beautiful, wears Scandal perfume, and has amazing lips that are always dressed in blood-red lipstick. But he held his tongue.

Peña looked at Jade. "Anything to add?"

"I think everyone needs to be reminded she's dangerous, probably armed," Jade answered. "And she may be inquiring about Ezmé."

Eladio raised an eyebrow, but Peña beat him to the question, "Hoping to find you?"

"Sarita may try to help if she can." Eladio held Jade's stare.

"That's what I think too." Jade looked at her phone. "Should we check with Juan Vega to see if she's reached out to him for help?"

"Humberto already contacted Vega to see if he knows anything about Raptor."

"Who the hell are these people?" Peña barked.

"They helped us in Mazatlán." Jade was back to sitting with her arms crossed over her chest.

Eladio pointed at her phone. "Sandrine?"

"Joy." Jade tapped the screen. "She's been picked up by the officers and is on her way here."

"Then we need to wrap this up." Eladio looked at Peña. "What do you know about Gwen's abduction?"

"She was taken somewhere between the Marriott and *Restaurante El Dorado* where she had dinner," Peña said. "The only reason we were alerted to her abduction is because she used the hand signal for help, and then a few people called the station."

"Can we assume Raptor's men took her, since he probably has her friend?" Jade asked.

"That is my guess," Eladio said. "But I am confused as to why Raptor would have Erica snatched."

"Because she is friends with Ezmé." Peña suggested. "We know he has his *halcones* watch women before they are taken, so someone probably observed Ezmé and Erica together."

"Possibly," Jade agreed.

"Or maybe she placed herself in danger by asking the wrong person about Ezmé," Eladio countered.

"Probably." Peña ran a hand through his hair.

"I want to discuss the undercover operation with you both before we return to the others." Eladio looked at Jade, then Peña, before continuing. "While I think the two of you would be the best team to go under, I also think your developing relationship could put one or both of you at risk."

Jade and Peña tried to speak at the same time, with Peña winning the shouting match. "We are not involved!"

"Seriously!" Jade shook her head. "Nothing happened at the Zoo."

Eladio held up a hand. "Now that Geovany has volunteered, I believe he should join Jade and Valéria."

Peña glared at Eladio. "I still do not think Agent Mendoza needs to be a part of this."

"Unbelievable!" Jade slapped the table.

"This is exactly why you do not get to decide, Lieutenant." Eladio looked at Peña as he stood. "We are finished." He headed for the exit. "I suggest you two stay and discuss your nonexistent relationship.

Eladio pulled the conference room door open and cast a last glance at Jade. He wanted to ask her what she saw in the sullen, disrespectful lieutenant. Thanks to his evening with Sienna, though, his yearning to get to know Sarita's daughter more intimately had waned. Eladio gave Jade a slight nod and stepped from the room.

CHAPTER TWENTY-FIVE

After Toro left his office, Raptor's plan to remove himself completely from trafficking women, willing or not, echoed through his mind. Stash as much money as possible in a safe place. Stay out of jail and stay alive. Find a replacement for his lovely Belen, and disappear. *Easier said than done,* he thought to himself.

After a lunch of *burritos de cerdo*, he now sat across from Milo. He opened a *Tecate*, and then handed Raptor the bottle.

"Do we have most of our females matched with a buyer?" Raptor sipped some beer.

"Sí." Milo nodded. "Most of the meet and greets have been completed too."

"Could you speed things along if we decided to close the compound sooner than planned?"

"Because of the hit?" Milo took a swig of beer.

"Sí." Raptor held Milo's questioning stare. "Toro is going to make an offer of a payoff, but I think we need to be prepared to—"

"Correr." Milo tipped up his beer bottle.

"Run, indeed." Raptor raised his beer in toast. "Milo, do you like this line of work?" Raptor took another drink.

"I did not like when we trafficked women." Milo raised an eyebrow. "But I do enjoy working for *Rafael, Protectora de la Mujer.*" Milo smiled.

He squinted at his lieutenant. Raptor knew he'd earned the nickname, Raphael, Protector of Women. And while he appreciated being compared to an archangel, Raptor knew his past would never allow him a set of wings.

"What would you do if you did not work for me?" Raptor leaned toward his lieutenant.

Milo's eyes grew round, and Raptor sensed his fear.

"It is okay," Raptor smiled. "You can tell me."

"My cousin has an agave farm in Tequila, near Guadalajara." Milo gave a slight grin. "I would like to work there and drink as much free tequila as possible."

"*¡Suena perfecto!*" Raptor laughed. "Do not tell the other men, but you are free to begin making plans to leave for Tequila."

"*No, Patrón.*" Milo shook his head. "I cannot leave you."

"You will not be leaving me here"—Raptor held his arms wide—"because I too will be gone."

Milo drained his beer bottle and Raptor imagined the plans already forming in the soldier's mind.

"Now, bring the lovely Ezmé to meet with me." Raptor said.

Milo stood, a slight smile on his lips. *"Sí, Patrón."*

Raptor finished his Tecate and enjoyed the view out his office window. He planned to have the same conversation with Toro, and he wondered if the *sicario* would welcome the chance to walk away from this life he hadn't been born into? Just as he hadn't been born to be a human trafficker, Raptor knew Toro had not been raised to be a *sicario*. Two boys who became men. Both with lost opportunities. which might have meant better lives.

Raptor had also decided to leave his legitimate business, *Ardiente Sol Galería*, to Edgar Dimas. He already ran everything by himself and deserved to own the gallery.

With millions stashed away, Raptor knew the time was right to leave Puerto Vallarta while he was still alive and before he landed in jail. Being arrested was a real possibility with Julio, Pablo and Cisco going rogue. If everything went according to plan, he could someday soon be on a beach far from Puerto Vallarta, discovering Ezmerelda Mendoza's treasures.

As if thinking about the young woman summoned her, Ezmé appeared in the doorway of his office. Milo waited behind her. When she stepped inside, he gave a nod, then departed.

"Por favor," Raptor stood and motioned to a chair in front of his desk.

When she sat, he resumed his seat. "Thank you for meeting with me."

"Like I have a choice." Ezmé crossed her arms.

"I wanted to apologize again for having you brought here." Raptor focused on keeping his tone cordial, even though a flicker of desire was warming his groin.

"If I accept your apology." Ezmé placed her hands in her lap and narrowed her brown eyes. "Will you let Novio and me leave?"

"You care for him very much?" Raptor hoped his disappointment didn't show on his face.

"Yes. We were friends but have become—" She looked down at her hands.

Now, jealousy snaked through his gut, and he knew he needed to make his offer before he said something to further alienate Ezmé.

"During one of our coffee dates at the café, I had hoped to ask you to dinner." He smiled. "But circumstances have caused me to remain here for the time being."

"And if I'd said no to dinner?" she asked.

"I would have kept asking."

"Yes, I'll have dinner with you. Then you can let me and Novio go."

"I will make arrangements for tonight." Raptor smiled and hoped his next request would also be granted.

"Fine." Ezmé stood. "What time do I need to be ready?"

"Please." He pointed to the chair, and she sat back down. "Since I do not have the luxury of wooing you until we have our third date." He grinned. "I would also like to request you spend the night with me."

Ezmé's eyes grew wide. "You want me to sleep with you?"

Raptor held her stare.

"Why? You know I am not your lost girlfriend, Belen."

"Because I want to take the memory of lying in your arms with me when I leave Puerto Vallarta for good."

Ezmé looked at him, and he relaxed when he didn't see hate in her eyes. She stood and extended her hand. Raptor came to his feet and grasped her hand with both of his.

"I will have dinner with you and spend the night." She gave his hand a firm shake, then withdrew hers. "And tomorrow you will let Novio and me leave here—without any trouble."

Smiling again, Raptor nodded, even though he'd already begun planning how to take the fair Ezmeralda Mendoza with him.

CHAPTER TWENTY-SIX

Jade shoved her chair back and headed for the exit. Peña cut her off before she reached the door. Staring at his lips, she noticed he'd trimmed his mustache, and tidied his usually scruffy beard. He wore a new, seductive-smelling cologne. Jade refocused her attention and looked into his dark eyes, blushing because she felt the same longing she saw reflected on his face.

"I do not want to fight with you." He shifted from one foot to the other. "You are a very capable agent and I mean no disre—"

Jade held up a hand. "This." She motioned between them with a finger. "This can't happen."

"*¡Maldita sea!*" He grabbed her by the shoulders and kissed her.

Jade pushed him away. "Stop!"

"You are very maddening." Reaching out, he brushed a stray strand of hair from her cheek. "*Hermosa y enloquecedora.*" He opened the conference room door.

"Wait!"

Peña whipped around to face her. "*¿Qué?*" He took a step forward.

Her phone chimed and she glanced at the screen. "Can we call a truce until we find Ezmé and the other missing women?"

He pointed to her phone, and she replied, "We're being summoned to Eladio's office."

Peña moved closer to her and whispered in her ear, "A truce." He pointed at her, then himself. "Then *this* will be resolved satisfactorily." He smiled at her and strutted from the conference room.

Jade took a deep breath and headed for Eladio's office. Licking Peña's salty kiss from her lips, she focused on containing her smile. His words, *beautiful and maddening*, echoed in her mind.

When Jade stepped into Eladio's office, Joy flew into her arms. "Jade!"

"Joy." Jade used a calm tone, and held her hysterical friend at arm's length. "Have a seat. Can someone get her some water?"

"I don't want water!" Joy looked unkempt. She wore a denim sundress and no makeup. Her blonde hair was clipped into a messy bun. "I want to know what you're doing to find Erica!"

"*Señora* Beck." Eladio placed a hand on Jade's shoulder. "Jade and our team are as anxious as you are to find your daughter and Ezmé Mendoza."

Joy took a breath and swiped away her tears. "I know you're doing everything you can, I'm just so worried."

The warmth of Eladio's touch had sparked a flicker of desire south of the border and Jade wanted to smack herself in the head to clear the confusion muddling her brain.

Instead, she did a mental head shake and asked, "Joy, when was the last time you heard from Erica?"

"Last night." Joy took the tissue Valéria offered her and blew her nose. "She texted she was having a drink with a friend at the Zoo, then coming home."

Jade tried to keep the concern fluttering in her gut from showing on her face. "Do you know who she was meeting?" She heard the rest of the team shifting their positions behind her, which told her they were worried too.

"No." Joy shook her head. "When she wasn't home by one, I started texting her friends, but no one had been with her at the bar. They hadn't seen her since some of them had dinner at *Bistró del Tucán*."

A policewoman stepped into Eladio's office and shook hands with Officer Herrera, who'd changed into attire similar to Peña's.

"Ms. Beck," Eladio said, handing Joy a notepad. "Officer Flores is going to escort you to the conference room, and I would like for you to write down the names of Erica's friends you have talked to so far."

Joy looked at Jade. "Can you come with me?"

"Jade's office is waiting for her to return a call." Eladio offered his hand to Joy. "I will see you are settled and have everything you need."

With a last pained look at Jade, Joy came to her feet.

"I'll come check on you as soon as I can." Jade hugged Joy. "Erica and Ezmé are strong." She looked into Joy's eyes. "They'll keep each other safe."

Joy nodded and Eladio guided her from his office.

"Benson called?" Jade asked Sandrine.

"No, Temple." She raised an eyebrow. "He talked to Eladio for a few minutes, then asked for you to call him back."

Peña hovered over Eladio's desk and tapped another pad lying in the middle. "I think it is about the white powder we found at *Casa de Bahía*."

"Why isn't it your lab calling?" Jade asked.

"Our lab did call." Eladio stepped back into his office. "I left a message for Agent Temple because the powder turned out to be fentanyl."

Jade looked at Peña and she could see the concern she felt etched on his face. "Shit." Jade said as Peña's, *"¡Mierda!"* echoed her sentiment.

"Exactly," Sandrine added.

"And a sweep of *Casa de Bahía*," Eladio continued. "Turned up six more Bibles with fentanyl between the pages."

"Is the drug showing up anywhere else in PV?" Geovany asked.

"Not so far." Eladio checked his notes. "According to the captain, there have not been any recently-reported deaths due to the drug." He glanced at Jade. "Maybe Agent Temple will have more information."

"Want me to call him on speaker?" Jade asked Eladio.

"Sí." Eladio returned to his desk. "I think we all need to hear what he has to say."

Jade nodded and touched Christopher's number on her phone as everyone settled into a chair or found wall space to lean against.

"Mendoza." Christopher's husky voice filled the room. "It's been a minute."

"Hey, C," Jade said. "You're on speaker with the troops in Eladio's office."

"Got it." Christopher's tone shifted to a professional cadence. "The PV lab notified Benson about their analysis of the white powder you and Peña found in a hotel room." He paused. Jade knew the hesitation was meant solely for her, because Christopher hadn't needed to add *hotel room*.

Avoiding eye contact with Peña, Jade said, "Right. I found the substance in a Bible."

"Jade." She heard a serious edge in his voice. "Benson and I think this is our unsub from Mazatlán."

Heat flushed her face. "Our alcohol-poisoning waiter?"

"Yes."

"But the fentanyl was in the pages of Bibles."

"Torres and his men were getting close in Mazatlán, and Benson thinks the heat caused the killer to run and choose a different weapon."

"But we have not had any deaths," Eladio stated.

"Possibly the killer was just passing through, and didn't succeed in poisoning anyone," Christopher suggested.

"Copy." Jade wasn't sure how she wanted him to answer her next question. "Are you being assigned here?"

"No. I'm following the money on another ML investigation and the trail is still in the states."

"Agent Temple," Eladio said. "There is a team here working the fentanyl case, but I have not been informed if the DEA or FBI have been invited."

"Correct. Benson reported that neither agency has been invited at this time." Christopher replied. "I also have info on the Devil's Breath you asked Benson about." Christopher's voice echoed through the small office. "Jade, the drug is coming from Columbia via the same trafficker you and Sandrine investigated a couple of years ago."

"Which means he's moving the substance through several channels before it reaches PV."

"Yes, and you also know he has his ear to the ground, so watch your six."

Jade heard worry in Christopher's tone and glanced at Sandrine.

"Thank you for the update," Eladio looked at Jade. "It would be appreciated if you would share any other information you learn on your end, and we will do the same."

"Will do." Christopher cleared his throat. "Jade, can I speak to you alone?"

She thumbed the speaker button, put the phone to her ear, and stepped into the hallway.

"C ..."

"Hey." Christopher's voice had reverted to the warm pitch she remembered from when they were a couple. "You sound tired."

"Thanks," Jade replied, thankful he couldn't see how exhaustion had left dark circles under her eyes.

"Heard your *mom* might be in PV." Christopher covered his phone and Jade heard him saying *yes* to someone else.

"Do you need to go?"

"No. Torres said Sarita has been sighted near you." Jade imagined worry clouding his blue eyes. "Has she tried to make contact?"

"Not yet." She didn't have any proof it had been Sarita watching her at the Zoo.

"I'm guessing you'll hear from her if she can make it happen."

"I think so too."

"Any new leads on Ezmé?"

"We've identified a bartender who has been drugging women, and we plan to arrest him tonight."

"Did you know Ortiz requested permission from Benson to put you undercover?"

"Yes," Jade lied. "I'm going under with Valéria and a PV officer."

Silence filled her ear for a second. "I know you've got this, but follow protocol and be safe."

"I will." Again, she wasn't sure she wanted to know the answer, but asked anyway, "How's Katelyn?"

"She's great." Christopher's tone shifted and Jade detected happiness in his voice. "I talked her into moving to LA, and we found a place in Malibu."

Jade still loved him, but she was no more ready to be committed to Special Agent Temple than she was to be involved with Lieutenant Peña.

"Jade," Christopher said. "Good?"

"Good," Jade replied.

"I'll come to PV if you need me."

"I've got this, Temple." Jade forced confidence into her voice. "Go catch your money launderers."

"Copy." Echoed through her phone, then silence filled her ear.

Jade stared at her phone. She could call him back and ask him to come to Puerto Vallarta and he would make it happen. But Christopher was right, she'd been trained for undercover work, and she had the support of a strong team.

And maybe, now that Benson had green-lighted her to go undercover, she could finally get a damn gun.

CHAPTER TWENTY-SEVEN

Eladio looked at Jade when she walked back into his office. "I am updating everyone on what we know about Sarita García."

"I've requested the FBI issue a BOLO for her." Valéria looked at Jade. "Anything you want to add to Eladio's description?"

"No, thanks." Jade looked at Eladio. "Did you mention Sarita might try to help locate Ezmé?"

"Yes." Eladio nodded, then looked at the notepad on his desk. "Before I left Joy in the conference room, I asked her to call Erica's phone."

"And?" Peña asked.

"No answer. I believe the phone has been turned off." Eladio stood when two officers entered his office. "I ordered lunch from *Fuego Tacos,* since we will need to work through the day." He pulled bills from his wallet and handed them to the officers. "Does anyone want something specific?"

"*¡Cervezas!*" Peña's answer elicited a few giggles.

Eladio frowned at Peña. "We have work to do, and your liver can probably use a break."

More stifled laughter, but no one added anything to the order before the officers left to fetch their lunch.

Eladio checked his notes. "I think the missing women's phones have all been turned off, but that they are being held in the same location as the captives." He motioned at Officer Herrera.

"*Sí*, that is what I believe also," Geovany said to the group. "In order for the phones to avoid being tracked, though, the location services have to be turned off immediately."

"So, when a female is grabbed," Sandrine began, "whoever takes her manipulates her phone so it can't be tracked?

"*Sí.*" Geovany nodded.

"Why not just leave the phone behind or in some random place?" Valéria asked.

"I'm guessing they keep the phones in case they need to make a ransom demand," Jade suggested.

"Agreed," Peña added. "The goal is to make money. If they cannot sell a *chica*, they will probably try to ransom her back to her family."

So if the phones are in the same location as the women," Eladio glanced at Jade, Valéria and Geovany, "then one of you may get the opportunity to use a phone to call us."

Jade sat in a chair next to Valéria. "Let's break down our plan. Are we arresting the Zoo bartender tonight?"

"*Sí,*" Eladio answered. "Sandrine and I will make the arrest, and Geovany and Valéria will stay at the Zoo while we bring the bartender back here to question him."

"We will have to move fast." Peña leaned forward, elbows on his knees. "He will be missed if we keep him too long."

"*Sí.*" Eladio nodded. "Geovany is going to step in as bartender, explaining there was an emergency."

"We need to be prepared for the *pendejo* to try to kill himself," Peña added. "Or to simply refuse our offer."

"Or he might alert Raptor," Sandrine said.

"Officer Herrera." Eladio looked at him.

"Right." Geovany cleared his throat. "If we can get him to cooperate, I will claim to be his *amigo* who's filling in until he's returned to the bar."

"You'll need a better backstory than that." Jade looked at Sandrine, who was a master at creating plausible cover stories.

"I'm on it." Sandrine picked up Eladio's laptop. "Do we know this guy's full name?"

"Ignacio Jiménez." Geovany nodded. "Goes by Nacho at the bar."

"All right." Sandrine's fingers flew across the keyboard. "I'll come up with something in a few."

The smell of food brought Eladio to his feet. Two officers carried in boxes of tacos, a bag with plates and napkins, and a case of water, placing everything on a table at the back of the office.

"Thanks." Eladio waved off the change. Once the officers departed, he said, "We should eat."

Jade stood. "I'll take some food to Joy and Officer Flores."

"Good idea." Eladio smiled. "I will join you."

Following Jade from his office, Eladio noticed Peña's frown. The surly lieutenant could deny having feelings for Agent Mendoza all he liked, but he'd need to do a better job of hiding his emotions.

Eladio carried two plates, and Jade held the door for him. As soon as they entered the conference room, Joy was on her feet.

"You found her?" Joy asked.

"No." Jade wrapped her friend in a hug as Eladio placed the food on the table. "We're still working on a plan to bring her home."

"Jade," Joy sobbed. "I can't stay here; I need to go back to my hotel and take care of things."

"Okay." Jade looked at Eladio, but he gave a slight head shake. He needed Jade to continue to prepare for tonight's mission. "We can have this officer take you back and stay—"

Joy shook her head. "I don't need her to stay."

"But it will give me comfort to know she is with you." Eladio stepped forward and took Joy's hands in his. "Officer Flores will know how to find us quickly should you need us."

Joy hugged Jade. "You'll call me as soon as you know something?"

"Yes." Jade smiled at Joy. "Try not to worry, and call if you need anything."

Joy waved off the food Eladio had plated for her. "Please find my Erica," she said on the way to the door. Turning, she added, "Alive." She exited the conference room, followed by Officer Flores.

Jade stepped toward the exit and Eladio touched her arm. "Can we eat in here?"

"Sure." She took a seat.

Eladio reviewed in his head what he wanted to say as he handed her a plate and bottle of water.

"I would like to discuss the undercover plan with you, since you will be lead." He held her questioning stare, then looked down at his tacos.

"I know you spoke with Benson."

"*Sí.*" Eladio wiped his hands with a napkin.

"If she's green-lighted me to go undercover, I'd like to have a gun."

"You are going undercover as a helpless female." Eladio sipped some water. "I do not think a gun suggests you are powerless."

"Fine!" Jade leaned back in her chair. "Tell me how you see this assignment playing out."

"I know you and Sandrine are knowledgeable in establishing backstories, so I would like you to create yours for this mission."

Jade shrugged.

"To me, you are a confident young woman who also likes to have a good time." Eladio began. "You are beautiful and intelligent, so you would not fall for the usual lure used by Raptor's men."

Jade stared at him and drank some water.

"I would like for Valéria to portray a vulnerable target and you will ser—"

"As her protector." Jade set the water bottle down. "Which could get me killed."

"Not if you are tipsy and play to these *pendejos'* need to capture one more sexy woman."

Jade raised an eyebrow at the suggestion. "And what about when they drug us?"

"Nacho, if he agrees to help us, will not be drugging you, but you will have to act accordingly."

Jade nodded. "Want to talk priorities?"

"*Sí.*" Eladio licked a finger, then pulled his little notebook from his back pocket. "Since you should be lucid, concentrate on the location of Raptor's compound." He looked at her and she pointed to her phone, which she'd set to record. "You will not have your phone with you."

Jade tapped her forehead. "I plan to memorize everything."

"*Bueno.*" Eladio looked back at his notes. "If you find the women's missing phones, hopefully yours will be among them. If not, maybe you can text us the GPS location from a different phone. If the other phones' screens are locked, and you do not find yours, try to use the Emergency SOS feature."

"Next, find the women and look for an escape route?" Jade asked.

She was an excellent agent, but Eladio worried she'd put herself in harm's way to ensure the women were rescued. He leaned forward and looked into her eyes, wishing he felt comfortable enough to reach across the table and take her hands in his.

"Jade," Eladio began. "This operation is going to be emotional since it is your sister you are rescuing. I know you will do everything you can to save Erica and the other women, but I need you to try and keep your emotions in check."

"If you," Jade began and stood, "don't think I'm up for the task, send Sandrine instead." She pushed her chair back.

Eladio shot to his feet and bolted around the table. He grabbed Jade by the shoulders and stared into her brown eyes. She leaned into him and rested her forehead against his chest, taking deep breaths. As he held her in a hug while she cried into his shoulder, he suddenly realized why Peña felt the need to protect Jade Mendoza.

"Sorry, weak moment," Jade mumbled, pushing away from him, and sitting down.

He sat in the chair next to hers. She dried her face with a napkin, finally looking at him.

"You are the best person for this assignment." Eladio attempted a smile. "But you know my job is to point out any areas that might be problematic."

"I get it." Jade nodded. "We can't fail like we did when Sarita escaped."

"You will not fail." Eladio took her hand in his, and she gave him a slight smile. "You are not the only one who will need to keep their emotions in check."

"Valéria?"

"*Sí.*" Eladio continued to hold her hand. "She will want to save her brother. While I do not have a problem rescuing him with the women, he cannot be her priority."

"Understood." Jade didn't try to withdraw her hand. "And I'm guessing you'd like any incriminating evidence we can find."

"Obviously, the more evidence the better." Eladio ran a thumb over the back of her hand, the action seeming natural—as if he'd done so before. "But rescuing the women and escaping without any injury to you or the others is the priority. *¿Copia?*"

"Copy." Jade nodded.

"If you have access to a landline." Eladio picked up her phone and entered a number. "I want you to call Captain Jack's and order the Pirate's Pizza with extra rum sauce."

Her dark eyebrows drew together.

"Ordering food should not cause alarm to anyone listening, because you do not know where you are," Eladio explained. "The owner, Jesús, will know to alert me, and we can try to trace the landline."

Jade withdrew her hand and stood. "We should get back to the others."

Eladio came to his feet and resisted the urge to pull her to him. "One last thing."

She looked at him. "What?"

"I think we agree Sarita knows about Ezmé from news reports. If she is here, she is probably following you."

"And will try to help if she can." Jade placed a hand on his chest.

"*Sí.*" Eladio tried to slow his accelerated heart rate.

"Maybe we can catch two fugitives at once." Jade smiled at him. "Thanks for walking me through your plan."

Eladio grasped her hand, then leaned in and kissed her. When Jade didn't resist, he wrapped her in his arms and devoured her lips. The noise of the door opening caused him to look toward the conference room entrance, where Lieutenant Amado Peña stood watching them.

CHAPTER TWENTY-EIGHT

Raptor held the spicy tequila under his nose. "You think the *policía* are closing in on us."

"Unfortunately." Toro took a sip. "Because our contact is not responding to my texts."

A trickle of concern seeped through Raptors veins. "Do you want to stay in México?" he asked.

Toro shrugged. "You have a suggestion?"

"Belize." Raptor finished his shot.

"Not Guatemala?" Toro tilted his head.

"Not for me, but I can make introductions for you if you would like." Raptor stood and reached behind the bar. He retrieved a money pouch that he'd taken out of his safe earlier. "This will help you relocate and get started." He laid the pouch on top of the map.

Toro's eyes grew wide, and he stared at Raptor. "You do not need to give me money."

"We need to walk away from this." Raptor circled a finger in the air, then poured them each another shot. "You are not only my most trusted employee, but you are also my friend. I am only paying you the bonus you deserve."

"What about the men?" Toro touched the pouch again and sipped some tequila.

"I have released Milo from service, and he has indicated he plans to move to Tequila and work on his cousin's agave farm."

"He talks about the farm all the time and how much tequila he will be able to drink." Toro smiled. "I worry he will become a *borracho*."

Raptor laughed. "He will probably marry a woman who will not let him drink!"

"Probablemente!" Toro laughed too.

"Ferdo will be the last to leave. After he returns the three recently-captured females to Puerto Vallarta, he should report to Edgar Dimas at *Ardiente Sol Galería*." Sipping from his glass, Raptor paused, then said, "I want Blake paid one hundred thousand US dollars."

"Incentive to keep her mouth shut?" Toro took a sip.

"Yes." Raptor looked out the window. Though he'd enjoyed his time with her, and something told him she'd be willing to run too, he only intended to leave with Ezmé. He looked back at Toro. "I will pay bonuses to each man, and they will all be free to go. Except Novio."

Toro raised an eyebrow. "You plan to finally kill the *pequeño bastardo*?"

Raptor didn't answer. He hadn't decided what to do with the little bastard. Did the young soldier deserve to die just because he fell in love with the same woman Raptor desired?

"I am not sure what will happen to Novio." Raptor held the *sicario's* questioning gaze. "Plans for my party have changed. I will be having dinner with Ezmé first at five-thirty, then would like the others to join us for dessert and after dinner drinks at eight."

"Sí." Toro nodded.

"Also, I would like cocktail dresses, makeup, and hair supplies given to the women."

"Bueno." Toro stood. "I will make sure they have everything they need."

After Toro departed, Raptor looked out the window of his office at the waning afternoon light. He leaned back in his chair and sipped more tequila, the memory of his and Ezmé's last coffee date seeping through his mind in a rosy haze.

"It's nice to see you again," Ezmé said when she stopped at his table at *Café de las Artes*.

"The pleasure is mine." Raptor stood and motioned to the seat across from him. She was dressed in a white sun dress with red roses and looked at her phone before sitting.

"I only have a few minutes." She flashed a dazzling smile. "So, tell me Handsome Stranger, how is the art world today?"

"It is filled with stunning paintings, but none as beautiful as you." Raptor grinned at the blush he brought to her cheeks.

Without having to ask him, the waiter brought their usual vanilla lattes, departing without a word.

"Since this is our third coffee date," Ezmé sipped from her cup, "is it not time for us to exchange names?"

Since he already knew her name, he wanted to tell her his. To ask her to dinner. To woo her into his bed. But he worried it was too soon to do so, and instead reached across the table, taking her hand in his.

"My name does not measure up to the name you've given me." He raised her hand to his lips.

"Then, Handsome Stranger," Ezmé smiled at him, "thank you for this delicious latte and for starting my day off with a smile."

A falcon calling to its mate stole the rest of the memory and brought Raptor back to the present. He tossed down the last of his shot and thought, *Maybe, if I remind Ezmé that I can be a gentleman, she will change her mind about wanting to ride off into the sunset with Novio.*

CHAPTER TWENTY-NINE

Jade stared at her reflection in the mirror as if she didn't know the woman looking back at her.

"What the hell am I doing?" She splashed cold water onto her face. When she looked at her image again, the only thing that had changed was that now her face was wet.

"Jesus, Jade!" She slapped the counter.

Sandrine popped into the women's bathroom. "What's going on?"

"Nothing." Jade snatched a paper towel from the dispenser and wiped her face.

"Bullshit! Something's happened." Sandrine stepped closer. "You're hiding in the loo, Eladio looks like he just became cock of the walk, and Peña's acting like someone shot his dog." She turned Jade to face her. "Now tell me what's going on!"

"I kissed Eladio in the conference room." She licked her lips as if she could still taste the hot sauce that had lingered on his mouth.

"Bloody hell!" Sandrine flashed a broad grin. "I know I encouraged you to pursue his interest, but your timing sucks."

"It wasn't intentional!" Jade ran her hands through her hair.

"Peña must have caught you in Eladio's arms, because his surliness is now ten-fold."

"But how?" Jade asked. "The conference room doesn't have any win—"

"Yep." Sandrine nodded. "He must have opened the door."

"Oh my God!" Jade covered her face with her hands. "I don't know what's the matter with me."

"The only thing wrong with you is you haven't had a good shagging since Temple, which was God knows how long ago." Sandrine pulled Jade's hands away from her face. "And I'm guessing talking to him brought up memories, which fanned fires simmering south of the border."

"But I've never been so unprofessional before." Jade shook her head. "I need to get my shit together."

"Or," Sandrine giggled. "You need to get laid."

"No, no, no!" Jade held up her hands. "I'm going to keep my distance from Ortiz and Peña."

"Jade, your anxiety about Ezmé is now complicated by Erica and Gwen's abductions." Sandrine waited until Jade looked at her. "There's nothing wrong with a little stress relief."

"I'm sure you miss Oliver, but you're not going around kissing random men."

"You know it's different when you're in a committed relationship," Sandrine said. "I miss him terribly, but I know missing Oliver will just make our reunion that much sweeter."

"We need to get back." Jade headed for the door, but Sandrine grabbed her elbow.

"What?" Jade narrowed her eyes at her friend.

"Just hear me out." Sandrine began. "You've been swimming upstream trying to avoid any encounter that might bring you pleasure."

Jade crossed her arms.

"For chrissake, swim to shore and take advantage of either the hot, handsome *Federale's* interest or the sultry, sullen lieutenant's blatant lust for you." Sandrine hugged Jade. "Of course, there's no shame in pursuing both opportunities."

Jade pushed away from Sandrine and marched from the bathroom, her bestie's giggle ringing in her ears. When she stepped into the hallway she collided with Peña, who placed his hands at her hips to steady her.

"Lo siento." He looked at her and removed his hands.

"No need to be sorry." Jade saw pain in his dark brown eyes, and touched his arm. "It was my fault."

"The others are waiting for us." He headed down the hallway.

"I didn't mean to hurt him," Jade said to Sandrine, who had appeared behind her.

"Come on, Love." Sandrine followed Peña. "I'm sure the brooding LT will recover."

When the scuffed brown tile of the hallway crossed another well-worn patch, leading to the station's exit, Jade wanted to run. How the hell was she going to manage being in the same room with two men, who, as Sandrine had suggested, had triggered a serious yearning for a mind-numbing sexual encounter. Sandrine had also been right about Christopher's call. While Jade hadn't been ready for a relationship, she missed being in his arms as he satisfied her every need.

Sandrine entered Eladio's office first, then turned and raised an eyebrow at Jade when she hesitated. Jade walked in and found her usual spot against the wall. She crossed her arms and leaned back. She focused on Geovany, who had paused his report.

"Herrera is updating us on a missing officer." Eladio indicated for Geovany to continue.

"Officer Marin has missed two shifts." Geovany glanced around the office. "We had men check his house, and it appears he is on the run."

"Married?" Peña asked.

Geovany nodded. *"Sí."*

"What would make him run?" Valéria said.

"Another officer had voiced his concerns to our captain. He believed Marin is an informant. But we do not know who he works for." Eladio looked at Geovany.

"But the consensus is he works for Raptor," Geovany added.

"Obviously we need to find him." Sandrine leaned back in her chair.

"Agreed," Eladio began. "With Marin in the wind, I think we should hit the Zoo now and arrest Nacho."

Peña looked at his watch. "Now would be a good time to pick him up, since the bar is usually slow from three to five." He glanced at Jade, and her cheeks warmed with the memory of their dirty dancing at the Zoo.

"*Sí.*" Eladio nodded. "Which gives us about an hour to bring him here and offer him a deal to cooperate with our undercover plan."

"Let's do it!" Sandrine stood and drilled Eladio with a dark stare. "I'm going to need a weapon."

Eladio came to his feet and retrieved his gun from his desk's top drawer. He smiled as he opened the next drawer, then handed her a holster and gun.

"About bloody time!" Sandrine slid the Glock 43 free and weighed the piece in her hand. "It's like you know me."

"I remembered the weapon you used at *Fiesta de Fuego*." He reached down again and withdrew another holstered gun. "And I believe this is what you prefer." Jade pushed off the wall and took the leather holster.

She removed the Glock 19M and met his dark eyes. "It's perfect. *Gracias*, Eladio."

"*De nada.*" Eladio flashed a warm smile. "Lieutenant Peña, would you and Jade mind preparing the office for our return with Nacho?"

Peña narrowed his eyes at Eladio and nodded. "*Sí.*"

"*Bueno.*" Eladio grabbed his car keys. "I will text when we are headed back."

Geovany led the way from Eladio's office, with Sandrine last in line.

Dropping the holster onto the counter, Sandrine tucked her gun into the waistband of her shorts at the small of her back. She stopped next to Jade and whispered, "Play nice." She winked at Jade, then followed the group.

Jade really wished she was leaving too. She turned to find Peña watching her. Then he began grabbing debris from their lunch and filling a garbage can. Jade joined him at the back table and picked up a half-empty box of tacos, the stale smell of cold meat wafting over her.

He pointed at the box. "Maybe I should take the leftovers to the station's break room."

"Good idea." Jade reached past him to retrieve the other partially-full box, and heard him suck in air when her arm brushed his taut chest.

Peña turned away and began adding scattered cups and plates to his wastebasket. Watching him bend to pick up a wad of napkins, it was Jade's turn to suck in air at the way his jeans fit his ass. She mentally admonished herself, and tossed clean plates into the taco box.

"I think this is ready." Jade waited for Peña to look at her. "If you tell me where to go, I'll deliver the box."

He crossed the space between them in long strides and took the box from her, their hands touching briefly.

Without looking at her, Peña said, "It will be better if I go."

Jade wanted to say, *Fine! But when you're back, we're going to talk.* But she held her tongue. The lieutenant left and Jade flipped him off behind his back.

"Well, this is all your fault." Jade scanned Eladio's office for more refuse to clean. Then, deciding things looked tidy enough, she sat at Eladio's desk, opened her voice memo app, and pressed play.

Eladio's warm cadence echoed through the room as he outlined his instructions for the upcoming undercover op. She tried to focus on what he was saying, but her mind recreated their kiss, and she closed her eyes to savor the memory.

"¿Necesitas una siesta?" Peña asked from the doorway.

Jade cut her eyes to him and stopped the playback. "Not napping, just mentally preparing for tonight."

Peña sat in a chair in front of Eladio's desk. "You will be fine."

Jade raised an eyebrow. "Thanks."

"Would you be interested in my input?" Peña's tone suggested he expected her to say no.

Jade leaned forward and set the app to record.

"I think you should write down my thoughts." Peña pointed at a blank notepad. "The process will help store what you hear." He tapped the side of his head.

Not wanting to argue with him, Jade nodded, then began searching the desk for a pen. When she didn't find anything in the middle drawer, where everyone keeps their pens, she opened the side drawers. She jumped to her feet after opening a bottom drawer.

"*¿Qué?*" Peña stood also.

Jade lifted a stack of photos and placed them in the center of the desk. As she sorted through them, Peña picked up a headshot and studied it.

"Your mom?" he asked.

"Why does Eladio have all of these photos of Sarita?" She continued to sift through the pile.

"A better question is: why does he have a shot of her standing outside the Zoo?"

"Unbelievable!" Jade snatched the picture from Peña's hand. "Why? Why wouldn't he admit she's here?"

A ding sounded from Peña's phone, and he looked at the screen. "You can ask him soon. He and Sandrine are on their way back with Nacho."

CHAPTER THIRTY

When Eladio returned to his office with Nacho, he hadn't expected to find Jade seated at his desk. She was glaring at him and photos of Sarita were fanned out across the desktop.

"Looks like you've got some explaining to do." Sandrine stepped past him, and placed Nacho in a chair.

Eladio held Jade's angry stare, then looked at Peña, who leaned against the back wall. The lieutenant's face was void of emotion, but his shrug suggested he, too, expected answers. While Eladio debated how to explain the surveillance shots of Sarita, Nacho reached out and picked up the photo of Sarita at the Zoo.

"Why you have her picture?" Nacho pointed at the eight-by-ten.

Jade shifted her attention to Nacho. She detected a sour odor which could be from lack of hygiene, or it could be the scent of fear. "Do you know this woman?" She tapped one of the pictures lying in front of her.

"*Sí.*" Nacho looked at Eladio, who nodded. "She has been in the bar." He returned his gaze to Jade. "Told me to give note to whoever came looking for her."

"Note?" Peña pushed off the wall and stepped toward Nacho.

Jade came to her feet and headed for the door. Eladio blocked her and grabbed her arm.

"Let go of me," Jade growled.

"This is not the time, but I can ex—" Eladio began.

"Not interested." Jade jerked her arm away. "Now get the hell out of my way."

"Jade." Sandrine met Jade's angry stare. "If the note's at the bar, we can have Geovany text us a picture." Sandrine looked at Nacho. "Right?"

"Sí, sí." His head bobbed again. "It is in the cash register under big bills envelope."

Pulling his phone from a pocket, Peña thumbed in Geovany's number, and put the phone to his ear. *"Sí,* they are here. I need you to look for a note at the bottom of the cash register drawer." As he waited, Peña looked at Jade. Eladio wanted to punch him in the face to eradicate his smugness. *"Bueno.* Now send me a picture."

Within seconds Peña's phone dinged. He looked at the photo then handed his phone to Jade, who glanced at the phone's screen, then handed it back to him.

"Care to share?" Sandrine asked.

"It's just a phone number written on a slip of paper with flamingo art at the bottom." Jade tapped the keys on her phone and hit the speaker button. After a couple of rings, an automated voice answered and a recording played, the words bouncing off the walls. *Come to this address, 1039 Casa Nuevo Vallarta Blvd, Nuevo Marina.*

Jade tried to step past Eladio again, but he blocked her exit.

"I cannot let you investigate this on your own."

"Get out of my way."

"She won't be alone." Sandrine motioned for him to move. "We'll text you when we get there."

"I will go." Peña moved from behind them, and Jade turned to face him. "Then I will report to you," he held Jade's stare, "what I discover."

Eladio nodded at Peña and said to Jade. "I need you here to prepare for the undercover op." Then to Peña he added, "Would you like Agent Mortieau to assist?"

Peña shook his head, then with another quick glance at Jade, he exited the office.

Jade turned and marched to the wall spot Peña had vacated, leaned back, and crossed her arms.

Eladio sat behind his desk, and Sandrine picked a chair close by. He stacked the photos of Sarita and set them aside. Pulling his small notebook from a pocket, he slid the pen free and looked at Nacho.

"As I explained at the bar, we know you are drugging women so Raptor's men can abduct them."

"No, no." Nacho waved his hands in defense. "I would nev—"

Jade stepped from the wall and pounded the desktop with a fist. "We don't have time for your bullshit! He has my sister!" Nacho shrank away from her as she continued, "Now tell us how the abductions work, or Agent Ortiz is going to announce you've come in and offered assistance in locating Raptor."

Nacho cut his eyes to Eladio, who nodded. Then Nacho looked back at Jade, but held his tongue.

"Okay." Sandrine stood. "I'll go tell the captain to release information that you're here at the station." She turned toward the door.

"*¡Espera!*" Nacho's eye twitched, and he looked like he might lose control of his bowels.

"I know you are afraid of Raptor," Eladio said, "and once we have him in custody, we can arrange for you to be relocated. But only if you cooperate."

"I am not afraid of Raptor, but you will not have to worry about me." Nacho scrubbed his face with his hands, then looked at them. "Because the cousins will know I am here, and will have me killed."

"Cousins?" Sandrine glanced at Jade.

"*Sí.*" Nacho ran a hand over his face. "They are the ones drugging and kidnapping women."

"But they work for Raptor, *¿sí?*" Eladio asked.

"They do … did." Nacho looked at Eladio. "Raptor changed his business years ago, and no longer traffics *mujeres*."

"Explain." Jade managed a calmer, tone with a touch of empathy.

"He now offers *chicas* a way out of street life or abusive relationships." Nacho leaned back in his chair. "He pays all of us a salary to not abduct women. Now he is known as *Rafael, Protectora de la Mujer*."

Eladio looked at Jade. If Raptor had earned the title of Raphael, Protector of Women, did this mean they were wrong. Had someone other than Raptor kidnapped Ezmé?

"Nacho," Eladio refrained from looking at Jade again, afraid his fear about her missing sister would show on his face, "break down how the operation is run now. What role do the cousins play?"

"The Gonzalez cousins, along with another soldier, Julio, have gone out on their own." Nacho took a sip of water from the bottle Sandrine had given him. "What I do not understand is why the women they are abducting are still being delivered to the compound."

"If Raptor has ordered no more kidnappings," Eladio began. "Will he retaliate against these rogue soldiers? Also, what will happen to the women?" He glanced at Jade and wished he could send her from his office before Nacho answered.

"*Sí.*" Nacho nodded. "I believe *Patrón* will order they be … dealt with."

"And the women?" Jade asked, her tone laced with worry.

"If he can, Raptor will let them go." Nacho's smile didn't reach his eyes.

Jade showed him her phone. "Do you know this woman?"

Nacho frowned, then nodded. "She was taken by Novio, then they were brought to the compound."

Eladio and Jade shared a look. The undercover operation was still a go and the sooner they infiltrated Raptor's complex, the better.

"Nacho, we know Raptor had an informant within the police department and he has gone missing." She looked at Eladio.

"Correct," Eladio said. "So, for now, we can keep you safe."

"But I am guessing you want me to go back to the Zoo and try to get the cousins or Julio to take your female officers, *¿sí?*"

"*Sí.*" Eladio pointed to Jade. "This officer, along with the female at the bar."

Nacho looked at Jade and raised an eyebrow. "She is not what the cousins like, but Julio will like the blonde."

Eladio wanted to touch Jade's arm when he saw her cheeks flush, but worried she would punch him with the fist she'd just made.

"Nacho, I need you to do your best." Eladio said. "The officer serving as bartender needs to be introduced as a trafficker looking for a new crew."

"That should be okay." Nacho sipped more water.

Jade and Sandrine still stood next to his desk, and Eladio motioned for them to sit. When Jade retreated to her wall space, he said, "Jade, would you please take a seat?"

She glared at him, stomped to the chair next to him, and plopped down.

"Let's start with a plausible emergency to explain why our officer stepped in for you at the Zoo," Sandrine said.

"My girlfriend is pregnant." Nacho sighed, suggesting he'd accepted his fate. "I can have her say she felt pain and asked me to come home."

"Do you know Raptor's real name?"

"No." Nacho looked at Jade. "I do not think anyone knows his real identity."

Sandrine glanced at Eladio, who nodded.

"Give us a rundown of how the abduction process works," Sandrine continued.

Nacho glanced at Jade. "Now, the cousins or Julio wait in the bar for *hembras* they like, then flirt with them. Once the female is drugged, they take her to the alley, put her in a car and drive away."

"What happens to their phones?" Jade asked.

"They are disabled before they leave," Nacho replied. "I do not know what happens to their belongings after they are taken."

"What time do they begin looking for women to abduct?" Eladio asked.

"When bar is busy. Ten or later," Nacho said. "But before two."

"Why before two?" Jade asked. "The nightclub is open until six AM."

"I do not know where Raptor's compound is, and neither do the *halcones* who drive the car. I believe it is in the mountains."

"Also," Eladio began, "they would want to travel under the cover of darkness."

"You know nothing about the compound? A name? Or a landmark close by?" Jade asked.

Eladio heard frustration in her voice.

Nacho shook his head. "When the *halcones* arrive at a designated place, they are met, and the *chicas* are handed off."

Eladio sensed, that, like him, both Jade and Sandrine were feeling apprehensive about the undercover operation. He'd hoped the kidnapped women were delivered directly to Raptor, which would have given them an opportunity to arrest a *halcón* and put Geovany in his place. Now he wondered if a falcon would let Geovany ride along. Mentally adapting their plan, he knew either he or Peña would have to follow the car when it left the Zoo.

"Nacho." Jade asked what Eladio was thinking. "What are the chances a falcon will take our male officer with him after the female officer and I are abducted?"

"I do not know." Nacho shrugged. "Or if one of the cousins will take you."

Eladio saw Sandrine place a hand on Jade's shoulder when she leaned toward Nacho.

"Here's what I *know*." Jade's razor sharp tone caused Nacho to lean back. "If you don't ensure I'm taken as well, we will arrest your girlfriend and make sure she has your baby in prison." Jade stood. "Assuming she survives long enough to give birth."

Eladio watched Jade Mendoza march from his office, wishing he had not kept the information he'd recently been given about Sarita García from her. He'd planned to tell her that her mom was in Puerto Vallarta as soon as they'd rescued Ezmé. Now he doubted she'd forgive his decision to wait, and he, too, would be on the receiving end of her wrath.

CHAPTER THIRTY-ONE

Raptor added a splash of *Mexican Soul*, a woody spicy scent he'd found at a clothing boutique close to *Ardiente Sol Galería*. The pretty salesgirl flirted with him to the point of making him finally ask her out. Though he'd enjoyed his time with her, he ended their relationship after a month because he could tell she had developed feelings for him.

He wanted to be in love, and a whisp of sorrow flitted across his heart. He thought about Belen and how he'd planned to propose to her when they reached Arizona.

Two raps on the suite door signaled Toro had arrived with Ezmé. Raptor took a last look in his mirror, pleased with the coral-colored shirt he'd selected for tonight's festivities. He'd paired the shirt with jeans that hung loosely on his hips. Anticipation fluttered in his gut as he padded barefoot to the living room, opening the door to find Toro standing alone. Toro stepped aside and Raptor's breath caught in his throat at the site of Ezmérelda Mendoza dressed in an aqua-colored cocktail dress.

Nodding at Toro, Raptor said to Ezmé, *"Por favor, entra."* He gave a slight bow and waved her inside.

Ezmé strode into the suite. Her head was held high and her shoulders back, accentuating her fabulous cleavage.

Raptor moved to the bar and retrieved two glasses of *sangría roja*. He stood in front of his guest and handed her a wine glass. "You look exquisite."

Her eyes darkened, but she smiled and took a sip. Raptor moved to a sitting area and sat on a red leather couch. He smiled and patted the space next to him.

Ezmé walked over and perched on the edge of a cushion, maintaining her perfect posture.

"Thank you for coming to dinner." He took her free hand in his.

She held his stare, her cheeks a light shade of pink.

"As I have told you, you remind me very much of Belen." Raptor raised her hand to his lips. "When I first saw you, I knew I wanted to get to know you better." He drank half of his sangria and placed his glass on the coffee table.

"I'm sorry you lost Belen." Ezmé placed her hand on his thigh. "You must miss her very much and wish she were here instead of me."

"It is true I miss Belen." Raptor leaned in and kissed Ezmé. "But I am honored to have you join me for dinner."

"I know you want more from me." Her hand still lay on his thigh. "And I am willing to enjoy the evening with you, but I can't replace Belen."

Raptor kissed her again, moving his lips to her throat, then following her soft flesh to the pinnacle of her cleavage. He raised his eyes to hers, took her glass, and set it next to his. Ezmé met his questioning gaze. When she didn't protest, he lowered the straps of her dress, revealing a vibrant purple dragonfly, the tattooed wings almost gossamer on her bronze skin. He lowered the straps further and breathed deeply at the site of her lovely breasts.

Ezmé stood and unzipped the dress, allowing it to fall to the floor.

"Dios mío, eres hermosa." Her beauty took his breath away.

Raptor stood and stepped toward Ezmé, who placed a hand on his chest. "Before we continue, I want three things."

He smiled at her. *"Hermosa y valiente."* He wrapped her in his arms, his hands finding her firm ass, and covered her lips. Her body fit perfectly against his. Despite his promise to let her leave with Novio, Raptor planned to keep her forever.

He freed her and asked, "What is it you want my beautiful, brave Ezmé?" He lifted her hair and ran the long strands through his fingers.

"What is your full name?" Ezmé asked.

He tilted his head. "Mateo Armas."

"It's nice to meet you, *Señor* Armas."

She extended her hand, which seemed odd given her nakedness. "The pleasure is all mine, *Señorita* Mendoza." He shook her hand.

Ezmé grasped his other hand. "You promise not to hurt me."

"I would never hurt you." He picked up their glasses, handing hers to her. "And your third request?"

"You may have me as much as you like for the night." Ezmé took a drink. "Then you must let me leave with Novio."

"Twenty-four hours." Raptor countered.

Ezmé parted her lips, hesitated, then raised her glass and finished her drink. She turned and marched to his bedroom, the rhinestones on her sandals sparkling with the ambient light of his suite.

"Time starts now," she called as she disappeared into his bedroom.

Raptor crossed to the bar, picked up his phone and texted Toro.

Raptor: *I will text you when I want food delivered to my suite.*

Toro: *Bien*

Raptor closed the distance to his bedroom in long strides. Ezmé looked out the window at the mountains beyond, painted in the soft light of the setting sun. Her dark silhouette was lovely, and he stood admiring the sight, burning the details into his memory.

When she turned and faced him, he expected tears, a change of mind, a plea to let her go, but she simply stood, waiting for him.

Raptor crossed to her, gently covering her lips with his. Ezmé wound her arms around his neck, then pulled at the back of his shirt. He raised his head and slipped the garment free while she worked the zipper of his jeans. Raptor pushed the pants down, stepping from them, then led Ezmé to the bed.

She reached toward his groin, but he intercepted her hand, partly because he was afraid he'd explode the minute she touched him, and partly because he needed to be sure.

Raptor lifted her chin and searched her eyes. For the first time since she'd arrived at the compound, he didn't see fear or defiance or anger. He also didn't see love.

"Since I do not want you to feel forced, are you sure you want to do this?" Raptor asked.

"Do you promise to keep your word?" Ezmé countered.

He hesitated. "I do."

Raptor continued to look into her eyes as she cupped him and stepped from her sandals. He lowered himself onto the bed and guided her down beside him. A whisp of a thing, she seemed small in the king-sized bed. His need for release sent his pulse racing, but he wanted to cherish his first time with Ezmé. He turned her face to his and kissed her, then began his exploration of her body.

Raptor followed his path back to her lips. Ezmé grasped his head and ran her fingers through his hair. She kissed him as if she wanted him. He freed her lips and laid on top of her, supporting himself as he nuzzled her neck.

"Mateo," she rasped.

He raised his eyes and met her dark stare as she traced the scar on his chest. "Ezmé."

"This is how you got your nickname?" She brushed the nipple next to the scar with a thumb, and he almost took her without regard for her attempt at intimacy.

"Yes." His voice, heavy with lust, rumbled.

Ezmé brought his lips back to hers and separated her legs. Raptor moved between her thighs but waited.

"I'm ready, Mateo," she whispered against his lips.

He entered slowly, ignoring his urgent desire, but stopped when she cried out in pain. The reality hit him like a baseball bat to the head, and he leapt from the bed. Ezmé had covered her face with her hands.

"You are a virgin!" Raptor exclaimed, running his hands through his hair. "I thought …" He stormed from the bedroom and headed for the bar.

As he poured his second shot of Patrón, Ezmé emerged from the bedroom wearing his shirt. He shook his head at her and tossed down the shot.

"You should have told me," Raptor growled.

"You didn't ask!" Ezmé barked.

He turned and faced her, a third shot in his hand. She crossed to him, took the shot, and drank the fiery liquid. She covered her mouth and bent at the waist as a coughing fit stole her breath. He touched her on the back, and she held up a finger.

After a few seconds, Ezmé righted herself. "We have a deal," she rasped.

Searching her dark eyes, he said, "I thought you and Novio already had sex." The memory of her and Novio kissing in his office filled his mind.

"Novio," Ezmé looked at Raptor with a dark stare, "was a gentlemen while he tried to rescue me from you."

Raptor blew out a breath. "You should have told me you are still a virgin."

"Why?" Ezmé jammed her hands onto her hips, which drew the hem of his shirt up, giving him a glimpse of her luscious treasure. "You do not strike me as a man who would care."

Raptor poured two more shots, handing her one. "You could have used your pureness to negotiate more favors." He smiled and clinked her glass.

Ezmé tossed down her shot. After a short coughing fit, she said, "I believe I'm still in possession of my virginity."

"Yes." Raptor emptied his glass. "Why do you choose to give me such a gift?"

Ezmé crossed to him, twined her arms around his neck, and kissed him. "You are not the only one curious about what it would be like to spend the night together."

He lifted her and she wrapped her legs around his waist as he carried her back to the bedroom. Raptor stopped beside the bed and set her on her feet. She lifted his shirt over her head, dropped it to the floor, then laid onto the bed.

"I believe you know where we left off, Mateo." Ezmé reached for him.

Raptor hovered above her, searching her eyes. When she raised her hips to his, he entered her. Ezmé cried out, but this time not in pain. She dug her nails into his ass and held him to her until they found their rhythm.

Knowing he was close, Raptor leaned down and whispered in her ear, "Open your eyes."

Ezmé looked at him and he felt relief when he saw no fear, pain, or anger in her beautiful dark orbs. Her panting breath was warm against his cheek as he moved to her lips and covered them with his.

He raised up when she arched her back, and shouted, "Oh God."

The intense explosion from his orgasm almost made him blackout, but he kissed her, then whispered. "You may not be Belen, but you have stolen my heart, dear Ezmé."

CHAPTER THIRTY-TWO

Jade returned to Eladio's office once she cooled down. Nacho stood in a corner, drinking from his bottle of water. Sandrine was nodding at something Eladio had said.

She looked at Jade and smiled. "I'm taking Nacho back to the bar, and then will babysit until you UCs return to the Zoo for Operation *Recovery*."

"Okay." Jade met Eladio's stare. "And you?"

"I, too, will be at the Zoo later." He waggled his phone. "Have you heard from Peña?"

"No." Jade looked at her phone and shook her head.

"Me either." Sandrine arched her eyebrows. "You don't suppose Sarita's kidnapped him?"

"No, but she won't hesitate to shoot someone she perceives to be a threat." Jade glared at Eladio. "Have you tried calling or texting him?"

"*Sí.*" Eladio's eyebrows drew together. "No response."

"Then you can take Nacho to the Zoo." Jade headed for the door. "Sandrine, we're going to check on Peña."

"Wait!" Eladio grabbed Jade by the arm.

She looked at his hand, then glared at him. "Let go."

"I know you are angry with me." He freed her arm. "I wanted to tell you about Sarita after the mission—when Ezmé was safe."

"How long have you known Sarita was here?" Jade barked.

"Valéria's boss sent an undercover agent here to investigate whether Sarita had landed in Puerta Vallarta—before you thought you saw her at the Zoo." Eladio crossed back to his desk, picked up the photos, and handed them to Jade. "These were delivered to me this morning."

Jade hated to admit he was right not to tell her, especially since he'd just found out, but he'd known when they kissed, which felt like a betrayal.

She gave the photos back to him. "I'm still going to check on Peña."

"The LT's probably fine, Jade," Sandrine said. "Let's stick to the plan."

"What effing plan?" Jade shouted. "Peña going missing isn't part of the plan."

"This is what we are going to do," Eladio began.

Jade narrowed her eyes at his authoritative tone.

"I will check on Lieutenant Peña." He directed his attention to Sandrine. "Please take Nacho to the Zoo and send Valéria back to the hotel. I want her to check in with Joy first and report to me if anything has changed."

"Come on." Sandrine waved for Nacho to follow her. "And second?"

Eladio looked at his watch. "Tell Valéria to rest, then change and return to the Zoo by ten."

"Copy." Stopping with Nacho as they stepped into the hallway, Sandrine said, "Listen, Love," she waited for Jade to look at her, "we have a real chance to get Ezmé back, then we can chase Sarita over the effing rainbow if you want. Right now, you need to get your shit together and focus."

Without waiting for a response, Sandrine led Nacho toward the parking lot.

Jade knew Eladio was going to tell her to go back to the hotel. Now she'd have to take a cab since Sandrine took the Kia. She looked at him standing, arms crossed, watching her.

"I will drop you at Joy's on my way to Nuevo Vallarta." He didn't wait for her response and left the office.

Jade trudged after him, once again irritated she was being told what to do. They reached Eladio's jeep, climbed inside, and rode to *El Mar Llama* in silence. He pulled into the parking lot and killed the engine.

After more silence and staring through the windshield at the swaying palms, Jade said, "I'll check on Joy and report to you."

"Copy." Eladio gazed through the windshield too.

As Jade grabbed the door handle, Eladio touched her arm. She turned and looked at him. She didn't want to be angry with him, especially before the mission. But controlling her emotions lately had been a challenge, particularly when it came to Ortiz and Peña.

"I may not have an opportunity to speak with you before you are taken from the Zoo." His eyes softened and he continued, "When the operation is complete and your sister is safe, I will help you find Sarita."

"We can talk about my *mom* once this is over." Jade opened the door and stepped out.

"Agent Mendoza." Eladio's professional tone halted her exit.

When she looked at him, concern mixed with longing clouded his face. Her heart skipped a beat.

"You are the best agent for this op." He shifted his gaze back through the windshield. "And I know you will keep everyone safe." Cranking the engine, he looked at her again. *"Por favor, asegúrese de volver sano y salvo también."*

She nodded and closed the door. Of course she'd come back safe; she planned to make him keep his promise to help her find Sarita. Plus, she knew she and the *Federale* had unfinished business between them.

The sun warmed her skin, and she could hear waves crashing onto the sand in front of *El Mar Llama*. God, she wished she could don a swimsuit, grab a couple of beers, and walk in the surf.

She entered the hotel and the scent of jasmine enveloped her as she passed an enormous vase with a multi-colored bouquet. Joy bolted from behind the reception desk and hurried to greet Jade.

"You've found her?" Joy asked.

Jade hugged her. "Not yet." She guided Joy to a sitting area and had her sit down. "We are fairly certain we know where Ezmé and Erica are and we have a plan to find them, but it could take a few days."

"The waiting is so hard," Joy cried.

"I know." Jade took her friend's hands in hers. "I wish there was a quicker way, but I believe we'll be able to bring them home soon."

Officer Flores joined them. "Agent Mendoza, I am ordering some food. What can I get you?"

"Nothing, thanks." Jade stood. "I'll be joining Agent Ortiz and the others for a meeting later. I'll grab something then."

"Copy." Officer Flores headed back to the reception desk.

"Officer," Jade called after her. "Do you have a replacement coming?"

"Yes, at ten." She nodded.

"Joy." Jade managed a reassuring smile.

"What?" Her friend came to her feet.

"After you eat, you should get some sleep." Jade hated seeing worry in Joy's dark brown eyes.

"I can sleep when you bring Erica and Ezmé home." She walked toward a clerk who was waving at her from the reception desk, wiping away a stray tear.

Jade took the elevator to her floor and used her keycard to unlock the door to her suite. The maid had cleaned and made the beds, and the thought of fresh sheets made Jade smile. She opened the fridge, grabbed a container of salsa, a *Corona*, and a lime. Placing her snack on the counter, she popped off the bottle cap, and opened a bag of tortilla chips. She squeezed the freshly-sliced lime into the *Corona* and drank half the contents.

Munching a chip, she checked her phone to see if Eladio had texted her. The screen showed nothing—no recent messages from anyone. She removed the lid to the salsa and dipped another chip into the spicy deliciousness. Jade leaned against the counter and washed down the bite with a swig of beer. It was almost six-thirty, which gave her four hours to rest—like that would be possible, shower, and get ready for her evening as a target.

She opened another *Corona* and carried it to her bedroom. As she pawed through her clothes, all she saw were boring pieces that would hardly create a sexy outfit. Beer bottle to her lips, she stepped into Sandrine's room and opened her closet. Sandrine had an eye for color, and way more style than Jade.

Nacho's comment about her not being the type of female the Gonzalez cousins would want to kidnap made Jade's blood boil all over again. Then she spied a red chiffon blouse and pulled the hanger from the rod. She moved in front of the full-length mirror attached to the back of the bedroom door and smiled. Since Sandrine was a few inches taller than Jade, the slinky top would fit like a minidress.

Jade grabbed her beer and raced back to her bedroom. She rifled through a drawer until she found the white lacey bra she wore with her suits. Another search of her suitcase produced a pair of dark red boy shorts that went with one of her swimsuits.

"Shoes?" She searched the jumble of sandals and flip flops on the closet floor, finally spotting the black heels she took everywhere.

Jade piled her selections on top of the dresser and headed for the shower. She'd never been a *linger under the hot water* girl, but the spray felt good against her skin. Deciding maybe she could indulge in a luxurious shower, she opened the frosted glass panel, stepped out and retrieved her Corona. When she turned back to the shower, she heard knocking on the door. *Joy*, she thought.

After turning off the water, she grabbed a towel and padded through the suite. She peeked through the peephole to find Lieutenant Peña standing in the hallway.

Anxious to know what he'd discovered, and forgetting she only wore a towel, she opened the door.

"Was she there?" She stepped back and waved him in.

"No." He shook his head. "The building seemed abandoned."

"Why haven't you been answering your phone?"

"Dead battery." He turned an envelope in his hands. "And the charger in my car isn't working."

Jade pointed, loosening her grip on her towel. "Is that for me?"

"Yes." Peña handed her the envelope.

Jade looked at her name scrawled across the front, then struggled to open the flap and maintain a grip on her towel. Peña pulled the flap up, the motion causing his hand to brush against her breast, and she couldn't contain the warm flush coloring her skin.

"Maybe I should …" she began, pointing at her towel and headed for her bedroom. "Help yourself to a beer."

Jade grabbed the terry robe hanging on the back of the bedroom door, slipped it on, and tied the belt around her waist. When she returned, she found Peña leaning in her spot against the counter, sipping a beer and reading the note.

She crossed the room, stood before him, and held out her hand. His dark eyes looked deeply into hers as he placed the paper into her palm.

Mi querida hija,
I am disappointed that it was not you who came today.
How lovely you looked the other night. I wish we'd
had a chance to catch up, but you were … busy.

Tell Eladio he is not off the hook.
Until next time *mi amor*,
Amor, Madre

"What did Ortiz do to earn her wrath?" Peña took a sip.

"He worked undercover and gained her trust as her business manager." Jade leaned next to him against the counter.

"Then the time came to arrest her." He glanced at Jade.

"Yes." She nodded.

"My apologies for not believing you saw your mother the other night." Peña headed for the door.

"I'm glad you're okay." Jade followed him. "And thanks for bringing me the message from Sarita."

Peña opened the door, then turned to face her. The yearning she saw on his face made her heart rate spike.

"I will see you later at the Zoo." He grinned and pointed at the robe. "I think you will need a better outfit." He stepped from the suite and pulled the door closed.

"Wait!" Jade yanked the door opened. "Do you want to see—"

Peña placed his hands on her cheeks and kissed her. Jade wrapped her arms around his neck and their backward momentum slammed her into a wall, the robe falling open. Peña kissed her dragonfly tattoo, then claimed a nipple. Jade moaned and clawed at his shirt, but the lusty lieutenant ignored her efforts to remove his clothing. He moved his lips to her other breast and Jade tried to reach his crotch, but he pressed his body against hers.

"Amado," She mumbled into his ear.

Peña raised his eyes to meet hers, then kissed her.

Jade took his face in her hands. "If you don't strip naked, I'm going to shoot you."

His lips curved in a salacious grin, and she yanked his shirt open, sending buttons flying across the tile floor. Peña shrugged out of the garment as she led the way to her bedroom. Working the zipper on his pants, he kicked off his shoes and she slipped out of the robe.

"Dios mío." Peña's eyes grew wide. "You are more—"

Jade crossed to him, placed her hands on his washboard abs and silenced his comment with a kiss. "And you're amazing too, but I don't have much time so if this ..." she pointed to him, then herself, "is happening less talk—"

Peña lifted her off her feet, carried her to the bed, and dropped her onto a comforter printed with dark green palm trees. Jade reached for him as he hovered over her, evidence of his desire growing in her hand. She sat up, pushed him onto his back, then straddled him. She wanted to satisfy the fire burning in her loins, but she also wanted to enjoy a moment of dominance. Lowering onto him, she smiled when he gasped and reached for her hips. Jade set the tone and they moved as one, her desire growing with every thrust.

Peña sat up and when she bent her head to touch his lips with hers, he used the opportunity to roll her onto her back. He increased their rhythm, and Jade had a clear understanding of two things.

The time had come to relieve some stress, and she knew she wanted a repeat performance with Amado Peña.

CHAPTER THIRTY-THREE

Eladio stared again at Jade's reply to his text.

Jade: *Peña is bringing me*

He'd sent a text offering to pick up Jade at the hotel when Valéria had arrived alone at the Zoo. A twinge of anger caused heat to bloom at the back of his neck. He wondered why Peña had gone to Jade's hotel after looking for Sarita in Nuevo Vallarta. Eladio had looked for him around the address in the automated phone message, but he'd been nowhere to be found. And the building belonging to the address appeared to be empty.

Eladio scanned the bar again, making sure he hadn't missed Jade and Peña's arrival. Other members of the task force were present. Sandrine sat at the bar. A few stools down from her, Valéria flirted with Geovany. Nacho worked behind the bar, the only indication he was nervous so far had been a dropped glass.

Eladio watched as a group of women trooped into the Zoo and was relieved to see they were accompanied by male companions. Lieutenant Peña followed the rowdy young people and headed for a tall table close to the bar. He motioned at Nacho to bring him a beer, then met Eladio's dark stare. Eladio wanted to march across the bar and demand to know where Jade was, but something about Peña's slight smile stoked his anger. He knew he needed to remain professional.

He checked his watch, noticing Jade was ten minutes late, and sipped his *Modelo*. A vision in a see-through red minidress walked in, and he spit beer across the table when he realized the stunning woman was Jade. She didn't acknowledge him, which of course was protocol, but he couldn't take his eyes off her. Eladio shot a look at Peña, instantly wishing he hadn't, because the lieutenant's smile had morphed into a smirk—suggesting he knew what lie beneath Jade's sparse outfit.

Fingering her hair off her shoulder, Jade glided to the bar. She hugged Valéria and kissed Geovany on the lips, causing him to blush. Leaning across the bar to get Nacho's attention, the shirt she wore as a dress crept up just enough to see ass-hugging red shorts beneath the garment. She curled her toned leg, lifting a black stiletto heel. Jade had ordered shots and *Coronas,* and the trio toasted each other before downing their tequila. Sipping her beer, Jade turned and looked right at him.

Eladio fought the urge to rush across the dance floor and drag Jade from the bar. Taking a deep breath, he reminded himself the op came first, and Jade was doing what she needed to as part of her undercover assignment.

Jade grabbed Geovany's hands and led him to the dance floor, pulling him close and moving to the rhythm. Eladio cut his eyes to Peña and took satisfaction in what he saw. A grim set to the lieutenant's lips replaced his previous obnoxious grin.

Geovany spun Jade around the floor, then wrapped her in his arms and whispered in her ear. She threw her head back and emitted a throaty laugh, a sound Eladio would've never imagined could come from the button-downed agent. He almost laughed when Geovany kissed Jade right in front of Peña, causing the lieutenant to slide off his stool.

Maybe it had been presumptuous of both Peña and him to think Jade could be interested in either of them. They were older than her and the young officer was closer to her age.

Valéria, stunning in a sexy black dress, joined them on the dance floor, wrapping her arm around Jade, then leaning in and kissing her. Jade twined her fingers into the blonde agent's hair. Eladio shifted in his chair, wishing the kiss would come to an end. When Geovany stepped in and began dancing with Valéria, Jade walked toward Eladio, a mischievous glint in her eyes. When she leaned toward him and grabbed his hand, a citrusy scent flowed over him. The red sheer blouse revealed a purple dragonfly tattoo on her breast just above the lace of her white bra. He raised his eyes to meet hers.

"¿Baila conmigo, papi?" She swayed her hips and smiled at him.

He cocked an eyebrow at the term *daddy* and as much as he wanted to dance with her, Eladio knew the act was intended to draw attention to herself.

"No, gracias." He lifted her hand to his lips. *"Otra vez."*

Jade set her red lips in a pout and sashayed to the next available man, leaving Eladio wondering if there would be another opportunity to accept her offer.

The next guy, a pale-skinned fellow with a slight paunch nearly knocked Jade over in his attempt to show her his best dance moves. She proved adept at staying just out of the guy's reach as she moved around the dance floor. When the song came to an end, she waved off his invitation to join his table and went back to the bar.

Peña whistled, which appeared to be directed at Nacho, but served as an alert to all of them that a falcon had arrived. Nacho brought Peña a beer and a shot, then pretended to be showing him items on a menu. Eladio knew it was a cover for telling the lieutenant something about the man who had just entered the bar.

The tall Hispanic, wore sunglasses even though it was nighttime. He waited for Nacho to finish with Peña, then followed him to the bar.

Eladio tried to see past the dark shades to decide if he'd ever seen the man before but too much of his face was obscured. When he motioned Nacho to the back of the bar, Nacho waved to Geovany, who hustled to take his place.

Jade whispered something to Valéria, and then they headed for the bathroom. Eladio looked at Sandrine. She nodded, waited a beat, then followed the two agents. Geovany also made eye contact, creating a small circle motion with his finger in front of his chest, which indicated to Eladio the man had come for *chicas*.

Laughter preceded the two women as Jade led them back to the dance floor, where they danced with each other. The paunchy pale guy, intent on impressing Jade, had joined them. That encouraged a couple of other men to circle the women like sharks looking for a hint of blood in the water.

Nacho was back behind the bar and the man took up a position at the end. He'd raised his sunglasses to the top of his head and nursed a *Tecate*. Jade and Valéria had captured his attention, and Eladio knew when he ordered three shots his intent was to dose the women. Geovany delivered the shots to the man, who stepped around the bar and shielded the drinks, then headed for Jade and Valéria. He glared at the other men, and they abandoned their hopes of ending the night with one of the lovely women, scattering like rats. The man handed a shot to each of the women, then they clinked their glasses.

When Valéria hesitated, Jade touched her glass again, laughed and downed her shot. Valéria followed Jade's lead, then took the man's hand and led him to the middle of the dance floor. Geovany was back as Jade's partner, pulling her close and whispering in her ear. Eladio noticed a glimpse of panic cross Jade's face. He feared the shots might have been spiked despite Nacho's promise not to drug the agents.

Jade turned and met Eladio's concerned stare. She held up five fingers on one hand, followed by two, then four on the other, then gave him a thumbs-up. Geovany put his arms around Jade and looked over her shoulder. The look on his face told Eladio he had a right to be afraid.

Valéria stumbled and fell into Peña, who jumped to his feet to steady her. She pawed at him as if looking for something until the man apologized and guided her away from the lieutenant. He barked something at Geovany who had his arm around Jade's waist. Before she was led from the dance floor, she made eye contact with Peña. Eladio stood, anticipating the possibility he may have to restrain the lieutenant to keep him from rescuing Jade.

Nacho followed the entourage to the back of the bar, returning after five minutes. Eladio and Peña converged on the bar at the same time, but Nacho waved them off. The two men sat on stools apart from each other, and then ordered drinks in turn. Nacho delivered Peña's *Pacifico* first, placing the bottle on a napkin. Next, he brought Eladio's shot and *Modelo*, adding a napkin to each drink.

Peña drained his beer and tossed one hundred pesos next to the empty bottle. Slipping the napkin into a pocket, he marched from the bar, followed by Sandrine. Eladio sipped his shot and tried to make eye contact with Nacho, who had been drawn into a conversation with a group of girls. When Nacho passed by him to grab their beers, he cut his eyes to Eladio, and pointed toward the entrance.

Eladio turned on his stool and looked at a large Mexican standing near the doorway. He had a scar running from his right temple across his nose to his ear. When he met Eladio's eyes, a chill coursed through him. To cover for what might seem like a stare, he waved at a group stumbling into the Zoo, thankful they were too drunk to acknowledge his effort. The man watched as they staggered toward Nacho, following them to take up a position at the end of the bar.

Eladio used the distraction to finish his beer, grab his napkins, and hurry from the Zoo. He raced up the side street to where he'd parked his Jeep, climbed behind the wheel, and looked at the napkins. One contained a message: *Sorry, 57-65.* And the other: *Jetta.* His heart seemed to jump into his throat when Peña slapped the car window. Eladio unlocked the doors and Peña climbed into the passenger seat, while Sandrine sat behind Eladio.

"Drive west." Peña ordered.

Eladio cranked the engine and punched the gas, the tires chirping as the Jeep jumped from the curb.

"What did Valéria give you?" Eladio asked without looking at Peña.

"A piece of toilet paper with three letters." Peña pointed. "Turn right."

"Where the hell are we going?" Eladio barked.

"The napkin from Nacho had the name of a liquor store." He pointed again. "It is in the next block on the right."

Eladio slowed and pulled into the curb a block before the store. "What are the three letters?"

"KKS." Peña looked at Eladio. "And you know the make and numbers, *¿sí?*"

"*Sí.*" Eladio nodded. "We are looking for a Jetta with a plate that reads KKS 57-65."

Peña opened the car door. "I will get closer."

Before Eladio could object, Peña exited the car and was on the sidewalk. The streetlights provided little light, but the liquor store's large window lit up the area next to the Jetta. Peña walked to the end of the block, then crossed the street, making his way back to Eladio's Jeep.

Eladio adjusted the rearview mirror until Sandrine met his eyes. "Did they say anything in the bathroom?"

A sob escaped her, and Sandrine covered her face with her hands.

"Sandrine!" His tone was harsh.

She looked at him, a tear running down her cheek. "Valéria said Nacho told Geovany the man was Pablo, one of the cousins, and he likes to control spiking the drinks."

Peña climbed inside and pounded the dash with a fist. "Jade and Valéria are passed out in the back seat." He rubbed his face, then added. "Their hands are zip-tied, and they have duct tape over their eyes."

"*¡Maldita sea!*" Eladio hit the steering wheel. "Sandrine, did Jade say anything?"

Peña turned to look at Sandrine and she let out another sob. "We're good." Sandrine wiped her cheeks with her palms. "That's all she said."

Peña looked forward again. "Valéria managed to whisper *cousin* before she was dragged away."

"Nacho wrote sorry on one of my napkins," Eladio added.

Peña's eyes were locked onto the entrance of the liquor store. "Here comes the *cabrón*. Geovany is with him and is headed to the driver's side."

"*Bueno.*" Eladio exhaled a small sigh of relief. "He knows we plan to tail the car, so he will not try to lose us."

"But according to Nacho." Peña leaned forward and looked out the windshield. "Jade and Valéria will be handed off at some point."

"*Sí.*" Eladio nodded. "We knew that was possible."

Peña looked at him. "You requested a helicopter with infrared, *¿sí?*"

"I did." Eladio smiled at him. "And if we are not successful tonight, I will be assigned as *un enlace* to ICE."

"We will succeed." Peña punched him in the arm. "The car is heading into the mountains."

"I see it." Slowing down, Eladio cut his lights. "I do not want to get too close."

"Right," Sandrine agreed. "I'm guessing there isn't much traffic this time of night."

"Sandrine." Eladio looked at her in the rearview mirror. "Your bag's on the seat. You should change."

Sandrine nodded, then pulled her low-cut blouse over her head. Eladio shifted his gaze back to the road.

They rode in silence for a few minutes and Eladio thought again about Jade's hand signals. Five fingers probably meant she would be incapacitated in five minutes. Two, then four could mean how many hours she thought she'd be out. And, obviously, the thumbs-up was her green light to continue.

Break lights flashed ahead, and it looked like the Jetta's headlights shined on a metal gate. Eladio pulled to the side of the road and turned off the interior lights. They opened their doors and exited the Jeep.

"We need to follow on foot." Eladio whispered.

Peña nodded, then met Eladio in front of the Jeep. "Ortiz."

Eladio faced the lieutenant, but the darkness made it impossible to see Peña's eyes. *"¿Sí?"*

"In case something happens," Peña began. "Make sure Jade and the others get out alive."

"That is the goal." Eladio inched forward through the dense shrubbery, the light from his flashlight casting a yellow glow in front of him.

"You, Lieutenant," Sandrine began as she tightened her tactical belt. "Are too ornery to die."

"Sí," Peña's tone was serious, "but the *cocodrilos* do not know that."

"Jesus," Sandrine whispered.

Eladio wished Peña had not mentioned the deadly reptile. If they made it through the jungle, they would have their hands full with the loyal crew of the person who had kidnapped Ezmé. And despite what Nacho had told them about Raptor's alleged metamorphosis, Eladio had no doubt that when cornered, a man nicknamed after an extinct predatory dinosaur would be willing to fight to the death to protect his prize.

CHAPTER THIRTY-FOUR

Raptor filled two champagne flutes, then turned and handed one to Ezmé, who once again wore her lovely aqua dress. She took the glass, crossed to the couch, and sat down.

Tonight, he thought, *will be my goodbye party. And in spite of my promise, I am leaving with Ezmé.*

She looked at him over the top of her flute. He worried his deception would show on his face, so he turned, picked up his glass, and took a sip.

Raptor escorted her to the dining table and clinked her glass. They sipped their champagne, then he leaned down and kissed her.

The kitchen had delivered their dinner on a cart. The aroma of *enchiladas de cerdo* and *sopa de pollo y tortilla* filled the suite. When his mouth began to water, he realized he was starving.

"What are you running from?" Ezmé asked, surprising him as he set a bowl of tortilla soup in front of her.

Raptor tilted his head and placed the platter of pork enchiladas on the table. "That is an odd question."

"You told me you have to stay here, but I'm guessing not forever." She looked around the suite. "And you probably can't go back to your regular life, which means you're planning to leave Puerto Vallarta."

"I am considering moving on." He smiled at her as he took his seat.

"What has kept you from finding Belen?" Ezmé sipped some soup.

"I did look for her, but was told she died." Raptor worried his tone sounded annoyed, so he smiled and continued, "For a time, I did not care about my life, but now I want something better."

"And you're leaving PV to start over?"

"Let's talk about you." He placed two enchiladas onto her plate.

"I'm afraid you'll find me boring." Ezmé took a drink of champagne.

"I find you nothing but intriguing." Raptor placed his hand on her neck and brought her lips to his.

He took a bite of enchilada, then spooned up a taste of soup. They ate in silence for a few minutes, then he refilled their glasses. Raptor thought about telling her the other women would be coming for dessert. He could take advantage of her current calm demeanor to explain why her friend was here, along with Blake and Gwen.

Then he imagined her anger, and decided not to ruin this delusion of normalcy.

Ezmé drained her glass and moved to straddle his lap. Raptor shoved his chair back to make room for her, and focused on not moaning when she pressed into him. He pulled her lips to his and she leaned against his chest.

"Would you like to return to the bedroom?" she asked.

"Sí." He stood and she wrapped her legs around his waist.

He carried her to the bed, then set her on her feet. She'd already begun removing her dress and he peeled off his clothes. Ezmé stepped to him, and he wrapped his arms around her, then kissed her.

"I know you are here so I will let you leave with Novio." Raptor searched her eyes. "But you act like you want to be with me."

"Men aren't the only ones with desires."

"What about Novio?"

Ezmé tilted her head and he thought he saw a flicker of regret in her dark eyes.

"Are you in love with him?" When she nodded, he wished he hadn't asked.

"Yes." She wound her hands around his neck and brought his lips to hers.

"Ezmé." He lowered her to the bed and sat next to her. "Why are you willing to be with me then?"

"Why are you asking so many questions?" Ezmé raised an eyebrow.

"I want to understand what changed from when you first arrived here."

"At first I was scared, then angry," she touched his cheek, "then you reminded me why I enjoyed our coffee dates."

"But this is more than a coffee date." Raptor kissed her. "Why are you embracing my need for you?"

"Because, Mateo, I don't feel like this when I'm with Novio." Ezmé laid back onto the pillows. "I only feel this way when I'm near you."

Raptor's mind spun with her revelation, his need for her almost overwhelming as he hovered over her. He covered her lips with his and she raised her hips to meet him.

A knock sounded against the door.

"*¡Mierda!*" Raptor jumped up and grabbed his jeans.

"Are you expecting someone?" Ezmé stood, reaching for her dress.

"*Sí.*" He touched her cheek. "Join me in the living room and I'll explain."

Raptor strode to the door and opened it. *"Entrar."*

A kitchen worker wheeled in another cart with a variety of desserts and a carafe of coffee.

"Should I take this away?" he asked, pointing to the dinner cart.

"*Sí, gracias.*" Raptor gave the worker a nod as he backed out of the suite.

"Dessert?" Ezmé stepped to the cart.

"I have invited some guests for a late night party." Raptor smiled. "I wanted to explain before they arrived, but we have been busy."

A double rap on the door signaled the arrival of the other three women. He opened the door to Toro, who stepped aside and motioned the women forward.

Once Erica spotted Ezmé she bolted toward her friend. "You're alive!" She hugged Ezmé, who glared at Raptor over Erica's shoulder.

Ezmé held Erica away from her. "What are you doing here?"

"I-I was looking for you and—"

Ezme rushed Raptor and slapped him across the face. "You kidnapped my friend?" She drew her hand back.

"No." Raptor grabbed her by the wrist. "I can explain."

Ezmé struggled to free herself. "Let go of me."

When he freed her, she rushed to stand next to Erica, who clutched Gwen's hand.

Blake, dressed in a white satin slip dress and red heels, sauntered toward him. Snaking her arms around his neck, she kissed him.

"Good to see you again, *Cariño*." Raptor put his arm around Blake's waist. "Would you like to introduce me to your friend?" They stepped toward Gwen, and he extended his hand.

"I tried to explain that they aren't here because you plan to hurt them, but as you can see …" Gwen clasped her hands in front of her as Blake looked at Raptor, "they're afraid nonetheless."

He removed his arm from around Blake's waist and left her standing next to Gwen, then stared at Ezmé and Erica.

"You need to let all of us go. Now!" Ezmé growled.

He offered his hand to Erica, who squared her shoulders.

"Erica Beck." She firmly grasped his hand. "May I know your name?"

Without responding, Raptor smiled at her and walked to the bar. "Please have a seat at the table." Hoisting two bottles of champagne, he returned to the dining area, then filled a glass in front of each one of them, ending with Ezmé.

"First, you all look very lovely." He sat and lifted his glass in toast. "Second, I did not have the three of you kidnapped." He took a large sip. "You may not know," he smiled, "but if you do not take a drink, it is bad luck."

Blake picked up her flute and drained the contents. She looked at Gwen, who took a small sip. Ezmé and Erica followed suit. Blake reached for the bottle and refilled her glass, then added more bubbly to Raptor's flute.

He covered Ezmé's hand with his, holding it tight when she tried to pull free.

"Then why the eff are we here?" Erica glared at Raptor.

"Due to a misunderstanding, you are my guests for the night." Raptor looked at Ezmé, then smiled at Erica. "I spent the day making arrangements for you to be returned to Puerto Vallarta."

His phone pinged and he shoved his chair back. *"Perdona."* He crossed to the bar and looked at an incoming text from Toro.

Toro: *Two more abducted tonight from Zoo.*

Raptor: *I thought we decided no more.*

Toro: *It was the loco cousins, Pablo and Cisco. Might need walk in the woods.*

Anger flooded Raptor. He wanted to order Toro to take the cousins deep into the woods and leave their carcasses for the *cocodrilos* to feed on. Of course, they'd have to find them first.

Raptor: *When do women arrive?*

Toro: *Half hour. Want to see them?*

Raptor: *Not tonight.*

Toro: *Entendido*

Raptor laid his phone on the bar and grabbed two more bottles of champagne. Then he crossed to the cart and selected a platter of chocolate cookies. He placed the bottles and platter on the table, then resumed his seat.

"Erica, you are not from here." Raptor smiled at her. "Where did you move from?"

"Canada." She held his stare.

"And do you like living in Puerto Vallarta?"

"I like the city just fine." Erica sipped some champagne. "I do not like being here with *you*."

Raptor narrowed his eyes at Erica. A resurgence of the old anger he'd harbored toward women washed over him. He had to resist the urge to grab Erica's hand and drag her to his bed. Another spark of anger over his ruined evening with Ezmé colored his cheeks, but how was he to know she wanted him as much as he desired her?

"Mateo, if you let my friends return to their guest rooms." Ezmé stood. "We can go back to the bedroom."

"Me too." Blake pushed back her chair.

Gwen gasped and grasped Blake's arm. "Please don't leave me."

Blake smoothed Gwen's auburn hair and freed her arm. "I won't be gone long."

She picked up her a flute and headed for the bedroom. "You coming, Baby?"

Raptor looked at Ezme, who glared at him and crossed her arms. He kissed her, wanting to backhand her when she bit his lip. He resisted the urge and followed Blake. He wished Ezmé would storm in and demand he not have sex with someone else. Then he stepped into the bedroom and found Blake naked and waiting for him, bringing only one goal to mind.

He pulled his phone from a pocket, checked the screen, then placed it on the dresser. He sipped from his glass, then walked to the bed and set the flute on a nightstand. He pulled his shirt over his head and Blake reached around him. She hugged him, her breasts firm against his back. He turned in her arms, fingered her hair away from her face, and kissed her. They fell onto the bed together and found a fast pace to satisfy their mutual need.

Raptor leaned into propped-up pillows and reached for his glass. Blake climbed from the bed, padded to the small bar, and filled her flute.

"The bottle is empty," she said. "Want me to fetch another?"

"Por favor." Raptor smiled at her and wondered why he couldn't choose to leave with Blake, since she wanted to be with him.

She blew him a kiss, then headed for the bar in the living room. He could hear her talking to the other women. He foolishly imagined Ezmé would be the one to return with the bottle of champagne, but Blake carried in two bottles, set them on the bar and strode to the bed. She sipped from her glass, and he raised his eyes to meet hers.

"¿Qué?" Raptor reached out and stroked her ass.

"Why did you have them captured?" Blake asked as she laid next to him.

"It was not my idea. I no longer wish to be a *secuestrador.*" He drained his glass. "I was forced into this life, and I very much want to leave it behind." He turned to Blake and kissed her. "But it would seem some of my men have other plans."

She pulled him on top of her and he covered a nipple with his mouth as she raised her hips to meet his.

"Please, Mateo," Blake rasped.

Raptor hesitated, since only Ezmé had called him by his given name, then met her arching hips. Blake clawed at his back, spurring him to a faster rhythm and they both said expletives as their climaxes consumed them.

Within minutes, Blake slept with her head on his chest. As tired as he was, Raptor knew he should sleep for a bit too. Knowing Ezmé sat in the other room, angry at him, kept him from closing his eyes.

His phone pinged and Raptor slid from beneath Blake, climbing from his bed. He crossed to the bar and looked at a text from Milo.

Milo: *Pardon me Patrón for knowing this, but I believe Ezmé has a purple libélula tattoo on her chest.*

He frowned, wondering how Milo would know about Ezmé's dragonfly tattoo.

Raptor: *Sí. ¿Por qué?*

Milo: *One of the new captives also has a purple libélula tattoo in the same place.*

Raptor walked to the doorway of his bedroom and stared at Ezmé Mendoza. She held hands with both Erica and Gwen, and spoke to them in a quiet voice. She must have felt his eyes on her because she met his stare, her face void of emotion.

His phone pinged again.

Milo: *¿Patrón?*

Raptor: *Bring the new captives to my suite.*

Who, he asked himself, *could be the person in Ezmé's life important enough to have a matching tattoo?*

CHAPTER THIRTY-FIVE

Stomach cramps brought Jade back to consciousness. Blinking, she tried to focus, but her eyes were full of tears. She swiped at them, her fingers hitting sticky residue on her skin. Slowly, her brain began to fit the pieces together.

Valéria lie next to her. Still unconscious, sweating, and breathing heavily. Jade shook her and the blonde agent's head lulled from side to side.

"Valéria," Jade whispered. "Wake up."

"Nah," she slurred. "Need sleep."

Jade's vision had cleared, and she took in their surroundings. They were in a bedroom with two twin beds, a closet, and a small bathroom. Blinds were drawn on the lone window. When she raised them, she could see iron bars covering the outside. She hustled to the bathroom, splashed cold water on her face, then wet a washcloth. Returning to the bedroom, she found Valéria trying to sit up.

"Here." Jade placed the cold cloth in Valéria's hands. "Run it over your face, it will help you feel better."

"Where are we—" Valéria began, then her eyes grew wide, and Jade knew she didn't have to answer.

"Geovany must have been able to give us the counter drug." Jade tried the bedroom door's knob, not expecting to find it unlocked. "Otherwise, we'd still be out."

Valéria tried to stand, wobbling at first, then raced to the bathroom. Jade could hear her retching and stepped to the doorway, the rancid smell causing her to gag. The bedroom door banged open, and Jade turned to see a wiry man watching her. She knew their best bet for survival was to appear as if they were still drugged.

"Hey." Jade stumbled toward him. "My friend's real sick." She took his hand. "Can you help her."

The man jerked his hand away and Jade saw a flash of anger in his eyes. "She drank too much." He stepped into the room, leaving two men in the hallway. "I am Milo. We have come to take you to meet *Patrón*."

"Patrón?" Jade gagged. "No, no, no more tequila." She weaved her way to one of the beds and plopped down.

"I'm cold." Valéria stepped into the bedroom and headed for the closet. "I hope there's warmer clothes in here." Looking at Milo, she giggled. "You didn't tell me we had company."

"Where are the guys that brought us?" Jade stood and pointed at Milo. "Do you know where they are? Cause I think one of them has my phone."

"¡Bastante!" Milo yelled. "Enough of this shit!" He turned, motioning two men forward. "Bring them to Raptor's suite."

Jade concentrated on not reacting to Raptor's name, but she heard Valéria gasp when the man in charge of her grabbed her arm. She wanted to turn and give her partner a reassuring smile, but the brute who had hold of her wrist was literally dragging her down a musty hallway. She was still having trouble seeing, but Jade tried to keep track of where they'd been and where they were going. The monochrome walls, ceiling and floor tile made it difficult to assess, though.

After a couple of turns, Milo stopped in front of a door and knocked. Jade heard a deep voice say, *"Entrar."* Before the door opened, Jade prayed her team knew where they were and had a plan to rescue them soon.

The soldier manhandling her shoved Jade inside, and Valéria came to a stop next to her. Jade's heart leapt into her throat when she saw her sister sitting on a red couch next to Erica. Jade wanted to warn Ezmé to stay quiet, but didn't need to. Her sister looked away from her and took Erica's hand. Both of them remained silent.

A tall, athletic man emerged from a bedroom, and Jade could see he'd left someone in his bed.

Noticing she looked past him, the man said, "Do not worry, she is tired from our tryst, but otherwise unharmed."

Jade met his dark eyes and knew she'd finally found Raptor. Her mind raced with different scenarios as to how to play him, and she decided to let him take the lead.

He touched his bare chest, drawing her eyes to the claw-like scar beneath his fingers. "My apologies." He walked toward them, and Jade felt Valéria move behind her. "I am Raptor." He extended his hand and continued, "But I believe you already know who I am."

Holding his stare, Jade shook his hand. "Pleased to finally meet you."

"I doubt you are finding any pleasure in being here." He released her hand. "Because, as you can see, the others are less than enthusiastic."

"I would imagine it is hard to be excited about being a captive."

Jade saw his jaw muscle jump before he reached out, grabbed Valéria and dragged her in front of Jade. "You should not hide your beauty."

He let go of Valéria. For a second, Jade thought the young agent might take a swing at him. Raptor moved to the bar and popped the top off a bottle of champagne, filling three flutes. He walked back and handed glasses to Valéria and Jade, then tipped his own glass to his lips.

"Por favor," He motioned for them to drink. "You are a little late, but we still have a few hours to enjoy ourselves before dawn."

Jade took a small drink, and Valéria emptied half of her glass. Jade's mind had cleared, and she decided the best way for the others to have a chance to leave Raptor's suite was to distract him. She tipped her glass and drained the contents.

"Are you inviting one of us to join you in the bedroom?" Jade kept her face neutral, but she could tell Valéria had reacted to Raptor's smile.

"You are offering yourself to me, *¿sí?*" Raptor took another sip.

Jade nodded and he closed the distance between them. He touched her lips with a finger, then kissed her, pulling her to him and grabbing her ass. His lips tasted citrusy, and Jade resisted the urge to bite him.

"Enough!" Ezmé stood, her hands jammed onto her hips, and glared at Raptor. She marched toward him, and he shot a warning look at her as he backed away from Jade. "Leave her alone," Ezmé growled at him.

He reached out and grabbed her by the neck, pulling her to him. "Why, *mi amor?*" He spun her around, then held her tight against his body, an arm around her neck. "Do you know this woman? Tell me is she a *Federale, policía* or FBI?"

"I'll go with you," Ezmé leaned her head against his chest, "if you let everyone else leave."

"Leave?" A naked blonde asked as she strutted from the bedroom. "I'm not ready to leave." She slinked next to Raptor, laid her head on his shoulder, and glared at Jade.

Raptor didn't remove his arm from Ezmé's neck or break eye contact with Jade. "Blake, maybe you should get dressed since I have new guests."

Blake ignored Raptor and approached Valéria. "She's pretty." Blake fingered one of the straps of Valéria's black cutout minidress. "I want what she's wearing." She took Valéria's hand and pulled her toward the bedroom.

"Blake." Anger echoed in his tone, and she stopped, then looked at him. "Let go of her and go put on your dress."

"Fine!" Blake stomped toward the bedroom. "But if you choose her, I get to participate." Before she disappeared into the dark room, Blake blew a kiss to Valéria.

"Please, Mateo," tears shone in Ezmé's eyes, "let it be just us—like it was a few hours ago."

Her sister's pleading caused Jade's stomach to lurch. The thought she'd been forced into this monster's bed made her want to kill him.

Raptor caressed Ezmé's shoulder with his other hand and kissed her cheek. As he lowered the strap on her dress, a grin blossomed on his lips. Jade's blood went cold. She took a step forward but was halted by Blake returning clad in a man's coral colored shirt.

When she reached Raptor, Blake turned in a circle and asked, "Better, Baby?"

Raptor still held Jade's stare. "Blake, I need you to assist me."

"Anything for you, Baby." She smiled at Jade, then asked, "Which one do you want me to bring to your bed?"

"Not quite yet, *Cariño*." He moved Ezmé's strap a little lower. "I need you to remove our guest's red blouse."

"Sure." Blake moved toward Jade.

"Don't touch me, bitch," Jade growled as she backed away.

"Oh, come on," Blake reached for Jade's shirt. "Live a little."

Jade grabbed Blake's wrist and twisted her arm behind her back. "Move and I'll break your arm."

"Mateo!" Blake yelled. "Make her let go."

Raptor lowered the strap of Ezmé's dress until her breast was exposed, along with her purple dragonfly tattoo. Jade let go of Blake and shoved her away, then ripped open her blouse, revealing her matching ink.

"No!" Ezmé cried and Raptor let go of her. "Please don't hurt her!" Ezmé stood between Raptor and Jade, her arms outstretched as if she could keep them apart.

"Get out of my way, Ezmé." Raptor growled.

Jade pulled her sister behind her. "If there's a way out of here." She kept her focus on Raptor. "Find it and run."

Raptor grabbed Jade and proceeded to drag her toward the bedroom.

Jade resisted and looked at Ezmé, then yelled again, "Run!"

"You can stop instructing them." Raptor shoved Jade down onto his bed. "It is a long shot, but *if* they managed to escape the compound," he began removing his jeans, "they would be eaten by *cocodrilos* before they could be rescued."

He stepped from his jeans and dread washed over Jade. She looked wildly around the bedroom for a weapon, her eyes landing on champagne bottles sitting on a small bar.

Blake stood in the doorway and pulled off the shirt she wore. "Me too, Baby?"

"Not yet," Raptor snarled. "I will call you when it is your turn."

"Can I have fun with the other girl then?" Blake asked.

"As much as you like." Raptor grabbed Jade's ankles and pulled her to the end of the bed. "You are just as beautiful as your sister." He reached for her red shorts. "But can you satisfy me the way she does?"

Jade knew she had to fight back enough to keep him engaged so the other women could try to escape. She kicked out at him and rolled off the bed. He smiled at her and blocked her attempt to reach the bar. Jade inched back toward the bed, intent on grabbing the lamp, but he was on her before she had a chance.

Raptor kissed her and Jade tried to push him away, but he was a powerful man and consumed with one thought—raping her.

"Mateo!" Ezmé shouted from the doorway. "Stop!"

Raptor raised his eyes to Jade and winked at her. Then turned and headed for Ezmé, who was shrugging off Blake's attempts to pull her away. Jade rushed across the room, surprised when he turned and punched her in the face. The last things she remembered before blacking out were Ezmé's screams and the sound of gunfire.

CHAPTER THIRTY-SIX

"There is a lot of blood." Eladio placed his hand on her chest. "But she is breathing."

Peña pointed at Jade's bloody face. "I think her nose is broken."

"The EMTs are here!" Sandrine shouted. "Make room!"

Someone had wrapped Jade in a blanket since she was naked from the waist up. Eladio and Peña stepped back from Jade so the first responders could attend to her. From the looks of her face, she'd taken a significant punch. It had knocked her out, and probably broken her nose. She stirred when one of the EMTs touched her nose, and Eladio exhaled the breath he'd been holding.

"Eladio," Sandrine touched his shoulder. "I'll stay with her." She looked at Peña. "You two need to check on the chaos going on at the main entrance."

"Sí." Eladio cast a last glance at Jade. "Keep us updated."

"Copy." Sandrine moved closer to her friend, who still sat slumped against a wall.

"Lieutenant." Eladio said to Peña.

Without a word, Peña looked at Jade once more too, then followed Eladio. "We were too late," Peña grumbled.

"Jade will be fine." Eladio continued down the hall leading back to the front of the compound. "You know we breached as soon as we could. We might have been able to make a silent entry if a guard had not seen our men on the east side."

"But we did not rescue Ezmé Mendoza," Peña said behind him, "and her sister is not going to be happy."

Eladio stopped, and Peña bumped into him.

"*¿Qué?*" Peña snapped.

"There must be a good reason Raptor has his rooms all the way to the back of the compound." Eladio met Peña's questioning stare.

"For a quick escape." Peña nodded. "I will check it out."

"Wait. We should wrap things up and make sure the rescued females are on their way to the hospital." Eladio halted the lieutenant's retreat. "Also, we can send Geovany to begin interrogating Raptor's captured men."

"But that will take time." Peña turned and headed back toward Raptor's suite.

"Amado."

Peña stopped and faced Eladio.

"You know if Raptor had an escape plan," Eladio said, looking at his phone, "he is long gone. All we will do is discover where the trail begins."

"*Bien.*" Peña marched past him.

"Geovany texted. We are needed." Eladio followed him. "Hopefully, we can wrap this up *pronto*."

A cloud of smoke still hung in the air, and the acrid smell of gunfire burned the back of his throat when they stepped outside.

Once their presence was known, a gunfight had ensued. Eladio knew most of Raptor's men had died, and he assumed he'd lost men as well. But the mission had succeeded, considering they had rescued Erica, Gwen, and five other women. Determining how many of Raptor's soldiers had escaped would take time, which was why he planned to give

Geovany the task. If Valéria felt up to it, he would have her work with Officer Flores to question the rescued women.

"Agent Ortiz," Geovany greeted him, giving Peña a head bob, "we have only been able to locate and arrest five of Raptor's men."

"Are any of them in charge?" Peña asked.

"Not that we have determined." Geovany answered.

"How many dead?" Eladio looked around the grounds, where bodies lay covered with sheets.

"First count is twenty." Geovany looked at the five captives. They were on their knees, their hands zip-tied behind their backs. "I heard one of them say a *sicario* named Toro escaped."

"What about our men?" Peña also took in the grisly scene.

"Four wounded, no fatalities."

"And the females?" Peña looked at Geovany. "Where are they being held?"

"In the *comedor*." Geovany replied. "We have also captured men that did not work for Raptor." Geovany headed toward six men who were being held away from the other group. "They are not talking, but one of Raptor's men said they were fighting these soldiers when we arrived."

Eladio exchanged a look with Peña, who shrugged and said, "Possibly another trafficking organization or a cartel."

"Make sure the two groups are transported and held separately at the station," Eladio said. "Now show us where the women are waiting."

Geovany nodded. Eladio and Peña trekked after the young officer down a hallway to a room that served as a mess hall. Several long tables with chairs were scattered around, and a cafeteria-style serving counter ran across the back of the room. A police officer, pad in hand, stood near a table. An older woman wearing a chef's hat and a dirty apron sat with a small group dressed in white shirts, black pants, and a clean version of the same apron.

Geovany stopped in front of the table occupied by the rescued females.

"This is Agent Ortiz," Geovany said in Spanish, then he repeated the introduction in English. "How many of you speak English?"

Two women of the five women raised their hands.

"I can translate if you want to continue in English." Valéria stood next to Erica, who held a half-empty champagne bottle. Gwen hovered close by clutching a shoe.

"Bueno." Eladio smiled at her. "We would like to ask you a few questions if that is okay." He waited while Valéria translated, and a ripple of nods indicated consent. "First, are any of you in need of medical attention?"

The question was followed by a round of headshakes, then a chorus of gasps echoed through the room. Eladio turned to see what had elicited their wave of shock. With Sandrine's aid, Jade shuffled into the mess hall. He and Peña rushed to her side, and she almost collapsed into Peña's arms.

"The EMTs think she has a bloody concussion." Sandrine shook her head. "But she refused to go to the hospital until she's sure Ezmé isn't here."

Geovany had grabbed a chair and Peña helped Jade sit down. Dark circles rimmed both of her eyes, and her nose had been packed and taped. She still had the blanket around her shoulders, but now wore a mishmash of sweats, an oversized T-shirt, and white socks.

"Jade." Eladio squatted and placed a hand on her knee. She met his eyes. "Are you sure you are up to staying?"

"Have you found Ezmé?" Her voice was a nasally whine.

Peña had also knelt beside her and took her hand in his. "Go to the hospital. We will—"

"I am not going anywhere." Jade narrowed her eyes at them and winced from the effort. "Ask them if they know where my sister is."

Erica inched forward, followed by the shoe-wielding Gwen, then Valéria.

"I can take the shoe, Gwen," Valéria said to her.

Gwen shook her head and stepped to Jade, followed by the other two women. Eladio and Peña came to their feet and made way for the trio.

"Jade," Erica began, her voice quivering. "Blake—"

"Give her the shoe." Valéria motioned to Gwen.

Her hands shook as she extended the shiny red high heel to Jade, yanking it back when Eladio tried to take the shoe.

"Thank you, Gwen." Jade let the young woman place the shoe in her hands.

"Jade." Valéria crouched down in front of her. "Blake wanted us to give the shoe to you."

Sandrine moved in front of Jade's chair and sat down, cris-crossing her legs. "Why?" she asked, her eyes focused on Jade.

"She said there's a message in the shoe, but only for Jade so ..." Erica began.

"I kept it safe." Gwen smiled at Jade.

"We didn't want to destroy anything looking for the message," Valéria said to Eladio.

"Give me the shoe, Love." Sandrine held her hands out.

"Let us see what we can find," Peña encouraged.

Jade handed Sandrine the red high heel and leaned forward. Sandrine turned the shoe over and checked the sole, which seemed well-worn but otherwise intact. She ran her fingers along the inside, looking at Jade when she reached the toe of the shoe.

"Who's got a small knife?" Sandrine asked.

Geovany pulled a penknife from his pocket and handed it to her. Sandrine worked the point of the knife along the edge of the insole, then peeled the flimsy material away. She looked up at Jade, slipped a piece of paper free, and handed it to her.

Jade unfolded the small sheet, scanned the note, then handed it back to Sandrine.

"Bloody hell!" Sandrine shot to her feet and handed the note to Eladio.

"What the fuck does it say?" Peña asked.

> *Querida hija,*
> I know you are worried about your sister, Ezmé.
> Blake works for me. She was to give you this note
> if Raptor left with Ezmé and Blake was able to
> join them. Once Raptor learns I hold his life in
> my hands, he will release Ezmé to me unharmed.
> All I require to return her to you is a chance to
> meet with you alone. Tell Eladio if he tries to
> join you, I will have him killed. I will see you
> soon *mija. Amor, Madre*

After reading the note out loud, Eladio refolded the paper and slipped the small missive into his back pocket.

"Come on, Love." Sandrine stood and extended her hand. "Let's get you checked out at the hospital so we can focus on getting Ezmé back.

Jade slowly came to her feet, but sat back down when Valéria said, "Wait, there's more."

All eyes were on the young agent, who was bookended by Erica and Gwen.

"Blake wanted us," Valéria indicated the other two women, "to tell you she's sorry."

"She tried to deter Raptor's interest in Ezmé by offering herself but—" Erica added.

"The crazy bastard only wants your sister." Gwen finished Erica's sentence.

"Blake also apologized to us, saying she was trying to protect us from Raptor and to—"

"To stay alive." This time it was Valéria who cut Erica off. "She said if she couldn't rescue Ezmé for you, Sarita would kill her."

Gwen emitted a squeak and Erica put her arm around her shoulder. Jade stood, and Eladio grabbed her arm.

"Has anyone found my brother, Novio?" Valéria asked.

"Not yet." Eladio shook his head. "If you think you are up to it, you can stay and help clear the building instead of going to the hospital with the others."

"I'm fine." Valéria squared her shoulders. "Who do I check in with?"

"Lieutenant." Eladio glanced at Peña. "Will you stay and help Geovany wrap up the scene?"

Peña narrowed his eyes at Eladio and answered by taking Jade's other arm.

Sandrine whistled at Geovany, who hustled over. "Can you assist Valéria in finishing up here?"

"Sí." He nodded, then said to Eladio. "One of the women, a former *prostituta*, claimed a soldier came to her to say goodbye."

Eladio raised an eyebrow and Peña said, *"¿Por qué?"*

Geovany looked at his notes. "His name is Milo and he had asked her if she wanted to move to Tequila with him in a couple of weeks," Geovany raised his eyes to the questioning stare of the team, "but told her he had to help Raptor escape. She has not seen him since."

"Thank you, Officer Herrera." Eladio smiled. "The scene is now in yours and Valéria's capable hands. Please text me when the compound has been cleared."

"Lo haré." Geovany nodded, then headed to the front of the compound.

"They'll do a good job," Sandrine said, watching Valéria follow Geovany. "Now can we get Jade to the effing hospital?"

"I think Raptor's escape route is through the mountains to the river that leads to the bay." Peña put his arm around Jade's waist.

"Agreed. Two men would be needed," Eladio hesitated.

"One to secure the women and one to shoot the crocodiles," Jade croaked, finishing his thought.

CHAPTER THIRTY-SEVEN

"¿*Patrón?*"

Raptor sat up and pointed his gun at Milo, who held his hands up in defense. Raptor lifted the barrel, then placed the gun next to him on the bed.

"How long have I been out?" Raptor closed his eyes and fell back into the pillows.

"Six hours," Milo said. "I am sorry to bother you, but Blake is not well."

Raptor looked at Milo. He sat up and placed his feet on the floor, despite exhaustion tugging at his body. He placed the gun in the drawer of the nightstand, then stood and pulled on a T-shirt.

"The bite wound?" He asked Milo as he padded from the bedroom.

"*Sí,*" Milo said, following him through the apartment. "Neither of them have slept, and Ezmé keeps asking for you."

Fleeing the compound replayed in Raptor's mind. He'd locked his bedroom door to keep Valéria from coming to Jade's aid. After donning his clothes and a pair of boots, he'd handed Blake a T-shirt to wear over her dress. He had to drag Ezmé away from her sister and had wrapped her in his coral shirt. Milo had retrieved a Glock for Raptor and a rifle for himself from a compartment at the back of the bedroom closet. Then the four of them had left the suite through a hidden door.

The image of the *cocodrilo's* jaws locked onto Blake's calf flashed in Raptor's mind. Milo had shot the beast, but the bite had punctured her flesh. Raptor had torn his T-shirt into strips to wrap Blake's leg, which had already begun to swell. He'd thrown Ezmé over his shoulder when they fled, and, in true Ezmé fashion, she'd pitched a fit, pounding his back and demanding to be put down. After Blake was bitten, Ezmé had no problem letting Raptor carry her through the dense jungle. Though he was strong for a skinny guy, Milo had struggled to help Blake as she limped alongside him, leaving a blood trail. Raptor worried the coppery scent would attract more *cocodrilos*.

When they reached the car he kept stashed at the end of the trail, they drove to his apartment. It took both Raptor and Milo to carry Blake inside. Their escape from the compound had taken them over an hour. They had no idea how much blood Blake had lost, but she was weak and lightheaded. Ezmé had gathered as many supplies as she could find, and the three of them did what they could to clean the wound and make Blake comfortable.

Now, when Raptor stopped next to an open door, he said to Milo. "I think there is coffee in the kitchen." He looked into the bedroom and continued, "There is probably not much food, but see what you can find."

"*Sí.*" Milo scrubbed his face with a hand. "There is no food, *Patrón*. I checked all the cupboards."

Raptor frowned. "You have cleaned the wound?"

"With soap and water." Milo nodded. "And I used tequila, but the bite is very bad."

Raptor rarely stayed at his apartment in the mountains. His last visit involved trying to save someone from a gunshot wound. But other than a few bandages and tequila, there wasn't anything else to treat Blake's *cocodrilo* bite. And he knew the worst thing about the injury would be the bacteria transferred from the beast's mouth to the wound, which could cause an immediate infection.

"Make the coffee for now, and then we will decide what to do next."

Milo hustled toward the kitchen and Raptor stepped into the bedroom. Blake was wearing one of his T-shirts and a pair of his sweats with the pant legs rolled up to her thighs. She reclined in the bed with her injured left leg propped up. An empty box supported her knee and her ankle rested on pillows to keep pressure off the wound. A swath of gauze had been wrapped loosely around her leg. Raptor lifted the bandage. Despite Milo's efforts, the flesh surrounding the bite was a dark red. Yellowish pus leaked from the larger punctures and emitted a foul, putrid odor. Her complexion was sallow, and perspiration dotted her forehead.

"Mateo." Ezmé stood from a chair and met him at the end of the bed. "Blake needs a doctor."

Raptor smiled at her, noticing she had chosen a tan linen shirt from his closet, which she wore over a pair of his shorts, then shifted his gaze to Blake.

"You are not planning to die on me, are you?" Raptor grinned at her.

"I'm trying not to," Blake said. "But I think a hospital sounds pretty good."

Raptor stared into her green eyes and could tell she knew letting her die would be a better choice for him.

"Ezmé," Blake rasped. "Would you get me a glass of water?"

"Yes." Ezmé gave Raptor a wary look before leaving the bedroom.

Blake tried to sit up and he gently grabbed her arm to support her. He stacked pillows behind her, which she leaned into with a moan.

"Mateo," she said. "I need to borrow a phone."

"I cannot let you call an ambulance."

"Not my plan." Blake gave a slight head shake. "But trust me, you want to let me use your phone."

"Tell me why first." Raptor frowned.

"Because if I die," she said, gasping when she tried to adjust her leg. "I won't be the only one who does." She held out her hand.

Raptor pulled his phone from his sweatpants pocket and unlocked the screen. After placing it in her hand, he moved to the head of the bed so he could see the phone's screen.

"Don't bother trying to remember what I'm doing," Blake said as her fingers tapped the keys. "As soon as I sign into this site it will shut down, so you won't be able to open it again."

Blake typed a quick message saying she'd been bitten by a crocodile, but would be fine. Then she handed him his phone and closed her eyes for a minute. As Raptor stood watching her, a whisper of an alarm echoed in his mind. *Who could the website belong to?*

"Milo made coffee." Ezmé entered with a glass of water and a chipped cup. "I brought both in case you want something warm." She set the drinks on the nightstand next to the bed, then used a cloth to wipe Blake's brow.

"Thanks, Ezmé." Blake reached for the water and Ezmé handed her the glass. After drinking half the contents, Blake said, "Would you mind giving us a few more minutes alone?"

Ezmé cut her eyes to Raptor, then looked at Blake. "You're not going to let him talk you out of the hospital, are you?"

"Not a chance." Blake smiled at Ezmé. "We're just trying to figure out the logistics."

Ezmé glared at Raptor. "Don't hurt her."

Raptor gave her a slight nod, then turned his attention back to Blake.

"Lock the door," she instructed him.

His jaw muscle jumped when he gritted his teeth, but he did as asked.

"What is so secretive that we need the door closed?" He cocked an eyebrow.

"I work for Sarita García." Blake grimaced as if talking caused her pain.

Raptor shrugged. "I do not know who that is."

"She is Jade Mendoza's mother."

Raptor's eyebrows drew together. "And Ezmé's?"

"No." Blake tried to shake her head, but the effort made her moan. "They were adopted separately by a couple in Arizona, so that's how they're sisters."

"García is Jade's birth mother, then?"

"Yes."

"And you work for her how?"

"It was my job to be abducted by your crew." She looked down and when she raised her eyes to his, tears pooled in the corners. "Lexi was supposed to stay below deck on the pirate cruise, but she followed me upstairs." She closed her eyes and leaned her head back against the pillows.

"And you did not realize my men work in pairs."

Blake opened her eyes, and his heart twinged at the pain he saw in them.

She shook her head and continued, "I don't care what happens to me, but I didn't mean to get Lexi killed."

"What could you possibly have done to be indebted to García enough you would allow yourself to be captured?" Raptor tilted his head.

"Remember I told you about being raped?"

"Sí."

"The reason the police never arrested him is because he disappeared." Blake sipped more water. "And I tracked him to Puerto Vallarta."

Blake's hand shook and Raptor took the glass, placing it on the nightstand.

"And?"

"I managed to drug him at a beach bar in Bucerias." She winced again when she tried to adjust her leg.

Stepping to the bed, Raptor asked, "What do you need?"

"A hospital." Blake held his stare. "How about more tequila?"

He lifted the bottle from a small dresser and waggled it. "You might as well finish it off." He handed her the almost-empty fifth.

She waved off the bottle. "You take a slug first."

Raptor tipped the tequila to his lips and took a pull, then handed Blake the remainder. She drank the rest before looking at him again.

"After I drugged him, I managed to get him into my rental car." She shook her head. "But I should've had a better plan, because he woke up on the way to the crocodile reserve."

Raptor raised his eyebrows and waited for her to continue.

"We fought in the car and crashed into a grove of coconut trees." She closed her eyes. "He pulled me from the car and tried to rape me again, telling me he was going to kill me this time. Then a gunshot rang out."

Blake took several deep breaths. "It was Sarita García. She'd shot him in the leg, then walked up to me and handed me the gun." Blake looked at him. "Without hesitating, I shot him in the chest and killed him."

"And she is now threatening to tell the *policía*."

"Yes."

"Blake." He took her hand in his. "I have enough money to help you relocate anywhere you would like—once you are well enough to travel."

"But not with you?" Her green eyes glistened with tears.

"Lo siento," Raptor brushed damp hair from her forehead, "but I only plan to leave with Ezmé." He kissed her, then headed for the door.

"Mateo."

Something in her tone made Raptor turn and face her.

"There's more, so sit your ass down." Blake pointed at the chair next to her bed.

"No." He unlocked the door. "We are done."

"You have a son."

Raptor relocked the door and tilted his head. He did not have time for her games and thought maybe he should dump her at a hospital, then leave with Ezmé. The sooner they left Puerto Vallarta, the better.

He turned and looked at her. "You are lying."

"I need your phone again."

He didn't move. "I believe you are not telling the truth, but instead a story you think will keep me from—"

"Letting me die?" Blake glared at him. "If you give me your phone, I can show you proof. Now!"

Raptor crossed back to the bed and handed her his phone. Blake's fingers worked the keys. She looked at him, then handed him the phone. A photo of a boy smiled at him from the screen. Raptor guessed he was about seven years old.

He raised his eyes to Blake. "Why do you think this is my son?"

"Because he is Belen's son."

Raptor stared at the photo again, then shook his head. "Belen is dead."

Blake held his stare. "She's alive, and lives in Texas with the man who bought her years ago."

"This is all a lie!" Raptor shot to his feet. "My investigator said she died a year after she was taken."

"Sarita had someone track Belen down." Blake nodded at the skeptical look on his face. "I don't know how she manages to get people to do her bidding, but I'm guessing blackmail plays a role."

Raptor paced the small bedroom, feeling like a caged animal looking for an escape route. He returned to the chair and asked, "What is his name?"

"Mateo."

He looked at the picture and tried to see the boy he once was in the smiling face, but his brain was splintering in several directions. *Belen was alive. He had a son. How could he rescue them from the monster who'd stolen his family long ago?*

"According to Sarita's PI, the man who bought Belen can't father a child. He married Belen when she told him she was pregnant with your child and gave the boy his last name."

"Where in Texas?" Raptor drilled Blake with his eyes.

"I don't know." Blake shrugged. "And if you try to find them, Sarita will have them killed."

"What the fuck does she want from me?" As soon as he asked the question, he answered it for himself. *Ezmé.*

Blake nodded, and he knew his realization had shown on his face.

"She wants us to deliver Ezmé to her tomorrow by five PM."

"What was your backup plan?" Raptor narrowed his eyes. "What if we had not been forced to leave the compound?"

"All I know is Sarita was confident Jade would rescue her sister." Blake looked down at her hands, then back at Raptor. "But if not, I was to stay with Ezmé—no matter what."

A knock sounded on the door and the knob jiggled. *"¿Patrón?"*

Raptor stood and opened the door to find Milo waiting in the hall, with Ezmé peering over his shoulder.

"¿Qué?" Raptor growled.

"Is Blake okay?" Ezmé pushed past Milo into the bedroom and stepped to the bed.

"I'm fine." Blake smiled. "Hurts like a son of a bitch, but I'm still alive."

"My *amiga* is a nurse. She can help with the wound and bring us food," Milo said.

"Can she come now?" Raptor asked.

"Sí." Milo nodded. "She will not tell anyone we are here."

"Bueno." Raptor looked at Blake and Ezmé. "Can she also bring them some clothes?"

Phone to his ear, Milo said, *"Sí."* He headed for the kitchen.

"And two bottles of tequila." Raptor called after him.

"Thanks for getting me some help." Blake smiled.

"And for the clothes," Ezmé added.

Raptor didn't want to let Ezmé go. But he also didn't want some bitch he didn't know to kill his beloved Belen and their son. The son he'd never met.

"Blake." Raptor forced a smile. "I hope you are ready to travel by tomorrow evening."

"I'm sure I will be." She gave him a slight nod.

He saw Ezmé stiffen, and wondered how she would respond to the news that he planned to deliver her to her sister's mother. She would finally have her freedom. Blake hadn't instructed him to refrain from enjoying his beautiful Ezmé one more time, but he could tell Blake wished he'd stay with her.

"Ezme." Raptor looked at Blake, whose green eyes had darkened. "Can I speak with you alone?"

Ezmé hesitated and looked at Blake. "I-I need to clean her wound again."

"Milo's *amiga* will be here soon." Raptor moved close to Ezmé. "Besides, I think Blake needs to rest."

Ezmé nodded and followed him from the bedroom. Raptor glanced at Blake, then closed the door. He wanted to draw Ezmé to him and kiss her, pretend they were anywhere but locked down in his apartment. But he knew she was angry with him after the way he'd treated her sister, and the questions circling in his mind had caused his own rage.

"There isn't any food, but we could sit in the kitchen and have coffee." Raptor said as they stood in the hallway.

"I haven't slept since you dragged us from your compound." Contempt darkened her brown eyes. She turned and marched toward his bedroom.

Raptor followed her but took a step back when she spun around and faced him, hands on hips.

"You're not welcome to join me!" Ezmé tried to close the door, but he blocked her attempt with a hand.

Raptor glared at her. "This is my home, and my bedroom."

"You know I won't try to leave without Blake, so you don't need to guard me while I sleep." She crossed her arms.

"I am not going to force you to—"

"I don't believe you!" Ezmé shouted. "You tried to rape Jade!" She slammed and locked the door.

"Ezme," His cheeks burned, but he kept his tone calm. "Open the door."

When she didn't respond, Raptor kicked in the door. Ezmé screamed and backed away.

"Get away from me, you monster!" She cried as he stormed across the room.

"You and your sister had this planned all along, *¿sí?*" Raptor grabbed her by the arms and yelled at her. "You flirted with me so I would be interested in you—all to lure me into a situation where Jade could arrest me."

"You know that's not true because you had me kidnapped!" Ezmé struggled against his hold. "Let go of me!"

"You are no different than a *prostituta*!" He shoved her onto the bed. "Whoring yourself to trap me!"

"I did not trap you!" Ezmé kicked him in the groin. "And it is you who pretended to be someone you aren't!"

Bent at the waist, Raptor sucked in air, blinking to clear tears from his eyes. He expected Ezmé to bolt from the room, but instead she patted his back as he had done when she coughed from her tequila shot.

"Mateo, all I want from you is for a doctor to treat Blake." She didn't back away when he straightened and looked at her. "And then for you to set us free."

He knew he should tell Ezmé of her impending freedom, but hoped she'd allow him one last time with her.

Raptor kissed her on the forehead and headed for the kitchen. Though Ezmé had admitted she desired him, he knew he could not force her into his bed. If he was to enjoy her sweetness before setting her free, she would have to come to him.

CHAPTER THIRTY-EIGHT

Jade woke with a start. The motion of sitting up abruptly caused her head to explode with pain. She leaned back into the pillows and thought about the last moments in Raptor's bedroom. If she'd just played along with him a little longer, she might have been able to rescue Ezmé when Ortiz and Peña breached the compound.

"Enough with the what-ifs." Jade shoved the sheet off and eased out of bed.

When the room didn't spin and she didn't feel nauseous, she padded to the bedroom door, hoping Sandrine had made coffee. Stepping into the small living room of their suite, she found Lieutenant Peña sitting at the dinette table staring at Sarita's recent note. A cup of coffee sat in front of him. As soon as he saw her, he jumped to his feet and raced to her side, causing Jade to contemplate the wisdom of popping out of her bedroom in her thin shorty pajamas.

"Are you sure you should be out of bed?" Peña put an arm around her waist.

"I'm afraid that line won't get you laid." Jade laughed, then winced.

"*¡Maldita sea!*" Peña growled. "That is not what I meant."

"No need to swear." Jade sat in a chair. "I'm just kidding."

"I will get you coffee." Peña marched into the kitchen, then returned with a cup for her and a box of *orejas*.

"These are my favorites." Jade lifted the lid and selected a puffy pastry.

Sliding a napkin toward her, he pointed at her nose. "You sound like you are under water."

"I feel like I got hit by a truck."

"You should have stayed in the hospital."

"No." Jade took a bite. "I want Sandrine to take me to the police station." She watched him over the rim of her cup.

"Sandrine is with Ortiz, checking the Nuevo Marina for any signs of Sarita García." Peña plucked an *orejas* from the box.

"What?" Jade stood. "Did Eladio not read the same note as us? She's threatened to kill him."

"You are not going anywhere."

"I don't want anyone else hurt."

"Jade." He stepped close to her and placed his hands on her hips, the warmth of his touch seeping through her cotton tank top. "You know García better than me, but do you think she would stay in a place we have connected to her?"

Jade shook her head. "Jesus, I need to stop moving my effing head."

"You should sit back down." Peña brushed her cheek with his fingertips.

"I should change." She headed toward her bedroom.

"Do you need help?" Jade smiled at him, and he continued, "You know what I mean."

"I'll be fine." She stepped inside and closed the door. Not feeling much like choosing an outfit, she picked up the blue knit skirt she'd worn a couple of days ago, then pulled a white V-neck T-shirt from a hanger. Dressed, she padded back to the kitchen.

"Por favor," he guided her toward her chair, "sit and tell me about Blake."

"Her behavior with Raptor makes sense now." Jade looked at him and saw what she was thinking written on his face. "But what will keep him from killing Blake, then going after Sarita so he can keep Ezmé?"

"Sarita must have some kind of leverage over Raptor."

"Maybe," Jade said, "and she might be wielding it to keep Blake alive."

"Do you know why he wants your sister so badly?"

"I have no idea." She couldn't control a wave of tears, and a sob escaped her.

Peña stood, pulled her to her feet, and wrapped her in his arms. "We will find her." He kissed the top of her head.

"Would you sit outside with me?" Jade looked up at him, touching his face with her hand. "I can't smell the damn sea air, but it would be nice to hear the waves."

"*Sí.*" His voice echoed with longing as he led her to the deck and guided her onto a lounge chair. "Do you want more coffee?"

"Amado," she took his hand, "can you sit and hold me?"

Peña slid onto the lounge chair and stretched out next to her. Jade curled herself against him and rested her head on his chest. He stroked her hair, and she closed her eyes. *Maybe a short nap is a good idea,* she thought. She could feel herself drifting toward a dark abyss.

Peña shifted, and she opened her eyes to see Eladio and Sandrine staring at them.

"She is sleeping," Peña whispered.

"I'm awake." Jade pushed herself up. "Did you find anything?

"My team searched every building within a mile of the address Peña went to." Eladio's dark eyes held hers. "And did not discover anything related to Sarita."

Peña stood and extended his hand to Jade to assist her as she came to her feet.

"I know it's been a while," Sandrine said. "But what do you recall from your investigation into García?" Sandrine led them back inside the suite without waiting for an answer. "Do you remember if she had any ties to PV?"

"No." Jade resisted shaking her head. "Should I call Temple and have him check our files for a link?"

"I will call him." Eladio tapped his phone alive and headed back to the deck.

Jade managed a small eyebrow raise and exchanged a look with Sandrine.

"If surfer boy hears your nasally voice, you'll be forced to tell him what happened, and he'll be on the next plane."

Peña cleared his throat and looked at Jade. She knew he probably had questions about her relationship with Christopher, but Jade didn't have the energy to explain something she herself didn't quite understand. Stepping into the kitchenette, Peña dropped his gaze and busied himself making another pot of coffee.

"Christopher's busy with a case, so he won't come." Jade sat in a dinette chair. "Probably he'll assign some minion to search our case notes."

"Okay." Sandrine sat too. "What about Vega? Do you think he'd know of anyone Sarita could use to help her orchestrate control over Raptor?"

"Maybe," Jade said. "We could call Marco or Humberto?"

Heading for her bedroom, Sandrine said, "I'll call all three."

Eladio joined Jade at the dinette table. "You are sure you are up to helping us investigate?"

"I'm fine. Okay, maybe not fine. I know I look like shit." Jade smiled at Eladio, whose dark eyes held a hint of concern. "Did Christopher share anything helpful?"

"I spoke with an agent who will relay the message to Agent Temple."

"The only person I can think of that might have the means and desire to help Sarita," Jade hesitated, "is her former lover, Dario Diaz."

"Do you think he could be persuaded to help you?" Peña set a mug in front of Eladio, then refilled his and Jade's cups. He placed the carafe onto a hot pad and sat next to Jade.

Jade picked up her cup and took a sip. Uncomfortable with both men's eyes focused on her, she looked toward Sandrine's closed bedroom door, wishing she'd join them.

"Possibly." Jade put her cup down. "Sarita left him her resort and a large sum of money." She looked at Eladio, then Peña. "He may feel he owes her."

"And," Eladio began. "From what I saw, he is very much in love with Sarita."

Sandrine popped out of her bedroom. "I talked to Torres first and he thinks the only person who might help Sarita is the boyfriend she left behind—" All eyes were focused on her. "What? Oh, you guys already came to that conclusion."

"Is Marco going to talk to him?" Jade asked.

"Yes." Sandrine nodded. "He's sending officers to bring him to the station."

"And Vega?" Jade tilted her head.

"You're not going to believe this." Sandrine paused for effect. "Vega said we should question Officer Marin."

Peña was on his feet, tapping his phone. "I will request a city-wide search for Marin."

Eladio stood and headed back to the deck. "Maybe Valéria can request a BOLO?"

"I left a message for Humberto." Sandrine picked up an empty cup and filled it with the last of the coffee. "You look awful." She sat in a chair. "I could help you take a shower," she smiled at Jade, "unless you'd like to ask one of your suitors."

"Funny." Jade narrowed her eyes at Sandrine. "If you can help me wash my hair, I can manage the rest." Tears stung her eyes.

"Look, Love," Sandrine began, reaching across the table and taking her hand. "I know it's hard to trust Sarita, but I believe she does plan to rescue Ezmé and return her to you."

Peña joined them, and Jade saw concern flash in his eyes. "My captain agreed to put out an arrest warrant for Marin."

"If he's still alive, and your men are able to find him, he might provide some answers." Sandrine said.

"Sí." Peña nodded.

"Valéria is requesting a BOLO for Marin." Eladio stood next to Jade. She could tell he had something to say, but was hesitant to speak.

Peña glared at Eladio. "Tell us what else she said."

"She has been questioning her brother, Novio." Eladio knelt next to Jade and placed his hand on her thigh. "Novio told Valéria he was ordered to bring Ezmé to Raptor."

Jade gritted her teeth. "Go on."

"Novio had hoped to escape Puerto Vallarta with Ezmé and take her to Arizona," Eladio cleared his throat, "because he is in love with her."

"That explains why they were at *Casa de Bahía*." Peña leaned forward. Jade cut her eyes to him, then looked back at Eladio.

"What are you not telling me?" Jade searched Eladio's face.

"Novio said Raptor is also in love with Ezmé. He is worried if Raptor cannot leave Puerto Vallarta with her, he may …" Eladio squeezed Jade's thigh, then stood, "kill her."

"Bloody hell!" Sandrine jumped to her feet and moved behind Jade's chair.

Peña remained seated, taking Jade's hand in his.

Feeling faint, Jade took a few deep breaths. For the first time since she'd learned Sarita was her birth mother, Jade wanted to believe Sarita loved her like a daughter and would make good on her promise to return Ezmé. She knew she'd let Sarita go free as long as the former drug queen delivered her little sister safely back to her.

CHAPTER THIRTY-NINE

Jade ignored their suggestions that she remain at the hotel and rest. Eladio reminded himself the reason Jade Mendoza now sat in a chair in front of his desk was because her sister was one of the women his task force had been assigned to find and rescue. Of course she wouldn't be left out now that they were close to saving Ezmé.

Jade had showered and dressed in a black cotton skirt and red tank top. Though she looked a little better, her injuries marred her beauty and created a sense of vulnerability.

"I have ordered lunch." Eladio looked at his watch. "It should be here in thirty minutes."

"While we wait," Peña said from his spot on the back wall, "we can review what has happened so far."

"*Sí.*" Eladio motioned and Geovany stepped forward.

"The final count of deceased at Raptor's compound is twenty-two." Geovany continued to look at his notepad. "Not all of the deceased are Raptor's men. Six of the soldiers we captured have been identified as working for the *Cartel de Cocos Pequeña*. Of the five we captured, only Pepe was willing to talk. He said Raptor's lieutenant, Milo, must have also escaped, along with his sicario, Toro."

"Makes sense because it would take at least two of them to navigate the jungle, especially in the dark." Peña pushed off the wall and stood next to Geovany.

"The helicopter that helped us locate the compound swept the area, but did not detect any heat signatures within a mile of the complex." Eladio looked up from a report.

"It is a very dense jungle." Peña shrugged. "Almost impossible to penetrate."

"Did Pepe have any thoughts as to where Raptor would hide in the city?" Sandrine asked.

"No." Geovany shook his head. "He said Raptor only trusted the *sicario* and his lieutenant."

Jade turned to look at Geovany as he studied his notes. "Do we know if Raptor or either of these two men were wounded during the shootout?"

Eladio noticed Peña studying Jade. The lieutenant's intense gaze brought color to her cheeks. He wanted to order the lieutenant from his office.

"The team that cleared the compound did not report any blood found in Raptor's suite." Geovany raised his gaze to Jade. "Except for yours."

"Where are the women you rescued?" Jade held Geovany's stare. "Still at the hospital?"

"We are holding them in a safe house, along with Novio." Geovany looked at Eladio, who nodded. "These women claim they voluntarily came to the compound and that Raptor was arranging for them to start new lives. They would start over in other countries with men they selected for themselves."

"Bullocks!" Sandrine said. Her cheeks reddened when they all looked at her. "Seriously, have any of you ever heard of such behavior from a human trafficker?"

"No." Eladio shook his head. "But it is also odd that we did not find more women being held at the compound."

"Once we arrest Marin," Peña said, "maybe he can confirm their claims."

"Jade," Eladio leaned forward and waited for her to look at him, "as soon as I could, I let Joy know we had rescued Erica. Then Officer Flores brought her to the hospital."

"They are back at the hotel now," Sandrine added, looking at Jade. "Erica wants to talk to you when you're ready."

Jade nodded, then asked, "And Gwen?"

"She is shaken." Eladio said. "Worried about Blake and devastated over Lexi's death."

"Herrera," Peña said, pointing to the young officer's notepad. "Did you question the female Milo planned to take with him to Tequila?"

"Valéria did." Geovany checked his notes, then looked at Peña. "All she could tell Valéria is Milo was kind to her, and she wanted to leave with him. She does not have any way of contacting the missing soldier, and says she does not know where he and Raptor might be hiding."

Jade shot to her feet, swaying from the action. She looked like she might faint. Peña stepped close and supported her under the armpits, lowering her down into her chair.

Standing, Sandrine said, "I'm taking you back to the hotel."

"No," Jade waved her friend off, "I just need some food."

"Which is here." Eladio intercepted the delivery person, handed him some cash, then carried two bags to the table at the back of his office. "I ordered *enchilada* plates." He took a Styrofoam container from a bag and brought a meal to Jade, along with a bottle of water. "Is *pollo* okay?"

"Chicken's perfect." Jade leaned back, making room for Eladio to set the container on the desktop. "Thanks, Eladio."

"De nada." He raised an eyebrow at Peña, who hovered behind Jade's chair.

"I hope you ordered at least one with *carnitas*." Peña moved to the table and looked into the bags.

"Tres." Eladio motioned for Geovany to select his lunch. "Sandrine, what would you prefer?"

"I'm guessing there's another chicken enchilada for the second *gringa.*" She smiled at Eladio.

Placing a container in front of Sandrine, Eladio looked at Jade. She hadn't opened her box. He held her stare as he resumed his seat. "You should eat."

Jade picked up her fork and lifted the lid, a savory aroma filling the air. "It's delicious." She swallowed, then asked. "Is Valéria going to take Novio home?"

Geovany had pulled a chair close. "Novio is refusing to leave until he knows Ezmé is safe."

"We are letting him leave?" Peña, who had returned to his spot against the wall, drilled Eladio with a dark stare. "He is a *secuestrador* and should be arrested."

Eladio leaned back in his chair and sipped some water. He knew Peña was right, but if they captured Raptor, they would need someone knowledgeable enough about his operation to testify against him. Novio and Nacho were the most logical candidates.

"You know," Eladio began, narrowing his eyes at Peña, "the prosecutor's office will want to use Novio and any of the other captured men to help build a case against Raptor."

Geovany held up a finger. "I have an update on Nacho."

Eladio broke eye contact with Peña when Sandrine said, "Let's hear it."

"His girlfriend had the baby, a boy," Geovany licked a finger and flipped a page in his notepad. "and Nacho is willing to do whatever it takes to stay out of jail."

Peña's phone dinged and he looked at the screen, then at Eladio. "One of my men spotted Marin near the airport, but then he lost him in traffic."

"Was he alone?" Eladio asked.

"They did not report seeing anyone else."

"Maybe we should do a grid search." Jade stood. "Raptor could be hiding near the airport."

"Sit down, Love," Sandrine said. "You aren't going anywhere." She looked at Peña. "You're going to have your men do a search, yes?"

"*Sí.*" Peña smiled, then said to Eladio, "What if we send—"

Geovany stood and tossed his empty container in the waste basket. "Me to do a search." He looked at Peña, then Eladio who nodded.

"You will blend in better than a group of officers." Eladio hesitated.

"And," Geovany smiled, "Marin does not know me."

"*Gracias, Officer Herrera,*" Eladio said. "Lieutenant can you and Geovany set parameters for the search and establish a reporting timeline?"

"*Sí.*" Peña glanced at Jade, who gave him a smile, then looked back at Eladio. "I will be back shortly." He left the office, Geovany following him.

Eladio racked his brain for a reason to send Sandrine away so he could be alone with Jade. He assumed any request he made would be met with a scathing look.

Instead, he smiled at the two agents. "It may be a while before Geovany has anything to report. Jade, maybe you should go back to Joy's hotel and rest."

"That's a bloody good idea." Sandrine stood and looked at Jade. Before she could encourage Jade to leave, her phone chirped. She met Jade's questioning glance. "It's Oliver." Sandrine headed from Eladio's office, and his phone rang.

"*Bueno.*" He answered, meeting Jade's eyes as she shifted her gaze to him. "*Entendido, gracias.*" Eladio wasn't sure how she'd react, but he had to tell her the news Marco had just shared.

"Who called?" Jade leaned forward. He thought she'd tried to narrow her eyes at him, but the bluish purple rings surrounding them made it hard to tell. "Temple?"

"Torres." Her hand lay next to her half-eaten enchilada, and he covered it with his. "He thought it better to call me than Sandrine," he began, "Dario Diaz is no longer in Mazatlán."

Jade held his stare until Sandrine walked back into the office, a grim set to her lips.

"What?" Jade stood. "Are you two trying to drive me crazy with these clandestine phone calls?" She jammed her hand onto her hips and glared at Sandrine. "Who the hell called you?"

"Temple." Sandrine bit her lip. "He wanted to know why you weren't the one to call and request the information about Sarita, and to quote him, 'What the eff has happened that Jade can't remember the details of our case?'"

Jade pulled her phone from her pocket and headed toward the door of Eladio's office. "I'll call him from the conference room." She turned and pointed a finger at them. "And I don't want any company." Weaving slightly, she bounced off the doorjamb, then marched into the hallway.

"Do you think Temple will come to Puerto Vallarta?" Eladio asked Sandrine, dreading an affirmative response.

"He asked for permission, but his handler, Ferris, said no." Sandrine dropped into a chair. "He wanted to know how badly Jade was hurt and where our investigation stands." She cradled her head with her fingertips. "He hung up on me after I told him about Raptor attacking Jade."

"They are very close, *¿sí?*" Eladio knew the answer to his question, and hated the jealousy snaking through his gut.

"Yes." Sandrine raised her eyes to his. "And I wouldn't be surprised if surfer boy risked his job to come to her aid."

CHAPTER FORTY

Raptor watched her sleep. He'd spent the night lying next to Ezmé, searching his mind for a way to hold onto her while also keeping Sarita García from killing Belen and his son. But he could not come up with a scenario in which he could have both.

He knew no matter how he tried to explain his actions, Ezmé would remain angry with him. It wouldn't help to tell her of his fear that he'd be arrested or that the cartel hit squad had finally found his compound.

She opened her eyes, then sat up. "Is it Blake?" She climbed from the bed.

"Blake is fine." As much as he wanted to be naked with her in bed, he couldn't help smiling at how cute she looked in his tan shirt, which fit her like a dress, covering the shorts she wore beneath. "Milo and his *amiga* gave her a shot of *antibióticos*, then cleaned and dressed her wound."

"Did you get any sleep?" Ezmé wandered to a small bistro table laden with plates of meats, cheese, crackers, and bread.

"*Sí.*" Raptor lifted a pitcher from a bucket of ice and poured hibiscus mimosas into two flutes. When he turned to set the glasses on the table, Ezmé sat watching him. The midday sun bled through the cracks in the blinds covering the bedroom window, and rays bathed her in a warm glow.

"I know you were in bed with me." Ezmé took a sip.

"Milo slept on the couch." He took his seat, his eyes probing hers. "And the tile floor is too hard."

"Why are you staring at me?" Ezmé glared at him. "Are you contemplating how you're going to kill me and Blake?"

"No, mi amor." Raptor smiled. "I would like to apologize for calling you a *prostituta*—."

"I believe you also accused me of being a whore." Ezmé popped a piece of cheese into her mouth.

"Obviously, you know I am different from the man you had coffee with at the café."

Continuing to hold his stare, Ezmé sipped her mimosa and didn't respond.

"Many years ago, the man I worked for sold the daughter of an influential man to another man. He took her to the states." Raptor took a large drink. "Shortly after, I killed my boss and began to plan my escape from a business I despised."

"You're a human trafficker." Ezmé stated, a hint of disgust in her tone.

"Not anymore." Raptor ran a hand through his hair. "But the father of the girl who was sold tracked her down and killed the man who bought her. Now he has assassins looking for me."

"But you had Novio kidnap me. And your men kidnapped Jade and the others."

"I already explained why I had Novio bring you to the compound." Raptor drank some mimosa. "My men have strict orders not to kidnap women, but I believe there are soldiers in my ranks who took Jade and the other women in an attempt to get me arrested."

"And someone took Blake, too." Ezmé raised an eyebrow.

"Yes." Raptor nodded. He didn't want to explain Blake's connection to Sarita García until it was time to tell Ezmé he was delivering her to her sister's mother. "But, again, not on my orders. With the help of Toro and Milo, I have become a facilitator."

"Explain." Ezmé nibbled a cracker stacked with salami and cheese.

"We still help men from all over the world find women to share their lives with."

Panic flitted across her face. He reached across and took her hand, relieved when she didn't try to pull free.

"The women come to us for help, and are never forced." He smiled, but Ezmé's eyes were still wary. "We do background checks to ensure the men are not potential abusers."

Raptor stood and retrieved the pitcher of mimosas, then refilled their glasses. "I know your sister came to rescue you and I am sorry for my behavior." He resumed his seat. "I have a plan to leave Puerto Vallarta. I want to avoid being arrested or killed."

"You could have left Blake and me at the compound," Ezmé said. "Then you could have made a clean getaway."

"Blake insisted on coming with us. I believe she sees herself as your protector." An almost true statement. "And I wanted to spend a few more hours with you, *mi amor*." He clinked her glass, then took a sip.

Ezmé narrowed her eyes and sipped some mimosa, then added a sampling of cold cuts to a saucer. They ate in silence for a few minutes and Raptor watched her over the top of his flute.

"You're staring at me again."

"Do you want to be a model?"

"What?" Ezmé tilted her head. "No. I thought it would be fun and I could earn some extra money."

"You are beautiful enough to be a model." Raptor touched her cheek. "Great bone structure." He loved that his compliment brought color to her cheeks. "If not a model, then what is it you would like to do with your life?"

"Books?" She giggled. "I love books, and want to own a bookstore someday."

"I am not much of a reader, but Belen—" He drained his glass, then refilled it.

"And you?" Ezmé brushed his forearm with a finger. "What will you do now?"

"I am not sure." Raptor took a sip. Of course, he knew what was in his immediate future, but he didn't want to ruin his remaining time with Ezmé.

"Do you think Novio survived the attack on the compound?" Ezmé asked. He was disappointed to see tears pooling in her eyes.

"Yes." Raptor cleared his throat and focused on a neutral tone. "He was being kept in a locked room so he would have been seen as a captive."

Raptor stood, then leaned down and kissed the top of her head. As much as he wanted to bring her to his bed and spend his remaining time making love, he knew he couldn't force himself on her.

"I will check on Blake." He headed for the door and Ezmé grasped his hand, surprising him.

He turned to her as she stood and placed her hand on his chest, then he leaned down and kissed her. She twined her arms around his neck and pressed her hips against his.

Ezmé led him to the bed and began to unbutton the shirt she wore. Though he wanted her more than she would ever know, he held her hands before she reached the third button.

"My beautiful Ezmé," his voice was thick with lust, "I need to tell you something."

"Mateo." She placed a finger on his lips. "I want this. You. One last time I want to pretend you're the sexy art dealer and you've whisked me away on a romantic weekend."

"Then come away with me." He kissed her.

"I care for you, Handsome Stranger." She placed a hand on his cheek. "But I want a life with Novio filled with domesticity and kids. You will always be looking over your shoulder, unable to settle down. And you certainly have no yearning to have kids."

Raptor knew she saw jealousy reflected in his eyes. She kissed him again, then removed the shirt and shorts. She stepped to him and lifted the hem of his T-shirt, then kissed the scar on his chest as he pulled the shirt over his head. Ezmé laid on the bed and he pushed off his sweats, then laid next to her.

He kissed her as he entered her. Though he wanted to explode with pleasure, he set a slow rhythm, waiting for Ezmé to move her hips to match his. He looked into her eyes and when he saw the same desire he felt reflected in their dark depths, he quickened his tempo. Ezmé lifted her hips, making them one, and he had to bite his lip to keep from telling her he loved her. Instead, he kissed her, and she twined her fingers in his hair.

When Ezmé cried out in ecstasy, Raptor prayed he'd be able to remember the sound of her bliss forever. He laid next to her, holding her in the crook of his shoulder, caressing her flat stomach.

Ezmé ran her fingers over his scar. "How did you get the scar?"

"I was ordered to kill a fellow soldier by my previous *Jefe*," he began. "The man had disrespected him by raping one of the females the boss had chosen for himself."

Ezmé sat up, and he followed her lead. They propped themselves up on pillows. "And?"

"When soldiers fight, they do so without any weaponry except for their hands." Raptor looked at her and his heart skipped a beat when he saw concern in her eyes. "The other soldier had hidden a claw-like weapon in his hand and attacked me before I realized what he hid."

"Why didn't your boss stop the fight when he saw the other man had cheated?" Her eyes were full of disgust.

"Once a fight begins it cannot be stopped—"

"You mean you have to fight until one of you is dead?"

"Sí." Raptor leaned back into the pillows and closed his eyes, the long-ago battle playing on behind his eyelids.

Ezmé leaned down and kissed the scar. "Did you choose the name Raptor?"

"No." He opened his eyes and looked at her. "The other men gave me the name. It was after I killed my boss because he wanted to turn me into his *sicario.*"

"Like an assassin?"

Raptor nodded. "He was a ruthless *bastardo* who enjoyed ordering his men to fight and kill each other. And I discovered he was killing captives if they resisted him."

"He deserved to die." Ezmé straddled him, then leaned down and kissed him. "I am sorry you have had such a hard life. You lost Belen and then circumstances turned you—"

"Into a monster you don't want to spend your life with." Raptor held her dark stare.

"I don't think you're a monster." Ezmé lifted her hips, then lowered her softness onto him. "But I can't run away with you, and you need to let me go."

Raptor groaned and placed his hands at her waist. "Ezmé," he rasped, "I have made arrange—"

She kissed him and silenced his attempt to tell her about releasing her to Sarita. "After," she whispered and raised her hips again, this time lowering onto him.

Raptor sat up, holding her to him and finding a nipple with his mouth when she arched her back. Ezmé held his head to her and once again they moved as one. His brain tried to focus on the reality that in a few hours Ezmé Mendoza would be gone from his life forever, but his body demanded he enjoy the beautiful young woman who'd stolen his heart.

CHAPTER FORTY-ONE

"What the hell, Jade!" Christopher's voice boomed in her ear.

"C, I can explain—" Jade began.

"You should have called me."

Silence filled her ear.

"You have your hands full with a case, and you're not here!" Jade wished she'd controlled her anger when the silence stretched on. "C?"

"You're right! I'm not there. But I wish I was because Sarita is *our* case."

"I know." Jade chewed a fingernail.

"Don't chew your nail," Christopher admonished.

"Wait?" Jade turned in a circle. "*Are* you here?"

"No, it's your go-to when you're worried." His sigh echoed through her phone. "How bad is your face?"

"It only hurts when I smile." Which she did despite the truth in her statement.

"You sound like you have a bad cold."

"What?" Jade laughed. "You don't recognize my sexy voice."

His laughter helped her relax.

"C," Jade began, "Eladio and I will do our best to bring Sarita in."

"Jade."

She heard concern in his voice. "Christopher."

"I want you to let García go, and just focus on getting Ezmé back."

"Okay, if you're sure." Jade knew she'd pick her sister's freedom over capturing her mother, but Christopher's support meant a lot to her.

"I'm sure."

Jade wished she could see his face. She imagined a frown creasing his brow.

"Do you ever feel like things weren't resolved between us?" Christopher's tone was warm.

"Yes." Tears sprang to her eyes. "I-I thought maybe you loved me more than I was ready to love you."

"Don't cry."

She closed her eyes, and he continued.

"I did—do love you. And I know you love me, but I also know we are in different places in our lives."

A moment of silence allowed her to rein in her emotions. "Christopher, I will always love you. And you're right. Our lives are not in sync, but we are destined to be part of each other's lives, forever."

"I'm okay with that. Now, promise me *you* will call me with an update after you get Ezmé back."

"Promise."

"I've gotta go, but you should know Marco Torres called to tell me Dario Diaz has left Mazatlán. Marco thinks he is in Puerto Vallarta helping Sarita."

"Ortiz just told me. And C, thanks." Jade took a deep breath, then exhaled.

"Remember, I'm just a plane ride away."

"I'll call you as soon as Ezmé's safe," Jade said, but Christopher had already disconnected.

Jade turned to find Sandrine watching her from the doorway of Eladio's office.

"Tall, blond and dreamy already on a plane here?" Sandrine asked.

Jade rolled her eyes, the effort causing a stab of pain across her forehead, and marched past her friend.

"What's Torres' position on arresting Sarita?" Jade asked Eladio. She had already decided it didn't matter. She planned to take Christopher's advice and let Sarita walk to get Ezmé back.

"He said to defer to you." Eladio held her gaze, and she saw the same longing that had been in his eyes during their lunch in the conference room.

"That's what Temple said too." Exhaustion pulled at her, and Jade took a seat. "I'm going to do whatever it takes to get Ezmé back."

"I agree." Sandrine sat in the chair next to Jade. "Sarita is not our mission."

"Look who I found wandering the halls." Peña stepped into Eladio's office followed by Valéria. He looked at Jade and moved toward the back of the room.

"Everyone," Valéria began, motioning to a young man who stood by her side. "This is my brother, Novio."

Novio wore the same racoon mask as Jade, albeit his bruises had faded. And though he'd been rescued from Raptor, he looked like he was ready to run at the first opportunity.

"*Bienvenido.*" Eladio extended his hand. "You are welcome here, so please have a seat."

Novio sat in the chair next to Eladio's desk, his eyes darting from Jade to Sandrine, then back to Eladio. Peña handed them water, then resumed his spot on the wall. Valéria stood behind her brother.

"Novio wants to share what he knows about Raptor," Valéria looked at Jade, "and Ezmé."

"Thanks, Novio." Jade smiled despite her anger at the young man for taking her sister in the first place. "Any information you can give us will help."

"Primero," Novio said, then cleared his throat and stared at Jade, "first, I apologize for taking Ezmé for Raptor." He rubbed his chin. "I should have been stronger and left Puerto Vallarta with her."

Jade saw pain in his dark eyes and wanted to accept his apology. If not for his actions, though, Jade wouldn't have to rely on Sarita García to get her sister back.

"We appreciate your apology." Sandrine glanced at Jade. "Can you tell us why Raptor wanted Ezmé kidnapped in the first place?"

"Segundo," Novio nodded and shifted in his chair, "second, I love Ezmé. But Raptor also love her."

Jade felt lightheaded, and gooseflesh bloomed at the base of her neck. They already knew Raptor was in love with Ezmé; the fear was he might not willingly surrender her.

"Do you know Raptor's real name?" Eladio's pen hovered over his notepad.

Novio shifted his gaze to Eladio. "His given name is Mateo."

"Last name?" Eladio met Novio's stare.

"I do not know." Shaking his head, Novio continued, "I think he is from Guatemala."

"We know from Valéria how you came to work for Raptor," Sandrine said. "Do you know how Raptor became a trafficker?"

"No." Novio looked at his clasped hands. "After I rescued my sister and became a soldier, Raptor became *Patrón* because he killed our boss."

"Agent Ortiz." Valéria's professional tone took everyone by surprise. "I request permission to leave the task force and return with my brother to Arizona."

"No, Valéria!" Novio jumped to his feet. "I will not leave until I know Ezmé is safe."

"Novio," Valéria said, putting a hand on her brother's shoulder, "you are not safe here. If no charges are going to be brought against you, we need to leave before that situation changes."

"Valéria." Eladio had stood also. "I cannot promise there will be no charges against Novio." He glanced at Jade. "It is possible my government will not pursue the matter, but I cannot speak for the US government."

Jade held Eladio's stare and contemplated a plausible scenario where Novio would not be charged for kidnapping Ezmé. "I can speak with Benson to see if she can arrange a deal Novio could become a protected witness for his testimony against Raptor."

Peña's phone dinged and they all looked at him. He raised his eyes from the screen. "Geovany followed Marin to a condo building near the airport."

Jade jumped to her feet, placing a hand on Eladio's desk as a wave of dizziness washed over her. "Let's go."

"It is too soon." Peña crossed to Jade. "We need to see if Geovany can determine which unit might belong to Raptor."

"I'm tired of doing nothing." Jade glared at Peña. Despite what he said, he looked like he wanted to grab her hand and run.

"He's right, Love." Sandrine touched Jade's arm. "We need to make sure we have the right location."

"Lieutenant Peña." Eladio stood. "Would you follow up on-site with Officer Herrera?" He looked at Jade. "I think we could all use more information."

Peña frowned at Eladio, then said to Jade. "Walk me out?"

Jade nodded and took a step toward the door.

"Wait." Valéria nodded at Novio. "Tell them."

Novio faced Jade. "I said before that Raptor might kill Ezmé rather than surrender her, but I do not believe he will hurt your sister." He looked at Valéria, then continued, "but he will never let her go."

Jade nodded at Novio, then followed Peña from the office, his long strides causing her to hurry and catch up. He pushed through the station doors at the back of the building, then crossed the parking lot to his car. Jade was out of breath when she caught up to him.

Peña turned to look at her, then wrapped her in his arms his sultry scent engulfing her. She expected him to kiss her, but after a few seconds he set her at arm's length.

"That *pendejo* should be locked up." Peña brushed her cheek with the back of his fingers.

"I'm angry with Novio too," Jade said, "but he was only trying to survive a difficult situation."

"You should go back to the hotel and get some rest." Peña opened the car door and climbed behind the wheel.

"You know I'm not going to be able to sleep until we have Ezmé back." Jade leaned in and kissed him. "Let me know what you find at the condo complex."

Peña smiled at her as she closed the car door, then gave her a salute, fired up the engine and drove away.

The heat had sapped her strength. Her knees gave way as she sunk down to the asphalt. But before she landed, Eladio put his arms around her. He turned her toward him and held her while she cried, smoothing her hair. Despite the comfort she felt in his arms, Jade pushed away from him. She gulped air through her mouth, since she couldn't breathe through her bandaged nose.

"I know the waiting is taking its toll. But we are close." Eladio took her hand in his. "I have a sketch artist coming, if you think you are up to meeting with her."

Jade nodded, then she headed back to the building entrance. She'd meet with the artist. Then, if she had to effing wait, she'd wait at the hospital where a doctor could remove the suffocating gauze from her nose.

Eladio beat her to the door and held it open for her.

Jade managed, "Thanks". Then marched toward his office.

CHAPTER FORTY-TWO

Eladio knew he should abandon his quest to get to know Jade more intimately because of her obvious interest in Peña, but his resolve withered whenever she was near. He let his thoughts wander to his previous encounter with Sienna and looked at the calendar. He had six days to find Ezmé Mendoza and reunite her with Jade before he could relax and enjoy his next date with the beguiling stranger. The memory of Sienna's fresh violet scent brought goosebumps to his skin when he thought about being with her again.

His office was quiet now. Sandrine had taken Jade to the hospital to have her nose attended to, and Peña had gone to meet Geovany at the condo building near the airport. After Jade and Novio met with the sketch artist, Eladio had sent Valéria and her brother back to the safe house.

Officer Flores knocked on the doorjamb and stepped into his office. "I have the flight information you requested." She handed him a stapled bundle of papers.

Eladio began to flip through the pages, and Flores added, "the name Dario Diaz is not on the list."

Eladio continued to scan the print-out anyway. If Diaz wasn't in Puerto Vallarta, then where the hell was he? And who else could be helping Sarita García? He reached the end and set the list on his desk.

"Can you ask someone in the Durango police department to see if anyone is staying at *Casa García*?" Eladio grabbed his notepad and jotted down the exact address of Sarita's family villa, then handed the slip of paper to Flores.

"*Copia.*" She nodded, then exited his office.

It made sense for Sarita to leave the villa to Dario, since she'd given him *Fiesta de Fuego*. He guessed Sarita had sent Dario to Durango just to create a false lead for them to investigate.

Eladio brought up a photo of the note Blake had been instructed to give Jade and reread the contents. Sarita's threat to have him killed if he tried to come with Jade to retrieve Ezmé meant she had someone who would carry out a hit. He knew that couldn't be the simpering Diaz. The missing puzzle piece clicked in his mind like a penny dropping.

"*¡Maldita sea!*" Eladio swore and snatched up his phone.

Eladio: *I think Marin is working for both Raptor and Sarita*

Peña: *¿Por qué?*

Eladio: *Explain later. Any luck locating condo?*

Peña: *No. Halfway through building.*

Eladio: *Copia. Report when you can.*

He set his phone down and tipped a water bottle to his lips, wishing it was a shot of tequila. It made sense would Sarita turn to a corrupt policeman to do her bidding. Initially, Eladio hadn't taken Sarita's threat to kill him seriously. With Marin under her thumb, he knew he had cause to worry.

Eladio tapped his laptop and the screen glowed in front of him. His intent was to bring up a map of the city showing the area where the condominium building was located to see if anything close by triggered an alarm. He was distracted when his inbox showed a new message. After opening the file, his screen filled with a reply from the prosecutor's office regarding Nacho.

Agent Ortiz:
It is our position that your informant,
Ignacio Jimenez, can serve as a witness
should your fugitive, Raptor, be brought
to trial. We recommend Señor Jimenez be
relocated to a safe location until such time
as he is needed for trial. Please inform me
of your plans for this witness.
Gracias, Bianca Rodríguez
Procurador General de la República

Eladio was pleased that they would be able to relocate Nacho and his family, but where in México would he be safe?

"Another matter to discuss with Lieutenant Peña." Eladio clicked the print icon and sent the email to the printer. When he stood to retrieve the printout, his phone rang. He frowned at the number.

"Bueno," he answered, and curiosity as to why his boss was calling raised sweat beads on his forehead.

"Ortiz." Agent Salas's voice vibrated with impatience. "Have you caught this *cabrón*, Raptor?"

Eladio stiffened in response to Salas's tone. "No, sir, but we have a solid lead and I expect to rescue the last missing females and make an arrest soon."

"Bueno. I have a new assignment for you."

Eladio gritted his teeth, his jaw muscle flexing with the action.

"You are headed to Zihuatanejo," Salas continued. "The killer poisoning *turistas* has turned up in Zihuat and I need you to head the investigation."

"When do I need to be there?" Eladio dreaded the answer.

"*¡Ayer!*" Salas barked. "I requested that the DEA agent working with you now be assigned to your new task force, so arrest this *bastardo* and get your ass on a plane!"

Eladio wanted to yell he had his hands full *yesterday* trying to locate Ezmé Mendoza, but his boss had ended the call.

The fact that Salas requested Jade for the serial killer assignment raced through Eladio's mind. He expected she would try to refuse the appointment in Zihuatanejo, but he planned to personally ask Jade for her assistance in tracking a serial killer who now used fentanyl as his weapon of choice.

CHAPTER FORTY-THREE

Raptor held Ezmé in his arms as she slept, inhaling the lemony aroma of verbena, which he recognized as the scent of the shampoo provided for the women at his compound. He'd resisted falling asleep, knowing these were his last moments with Ezmé. He had occupied his mind imaging the possible outcomes of the battle that had continued after he and Milo had fled with Ezmé and Blake.

Had Toro survived and escaped, or had he stayed to defend the compound to the bitter end? How many men died during the gunfight? Could Julio and the Gonzalez cousins be behind the raid, or had they attacked at the same time as the *policía*?

Ezmé stirred when Milo knocked. Raptor kissed her, then climbed from the bed and padded to the door.

"Patrón," Milo said when he cracked the door.

"We are getting ready to leave," Raptor said. "How's Blake?"

"She is good, and we are ready too." Milo gave a head bob, then headed back down the hallway.

When he turned, Ezmé stood naked behind him, and it was all he could do to not wrap her in his arms.

"Is Blake okay?" Ezmé asked.

"Sí." Raptor nodded. "Milo and Blake are waiting for us in the kitchen."

"What are they ready for?" Ezmé tilted her head.

"After you shower, join us and I will tell you everything." Raptor reached for his sweats.

"Mateo." She touched his face, then took his hand and led him toward the bathroom. "I don't believe our time is over yet."

Raptor's last moments with the exquisite Ezmé were forever burned in his memory. He'd left her washing her hair, then dressed in clean clothes and placed the outfit Milo's *amiga* had brought for Ezmé on the bed. Frowning at the simple sundress, he wished he'd been able to buy her something more extravagant.

He cast a last glance at the tangled sheets and a thread of desire slid through his loins. *God, I am going to miss her*, he thought to himself. But until he could rescue Belen and his son from the *cabrón* in Texas, he knew he'd have to comply with Sarita García's demands. He would deliver his darling Ezmé to the former drug queen this evening.

Raptor walked past the bedroom where Blake had been laid up and found it empty, then continued down the hallway to the kitchen. Milo and Blake sat at the table with Blake's injured leg propped on a chair.

"Patrón." Milo came to his feet. "The car is packed and ready."

"Gracias, Milo." Raptor gave his lieutenant a nod, then shifted his attention to Blake. "How's the leg?

"Better." Blake smiled. "Thanks for allowing Fatima to tend to the wound."

"I am guessing Sarita García would not appreciate you dying in my care."

"Blake!" Ezmé burst into the kitchen. "You look so much better." She knelt next to Blake's chair.

"That's what an ass-full of antibiotics will do for a girl." Blake laughed. "I even managed a sponge bath and washed my hair."

Raptor pulled out the chair next to Blake's for Ezmé and she took a seat. He moved to the kitchen window and looked past the cliff to the ocean. He may have to leave Puerto Vallarta, but whatever his next destination was, Raptor knew he would need to relocate somewhere near the sea.

"Would someone like to tell me what's going on?" Ezmé asked.

Raptor turned to face her, and Milo poured four shots, then placed the bottle of *Patrón* on the table. Raptor set glasses in front of Blake and Ezmé, then handed one to Milo. He held the last shot in his hand.

Ezmé stood took Blake's hand, looking as if she planned to run.

"Blake has an *amiga influyente* who has negotiated your release and eventual return to your sister." Raptor held her wide-eyed stare. Anger marred her beautiful face, and he knew that she understood he would never willingly let her go.

Ezmé shifted her gaze to Blake. "Who?"

"Her name is," Blake began, "Sarita García. Jade knows her from Mazatlán."

It was only a half-truth, but the fact that García was Jade's birth mother was not Blake's to share with Ezmé.

"And you are bringing me to this García woman?" Ezmé's eyes still held a hint of fear. "You are not selling me to her, are you?"

Raptor fought the urge to grab Ezmé and leave right then, with just her. He wanted to tell her the price of her freedom was paid for with Belen's and his son's lives, but he just shook his head. It would take time to plan how to kill García and bring Belen and young Mateo home. And to decide if he wanted to find Ezmé and bring her back to him too.

"I promise." Blake squeezed Ezmé's hand. "Sarita plans to return you to Jade and Mateo knows this is what is best for you."

"What about you?" Ezmé asked Blake. She looked at Raptor, tears pooling in her eyes. "You are setting us both free, right?"

"*Sí.*" Raptor forced a smile. "You will both be freed once we arrive at García's." He lifted his shot glass in toast. "To new beginnings."

Raptor tossed back his tequila while Ezmé clinked glasses with Blake and Milo. When she angled her shot toward Raptor's empty glass, he reached for the bottle and poured the last of the tequila. He touched her glass, took a sip, and watched as she tried to drink the whole shot. As before, it made her cough. Ezmé doubled over, sucking in air, and he rubbed her back.

Raptor lowered his face to hers. *"¿Bien?"*

"Okay," she said on a citrusy breath, then smiled at him.

"Patrón," Milo cleared his throat, "we need to go."

Raptor nodded at Milo. *"Estamos listos, ¿sí?"* He looked at Blake, then Ezmé.

"Ready." Blake tried to stand. He and Milo both stepped forward to help her.

"Milo." Raptor lifted Blake into his arms. "If you will lock up behind us, Ezmé can lead the way."

Ezmé stepped into the garage, then opened the back passenger door and looked at Raptor. "I don't think she'll fit."

"We will put her up front." Raptor smiled at Ezmé, and she nodded.

"Thanks, Mateo." Blake winced when he set her onto the seat, then helped guide her injured leg inside.

Ezmé squatted next to Blake. "Do you need a pillow for your leg?"

"No." Blake shook her head. "Thanks. Let's just get on the road."

Milo climbed behind the wheel and Raptor helped Ezmé into the backseat, then slid in next to her. As Milo exited the garage and navigated the road's steep descent toward the city, Raptor wondered if he'd ever return to Puerto Vallarta or *La Pedrera.* He looked past Ezmé who stared out the window at the spectacular view of *Bahía de Banderas* stretching toward Nuevo Vallarta.

She turned and smiled at him, and his heart lurched into his throat. She took his hand in hers and he wanted to kiss her. He placed their twined hands in his lap, and she returned her to gazing out the window.

Traffic was light, making the silent car ride shorter than he'd anticipated. When they hit the highway that would take them to the airport, Blake directed Milo. She told him when and where to turn—until they reached a large condominium tower.

"Stop at the first garage entrance." Blake said.

Milo rolled down his window when a guard approached.

"Name?" the guard asked.

"Blake Jensen for Sarita García."

The guard looked at each of them, made a note on a clipboard, then raised the red and white striped barrier.

"The elevator we need is at the back of the garage." Blake pointed to a sign showing the way.

Milo pulled into a parking slot, cut the engine, and exited the car. He opened the door for Ezme. Raptor hesitated, then lifted her hand to his lips and kissed her soft skin. Before he could change his mind, he let go and climbed from the back seat.

Blake opened her door and swung her legs out of the car. Raptor placed his hands under her armpits and helped her up, then he swept her into his arms. Milo and Ezmé waited for them at the front of the car.

"Milo." Raptor smiled at his lieutenant. "Leave the keys under the floormat and be on your way."

"*¿Patrón?*" Milo shook his head. "No, I will help you leave the city."

"*Teniente.*" Raptor leaned against the hood of the car. "You will go and find your ride to Tequila. Do not argue because, regardless of Blake's waif-like appearance she is still heavy."

"But, how can I—" Milo frowned at his boss.

"You are not disregarding a direct order are you lieutenant?" Raptor barked.

"*No, Patrón.*" Milo gave a salute, then turned and headed for the garage exit.

"Milo!" Raptor called after his soldier. Milo stopped and looked at him. "Toast me when you get home."

Milo flashed a wide smile, then disappeared into the waning afternoon sunshine.

Raptor pushed off the car, repositioned Blake in his arms, and headed toward the elevators. Ezmé walked quietly next to him, and pushed the UP arrow when they arrived.

The trio stepped inside, and Blake said, "The PENTHOUSE."

Ezmé pushed the button and the elevator whooshed upward. Raptor's stomach dropped the higher they rose. He searched his mind for a way to keep Ezmé and protect his family at the same time. But each scenario he contemplated raised red flags and dashed his hopes.

The elevator ride was swift, and the doors opened onto a lavish lobby. Ezmé stepped from the car first, then held the door for Raptor and Blake. Before they could push a large ornate doorbell, an elaborate set of double doors swung open.

"Blake." A stunning woman dressed in black capris and a bloodred sleeveless blouse stood before them. "Please come in." She stepped aside and motioned them to enter.

Ezmé stood back and waited for Raptor to walk in first. He closed the distance to an armchair, where he carefully placed Blake. He returned to the door and offered Ezmé his hand, which she took. They walked in together, finding themselves in a large room with floor to ceiling windows looking out on the south end of *Bahía de Banderas*.

When the doors closed behind him, Raptor's pulse quickened and he squared his shoulders, bracing for what might come next.

Sarita smiled at him, then extended her hand to Ezmé. "It is so nice to finally meet you."

Ezmé shook her hand, looked up at Raptor, then shifted her attention back to Sarita. "It is nice to meet you too." Ezmé withdrew her hand and looked around the living room. "Is Jade here?"

"Jade will be here tomorrow." Sarita crossed to Blake. "How is your leg?"

"Better, thanks." Blake smiled at her hostess.

"I have a doctor coming to check the wound and give you a shot of antibiotics." Sarita touched Blake's cheek. "I am glad you did not die, *mija*." She turned to Raptor. "You must have questions."

"Sí." He focused on controlling the rage bubbling within him. "I would like to speak to you alone."

"No." Sarita walked to a bar and reached for a bottle of *Kah* tequila and four shot glasses. She then carried them to a large glass-topped coffee table. "Come sit." Sarita took a seat at the end of an oversized brown leather couch closest to Blake's armchair.

Raptor motioned Ezmé before him, then followed her. He sat in the chair next to Blake and Ezmé perched on a cushion of the couch. Sarita poured the tequila and picked up her glass, but left the other three on the table. Raptor stood and handed a glass to Blake, then one to Ezme, before returning to his seat with his.

"What would you like to know?" Sarita sipped tequila.

"How did you find Belen?" Ezmé looked at him, eyes wide, then shifted her gaze to Sarita.

"Once I know who the enemy is." Sarita's lips curved slightly. "I make it a priority to learn everything I can about them."

"I do not know you, and I am not your enemy." Raptor tipped his glass and took a sip.

"Your actions, or rather those of your men," Sarita's eyes darkened, "hurt my daughter. That makes you my enemy."

"Wait." Ezmé held up a finger. "I'm not your daughter."

"No, *mija*." Sarita looked at Ezmé. "I am Jade's mother."

"What?" Ezmé was on her feet. "Blake, did you know this?"

"Yes." Blake nodded.

Ezmé crossed the room and hugged Blake. "I don't know what you had to do to come to my rescue," Ezmé began, then cut her eyes to

Raptor, "and I hope no one hurt you, but I'm so glad you sacrificed yourself."

Blake swiped a tear from her cheek. "You belong home with your family."

"But what about you?" Ezmé faced Sarita. "Is Blake's family coming for her too?

Before Sarita could respond, Blake said, "Ezmé."

Ezmé turned to Blake. "You are all alone, aren't you?"

"Yes, but I'll be fine." Blake attempted a smile. "Sarita will make sure I'm patched up and I'll be good as new."

"Then you will come back to Arizona with me." Ezmé hugged Blake again and glanced at Raptor before returning to her seat.

"Mateo, I can see why you wanted to meet alone." Sarita laughed, then continued, "I found Belen via a private eye. I did not expect to learn you had a son." Sarita held his stare. "I, too, know what it is like to suddenly discover you have a child."

Raptor sucked in a breath. He focused on not strangling the dark haired bitch to remove the smug look from her face.

"I would like their location." Raptor fought to keep anger from his tone.

"Possibly, in time." Sarita took another sip. "But for now, I need to know you will not come for Ezmé or Blake after I let you leave."

Raptor noticed Sarita did not include using the information about Belen and his son to protect herself as well.

The doorbell chimed, signaling someone's arrival. A female servant entered through a side entry, then opened the double doors.

An older gentleman strode into the room carrying a small black bag, and Sarita moved toward Blake.

"Doctor Colón." She extended her hand. "Thank you for coming."

"*De nada.*" After shaking Sarita's hand, he stopped next to Blake's chair. "*¿Y tú eres la paciente?*"

Blake looked at Sarita, who said, "Yes, this is Blake your patient."

"Do you have a room for us?" The doctor scanned the large living room.

"I-I'd like to stay here if that's okay." Blake looked at Raptor.

"Bien." Doctor Colón shrugged, then looked at Sarita. "I need a basin of hot water and small towels."

Sarita nodded at the maid who disappeared through the side door. Sarita turned, almost bumping into Ezmé who had moved close to Blake's chair. Sarita smiled at Ezmé, then returned to the couch. Ezmé took Blake's hand.

"I will need you to roll to your side and raise your dress." The doctor prepared a syringe and Blake rolled toward Ezmé.

Raptor met Ezmé's eyes as Blake tugged her sundress up, revealing her ass. A wave of regret washed over him, but he knew better than to indulge his self-pity. His greedy desire to have Ezmérelda Mendoza for himself had brought him to this moment—and the inevitable fact that he would leave this penthouse without either woman.

Blake emitted a small cry as the doctor stuck the needle into a butt cheek and pressed the plunger. When she moved back to a sitting position, Ezmé still held her hand. Raptor saw tears in both of their eyes.

The doctor cleaned the wound with hot water and gave her a shot to numb the area so he could suture the larger holes left by the bite.

"Take these pills two times a day." The doctor handed Blake a small bottle. "And be sure to take them all." Then he looked at Sarita. "You overpaid me, but I do not plan to offer you a refund."

"Gracias, Doctor Colón." Sarita walked him to the door.

"Señor Armas," Sarita said after the doctor left, "I believe it is time for you to go."

Raptor glared at her and stood. "How will I contact you in the future?"

Matching his dark stare, Sarita smiled. "I will contact you when I believe you are not a threat to my daughter, her sister, or Blake."

He glanced at Blake and Ezmé, then headed for the door.

"Mateo," Sarita said, and he turned to face her. "I know it will be hard to resist the urge to find Belen and your son, but I advise you to wait on this endeavor as well."

Raptor glared at her, his rage turning his cheeks red.

She walked toward him and handed him an envelope. "I have a parting gift for you."

Raptor opened the flap and emptied the contents into his hand. He stared at the passport, wallet, and airline ticket, then raised his gaze to meet hers.

"I know the *policía* are looking for you, and though returning Ezmé to Jade will deter their hunt temporarily." She returned to the couch and flashed a smile. "I know my daughter and Eladio Ortiz will continue to search for you."

Raptor looked at the passport, noting his new name, then checked the wallet, which was full of *dinero*. Finally, he studied the ticket with the airport designation GAU. She was sending him back to Guatemala via Manzanillo.

"Gracias por el regalo generoso." Raptor walked back to the coffee table and placed the envelope onto the glass top. "But I cannot accept such a generous gift."

With Ezmé's help, Blake had come to her feet. The two ambled toward him.

"Mateo," Blake took his hand, "take me with you." He looked down at her and wiped away her tears with his thumb. "We can start over together."

Blake almost fell into the coffee table when she bent to pick up the envelope. Raptor grabbed her by the hips to steady her. She turned in his arms and kissed him. He looked into her green eyes, then touched his forehead to hers. Blake put the envelope into his hand, and he nodded.

"I anticipated this might be your choice." Sarita crossed to the bar and retrieved a second packet. "Everything you need to start over, *mija*."

She handed Blake the envelope, nodded at Raptor then moved to stand by Ezmé.

Blake angled enough to face Sarita. "And my debt to you is now paid." Blake stated.

"*Sí*. In full." Sarita nodded. "I will delay my meeting with Jade to give you a head start."

Blake looked at Raptor. He tightened his arm around her waist, then headed for the large double doors. He glanced at Ezmé one last time, smiled at her, then reached for the knob.

"Mateo, wait!" Ezmé shouted and rushed to him.

Blake palmed the wall to support herself as Raptor wrapped Ezmé in his arms and kissed her. He wanted to yank the door open and leave with her, running toward freedom, but when she pushed against his chest and stepped from his arms, he knew he'd be leaving her behind.

"I hope you find you Belen and your son someday." She touched his cheek.

Raptor cast a glance at Sarita. "As do I."

"*Muchas gracias,*" Ezmé held his hands, "for setting me free."

"*Adiós, mi amor.*" He kissed the top of her head and waited while she hugged Blake.

Then, Mateo Armas opened the large doors, lifted Blake into his arms and took his first steps back to where he'd come from.

CHAPTER FORTY-FOUR

"You look awful." Joy hugged Jade and a hint of coconut enveloped her. "Come, we have the hotel bar all to ourselves." She led Jade and Sandrine through the lobby into the cozy *Libélula Lounge*. The wall behind the bar featured a large blue dragonfly hovering over a colorful field of Mexican daisies. The spectacular artwork had been created entirely with pieces of Mexican tile and clear glass to create the gossamer wings of the lovely *libélula*.

Glass shelves dotted the wall and showcased bottles of the small batch blend of *Libélula Tequila*, a product of *Jalisco* state which included the basics: *reposado* and *blanco* tequilas. Various drink glasses featuring vibrant dragonflies shared space on the glass shelves. A bank of windows sat at offered a stunning view of *Bahía de Banderas*. Tall fake palm trees strung with lights occupied the corners the windows and showcased a variety of dragonfly ornaments people had gifted Joy.

Erica, Gwen, and Valéria were seated at a large table, and came to their feet as Jade and Sandrine approached. Various dishes of appetizers were arrayed along the middle of the table, with two pitchers of margaritas sitting in the center like sentries waiting for their orders.

After embracing Jade, Erica touched her nose. "Does it hurt?"

"It's better now that the gauze is gone." The bridge of her nose was now taped. Jade still sounded a little stuffy, but was thankful to be able to breathe again.

Gwen hovered behind Erica and Jade worried the young woman wouldn't recover from her horrific vacation in Puerto Vallarta.

"Do you know what's happened to Ezmé and Blake?" Erica asked. Gwen stepped closer to Jade.

Jade knew she couldn't share information about Sarita, because it only made sense to her and Sandrine. "We have a lead on a possible location for Raptor and believe he still has Blake and Ezmé with him."

"Let's sit and drink these margaritas before the ice waters them down." Joy pulled out a chair.

The women returned to their seats. Jade sat next to Joy, with Sandrine sitting across from her. Her BFF hadn't left her side and watched her like a hawk, making sure Jade didn't fall or faint. Jade still looked like a prize fighter, but felt stronger with each passing hour.

"Gwen is thinking of coming to Arizona with Novio and me, since her parents retired in Florida." Valéria held Jade's stare, but Jade knew the new agent couldn't be blamed for her brother's actions.

"Where are you from originally?" Jade asked Gwen.

"Bend, Oregon." Gwen looked at Erica. "I might stay here too. I can't imagine leaving without Blake."

"Is that a platter of imperial shrimp?" Sandrine pointed down the table.

"Yes." Joy lifted the dish and passed it to Sandrine.

"This is one of my favorite ways to cook shrimp." Sandrine placed three pieces on her plate and two onto Jade's.

Jade raised her eyebrows and Sandrine said, "You need to eat."

"What else do you like?" Joy selected another dish. "These are chicken *flautas*." She passed the platter to Sandrine.

Within a few minutes, Jade's plate was loaded with delectable food.

Joy poured everyone a margarita. Her glass was etched with a fuchsia dragonfly, and she lifted it in toast. "To bringing Ezmé and Blake back safely."

Jade drank half of her margarita, then forked in a bit of *barbacoa*, the savory shredded beef almost melting in her mouth. When all eyes focused on Jade, she thought maybe remnants of food clung to her lips. She used her napkin to wipe her mouth.

Sandrine stood. "Agent Ortiz."

Coming to her feet, Jade turned to find Eladio standing behind her. "You have a location?" Jade cut her eyes to Peña, who was headed their way. "Damn it!" Jade stamped a foot. "Tell me what's going on."

As Peña grew closer, Geovany stepped into the lounge with another man.

"Officer Marin turned himself into Lieutenant Peña." Eladio shifted his focus to Peña. "Marin has a message for you." Eladio motioned Geovany forward.

A middle-aged man, Marin looked like he hadn't slept in days. "Agent Mendoza." Marin extended his hand.

Jade hesitated, then shook his hand. "Do you know where Sarita is?"

Reaching into his back pocket, Marin withdrew a crumpled envelope and handed it to Jade. She studied her name written on the front in cursive, then raised her eyes to the quartet of men.

"I am very sorry about your sister." Sadness clouded Marin's dark eyes.

"What?" Dread slithered through Jade's gut. "Has something happened to Ezmé?" Jade's focused whipped from Eladio, to Peña, to Geovany.

"Jade," Peña stepped forward, "as far as we know, your sister is fine."

"Raptor delivered her to Sarita this evening," Eladio began.

"Then I'm assuming you know where Sarita is keeping Ezmé." Jade marched from the lounge. "Let's go get her."

Peña followed and grabbed her elbow. "You need to read the note." He placed his hands on her arms. "We are close Jade." She saw concern in his eyes and her stomach knotted. "Want me to read it first?"

Jade shook her head and ripped open the envelope. *Now that Sarita had Ezmé, what would she want from Jade in exchange for her sister? Jade to guarantee her freedom? Revenge for being forced to leave her lavish lifestyle? Or, God forbid, a relationship with her daughter?*

Jade slid the small note free and unfolded the paper.

*Querida Jade ~ I am enjoying getting to know
your sister, Ezmé. Such a lovely young woman
I do hope you will allow me the same
opportunity with you.*

*I know you are anxious to rescue your sister, but
I promised Blake I would delay our meeting so she
and Mateo could leave town. Officer Marin will
share his reason for helping me, then you will
understand why he cannot give you my address
until tomorrow.*

*Ezmé is asking about Novio and her friends. I
told her you would be able to update her when
you arrive. Please dissuade Eladio, or anyone
else, from accompanying you. I would hate for
someone's death to ruin our time together. I look
forward to seeing you for brunch at eleven
Que tengas una velada encantadora, Amor, Madre*

"It sounds like Blake willingly left with Raptor." Jade raised her eyes to the group.

"Want me to talk to Gwen to see if she knows anything?" Sandrine placed a hand on Jade's shoulder.

"No." Jade looked at Sandrine. "I don't want to upset her until we know for sure."

"What else does the note say?" Peña asked.

"She wants me to come to brunch tomorrow at eleven. Alone." She shifted her gaze to Eladio. "Is there any way we can go sooner?"

Eladio waved at Marin. "Tell her why you work for Sarita."

Marin shuffled his feet. "She found me drunk in *Cantina del Diablo* and told me she knew I worked for Raptor."

"And threatened to turn you in?" Sandrine asked.

Marin shook his head. "She threatened my family." He looked at Jade and she saw worry in his eyes. "García said she would tell my wife who I worked for, then kidnap my daughters and take them away."

"You have daughters and you worked for a sex trafficker?" Sandrine stepped closer to Marin, who hung his head. "We should let Jade shoot you, since you played a role in having her sister kidnapped, then delivered to Sarita García!"

Jade agreed with Sandrine, but she empathized with how Marin felt about having his family threatened. She didn't know what fate awaited Officer Marin, but once his family was safe, she hoped being locked up was in his future.

"I want you to tell me as much as you can about what Sarita's up too." Jade stepped close to Marin.

"Joy," Peña glanced at Jade, then looked at Joy, "do you have a room we can use?"

"Yes," She turned to Erica, "Era-K, will you please fill in as hostess?"

"Of course." Erica smiled at her mother.

"I'll be back in a few." Joy motioned for them to follow her.

Geovany and Marin trailed after Sandrine, leaving Jade with Ortiz and Peña. Eladio held her stare and she thought she detected something unsaid in his dark eyes. Peña hung back too as if he wanted to be alone with her. Jade rolled her eyes and headed down the hallway leaving them to follow or not.

Sandrine stood by an open door and Jade stepped into a suite like the one she and Sandrine were in—except this setup only had one bedroom. Marin sat at the dinette and Geovany leaned against the small bar separating the kitchen from the living room. Joy had her head in the fridge. When she emerged, she had an armful of beverages, which she placed on the counter behind Geovany.

Jade and Sandrine sat at the table with Marin, their counterparts stood next to Geovany, and Valéria lingered by the door.

"What's your first name?" Jade asked Marin.

"Alberto." He looked up at Joy as she placed water and sodas in the middle of the table.

"I also have *cervezas*." She headed to the slider at the other end of the living room and opened the drapes. Bright sunshine striped the sand-colored tile at the base of the door. "I'll be in the lounge if you need anything." Joy gave a wave over her shoulder as she left the suite.

Jade returned her focus to Marin. "I know your involvement with Raptor put you in a difficult situation, and now your family is in danger." Jade took a water bottle and cracked it open. "And I don't know if Agent Ortiz can offer you a deal if you help us capture Raptor, but you need to tell us what you know."

Eladio sat in the chair next to Jade. "Agent Mendoza is correct. Though corruption is common among our ranks, you broke the law and got caught." He looked at Jade. "But I believe it is in your best interest to cooperate with us."

Marin selected a Coke and tapped the top with his finger. He lifted the tab, releasing a hiss from the can.

"I was enjoying a *cerveza* at the Zoo after my shift." He took a sip of Coke. "A *cabrón* was fighting with a *chica* and I saw him kick her in the face before he closed the back passenger door." Another swig of soda. "I believed his story about the girl being drunk and needing to defend himself." He looked at Jade, and a hint of sadness flitted across his face. "He had scratches and a cut lip." He ran a hand through his close-cropped hair. "I let him go. Two days later, I received an envelope with a photo of me shaking hands with the *bastardo* and five thousand US dollars."

Peña grumbled something under his breath, marched to the fridge, and grabbed a *Pacifico*.

"Did you ever meet with Raptor?" Eladio asked as Peña sat in the last remaining chair.

"No. I only dealt with Milo and Toro by text." Marin shook his head. "Lately, it has been Julio who texts me. I believe he is trying to take over Raptor's organization."

Peña banged his bottle onto the table. "And you fed them information about our task force?"

"I only reported if there were *policía* in or near the Zoo." Marin held up his hands and did another head shake. "I told Milo someone on the pirate ship saw the girl from the beach go overboard. But I never shared any information about the task force."

"I do not believe you!" Peña slapped the table.

"*¡Teniente!*" Eladio barked.

"This *pendejo* is lying!" Peña jumped to his feet. "He is covering for this man Milo, and for Raptor." Peña drank half of his beer. "Probably helped them get away."

"I was hiding from Milo and Julio because of García's threat against my family." Marin stood also. "And I know you have no reason to believe me, but I want to help."

Valéria had stepped to the table, her cheeks wet with tears. "Did you tell Raptor we were undercover officers?"

"*¡Dios, no!*" Marin swore. "I would never—"

"It is too late to have a conscience now—" Peña began.

"Enough!" Jade glared at Peña. "Valéria, Raptor knew I was Ezmé's sister because of our matching dragonfly tattoos." Jade waited for Valéria to nod in understanding. "Maybe you'd rather wait in the lounge?"

"No." Valéria glared at Marin. "I want to hear what he has to say."

Peña stalked off to the fridge, grabbed another beer, and returned to a spot next to Geovany.

"Por favor, siéntate." Eladio stood and offered his seat to Valéria.

"Is there anything you can tell us about Raptor that might help us catch him?" Jade asked.

Marin drained his can of Coke, then nodded. "I know where he went when he left the compound during your raid."

Jade looked around the room at the ragtag task force. She could tell by their expressions they felt the same as she did: this assignment was not over yet. Not only did they need to get Ezmé back from Sarita, but they still needed to bring down a human trafficker, despite his attempt to change his business practices, and make him pay for his crimes.

CHAPTER FORTY-FIVE

The sun hung low in the sky and Eladio wished he was sipping tequila at Captain Jack's waiting, on another spectacular sunset. Instead, he was standing on a patio flipping an envelope over and over in his hands.

He turned from the ocean view and studied the movement inside the suite. Officer Marin still sat in a chair at the table. Geovany and Valéria had their heads bent together, and Eladio assumed they were discussing the specifics of their night of guard duty. Valéria had asked if Novio could join her at the hotel, which Eladio granted, so the young man was cooling his heels in her room.

Sandrine had gone to their suite to fetch sweatshirts and tennis shoes for herself and Jade, because the temperature in the mountains can be considerably cooler than at sea level. Jade and Peña stood in the kitchen. Eladio's pulse quickened when he saw Peña tuck a strand of her hair behind an ear.

Eladio chewed the corner of his lip and turned back to the sunset. The fiery orb had kissed the horizon, turning the ocean a slate blue and painting the sky with warm hues of golden yellow, burnt orange, and dark red. Once again, he wished he had a shot of tequila.

"Eladio?" Jade said behind him.

He turned to face her and hated the wave of longing that washed over him. "Have you decided to take my advice and stay here?"

"No." She tilted her head. "I need to see Raptor's apartment—"

"But you know where Ezmé is, so I do not under—"

"Do you really think," Jade began, "I'm only interested in getting my sister back?"

"No." Eladio frowned. "I guess neither of us needs another unresolved case on our hands."

"I recognize her handwriting." Jade pointed at the envelope in his hands. "Are you going to read Sarita's note?"

Eladio looked at his name and recalled the last time he and Sarita had exchanged an envelope. Then, though, it had been because he provided her with information to help her recover millions stolen by some crooked American bankers.

He lifted the flap and slid the cream-colored paper free. Eladio raised his eyes to meet Jade's inquisitive stare, then unfolded the note.

Eladio ~
I would like to say it has been nice to see
you, even from afar. But seeing you only
reminds me of all I have lost, thanks to you.
As I have said in previous missives, I advise
you not to come with Jade tomorrow. My
fondness for you has waned, and I will have
you killed if you interfere in my reunion with
my daughter. And as much as I know you
would like to arrest me, I trust Jade will feel
that having her sister returned to her is more
important. I do hate to resort to threatening
you, but if you persist in hunting me, I may
have to pay a visit to your parents and sister,

lovely Isla, in Monterrey.
Adiós para siempre, Sarita

Eladio handed the note to Jade and looked back at the darkening ocean. His training told him not to be afraid of Sarita's threat against his family. Given what she had accomplished since her disappearance, though, a whisper of fear fluttered through his gut.

Jade stepped next to him and handed back the note. "I'm sure your family's fine."

Eladio nodded and resisted the urge to move closer to her. "Since we now have Marin in custody, I wonder who she has recruited to kill me if I disregard her wishes."

"It doesn't matter, because you're not coming with me." Jade turned from the view and faced him.

"I will be close by, in spite of your stubbornness." Eladio smiled at her and wanted to kiss her when she responded with a grin.

"Do you think we should turn over these notes to our bosses?" Jade asked.

"Maybe." Eladio returned his gaze to the sea. "I also think we need to request a different team be assigned to arresting Sarita."

"Agreed. How do you think she's managing all of this?" Jade touched his arm when he didn't answer. "Eladio?"

He looked at her and was once again struck by how much Jade looked like Sarita. How could he tell her his theory was that, in addition to blackmail and threats, Sarita probably used her feminine wiles to manipulate vulnerable men into doing her bidding.

"I do not know." Eladio smiled at her. "But she does have access to funds she hid before she escaped and—"

When Sandrine entered the suite, Peña headed their way.

"It is time to go." Peña stood at the open sliding door.

Jade returned Eladio's smile, then stepped past Peña into the living room. Eladio met Peña's questioning stare, then pushed past him and followed Jade. He liked the idea that, for once, the lieutenant might be jealous of him.

"Officer Marin." Eladio stopped next to the disgraced policeman. "I know it is not your intention to cause Geovany or Valéria any trouble, but I have instructed them to have you delivered to the *cárcel* and placed in general population if you try to escape or become a problem. *¿Entender?*"

A look of dread crumpled Marin's face and he nodded. "Understood."

Jade finished tying her shoes and stood from the couch. Sandrine grabbed water bottles from the fridge.

"*¿Listo?*" Peña said at the open suite door.

"Yep." Sandrine handed Jade a bottle and stepped into the hallway. Jade followed her.

Eladio said to Geovany. "I will text when we arrive and are headed back."

"*Copia.*" Geovany nodded.

Eladio stepped past Peña and heard the door close behind him. When they reached the lobby, Jade popped into the lounge and Eladio noticed that Peña stopped at the hotel entrance to wait for her. Sandrine reached his Jeep, and he beeped the locks open. She climbed in behind him and he cranked the engine when Jade and Peña exited the hotel.

"Did you replace the flashlight batteries?" Peña held the back door for Jade, then settled into the passenger seat.

"*Sí.*" Eladio pulled into traffic and headed for *La Pedrera*. "And checked the tactical gear in the back."

"You don't think we'll find someone at the apartment, do you?" Sandrine leaned forward.

"No." Peña shook his head. "But it will be dark when we arrive, and we may have to deal with *vecinos curiosos*."

"If we are approached by neighbors, I think our story should be that we are investigating a reported prowler." Eladio flipped his blinker and turned up a winding two-lane road.

"Well, we're obviously not teenagers looking for a place to party." Sandrine laughed at her joke.

"Let's hope we find something useful to track Raptor," Jade added.

"It sounds like your *mum* has already helped him escape." Sandrine met Eladio's stare in the rearview mirror.

"But we need to know for sure if Blake went willingly, or if she's still a captive." Jade chewed a fingernail. "There has to be clues at his place."

"We will know soon." Eladio pulled into a driveway. As instructed by Marin, he drove through a small complex toward the last building, which sat on the edge of the cliffs.

"These look more like individual units than an apartment building." Sandrine lowered her window, letting in cool air that carried the scent of rain.

Eladio parked in the driveway. "There is a flashlight in the glove box."

He exited the Jeep and headed for the keypad attached to the jamb of the garage door, where he punched in the four digit code. The door came alive and rolled upward as the others gathered behind him. Though it was hard to understand why Marin had become involved with Raptor, Eladio was thankful Marin had once been instructed to stock the apartment with medical supplies, food, and tequila.

Peña clicked the flashlight on and swept the garage with a bright stream of light, highlighting a door at the back of the space. He led the way and tried the knob, which was locked. He used his picks, entered the code to silence the beeping alarm, then moved forward into the kitchen.

Once again, he used the flashlight to search the room, then hit the wall switch, flooding the small space in bright light.

Jade circled the room, opening cabinets, as Sandrine checked out the refrigerator.

"There's a bit of food in here." Sandrine closed the fridge door.

Jade had moved to the small table, where an empty bottle of *Patrón* sat next to four shot glasses. Eladio watched her cheeks color and wondered if she had the same question as he did: *Who would willingly drink with Raptor?*

Peña had knelt next to a chair and studied a dark stain on the floor. "I think this is blood."

"Sarita's note didn't mention anyone being injured, right?" Sandrine asked.

"No." Jade squatted and looked at the stain, then exchanged a look with Peña before they both stood.

Eladio ignored the flicker of chemistry between them and headed down a hallway. A small living room branched off across from a bedroom. When he stepped inside the bedroom, he saw blood stains on the bed sheets. Pillows had been propped up against the headboard and a makeshift support still sat in the middle of the bed.

"Jesus." Sandrine said from the door.

"I think one of them was attacked by a *cocodrilo*." Peña pushed into the bedroom and kicked a pile of bloodstained towels and bandages. He bent and retrieved an empty syringe, then held it out to Eladio.

"*¿Antibiótico?*" Eladio turned the needle in his fingers.

"*Sí.*" Peña looked at Jade. "I do not believe whoever was bitten suffered a life-threatening wound."

Sandrine moved next to Jade. "And if Sarita knew of the injury, she'd arrange for them to get care."

"Unless it was Raptor." Jade hurried to the end of the hall.

Peña scanned the living room, Sandrine checked out a small bathroom, and Eladio followed Jade into a larger bedroom. A king-size bed sat in the middle of the room and a heap of sheets told the story of what had happened.

The others stepped into the bedroom as Jade began her search. She cast a quick glance at the bed, then opened drawers in a dresser. Two empty flutes sat on top of the dresser. She lifted a towel from the back of a bistro chair and carried it to the bathroom on the other side of the room.

Not wanting to disturb her process, Eladio observed from the doorway. Jade partially closed the bathroom door before reopening it and meeting his eyes, holding a dirt-stained, aqua-colored cocktail dress in her hands.

"Ezmé was definitely here." Jade turned in a circle. "Does anything look out of place?" Her eyes darted around the room.

"There is no blood on the dress." Peña took it from her hands. "Which means Ezmé was not likely the one who was injured."

Jade nodded, reached for the sheets, and yanked them from the bed, the wad billowing around her.

"I found something!" Sandrine hit the tile floor on her knees and gathered slips of paper. "Notes." She stood and handed them to Jade. "I think they're from Ezmé."

Jade read one, then passed it to Eladio. He couldn't help but smile when a grin curved Jade's lips.

"What the bloody hell do they say?" Sandrine asked.

Eladio passed the notes to Peña, then said. "She wrote down the make of the car and a plate number."

"This one says Blake was attacked and treated." Peña looked at Jade. "She wrote down the names Milo and Armas."

"And." Jade waved the last piece of paper, tears streaming down her cheeks. She read the note to them, "Jade, I am not hurt or afraid. I know you will find me soon. E~"

CHAPTER FORTY-SIX

Blake had slept the first two hours of their trip south, leaving him alone with his thoughts. He'd tried to distract himself with the radio, but the only sounds were static and an occasional musical note. His last moments with Ezmé jerked through his mind: snippets of their lovemaking, telling her about Sarita García, her goodbye kiss.

When Ezmé had rushed into his arms before he left the penthouse, hope that she'd come with him had flooded his senses. But unlike Blake, Ezmé had chosen to stay behind.

As the sun drifted below the horizon, Raptor tried to focus on his plan to get Belen and young Mateo back, but each scenario was countered with concern over what Sarita might do if he acted too soon. He ran a hand through his hair and refocused on the darkening road. He had initially thought he'd drive straight through to Manzanillo, but as the monotonous miles passed by, he longed for a shower, a bed and a fifth of *Patrón*.

Blake stirred in her seat, wincing when she moved her leg. Adjusting again, she rubbed her eyes. "Where are we?

"Outside of Tomatlán." Raptor glanced at her. "Would you like to stop or keep going?"

"How far to Manzanillo?" She brushed hair from her face.

"Two and a half hours." He slowed for a breaking car.

"I can keep going, but I need a bathroom." Blake grimaced again and laid back against the seat.

"We will stop for the night." Raptor smiled at her. "I need a drink."

He had no idea where they would stay, but as the car in front of him slowed to turn, he saw a small market and whipped the sedan into a gravel parking lot.

"I will check to see if they have a bathroom."

"What about the restaurant?" She pointed to a ramshackle building.

"Bien." Raptor nodded. "Can you wait, and I will help you?"

Blake gave him a thumbs-up and he headed inside the store. Scanning shelves, he finally spotted *cervezas* in a cooler on the back wall. Raptor grabbed a six pack of *Pacifico* and two jugs of water. As he made his way back to the cashier, he stopped in front of a shelf with hair dye. He wasn't sure how Blake would feel about dying her blonde hair, probably as thrilled as he was about lopping off his curls. He grabbed a box of red dye and a pair of scissors. In the next section he added bandages to the pile in his arms. The cashier's eyes grew wide when he dumped his purchases onto the counter.

"Buenas noches." Raptor smiled at the young woman and perused the tequila selection behind her.

"Buenas noches." She began tallying the items on an old calculator.

The tequila choices were abysmal. He would probably require a whole fifth to achieve any semblance of calm.

"And a bottle of *El Jimador*." Raptor pulled the wallet Sarita had given him from his back pocket and extracted one thousand *pesos*.

The clerk added his items to plastic bags, then took the bill and handed him his change.

"Gracias." He smiled again and left the store.

Blake sat in the car with her door open and legs angled out. Raptor placed the bags onto the backseat, then walked around the car.

"I really have to go." Blake tried to stand.

Raptor placed his hands under her armpits, helped her up, and wrapped an arm around her waist. *"¿Listo?"* He waited for her to look at him.

Blake nodded. "Ready."

As they hobbled toward *Fresco Ayer*, Raptor laughed when the name of the restaurant registered in his muddled brain.

"What's so funny?" She looked up at him.

"The restaurant's name is Fresh Yesterday." Blake stumbled and he steadied her.

"Maybe we should just get junk food from the store."

"You use the bathroom first, then we will decide."

She nodded and he guided her inside. Taking in the festive interior decorated in bright colors, they both grinned. Mexican pine tables and chairs dotted a gleaming tile floor, and a small bar took up part of the back wall.

A plump woman stepped from a doorway and yelled over her shoulder, *"¡Clientela!"*

"Baño, ¿por favor?" Blake asked.

"Esquina." She pointed and Blake limped toward the bathroom tucked into the back corner of the restaurant. *"¿Aquí?"* The woman pulled out a chair.

"Sí. Here is fine." Raptor sat in the other chair at the table, and she scurried off.

Blake rejoined him as their hostess returned with a basket of chips, a bowl of salsa, and a plate of pickled vegetables.

"Dos cervezas, por favor." Raptor ordered.

"Bien." She glanced at Blake's bandaged leg. *"¿Comida?"* She pointed to a board hanging on the wall behind a counter. An ancient cash register sat at one end of the counter.

Blake raised an eyebrow at the menu items—all written in Spanish. "You order for us."

"Dos platos de enchilada de pollo," Raptor said.

"Bueno." The hostess headed to the counter, then yelled their order to someone in the kitchen.

"Chicken enchiladas, right?" Blake dipped a chip into the salsa. "Good call."

Raptor nodded as their hostess delivered two bottles of *Modelo.* "How is your leg?"

"It hurts, but also itches." Blake took a sip of beer.

"I am sorry you were attacked." Raptor drained half of his bottle.

Blake shrugged. "I'm just glad Milo was there to shoot the prehistoric beast."

Raptor wondered if Milo had found his ride to Tequila. Since he hadn't heard from Toro, he imagined the *sicario* had fought to the end alongside his men to protect Raptor and the compound.

"I'm sorry about Ezmé." Blake said, mistaking whatever showed on his face as regret for having to leave the young woman behind.

"Ezmé made the choice of what is best for her." He smiled and took another sip.

"And you did what you needed to do to protect Belen and Mateo." Blake tipped the *Modelo* to her lips.

He wanted to ask why Blake had chosen to come with him, but just then the hostess delivered their food. The savory aroma reminded Raptor he hadn't eaten much for almost a day. He and Blake ate in silence for a few minutes, and he thought about how well she fit into his life. Of course, she was willing to follow him anywhere, but she also cared about him. And while it wasn't the first time he'd had a woman fall in love with him, Raptor was surprised he wasn't contemplating how he would end his time with Blake.

"This is so good," she said around a mouthful, then took a long pull from her beer.

Smiling, he chewed his own bite, the flavors reminding him of his mother's cooking. The memory of waiting for her famous *carnitas de cerdo* flitted through his mind. He wondered what he would find when he returned home. Sadness replaced the fond memories when the reality that Belen would not be there struck him. And he would not be able to stay in his small hometown because the *policía* would be looking for him.

"Mateo?" Blake touched his hand.

"*¿Sí?*" He blinked to clear his mind.

"If you want to continue, I can manage the rest of the drive." Blake finished her beer.

"No." He shook his head. "There is a small hotel across the parking lot, and we will get a room for the night."

"I have to say I'm relieved." Blake smiled.

"Would you like any food to go?" Raptor waved at the hostess who stood at the cash register.

"No, I'm more than full." Blake patted her flat stomach.

"*La cuenta por favor,*" Raptor said to their hostess.

She placed a slip of paper on the table in front of him, collected dishes and disappeared into the kitchen. Raptor almost laughed at the amount due for their meal. It was one hundred and twenty-three *pesos*— approximately seven US dollars. He wanted to leave a large tip, but knew it wasn't wise to draw attention to himself and Blake.

"*Muchas gracias.*" Raptor stood and placed one hundred and fifty *pesos* on top of the bill. "*Nuestra comida estuvo muy deliciosa.*"

"*De nada,*" she said, giving them a little wave as they headed for the exit.

Raptor held the door for Blake, who returned the hostess's wave before hobbling outside. He followed her, placing his arm around her waist, and they walked to the car. The temperature was perfect, and he inhaled the briny sea air. The thought of sitting outside as he nursed the tequila almost brought him a sense of calm.

He opened the passenger door for Blake. "I want to move the car closer to the hotel."

She lowered onto the seat, and he helped guide her injured leg inside, then rounded the bumper and sat behind the wheel. The drive was short, and he laughed at the hotel sign. Below the name *La Posada Pacifica*, the sign announced *Proporcionamos sában, as limpias, tú traes la diversión.*

"What's funny this time?" Blake looked at him.

"The sign says, 'We provide clean sheets, you bring the fun.'" Stepping from the car, he came to help her out. "I will bring in our things once we have a room."

They shuffled into the vacant lobby, a bell sounding their arrival. A scruffy, middle-aged man appeared through a door located behind the check-in desk.

"Buenas noches," Raptor said, placing his new passport onto the counter. *"Una habitación para dos, por favor."*

"Good evening." The man smirked, showing tobacco-stained teeth, "I speak English." Turning to a rack behind him, he pulled an old school key hanging from a tag with the number four printed in white. "This is very good room for two." He winked at Blake. "Clean sheets."

"Thank you." Raptor took the key. "How much for one night?"

The clerk squinted and Raptor knew he was debating whether to charge more than the nightly rate posted on his sign.

"Seiscientos cincuenta pesos." His eyes still wary.

"Bien." Raptor counted out the equivalent of one hundred and fifty US dollars in *pesos* and handed the money to the man.

"Okay." A broad grin curved the clerk's lips. "Have a good night." He winked at Blake again.

Raptor helped Blake navigate back outside, then escorted her to their room.

"You should check for cameras." Blake limped inside. "I think that pervert is expecting a show."

Raptor cocked an eyebrow, then headed for the car. Lifting their duffels from the trunk, he grabbed the bags from the backseat and walked back to the room. He pushed the door open and set everything onto a bed. Blake wasn't in the room. For a beat, he worried the creepy clerk had snatched her. Then he heard the water running. After locking the door, he stood at the edge of the bathroom and admired Blake's luscious round breasts, the familiar burning need for release crawling through his loins. Eyes closed, head resting against the wall, she'd propped her injured leg on the side of the tub.

Raptor moved close and grabbed a washcloth from the rack above the toilet. He knelt and dipped the cloth into the hot water, then washed her neck and shoulders. Blake opened her eyes and he saw desire flickering in their green depths. He leaned in and kissed her, careful not to bump her leg. She twined her hands into his hair and pulled him closer.

Raptor abandoned the washcloth and covered a nipple with his mouth, eliciting a deep moan from Blake. He kissed her and moved a hand between her legs. Lifting her hips to meet his touch, she whimpered.

"*Lo siento.*" Raptor stood. "I do not want to hurt you."

"Mateo," Blake placed her hands on the side of the tub and tried to stand, "move me to the bed."

Raptor searched her eyes, which showed the same longing he felt, then lifted her from the tub. He grabbed a towel, carried her to the empty bed and patted her skin dry. Placing a pillow under the ankle of her wounded leg, he kissed her and she pulled at his shirt. Raptor stripped naked and laid next to her, caressing her body as she reached for him.

He moved his hips away. "We will go slow."

"And I'm sure the desk clerk will appreciate every second." Blake raised up and kissed him.

Raptor moved his lips to her breasts, then kissed his way to the border of her alluring mound.

"Now," Blake rasped, "Mateo, now."

Raptor moved carefully between Blake's legs, then lowered himself to meet her arching hips. When he entered her, she groaned and dug her nails into his back. They moved as if their bodies had been made to fit together. For the first time since he'd learned of Belen's fate, discovered the news he had a son, and said goodbye to Ezmé, Raptor felt at peace.

CHAPTER FORTY-SEVEN

Showered and dressed in brown cotton shorts and a cream-colored tank top she wore for pajamas, Jade brushed her hair into a ponytail. She padded to the fridge, plucked a *Corona* from the shelf, and headed to the deck. The sun had set over an hour ago. Sandrine had called it a night even though it was only nine o'clock. Too restless to sleep, Jade knew she had a long night ahead of her. She was thankful for the cool breeze blowing in from Banderas Bay.

When she and Sandrine had left the suite Joy had provided for their meeting, everyone was dispersing for the night. Peña had hugged her before leaving and told her to get some sleep. Valéria checked in with Novio, then she and Geovany settled on a schedule for guarding Marin through the night. Jade had offered to do a shift, but Eladio had encouraged her to get some sleep before her meeting with Sarita in the morning.

She sipped some *Corona* and wondered if the BOLO Valéria had requested would provide any leads on Raptor's Ford Fusion. Sketches of Mateo Armas and Blake Jensen had been distributed to local law enforcement, then sent to the airport, the cruise ship ports, car rental agencies, and bus stations. But the fact that Sarita had given Raptor and Blake a head start would make it harder to locate them.

Jade emptied her bottle and headed back to the kitchen. She eyeballed the fifth of *Libélula* tequila Joy had left for them, but decided being tired was going to be rough enough without the extra cloudiness of a hangover.

"Soon, my citrusy dragonfly friend." She popped the top of the *Corona* bottle. "We'll celebrate when Ezmé is safe."

Jade sloshed beer onto her tank top when a knock sounded on the door. She stepped to the peephole and saw Eladio Ortiz standing in the hallway.

She opened the door. "Hey."

"Do you have a minute?" Eladio looked at his watch. "Or is it too late?"

"Not too late." Jade stepped aside. "Come in."

He entered the suite, stopping next to the kitchen bar. "I wanted to talk to you before your meeting tomorrow."

She thought about rolling her eyes, but something about the seriousness etched on his face kept her from doing so.

"Want a beer?" She tipped her bottle to her lips.

Pointing to the tequila bottle, he said, "A shot would be better."

Jade nodded, grabbed two glasses and the *Libélula*, then headed back to the deck. "Sandrine's sleeping, so let's talk out here." She sat on one of the lounge chairs.

Eladio followed her lead, sitting across from her. She handed him the bottle of tequila and held the glasses toward him. He filled them, put the stopper back in the bottle, then took a glass from her.

"To Ezmé." He clinked her glass, then tossed down the shot.

Jade swallowed the tequila, a spiciness lingering on her tongue. She noticed Eladio looked tired. She could tell something bothered him, but waited until he was ready to talk.

"I liked Sarita very much." He reached for her *Corona* and took a long drink. "She is … was, fun and easy to be around."

Dreading the answer, Jade asked, "Did you have a fling with my *mom*?"

"No," Eladio shook his head, "but we grew very close, and she considered me her friend."

"Then she felt you betrayed her." Jade took back her beer.

"Sí." He stood and walked to the railing. "I tried to warn her, and delayed my report to my boss as long as I could, but—"

"But Sarita García," she continued his thought and joined him at the railing, *"puede ser muy terco."*

"Very stubborn indeed." He laughed.

Heading back inside, Jade said, "I'm getting more beer."

When she returned, she found him watching her. She thought she saw desire lurking in his brown eyes. He turned and looked back at the dark ocean. Jade stood next to him, their hips touching, and handed him a *Corona.*

"You do know this is not real Mexican beer, *¿sí?*" He touched the neck of her bottle and took a drink.

"What?" Jade smiled at him. "I love this beer." She took a sip, then released her hair from the rubber band.

"I want you to know," Eladio began, then tipped his bottle to his lips.

Jade almost touched her lips as she remembered their kiss. "Want me to know what?" She turned and faced him.

"I am okay with you letting Sarita walk after you get Ezmé." He took her hand in his. "I am assuming Temple is also good with this idea."

"He is." Jade nodded. "Are you in love with Sarita?"

Tilting his head as if the question confused him, he said, "No." He let go of her hand. "I have written a note to Sarita and would like you to deliver it tomorrow."

"Okay." Jade nodded.

"And I would also like you to read what I wrote." He pulled a folded piece of paper from his pocket and handed it to her.

Jade looked at the small square, then stepped to the wall and flipped on the outside light. She looked at Eladio. "You're sure?"

"*Sí.*" He shifted his gaze back to the dark bay.

Jade unfolded the note, took a deep breath, and read Eladio's message to her mother.

> *Sarita,*
> *I wanted to address your threats to take my*
> *life, which of course, I do not wish to lose.*
> *You have managed to gain the upper hand by*
> *rescuing Ezmé for Jade, and she is very grateful.*
> *I know you may not believe me, but I wish you*
> *no harm. If you are pursued by law enforcement,*
> *it will not be because of me. Our time together*
> *was a chess match, and you won. Por favor, ve a*
> *vivir una vida increíble, encontrar paz, encuéntrate*
> *a ti mismo, encuentra el amor de nuevo.*
> *Always, Eladio*

Jade wiped tears from her cheeks as she read the last line: *Please go live an amazing life, find peace, find yourself, find love again.* Jade believed Eladio didn't have feelings for Sarita now. He had cared for her when they worked together, though, despite his assignment to arrest her.

She refolded the note and moved next to him at the rail. "I'll deliver this for you, but are you sure you don't want to try to see her yourself after we get Ezmé back?"

"*Sí*, I am sure." He looked at her. "I also want to discuss the plan for tomorrow."

"Okay." Jade picked her beer up from the floor and took a sip. "I think it's pretty straightforward."

"Nothing with Sarita is ever as it seems." Eladio sipped some beer. "The key is to let her believe she is in charge."

Jade laughed. "A trait I think we share."

"You are nothing like her." Clearing his throat, he continued, "Sandrine, Peña and I will be as close as possible." He emptied his beer. "I wish I could swoop in like a white knight and whisk you and Ezmé to safety, but Sarita will control the timing of your departure."

Jade stepped back to the chairs and picked up the tequila bottle. She refilled their glasses, then carried them to where Eladio stood at the rail and handed him a shot.

"To putting Sarita García in our rearview soon." Jade clinked his glass.

Before she could take a sip, Eladio kissed her, his spicy, woody cologne mingling with the night air. Still looking into her eyes, he raised his glass and tossed down the tequila. Jade held his dark stare and finished her shot.

Eladio looked at his watch. "I should let you get some sleep." He headed from the deck into the suite and crossed to the door.

Jade grabbed the tequila bottle and followed him. "I doubt sleep is in the cards for me tonight."

Eladio placed his hand on the knob, then turned and closed the distance between them. He kissed her and Jade wrapped an arm around his neck, pulling him close. He held her away from him.

"*Dios mío*, I want you, but—" Eladio looked into her eyes.

"Quiet." Jade took his hand and led him into her bedroom. "We don't want to wake Sandrine."

She closed the door and put the *Libélula* bottle onto the dresser. Standing close to Eladio, she pulled her tank top over her head and dropped it to the floor, then stepped out of her shorts.

"I want you too." A whisp of guilt brought color to her skin when she thought about Peña.

Eladio unbuttoned his shirt and shrugged out of it. As if he read her mind, he said, "I do not want to come between you and Lieutenant—"

Jade silenced him with a kiss and worked the button on his khakis as he kicked off his shoes. He lowered the zipper, letting his pants slide to the floor.

It must be the heat, Jade thought, *that causes men in México to go commando.* She reached for him, but he trapped her wrists behind her back and bent his head to her breasts. Jade liked a little dominance and didn't fight his hold on her, but when he'd raised both nipples to attention, she wanted to participate in the fun. She turned away from him and he freed her hands.

Jade picked up the tequila, moved to the bed, and laid on her back. She pulled out the stopper and smiled at him.

"Would you like another shot?" She dribbled tequila into her bellybutton.

A wide grin lit up his face as he climbed onto the end of the bed and moved up until he reached her stomach. He sucked the tequila from her skin, then kissed his way back to her lips. Jade tried to guide him with her hips, but he managed to hold himself just above her.

He freed her lips and smiled down at her. "You are very *hermosa.* In case I am not invited to enjoy seconds," he teased her with his hardness, "I plan to savor every inch of your sweetness."

"Oh, I promise there will be more." Jade raised up and kissed him. "As much as we can manage before the night slips away." She grabbed his ass and held him tight until he plunged into her.

Eladio held her stare, his eyes soft and warm. Their rhythm felt familiar and neither of them hurried, setting a slow erotic pace. He leaned down and kissed her and she could feel urgency in his lips. Jade wrapped her legs around Eladio's waist, and he rocked back on his knees, raising her to his chest.

"I definitely want seconds." He held her face in his hands, then kissed her as she exploded in a bright burst of ecstasy.

CHAPTER FORTY-EIGHT

Eladio thought he'd dreamed his amazing night with Jade. Then he opened his eyes and found her lying in his arms. Sunlight brightened the bedroom curtains, and he knew their time together was coming to an end. *But only for now*, he hoped.

Jade shifted in his arms, a floral, musky aroma drawing him closer. Her eyes fluttered open, and she smiled at him.

He kissed her, then said, "Good morning."

"Morning." She lowered her hand to his crotch.

Eladio threw the covers from their bodies, and she turned to him. Her lips, salty from their previous night's passion, touched his. He knew he should pace himself, but they did not have much time.

Jade pushed him onto his back, straddled him and teased him until he throbbed. Eladio grabbed her hips, then matched her rhythm. She leaned down and kissed him, then placed a breast near his mouth. He sucked one, then the other and Jade increased her pace.

"Oh my God," she whispered.

He silently thanked God for allowing him a night with this incredible woman.

Jade raised her torso, and he gasped at the magnificent sight. Eladio held her hips tight to his and matched her movements. He wanted this moment to last forever and waited for Jade to reach her peak of passion first. Jade leaned down and kissed him as he found his release too.

Eladio held her to him, then adjusted until she lay in his arms again. She caressed his chest as he stroked her hair. The quiet, combined with the feeling of satiation, almost lulled him back to sleep.

"I wish we could stay here all day." Jade propped herself up on an elbow, then reached across him and grabbed her phone from the nightstand. "We have an hour before we need to meet everyone in the other suite."

"An hour." Eladio smiled at her.

Jade laughed. "And I need to eat something. I'm famished." She climbed from the bed.

Eladio's phone buzzed. He checked the screen, then stood and reached for his pants. Jade donned her shorts outfit from the night before, pulled her hair into a ponytail, and then brought him his shirt. He knew she'd be fine today because he felt Sarita truly wanted to get to know her daughter. After she read his note, she would also know he and Jade no longer planned to hunt her.

"Maybe we can have dinner tonight after you get Ezmé settled." He buttoned his shirt, hoping he didn't sound like a lovesick schoolboy.

"If Ezmé is okay, it would be fun to celebrate with the whole gang." Jade touched his lips with hers in a quick kiss.

"*Sí.*" He focused on keeping disappointment from his tone. "I will have Jesús reserve a table for us."

"Perfect." Jade headed toward the door.

"Jade." He waited until she faced him. "Will it be uncomfortable if both Peña and I are there?"

She walked back to him and took his hands in hers. "I had a fabulous time last night and I care about you both. But I'll be leaving soon, so I think we can all be adults about our interludes." She turned toward the door again.

"I have to tell you something." Dread churned his empty acidic stomach.

Jade faced him, hands jammed onto her hips. "I already don't like what you're about to say."

"I am being sent to Zihuatanejo to head the task force hunting the fentanyl serial killer." Eladio rubbed his chin, then continued, "And my boss requested you be assigned as the DEA agent."

"Well, I'm not going." Jade glared at him. "I'm just getting Ezmé back, and I'm exhausted."

Eladio didn't suppress his grin in time, and Jade rushed toward him with an open hand. He caught her by the wrist and trapped her hands behind her.

"Let me go!" Jade tried to stomp on his foot. "This is the second time you've withheld information from me and, and—"

He released her and ducked as she took a swing at him. "I wanted to tell you earlier, but—"

"But you wanted to have your fun before you dropped another bombshell on my head!"

"I did not know for sure until now." He turned his phone screen toward her. "I just received the text saying Benson approved your assignment."

"Unbelievable!" Jade threw her hands in the air. "I'm so sick of people telling me what the fuck to do!"

"This is out of my control." Eladio took a step toward her.

The bedroom door swung open, and Sandrine stared at them, arms crossed, scowl in place. "If you kids are through," she looked at the bed, then back at them, "Lieutenant Peña's here." Sandrine grinned at Jade, then closed the door.

"I will leave first." Eladio stepped forward.

Jade shot him a hateful look and stormed from the room. He heard her kiss Peña, then say, "Amado, if you give me a few minutes, I'll be ready to go."

"No hurry," Peña replied, "I can wait."

"Why don't I meet you downstairs," Jade said, followed by the door opening and closing.

Jade marched back into the bedroom, stripping off her clothes on the way to the bathroom. She turned and faced him, giving him a last look at her stunning body before slamming the door closed.

Eladio had been mistaken when he'd said she was nothing like her mother, because Jade Mendoza had the same fiery temper as Sarita García.

CHAPTER FORTY-NINE

Raptor smiled at Belen and ruffled his son's dark curly hair. Young Mateo smiled up at him, then raced ahead into his grandmother's open arms. Belen kissed him and he tried to tell her he loved her, but the words wouldn't come. His mouth was dry, and he licked his lips. When he tried to speak to Belen again, she was too far away to hear him. The warm image faded to black, and he woke to find himself alone in the motel room.

He closed his eyes and thought about last night. Despite her wounded leg, Blake had been zealous in her lovemaking. Raptor wondered if her intent was to erase his time with Ezmé from his memory.

When they were satisfied, he'd helped her dye her blonde hair red, causing the black color block to look like a shadow, then she'd cut his hair. After sweeping his curls into a small pile, she'd cried before depositing them into the trash can. He showered and helped Blake with a sponge bath before they fell into bed, exhausted.

Raptor swung his legs free from the sheet and stood, wishing the room came with a coffeepot. A slip of paper sat on the rickety table by the window, and he read the note: *Went for coffee, be back in a few. B*

Raptor found his clothes and dressed, tucking his gun into the waistband of his jeans. He frowned at his reflection and touched his short hair. "It will grow back."

A knock echoed through the small space. He smiled, imagining Blake trying to balance two cups of coffee and use the key.

Raptor pulled the door open and found the creepy clerk leering at him from the sidewalk. Something besides the thought of the weird little man being a voyeur bothered Raptor. He glared at the clerk and waited.

"You are famous." He showed Raptor a screenshot on his phone.

A pencil drawing of his face stared back at Raptor. Then the clerk swiped the screen to a photo of Blake. He didn't let the thread of worry spinning through his mind show on his face.

"What do you want?" Raptor growled.

The clerk stepped inside the room. "Give me the *chica*." He faced Raptor.

"She is not mine to give," Raptor moved to his duffle bag and stuffed clothes inside, "but feel free to ask her to stay." He smirked at the clerk.

"Then you will pay me not to call the *policía*."

Raptor popped the cap off the small bottle of Devil's Breath. It had been a long time since he'd used the powder. He was thankful Milo had thought to tuck the vial into the duffle. He tapped a small amount into his hand, then loosely closed his fingers around the white substance, and faced his uninvited guest.

"*¿Cómo te llamas?*" Raptor smiled.

"Felix." He grinned. "And you are Mateo Armas."

Raptor opened his hand and blew Devil's Breath into Felix's face. The clerk coughed and sputtered, then clawed at his throat. His eyes watered and he bent at the waist, trying to catch his breath.

After a few minutes, Felix stared at Raptor with cloudy eyes. A dribble of drool hung from his lips, and he looked like he might pass out. Raptor knew the powder had taken effect and he'd now be able to get the slimy clerk to do anything he requested.

"Felix." Raptor stepped to the door. "Show me where you watch the people in these rooms."

Felix exited and shuffled to his office. He walked past the check-in counter and into a small room. At first, he seemed confused as to why he was there, then he sat at a desk and fingered the mouse. While Felix closed a couple of programs, Raptor took in the state of the dilapidated room. It contained an old, stained tan recliner, a double bed with filthy sheets. A large flat screen TV hung on the wall opposite the end of the bed.

Felix sat with his hands in his lap and Raptor looked over his shoulder at a split screen of his and Blake's motel room. One half showed the bathroom and the other a shot of the beds.

"Where do you store the recorded tapes?" Raptor asked.

Hand back on the mouse, Felix brought up the desktop screen and clicked on an icon called: OLD RECORDS. Hundreds of subfolders populated the screen.

"Which folder contains video from my room?" Raptor scanned the screen.

Felix double-clicked the folder titled: BLONDE

The first video played. It showed Blake undressing then settling into the bathtub, followed by Raptor entering and kneeling by the tub. The next clip was of the two of them in bed. The third showed them doing each other's hair and him helping Blake with her sponge bath.

Raptor wanted to snap the pervert's neck and leave him watching the video with eyes that couldn't see. But now that he knew BOLOS had been issued for him and Blake, and probably the Ford, he needed to cover their tracks.

"Felix, where are the keys to your car?" Raptor slid his gun free.

Felix opened the center drawer of the desk and withdrew a set of keys with a Chevrolet tag. Raptor took them from him. He found a notepad with disturbing doodles and set it in front of Felix, laying a pen next to the pad.

"I want you to write this down."

Felix picked up the pen.

"Lamento mis acciones." Raptor waited for Felix to write the words, which were barely legible. He continued, *"Ya no puedo vivir conmigo mismo."* When Felix finally completed the sentence, Raptor told him to sign his name.

"Wait here," Raptor instructed, returned his gun to the small of his back, and marched to the front desk. He searched the check-in cards until he found his, then stuffed the card into his back pocket. Raptor glanced through the grimy windows looking onto the parking lot. The Chevrolet Aveo sat to the left of the motel. There were no other cars in the lot.

He stepped back into the office and found Felix slumped in his chair. At first Raptor thought he'd died from the Devil's Breath, but the *pendejo* was sleeping. Raptor read Felix's note again:

I regret my actions and can no longer live with myself.

Raptor left the clerk sleeping and hung a NO VACANCY sign on the door, then returned to his room. He threw Blake's clothes into her duffle, put their store items into the plastic bags, and stacked the remainder of the beer next to the door. The water jugs were empty, but he planned to leave nothing behind.

He grabbed the Ford's keys and the duffels, then stepped from the room and walked to the trunk of the car. He loaded everything, then returned to the room. After checking the bathroom, he grabbed the trash can liner full of Blake's discarded bloody bandages and the empty hair products. When he moved back into the main room, he found Blake watching him from the open door.

"Leaving without me?" She held two paper cups, and looked more hurt than angry.

"No." Raptor shook his head. "But we have to go." He handed her the Ford's keys. "You will have to drive, so get settled behind the wheel."

Raptor pulled the sheets from the bed they'd slept in and added the heap to the towels from the bathroom. He scooped up the dirty linens and headed for a laundry room that occupied space next to the office. After stuffing in his load, he added Felix's phone. Once he started the washer, he returned to the motel entrance and marched back to Felix's office.

The clerk was awake, watching the video of Raptor and Blake, drool seeping down his chin.

Raptor leaned close to Felix and said, "Delete this video and empty the trash folder, then pick another one to watch."

Felix did as instructed. When he opened the next clip, bile rose in the back of Raptor's throat. The video showed a mother and her teenage daughter, naked and taking turns in the bathroom, dressing for bed, getting ready in the morning.

Raptor wanted to kill the miserable deviant himself, but knew he should stick to his plan. He pulled his gun free, wiped it clean, and laid the piece on the desk next to Felix's right hand. Raptor knew once the gun was fired, it would draw attention to the motel and he would have to act fast.

"Felix," Raptor whispered in the clerk's ear. "You need to shoot yourself in the head when I reach the count of five."

Nodding, Felix picked up the gun and placed the barrel next to his temple. Raptor backed toward the door, counting out loud. When he reached five, he shouted, *"¡Cinco!"* He bolted for the motel door, the acrid smell of gunfire trailing after him.

When she heard the gunshot, Blake had opened the Ford's driver door. He motioned for her to stay, then pointed at the Aveo. Raptor hurried to Felix's car, clicked the locks open, and climbed behind the wheel. Blake had already pulled close to the Chevrolet. He cranked the engine, threw the car into reverse, then raced across the parking lot.

Checking the rearview mirror which had a leather cross hanging from the bracket, he could see people milling about in front of the motel.

Raptor pulled onto the highway, with Blake on his bumper and headed south toward Manzanillo. As disgusted as he was with Felix, Raptor knew his past actions as a trafficker were just as despicable.

Once again, alone with his thoughts, he wondered if he, too, didn't deserve a bullet to the brain.

CHAPTER FIFTY

Jade stood in the kitchen, her back against the wall, holding a cold cup of coffee. By the time she'd showered and dressed in a navy blue blouse and black cotton skirt, she'd calmed down enough to join the others. They met in the suite where they'd stashed Marin.

Joy had provided pastries, coffee, and juice for them, then had asked Gwen and Novio to help her move tables and chairs in a conference room for an upcoming meeting. Hugging Jade before she left, Joy said, "Be safe."

Now, Jade observed an argument between Sandrine, Peña and Eladio. They couldn't agree on the best place to wait for her and Ezmé. Peña wanted to be in the parking garage, engine running and ready to roll. Eladio insisted they sit at a café across the street where they would blend-in if Sarita had someone watching for them. Sandrine wanted to go with Jade.

"You know Sarita said no one is to accompany Jade." Eladio held Sandrine's angry stare.

"It's you she doesn't want tagging along." Sandrine crossed her arms.

"No one is going with Jade." Peña glanced at her. "But we do need to be closer than the coffee shop."

Geovany stood on the deck talking on his phone. Valéria stepped to the coffee pot. She poured a cup, perused the pastry selection, and then met Jade's eyes. "For Marin." She selected a *concha* roll and placed it on a napkin. "How are you holding up?"

Jade shrugged and set her cup on the counter. "I'm going to sneak out." She watched her backup crew—still arguing their best approach to support her. "Can you cover for me?"

Valéria nodded. "You have your phone and—"

Jade patted her skirt pocket and touched the small of her back. She put a finger to her lips and moved to the suite door. Thankfully, it opened without a sound. As Jade slipped out, she heard Valéria say, "Anyone want a pastry or more coffee?"

Hustling down the hall, Jade wished she'd thought to grab the Kia keys. She knew she didn't have time to go back to her suite. She caught Joy's eye as she walked through the lobby, and her friend gave her a nod and thumbs-up. The lobby doors whooshed open, and Jade stepped outside into bright sunshine. She pulled her sunglasses from the neckline of her blouse and slid them in place. A cab honked as it approached, and Jade waved him to a stop. She climbed in and gave him Sarita's address.

The cabbie whipped in and out of traffic as he headed toward the airport. The city seemed crowded for a Tuesday, and Jade envied the tourists wandering in and out of shops, having an early lunch at a sidewalk café', or heading toward the sandy beaches of the bay loaded with beach supplies.

As they approached the airport highway, the driver made a couple of turns, then pulled into the parking lot. He stopped at a barrier that prevented them from entering a garage beneath a massive condominium tower.

A guard approached, and the cabbie rolled down his window.

"Name?" The guard had his clipboard ready.

Jade leaned forward and gave him her name, then Sarita's. Checking his list, he made a notation, then pressed a button and the barrier swooped upward.

"You want me to drive you inside?" The driver looked at her.

"No." She handed him his fare, plus a generous tip, and climbed from the backseat.

The guard watched her as she headed down the sidewalk into the garage. According to Marin, Jade needed to take an elevator at the back of the garage, which would deliver her to Sarita's penthouse.

Jade checked the time on her phone, it showed she'd be five minutes early. She found the correct elevator bank and pushed the UP arrow. The doors opened with a ping and Jade stepped inside. Her image was reflected in the mirrored back wall of the elevator. Knowing Sarita had a penchant for striking makeup and bloodred lipstick, Jade had used minimal enhancements. And, despite her night with Eladio, she still felt tension in her shoulders.

The doors whooshed open and Jade stepped into a lavishly decorated lobby. A massive set of double doors opened and a young woman in a maid outfit waited for her to approach.

Jade walked through the entry and found herself face to face with Sarita García.

"My darling daughter." Sarita opened her arms as if she thought Jade would welcome a hug. "Please, come in." She waved Jade toward her.

"Where is Ezmé?" Jade took a couple of tentative steps.

"She is freshening up." Sarita motioned at the maid, who nodded then disappeared through a side door. "I have champagne to celebrate our first meal together." She pulled a bottle from a bucket of ice and filled two flutes.

"This isn't a social call." Jade noticed that Sarita's eyes grew darker, though she maintained her smile.

"I know you are anxious to see your sister, but please, sit and have a drink with me." Sarita offered her a flute.

Jade crossed the space between them and took the glass. When Sarita touched her flute to Jade's, a crisp ping rang out. Her mother took a sip and Jade hesitated, then sipped from her glass. Sarita sat on a leather couch the color of milk chocolate and pointed to a chair on the other side of a glass coffee table. Until she saw Ezmé and knew she was safe, Jade would have to play along with this charade.

Sarita's phone chimed and she checked the screen. "Thank you for respecting my wishes and coming alone."

Jade pulled Eladio's note from her pocket and slid it across the coffee table. Sarita cocked a perfectly-shaped eyebrow, then picked up the folded square. As she read the message, she raised her eyes to Jade's, then touched the page at the bottom.

"I trust Eladio is well?" Sarita refolded the paper.

"He is." Jade could still feel his touch on her skin, and focused on keeping color from her cheeks.

"And you agree with not arresting me?" Sarita smiled.

"I do." Jade's stomach churned. She wasn't sure she could resist the opportunity to arrest García right now.

The maid appeared at the edge of the room, nodding when Sarita looked at her.

"*¡Bueno!*" Sarita stood. "Brunch is ready." Carrying her flute, she headed for a long table positioned behind a bar.

Jade was tired of this little dance but followed her mother anyway. A bank of windows provided a stunning view of Banderas Bay that took her breath away. She didn't know how García was managing such an extravagant lifestyle when she was on the run. Then it occurred to Jade that maybe Sarita was willing to spend whatever it took to impress her daughter, even if it jeopardized her freedom.

Sarita sat at the head of the table and indicated for Jade to sit next to her.

Jade set down her glass. "Enough of this pretending we're a happy mother-daughter duo." She crossed her arms. "Where the hell is my sister?"

"Here," Ezmé said behind Jade.

Jade whirled around, rushed to Ezmé, and hugged her. "Thank God you're okay."

"Jade," Ezmé rasped, "I can't breathe."

Jade released her. "Sorry," she kissed her on the forehead, "I'm just damn glad to see you."

"I have so many questions. Were you hurt badly when Mateo punched you?" Ezmé searched Jade's eyes. "Are Erica, Gwen and Valéria safe? Is Novio alive?"

"I'm fine and yes to your other two questions." Jade smiled at her sister, stunning in a red sleeveless hourglass dress. "Everyone is excited you're safe too."

"*Señorita García,*" the maid's tone was timid, "do you need anything else?"

"That will be all for now." Sarita waved her away. "Please bring the soufflé in fifteen minutes."

Jade took Ezmé's hand and led her to the table. She pulled out the chair next to hers, but Ezmé pointed to the other side of the table and headed in that direction.

"Ezmé," Sarita touched her hand after she took her seat, "you look lovely."

"Thank you for the dress." Ezmé smiled at Sarita.

"*De nada.* You will take Novio's breath away." Sarita poured champagne into the flute in front of Ezmé from a fresh bottle, then raised her glass. "To beautiful sisters, finally reunited."

Ezmé took a long sip and looked at Jade, who picked up her glass and took a drink. A fruit tart had been placed at each of their spots, and Sarita forked in a small bite. Ezmé broke hers apart with her fingers and popped a morsel into her mouth.

Jade ignored hers and drilled Sarita with a stare. "Is there something specific you want to know about me?"

Sarita sipped from her glass. "I do not believe we can cover almost twenty-three years with a few questions."

"Would it help speed this along if I told you I'm not interested in getting to know you?"

"Jade!" Ezmé glared at her. "Sarita convinced Mateo …" she cast a glance at Sarita, then continued, "to bring me here. And Blake sacrificed herself so I can go home." Tears sprang to her sister's eyes.

"And I'm grateful you're safe," Jade didn't intend to back down, "but Sarita gained her permanent freedom by negotiating your release from Armas."

Sarita narrowed her eyes at Jade, then smiled at Ezmé. "I understand your sister's frustration in not being able to arrest me and her desire to ban me from her life."

The maid was back. She set a cheese soufflé onto a hot pad in the middle of the table, the aroma of creamy cheddar wafting through the air. "Would you like me to serve?"

"Si." Sarita nodded.

The maid spooned small servings onto the empty plates in front of them.

"Can I bring you anything else?" She stood at attention.

"No, gracias." Sarita pushed her chair back and walked to the bar.

Jade watched Ezmé take small bites of the food in front of her. She'd expected Ezmé to be fragile from her time with Raptor, and anxious to leave Sarita García's manipulative control. But her sister seemed fine, and her use of Armas's first name told Jade she hadn't been afraid of her captor.

Sarita returned to the table with a bottle of *Kah* tequila, three shot glasses, and an envelope. She placed the items within arm's reach and resumed her seat.

"I knew you would learn Raptor's real name in due time, but I believe he and Blake will be long gone before you can catch him."

Jade held her dark stare but didn't respond.

"You have made it clear you do not want to enjoy this lovely brunch, or my company." Sarita poured three shots of tequila, handed one to Ezmé, then placed Jade's by her plate. "Tell me one personal thing about yourself, and then you and your sister may leave." Sarita lifted her glass in toast, then took a sip.

Ezmé sipped some tequila and looked at Jade, expecting her to honor the tradition of taking a drink after a toast. She picked up the shot glass and tossed down the tequila.

"And," Sarita laughed, "do not say you like tequila like me."

"I," Jade began, "Ezmé and I, had a wonderful childhood." Jade poured herself more tequila. "I became a DEA agent to stop the insidious spread of drugs throughout the world." She sipped some tequila. "Imagine my dismay when I learn my bio-mom is a drug queen." This time she took a bigger drink. "I fell in love with my FBI partner, and am now torn between the attentions of two men." Sarita cocked an eyebrow as Jade finished the shot, then reached for the bottle again. "I have been telling myself you and I are nothing alike, but that's not the case."

Jade lifted her glass and said, "I, too, love bloodred lipstick. I enjoy having a little power over the men in my life. I also enjoy fine tequila, and I work hard to protect the people I love." Jade emptied her shot glass, coughed, and continued, "And I am very grateful to you for rescuing my sister."

Ezmé took a small sip of tequila and Sarita tossed down her shot. Jade stood, as did Sarita, followed by Ezmé.

"May I please have a hug before you leave?" Sarita asked, and Jade was surprised to see tears in her mother's eyes. She stepped toward Jade and held her arms wide.

Jade let Sarita hug her and was shocked by how good it felt to have her mom hold her. Jade stepped away from Sarita, and gave her a small smile.

"We need to go." Jade looked at Ezmé, who moved toward Sarita.

"Thank you for everything, Sarita." Ezmé hugged her, then wiped tears from her cheeks. "I, too, am very grateful."

"It was my pleasure, *mija*." Sarita tucked a strand of Ezmé's hair behind her ear.

"Thank you for brunch." Jade had reached the massive doors. "You should take Eladio's advice and go live your life." Ezmé joined Jade as she reached for the knob.

"Jade." Sarita crossed to her, holding the envelope. "Thank you for sharing a little about yourself. You should pick Eladio." Sarita tilted her head. "He is a good man."

Jade held her stare but didn't respond.

Extending the envelope, Sarita continued, "I think this last note will answer any remaining questions you might have." Jade took the envelope and Sarita touched her cheek.

"Hasta luego, hija." Sarita turned and headed back to the bar.

Jade opened the door, ushered Ezmé into the lobby, then pushed the DOWN arrow for the elevator. The sisters stepped inside and Ezmé pushed the GARAGE button.

Ezmé pointed to the envelope and asked, "Are you going to read her note?"

"Yes." Jade put her arm around her little sister's shoulder. "But I'm guessing it's going to take a fifth of tequila to do so."

CHAPTER FIFTY-ONE

After Jade slipped out unnoticed, chaos had erupted in the suite. No longer arguing, Eladio, Peña and Sandrine had raced to Sarita's condominium building and waited in Eladio's Jeep. He'd only had to talk them out of storming Sarita's condo once.

Eladio had expected to wait an hour or more for Jade and Ezmé, but the sisters appeared at the garage entrance forty-five minutes after he'd parked at the curb. The three women sat in the back together, all talking at once, laughing and crying. He'd tried to make eye contact with Jade, but she'd ignored his efforts.

While they'd been waiting for Jade, Eladio had arranged for two police officers to retrieve Marin and take him to the city jail. He felt bad for Marin, but the ex-policeman had told Geovany he was thankful his family was safe. He would take whatever punishment he deserved.

Now they were crowded into the first floor suite they'd been using for two days. He looked around the room and almost laughed at the dynamics: Jade, Sandrine, Joy, Ezmé, Erica and Gwen commandeered the table, drinking margaritas, while he, Peña, and Geovany hovered on the outer band of their enthusiasm, nursing *Pacificos*.

He'd tried to talk to Jade about her time with Sarita, but she'd given him the cold shoulder. He did, however, take comfort in the fact that she also wasn't cozying up to Peña.

"When can I see Novio?" Ezmé asked for the third time.

Jade glanced at him. He nodded, then pulled his phone from his pocket and texted Valéria.

Eladio: *If he is ready, you can bring Novio to the suite.*

Valéria: *On our way.*

He looked at Jade and smiled when she met his gaze. She raised an eyebrow, so he gave her a thumbs-up to indicate Novio was on his way. Initially, Novio had asked to meet with Ezmé alone, but Jade's response had been a colorful *no.* Valéria explained Novio was nervous about being around all of them when he saw Ezmé. Eladio thought the young man should be more nervous about what might be next for him.

The suite door opened and Valéria walked in alone. She turned and headed back to the hallway, then she and Novio both entered the room.

Ezmé jumped to her feet and ran into his arms. They hugged and whispered to each other. Jade stood directly behind her sister and watched Novio—as if waiting for him to misstep so she could coldcock him.

Stepping forward, Eladio said, "Novio, I would like you and Valéria to come to the station in an hour so we can discuss what is next for you."

The former soldier's face crumpled with dread. He looked at his sister, then back at Eladio.

"Eladio," Valéria began. "Can our meeting wait until tomorrow?"

"No." Peña said from behind her. She whipped around, glaring at the lieutenant.

"Peña is right," Eladio drew Valéria's attention back to him, "if we are going to offer you a deal," he continued, looking at Novio, "we need to do so soon."

"He tried to protect me from Raptor," Ezmé said. "Can't you just let him go?"

"Ezmé." Jade stepped closer to her sister. "He may have been protecting you, but he also kidnapped you."

"No!" Ezmé stomped her foot. "I went with him willingly." Tears pooled in her eyes.

Jade exchanged a look with Eladio. "Agent Mendoza, would you like to join us for the meeting?"

"No." Jade shook her head. "I trust you and Lieutenant Peña."

Joy joined their circle. "I should have the kitchen make a special dinner to celebrate being together." She looked at Jade. "And everyone finally being safe."

"Joy," Eladio smiled at her, "you have already done so much for us, I would like to treat everyone to dinner at Captain Jack's." He looked at his watch. "And I have made reservations for six."

"That is very kind of you." Joy hugged him. "Ladies, Eladio has invited us to dinner." She headed for the door. "Let's move the party to my suite."

"I need something nice to wear," Gwen said.

"We'll raid my closet." Erica grabbed the empty margarita pitcher. "Mom, can I order drinks from the bar for our dress-up party?"

"Sure, Era-K." Joy smiled at her daughter. "Jade, are you girls joining us?"

"Yes." Jade nodded. "Ezmé's coming now, and Sandrine and I will be there soon."

Ezmé kissed Novio, then followed the others.

When the door closed, Jade touched Eladio's arm and motioned him away from the group. He noticed Peña's scowl before he followed Jade out to the deck.

"Look," she began, facing him, "I don't have a problem with Novio getting a pass."

"Jade, he broke—" Eladio began.

"Yes, and so did Sarita and Raptor and Nacho."

She covered her face with her hands, and he placed his hands on her arms. He wanted to draw her to him, but given their argument this morning he decided to let her make the next move.

"I will see what I can do for Novio."

Warm, briny sea air blew her hair across her face. Eladio kept his hands on her arms until she brushed the strands away and swiped tears from her cheeks. She nodded and walked back into the suite. He watched her as she headed for the door, Sandrine on her heels, and wondered if she'd carry her anger at him to Zihuatanejo.

Or maybe, once Ezmé was home safe, this task force was disbanded, and they were no longer in Puerto Vallarta, she'd give him another chance.

CHAPTER FIFTY-TWO

Raptor surveyed the damage to the Ford's right front fender. The car was still drivable, even after using it to push the Chevrolet off the road. It would make the final hour of their trip to Manzanillo. He peered over the cliff at the Aveo still smoldering after it exploded on the rocks below. The scent of burnt rubber drifted upward. Though he doubted anyone would see the wreckage, he hoped the Ford's license plates had been destroyed in the fire.

He climbed behind the wheel and pulled back onto the highway. Blake stared out her window at the vast Pacific Ocean, the sunlight sparking diamonds on the tips of waves they couldn't see.

"So they're looking for us?" She shifted her gaze to him.

"Yes," he nodded, "and this car with the original plates."

"If they're looking for me," Blake began, "does that make me a fugitive?"

"No." Raptor looked at her. "You are probably still consider a captive."

Blake placed her hand on his thigh. "I think I've proved I'm not your prisoner."

"Why are you coming with me?" He returned his focus to the road.

"Because you and I are broken." She removed her hand from his lap and fingered her new red hair. "If I go back to Portland, Lexi's parents will want answers and Gwen will never forgive me for putting her in danger."

"Once you crossed paths with Sarita García, your choices were limited." He glanced at her. "What about your family?"

"My mom, who has Alzheimer's lives in assisted care. She's all I have left—besides a sister I don't speak to anymore." She rubbed the skin on her leg above the bandage. "Do you have family?"

"*Sí*, but I cannot return to them either."

"Because Belen's family would want to know what happened to her?"

Raptor didn't answer, and Blake sat quietly staring out at the passing ocean. It was possible Belen's husband trusted her enough to allow her to contact her parents. But even if she did he didn't think she'd share what had happened to them.

After a few minutes, he said, "The *policía* will look for me in my hometown."

Memories of his mom cooking Sunday dinner and slapping his hand when he tried to sneak a taste of his favorite dish, *pepián de pollo*, flooded his mind. He could almost taste the spicy chicken stew.

"Running with me," he glanced at Blake, "will put you in danger."

"Is that why," she began and looked at him, sadness in her green eyes, "you were leaving me at the motel?"

"I was not leaving you behind." Raptor reached for her hand. "Just making sure our tracks were covered. But what took you so long to get coffee?"

"Alma, the owner of the restaurant," Blake began and twined her fingers into his, "had to brew a pot. While we waited, she gave me some of her daughter's clothes."

Raptor shot her a look. "You did not tell her anything about us, did you?"

"No. She said her daughter ran off a year ago, and she couldn't bear to keep the clothes any longer." Blake looked into the backseat, then back at him. "One of the items is a long dress to hide my injured leg."

The slimy clerk's face flashed in Raptor's mind, and he wondered if Alma's daughter had run away or if she'd been murdered by the demented motel owner.

"What are you thinking?" Blake squeezed his hand.

"That persuading the clerk to kill himself was a good idea."

"Why?" Her eyebrows shot to her hairline.

"You were right about him watching the guests in their rooms." Raptor sped around a slow moving bus. "When he saw our pictures on the news, he tried to blackmail me and asked that I give you to him."

"Bastard!" Blake slapped the dashboard. "But how did you get him to shoot himself?"

"I had a little help from the devil." He smiled at her.

Blake tilted her head but didn't pursue the matter. "How are we going to avoid being identified at the airport?"

"We will split up." Raptor noticed a car following too close in the rearview mirror and pulled onto the shoulder of the highway. "Do you need to use the outdoor facilities?"

Blake wrinkled her nose. "I'm good."

Raptor stood facing the rocky cliff, looking at the steely blue ocean stretching toward the horizon, and relieved himself. He hated the idea of getting into a car chase along this stretch of road and hoped he was just being paranoid about a tail. He returned to the driver's seat and found himself behind the slow bus once again. Deciding the battered, former school bus would provide good cover, he lagged behind. They were close to the city and would soon see signs for the *aeropuerto*.

"Explain your plan." Blake looked at him, but he focused on the bus's taillights.

"I will drop you at the airport entrance, then park the car." The bus slowed and he hit the brakes. "You will check in, go through security, and find a seat at the gate."

"Okay." Blake nodded. "Act like we're strangers."

"*Sí.*" Raptor didn't tell her that if he was being followed, he wouldn't board the plane. "I will meet you at our seats."

"Mateo," Blake began, "maybe we should start going by our new names." Laughing, she continued, "Although, I'm not sure you look like Gabriel Santos."

"Because I am neither an angel nor a saint?" Raptor winked at her.

Her laughter increased until she was in tears. "Exactly."

"And may I ask your new name, *mi amor*?" Raptor thought he'd said something wrong, because her happy tears dissolved into sobs. He'd never been good with crying women and waited until Blake was calm. "Is your new name so awful?"

"No." She used her tank top to dry her eyes, exposing her toned abs. "You said *mi amor—*"

"*¿Qué?*" He raised an eyebrow.

"I know I'm not Belen, and I'm sorry Ezmé did not come with you." Another little sob escaped her, and she covered her face with her hands.

"Blake, look at me."

She turned her tear-stained face to him.

"I do love Ezmé, but I want her to have a happier life than I can provide." And though he meant what he said, sorrow tugged at his heart. He knew Ezmé would eventually get married, have kids, and live her life without him.

The *aeropuerto* sign indicated he needed to make a right turn soon, and he focused on driving for a few minutes.

"And while I am sad not to have Belen and my son in my life," he flipped the blinker and made the turn, "I am grateful to you. Without you, I would think Belen was lost forever and I would not know I have a child."

He navigated the maze of streets leading to the airport and Blake looked back out her window.

"I am happy to continue to call you my love." He reached for her hand. "If your new name is truly terrible."

"Eva." She smiled at him. "Eva Delgado."

"*Mucho gusto, Eva Delgado.*" He brought their hands to his lips and kissed hers. "Now I must let you out because the last leg of our journey home has arrived."

He stopped next to the curb and Blake climbed out. She grabbed the duffle and the clothes Alma had given her from the backseat.

Blake closed both doors, leaned in the passenger window and said, "I'll see you on the plane, Gabriel."

"Be safe." Raptor held her stare for a beat, then pulled away as she headed for the airport entrance.

He parked as far back in the parking lot as possible, took his duffle from the backseat and placed it on the trunk. The vial of Devil's Breath would never make it through security, so he carried the small bottle to the dirt lining the asphalt and dumped the powder onto the ground. He scuffed the area with the toe of his shoe to keep the residue from wafting through the air.

As he approached the airport, he swept the sidewalk with a discerning look and didn't see anything or anyone out of place. When he was within fifty yards of the building, he noticed two *policía* studying people as they entered the airport.

"*Mierda.*" Raptor searched his mind for an alternative plan.

He slowed his pace and scanned the parking lot. A woman and three kids were struggling with their luggage, and he rushed to help.

"*¿Puedo ayudar?*" He smiled at the mom.

"*No, no, gracias.*" She shouldered a large bag, then tried to pick up her youngest.

"*Por favor.*" He took the bag and held his arms out for the boy.

She gave him a tired smile, handed him the child, and herded her older daughter and son toward the entrance. The boy was wearing a large *sombrero* and it flew off his head when he took off running. Raptor scooped up the hat and slapped it onto his head.

"*¡Pino, para!*" The mom called after him, but the boy kept sprinting through the parked cars.

Raptor saw a small car looking for a parking spot. He realized if the boy didn't stop, the vehicle might hit him.

"Take him." Raptor handed off the toddler and bolted after Pino.

The kid was fast, but Raptor's long strides were closing the distance. The car was approaching, and Julio had turned to see who was chasing him, laughing but not stopping. Raptor grabbed the boy's shirt, then wrapped an arm around his waist just before he ran into the path of the car. The car screeched to a halt and Raptor waved them on.

"Let go of me." Pino squirmed and Raptor tightened his grip.

"Calm down, little man." Raptor held onto him until his mom caught up.

"Pino." The mom took him by the hand. "*No puedes huir así.*"

Pino sulked at being scolded and Raptor winked at him, then offered to carry the toddler again. The mom handed the child back to Raptor, and the little girl handed him the *sombrero*. He smiled at her and placed the hat on his head. He and his charges crossed the street to the main building. Raptor didn't see the police lurking near the entrance. The mom shooed them all inside, then headed toward a different flight from Raptor's.

"*Perdona,*" he said, and she turned to face him. "*Estoy en un vuelo diferente, así que debo decir adiós.*"

"*Muchas gracias por tu ayuda y por salvar a Pino.*" She took the toddler from his arms.

"*De nada.*" Raptor put the *sombrero* back on Pino's head and walked to the check in counter.

Pino ran after him and handed back the *sombrero*, then hurried back to his mom. Raptor set the hat on his head, adjusted his duffle, and stepped in line. He was waved forward, and the attendant checked his identification.

Handing him his passport and boarding pass, she said, "Have a good flight, *Señor* Santos."

Raptor gave her a nod, then headed for his gate. He caught sudden movement out of the corner of his eye. Without looking, he knew he was being followed. Checking the time on a wall clock, he estimated he had twenty minutes before they closed the gate for his flight. He picked up the pace and pushed his way into the crowd waiting in the security line. People grumbled, but no one tried to keep him from advancing.

When the security agent motioned him forward, Raptor took a cleansing breath and focused on being calm. The agent studied his passport and looked at him twice before waving him through. As soon as he cleared security, he set the *sombrero* onto a table near a hallway leading to a different set of gates, then headed for his. He breathed a sigh of relief when an elderly couple was being assisted down the jetway.

Raptor handed his boarding pass to the gate attendant, and she ran the slip past her scanner.

"Cutting it close." She gave him a flirtatious grin and handed back his pass.

"It was a gauntlet to get here." Raptor hurried down the jetway and stepped onto the plane.

Scanning first class, he spotted Blake looking out a small window.

"Sir," the flight attendant said. "I need you to take your seat."

Raptor nodded and moved to his row. "Is this seat taken?"

Blake looked up at him and he could see she'd been crying.

"No." She smoothed her dark hair. "I think my friend Mateo missed the flight." She extended her hand. "Eva Delgado." Raptor shook her hand. "Please join me."

"Nice to meet you, Eva." He sat next to her. "I am Gabriel Santos." He placed his hand on her cheek and was happy to see her green eyes twinkle. "I think we are going to be very happy in my home country."

She leaned in and kissed him. He made a mental promise to her to try to leave Ezmé in the past. And when he began his search for Belen and his son, he would try not to hurt Eva Delgado.

CHAPTER FIFTY-THREE

Jade looked at the unopened envelope Sarita had given her.

Sandrine hovered behind her. "Are you going to open the damn thing, or do you have x-ray vision?"

Jade shifted her gaze to Sandrine, then lifted the flap on the envelope. She slid a folded slip of paper free and read the note from Sarita, with Sandrine looking over her shoulder.

Querida Jade ~
I thought you might have questions about
your birth, your father, and why I did not
raise you. My parents told me you died at
birth, and then they put you up for adoption.

I am thankful you and Ezmé were raised by
nice people, but very sad I did not get to be
your mother. You have already met your birth
father, Marco Torres. After our encounter, I
did not tell him I was pregnant, so he does not
know you are his daughter.

*It may be impossible for us to have a normal
relationship, but I will always be here for you.
Amor de tu madre, Sarita*

"I told you I thought you looked like Torres," Sandrine grabbed the *Libélula* bottle and two shot glasses. "Are you going to reach out to him?"

"No." Jade shrugged. "I don't know." She folded the note and returned it to the envelope.

"What's going on with you?" Sandrine poured the tequila. "I thought you'd be happy to finally have some answers."

"I'm just tired and ready to go home."

Jade touched her glass to Sandrine's and took a sip. Sandrine had a taste and looked at Jade, a touch of amusement glinting in her brown eyes.

"What?" Jade couldn't imagine why Sandrine would think the news about her birth would be funny.

"Tell me about the two men in your life." A broad grin curved Sandrine's lips.

"There's nothing to tell." Jade sipped more tequila.

"I will stay in Puerto Vallarta," Sandrine declared, crossing her arms, "until you tell me what's going on in your little love triangle."

Jade tossed down her shot. "I think *love triangle* is an exaggeration." She reached for the *Libélula* bottle again, but Sandrine snatched it away.

"No more until you give me the details." Sandrine set the bottle on the counter.

Jade leaned against the chair back and closed her eyes, which proved to be a bad idea. The images behind her lids switched from hot, steamy sex with Amado to her sultry, sensual encounter with Eladio. She opened her eyes and smiled at the shot of tequila sitting in front of her.

"I didn't mean to sleep with either of them. It just happened and …" She sipped from her glass.

"And now you don't want to hurt one of them."

"Actually, I wish that was the problem." Jade ran her hands through her hair. "Benson is sending me to Zihuatanejo to serve on another effing task force investigating the fentanyl serial killer."

"Is agent tall, blond, and handsome being sent too?"

Another sip of tequila and a shake of her head. "Ortiz."

Sandrine's eyebrows shot to her forehead. "And?"

"I want to go home." Sobs racked her shoulders. "I want to make sure Ezmé recovers from her ordeal. I need some downtime."

"I'll go in your place." Sandrine poured herself a shot of tequila.

"Thanks, but you need to go home too." Jade took a sip.

Sandrine followed her lead, then said, "If you could pick between the sullen lieutenant and the stoic *Federale*, which one wins the trip to Zihuat?"

Jade grinned. "I kind of like the idea of both of them being at my beck and call." Her phone chimed and she checked the screen. "It's Christopher."

Temple: *Sorry I missed your call but glad Ezmé's safe.*

Jade: *We'll talk soon.*

Temple: *Call when you're settled in Zihuat.*

Jade: *Will do.*

"Temple offering to take Ortiz's place?" Sandrine giggled.

A knock sounded on the door and Sandrine crossed to open it. "Come in, Lieutenant." She gave Jade a questioning glance as she moved to the fridge.

Jade stood. "What's up?"

Peña looked at Sandrine, who handed him a *Pacifico*, then at Jade. "Can I speak to you alone?"

"Perfect timing." Sandrine headed for her bedroom. "I need to shower and dress for dinner." She glanced at Jade before she closed the door. Jade narrowed her eyes at the merriment in Sandrine's smile.

Jade pulled a *Corona* from the refrigerator and popped off the cap. She searched the countertop for the bowl of limes, but found nothing.

"That skunky beer might taste better if you did not add *lima*." Peña stepped close to her.

"What do you want to talk about?" She leaned against the counter.

He kissed her, then searched her eyes. "I do not care what happened between you and Ortiz."

"Amado—"

He put a finger to her lips. "We knew this case would be over at some point, sending us back to our lives." He brushed her hair back and touched his lips to her forehead. "And as much as I would like for this"—he pointed to her, then himself—"to last a little longer, I would settle for a night with you before you leave."

Jade wrapped her arms around his neck and pulled his lips back to hers, sparking a whisp of desire in her loins. Peña pressed his hardness against her, and Jade wondered if it would be rude to skip dinner at Captain Jack's. He unbuttoned the top of her blouse and moved his lips to her dragonfly tattoo. Her conscience was telling her now was not a good time, but her body disagreed and responded to his touch.

Jade's phone chimed and she tried to stop Peña's advance on her breasts, but he ignored her attempts to extricate herself.

Another chime caused him to raise his eyes to hers. He kissed her, then stepped away. Jade walked to the table and looked at her phone.

"Ezmé." She moved back to stand next to him. "She wants Sandrine and I to come to Joy's suite, so I need to change."

"*¿Por qué?*" Peña looked her up and down. "You look *muy bonita*."

Jade took him by the hand and led him to the door. "I will see you at dinner."

"But to be clear," he drew her close and covered her lips, "tonight is not our date."

"I hope not." Jade opened the door and he stepped into the hallway. "Because I'm looking forward," she whispered and placed a hand on his chest, then put his on hers, "to this happening again." She grinned at him, pulled away, and closed the door.

"Glad I didn't find you two shagging on the couch," Sandrine, stunning in a periwinkle sundress, had walked up behind her.

"Almost." Jade laughed and headed to her bedroom. "I just need a minute to change."

"No hurry, it looks like I have a shot and two beers to drink."

Jade dressed in a slinky, off-the-shoulder white dress and stepped from her bedroom, noticing Sandrine had cleaned up the kitchen. "You didn't really finish the drinks, did you?"

"God, no." Sandrine wrinkled her nose. "I'm so tired of Mexican beer, tequila, and margaritas. I need a large glass of a nice, full-bodied cabernet."

Jade applied bloodred lipstick without a mirror and Sandrine tilted her head.

"What?" Jade asked.

"How do you put on lipstick without a mirror?"

Jade shrugged. "Practice." Her phone pinged and she looked at the screen.

Ezmé: *Are you coming?*

Jade: *On our way.*

Sandrine held the door for Jade, and they walked to the elevator, finding the doors open. They stepped inside and Sandrine tapped the UP arrow.

"I wouldn't push Ezmé about her time with Raptor." Sandrine cautioned.

Jade raised an eyebrow, but she knew Sandrine was right. The best way to know what happened would be to let Ezmé tell her when she was ready.

They exited the elevator and arrived at Joy's penthouse. The door was open, so they stepped inside and found the other women laughing and doing their hair and makeup. Ezmé had changed and pulled her hair into a clip, creating a cascade of wavy dark locks.

"You two are a vision of loveliness," Joy said and handed them each a margarita.

Jade smiled at Sandrine, then took a sip. "Looks like you're all having fun."

"We are," Erica called from her seat at a table strewn with cosmetics, perfume, and hair supplies.

Sandrine bumped Jade's shoulder and tilted her head toward Gwen who sat alone on a couch. Jade nodded and walked toward the young woman.

"Gwen?" Jade sat next to her. "Are you okay?"

Gwen frowned and shook her head. "I'm worried about Blake."

Ezmé overheard Gwen, and moved to an armchair near the couch. "Gwen," Ezmé looked at Jade, "Blake went with Mateo willingly."

"But why?" Tear's pooled in Gwen's eyes.

"I think she's in love with him," Ezme reached out and touched Gwen's arm, "and he won't hurt her."

"How can you say that?" Gwen dabbed her eyes with a tissue. "He had us kidnapped!"

"And he forced himself—" Jade caught Sandrine shaking her head from behind Ezmé.

"He didn't make me do anything I didn't—" Anger flashed in Ezmé's eyes when she looked at Jade.

Joy and Erica had joined the quasi-therapy session.

"I think Blake was brave in trying to protect us, and for what she did to help rescue Ezmé," Erica said.

"Blake doesn't have anyone waiting for her at home," Gwen said with a shrug. "And she may be afraid to face Lexi's parents, so maybe she wanted to run away."

"Maybe Raptor," Jade held Ezmé's stare, "is filling a void in her life."

"And she's a survivor." Gwen blew her nose. "She was kidnapped before and almost died."

Jade exchanged a look with Sandrine. Ezmé had shared with them what she'd learned from Blake. Sarita had saved Blake from being raped, again, and then killed by her rapist in Puerto Vallarta. But when Blake shot and killed her rapist with Sarita's gun, Sarita kept the weapon as evidence of Blake's crime. Then she blackmailed Blake into being captured by Raptor so she could assist with Ezmé's rescue.

Ezmé said she knew Blake was in love with Raptor when she asked him to take her with him before he left Sarita's penthouse.

If what Ezmé said about Mateo Armas not hurting her was true, then he may treat Blake well too. But Jade struggled with the thought that a human trafficker could change. Or the idea that a man who would kidnap her sister would forgive the woman who'd help rescue her from him.

CHAPTER FIFTY-FOUR

Eladio reviewed his notes as he waited for Valéria and Novio. He had plenty of time to meet with them—and Peña if he showed—before going home to change for the celebration dinner at Captain Jack's.

Though they hadn't captured Raptor, the task force had been successful in rescuing five women in addition to Erica, Gwen, Valéria, and Jade. He was still trying to wrap his head around the claims the rescued women were making, saying that Raptor and his crew were arranging for them to have better lives. One *prostituta* who was still recovering from a severe beating had begged Eladio to help her. She wanted to contact the man from the Dominican Republic she'd recently met—and planned to marry.

It was Peña's theory that Basilia Casas, the owner of *Casa de Bahía*, was providing a safe haven for *prostitutas* running from abusive pimps. The hotel's security guard, Fonsie, was still missing, and his girlfriend reported he'd recently been paid a large sum of money. If Julio and the Gonzalez cousins were trying to bring down Raptor's operation, they could be responsible for the missing guard. That would leave the hotel vulnerable to a takeover by the *Cartel de Cocos Pequeña* once Raptor was either arrested or dead. Raptor had placed his own men at the hotel after Novio and Ezmé were removed, linking him further to the hotel and the *prostitutas.*

Eladio and Peña had decided it didn't matter if Mateo Armas had changed his stripes. He'd been a human trafficker once and was behind Ezmé Mendoza's kidnapping. Although she wouldn't admit it, Eladio was sure Raptor had tried to rape Jade.

They managed to arrest six of Raptor's men. One of them was Cisco Gonzalez, who had kidnapped Jade and Valéria. His cousin, Pablo Gonzalez, had been arrested fleeing Puerto Vallarta after eluding capture at Raptor's compound. Still in the wind was a soldier named Julio Mora. According to the men captured from the *Cartel de Cocos Pequeña*, he and the Gonzalez cousins were in charge of the raid on Raptor's compound.

Another piece of evidence came from the recovered bit of flesh pulled from Lexi's teeth, which had produced a DNA profile so all they needed was someone to provide a match. The young woman's dental records had confirmed her identity and her body had been returned to her distraught parents.

For the past half hour, Eladio had struggled to write his report outlining Mateo Armas' escape with Ezmé and Blake. The facts, though true, sounded bizarre even to him. Once he filed his final report with his recommendations for Nacho and Novio, Eladio knew other *Federale* agents would partner with the FBI to take over the hunt for Armas. *Fine by me,* he thought.

The Gonzalez cousins would be charged with human trafficking. If they survived jail, before their trials, they would be sent to *Jalisco* State Prison once they were convicted. Bianca Rodríguez had agreed to honor her office's offer to relocate Nacho if he testified against Pablo and Cisco and the other five soldiers captured in the raid. Deciding where to safely stash Nacho and his family until the trial was at the top of Eladio's list.

A knuckle rap announced Valéria and Novio's arrival, and Eladio stood as they entered his office.

"Por favor." he pointed to the chairs in front of his desk, *"sentarse."*

Valéria took her seat, but Novio hesitated. Eladio held the young man's nervous stare.

"Novio." Valéria waited for him to look at her, then pointed to a chair.

Her brother sat, ramrod straight, looking like he would bolt if Eladio produced a set of handcuffs.

"I know you feel as if you have done nothing wrong," Eladio held the young man's nervous stare, "but you did, in fact, kidnap Ezmé Mendoza."

"Agent Ortiz," Valéria began, "Ezmé herself told you my brother was trying to rescue her and keep her safe," she touched Novio's arm, "and you know the circumstances that trapped him into working for Raptor."

Eladio also knew he had no hard evidence linking the young soldier to the human trafficking ring. If he charged Novio and added him to the others already arrested, he had no doubt Novio would be found guilty by default. Besides, hadn't he already served a four-year sentence for putting Valéria on the radar of a human trafficker's *halcones*?

"Novio, you and I both know you participated, willingly or not, in Raptor's operation."

Valéria leaned forward, a glint in her eyes suggesting she planned to argue against Eladio's decision.

"However," Eladio continued, "I do not have any proof of your crimes." He met Valéria's intent stare, "since I cannot offer you a deal, I suggest you leave Puerto Vallarta as soon as possible."

"Our parents have Novio's passport, which is still valid." Valéria smiled at her brother. "I will have them overnight it to us. We will make arrangements to return to Arizona." She and Novio came to their feet.

"Muchas gracias, Agente Ortiz." Novio offered his hand.

As Eladio rose and shook the young man's hand, Peña appeared in the office doorway. He glared at Eladio, then walked to the back of the room.

Valéria glanced at Peña, then shook Eladio's hand too. "I will let you know as soon as I've booked our flights."

"Bueno." After they exited his office, Eladio sat down and shuffled the paperwork on his desk.

"You are letting him go?" Peña occupied the chair Valéria had vacated.

"Sí." Eladio didn't raise his gaze to the lieutenant. "We do not have any evidence against him."

"It is what Jade would want for her sister—to have her *joven amante* set free," Peña said.

He leaned back in his chair and met Peña's dark stare. Eladio knew the lieutenant had heard him and Jade arguing in her bedroom this morning and was somewhat surprised Peña hadn't demanded he step aside. Maybe Peña knew Jade was angry with him. Eladio didn't expect that to subside quickly.

"I heard you are being sent to Zihuatanejo." Peña's face showed no emotion.

"Sí." Eladio wondered if the lieutenant knew Jade had also been assigned to the fentanyl task force.

"When do you leave?" Peña asked.

"According to my boss," Eladio lamented. "Yesterday."

"Then tonight is your farewell dinner?" Peña stood.

Eladio thought he saw a flicker of satisfaction in the lieutenant's eyes.

"I will walk you out." Eladio closed the file on his desk and stood as well. "Since I am hosting tonight's festivities, I do not want to be late."

They walked to the back of the building and pushed through the door. The cool evening air carried the scent of mesquite from a nearby restaurant specializing in steaks cooked on an open grill. Without another word, Peña walked to his Nissan, climbed inside, and fired up the engine. Eladio got behind the wheel of the Jeep and headed in the opposite direction. He wanted to arrive early at Captain Jack's to ensure everything was ready for his guests' arrival.

As he navigated the busy afternoon traffic, Eladio let his mind relive his night and morning with Jade, the memory bringing him to attention. He wanted her to accompany him to Zihuat. He knew she was the best agent to work with him on the task force, since she was familiar with the serial killer poisoning *turistas*.

If it meant she'd no longer be angry with him, though, he'd offer to request a different DEA agent. Of course, he hoped she'd forgive him and join the task force in Zihuatanejo.

CHAPTER FIFTY-FIVE

"I asked the bellman captain to get us a taxi and he just texted. Our van awaits us." Joy smoothed a wrinkle from her beige sleeveless blouse and strung the strap of a small leather purse on her shoulder.

Erica, Gwen, and Ezmé, all dressed in floral print sundresses covering the color pallet of the rainbow, headed for the elevators. Jade allowed a small sigh of relief as Ezmé smiled and followed her friends.

The doors whooshed open, and a delivery man stepped into the penthouse's lobby. He held a bouquet of orange lilies. The arrangement also contained two birds of paradise and was dotted with sprigs of plumeria.

He looked at the group of women. "Jade Mendoza?"

Her cheeks warmed and she stepped forward. "That's me."

He handed Jade the bouquet and returned to the elevator, the doors closing before she could tip him.

"There's a card." Sandrine pointed to a small white envelope, and took the flowers from Jade while she plucked the card free.

Jade felt all eyes on her as she slipped out the note and read the simple message.

"Stay with me tonight," whispered the moon.
"The sun will walk you home in the morning."

The note wasn't signed. Jade thought the sender had to be Peña, since he knew she'd be in Joy's suite.

"Which Romeo sent the flowers?" Sandrine handed her back the bouquet.

Jade shrugged.

"Give them to me," Joy held out a hand, "I'll put them in water."

"Wait." Ezmé stepped close to Joy and snapped the stem of one of the lilies. "This will look beautiful in your hair."

"It's a lovely idea," Jade began, "but I think the flower's too heavy."

"I can fix that." Erica dug in her purse until she found a couple of bobby pins.

"The flower will be a nice *thank you* to whoever sent the bouquet." Gwen smiled at her.

"Okay, lovelies," Joy pushed the DOWN arrow, "let's be on our way."

The women crowded into the elevator car, and a myriad of perfume scents filled the small space. Sandrine had a sly grin on her face, and Jade wondered if she knew who had sent the flowers.

They reached the lobby and the young women hurried to the van. Joy checked in with the desk before joining Sandrine and Jade. Jade held the sliding door for her friends, then climbed in next to the driver.

"Capitán Jack's, ¿sí?"

"Sí." Jade nodded, then looked out her window.

As they drove south, Banderas Bay stretched out to the west with the sun drifting toward the horizon like a fiery orange orb. Jade asked herself if she'd miss Puerto Vallarta, and she wasn't quite sure of the answer. Of course, she couldn't stay—no matter what happened between her and Amado Peña. If she didn't go to Zihuat, she'd eventually have to return to Phoenix. Right now, that sounded more appealing than another task force hunting a serial killer.

"Penny for your thoughts." Sandrine leaned over her shoulder.

"I'm thinking I might want a glass of cabernet too," Jade replied.

She was a tad nervous about being in a non-work environment with her two lovers at the same time. And she was about to find out if they were uncomfortable too. The van pulled next to the curb in front of the restaurant. Jade hopped out and paid the driver. Sandrine offered a hand to Joy, and then the trio of new friends gracefully exited from the back. Joy led the way into Captain Jack's.

Sandrine hung back and waited for Jade. "It doesn't matter who sent the flowers and the esoteric note." She smiled. "What matters is, you choose what or who is best for you." Sandrine headed for the entrance. "Now come on, I hear a glass of wine calling my name."

Jade touched the flower in her hair, lowered the neckline of her dress a smidge, and strutted into the restaurant. Erica, Gwen and Ezmé had joined Valéria and Novio at a tall table. Novio pulled his arm from around Ezmé's waist when Jade appeared, and she tried to give him a reassuring smile. After all, if Novio wasn't in jail, it meant Eladio had decided not to charge him with a crime.

Amado Peña stood, *Pacifico* in hand, talking to Geovany. He hadn't noticed her yet, so she took advantage of the opportunity to admire his sinewy, athletic frame. He wore a white cotton Henley shirt, slim-fitting denim jeans, and cowboy boots. Jade loved the way his smile softened his eyes, and it was hard not to focus on his lips and the mustache that tickled her upper lip when he kissed her.

Sandrine handed her a glass of cabernet. When Peña finally saw her, he lifted his beer in toast.

"I'm super glad I don't have to choose between the hot, handsome lieutenant and the cool, elegant *Federale*," Sandrine whispered in her ear. "Good luck love, because here they both come."

"Sandrine," Jade muttered, "don't leav—"

"Buenas noches." Eladio pointed at her drink. "I was going to offer to get you a shot of tequila, but I see you have chosen something already."

Peña joined them. "Red wine, interesting choice." He touched her glass with the neck of his bottle, then looked at Eladio. "If we are to toast our beautiful DEA *amiga*, you will need a *bebida*."

Eladio waved at Jesús, who approached with a tray of champagne.

"I have placed *aperitivos* on the tables." Jesús balanced the tray as Eladio took a flute. "Do you want these passed around?"

"Sí. Then can you place glasses and a bottle on this table?" Eladio turned to Jade and Peña. "I would like you to meet the owner of Captain Jack's, and my friend, Jesús Medina."

"It is nice to meet you." He smiled at Jade and gave Peña a nod. "I will let you know when dinner is close," Jesús said to Eladio.

"Bueno," Eladio replied as his friend delivered appetizers to the younger group, which now included Geovany.

"Geovany is asking about becoming a *Federale*." Peña took a sip from his bottle.

Eladio glanced at Geovany. "I will speak with him." He headed toward the officer who had been an integral part of the raid on Raptor's compound.

"It suits you," Peña touched the lily in Jade's hair, "and this dress." He grinned at her. *"Es muy impresionante."*

"Muchas gracias." Jade's cheeks warmed, and she sipped some wine. "You look very handsome too." She placed a hand inside the shirt's open buttons onto his chest.

Peña stepped closer, his musky cologne invading her senses. "I would like to take you to dinner tomorrow night."

"And when you say dinner," Jade winked, "do you mean takeout at your place, enjoyed in bed?"

"As much as I am hungry for you too," Peña kissed her, "I insist on treating you to a meal before I ravage you throughout the night."

Jade tipped up her glass again. His phone dinged and he frowned at the screen.

"I need another beer." Peña tucked his phone into his back pocket. "Can I get you another glass of wine?"

"Sí, por favor." Jade watched him stride to the bar, ogling his ass as he consulted his phone again.

"Points for the lieutenant fetching you some vino," Sandrine said behind her.

"You really have to stop lurking and listening." Jade laughed.

"I've been on the phone with Oliver, who misses me terribly." Sandrine drained her glass. "I'm afraid the time has come for me to return to San Diego, Love."

Jade hugged her. "When do you leave?"

"I'll have to check flights, but I'm hoping by the end of the week." Sandrine plucked a flute of champagne from the tray. "Should we join the others at the table?"

Jade glanced at Peña, who stood at the bar. His back was to her, and he was on his phone. She scanned the restaurant for Eladio, who was also on his phone.

"You go." Jade grabbed a glass of champagne. "I'll be there in a minute."

She wanted to give Peña a chance to return with her wine. And in the meantime, she'd take advantage of the *Federale's* unguarded moment. He was smiling at whatever was being said by the caller, his merriment reaching his eyes. Unlike Amado, Eladio had more of a runner's body, toned and lean. He threw back his head and laughed, and a wave of jealousy colored her cheeks.

As if he knew she was watching him, Eladio met her eyes and tilted his head. He ended his call and walked toward her."

"Good news?" Jade asked as he approached.

He raised an eyebrow.

She pointed to his phone. "Your phone call."

"My sister, Isla." Eladio smiled and tucked the phone in his back pocket. "She is making plans for after she graduates from university."

"Oh." Jade's cheeks grew hot. "That's exciting news."

Eladio grinned at her. "I am glad to have you alone for a few minutes." He picked up a glass of champagne, touched hers, and took a sip.

Jade sipped some bubbly too. "It is very nice of you and Jesús to throw this party."

"It is my pleasure." He looked at the table with the young people. "I do not know why, but they make me feel old."

Jade laughed and he joined in. "I am sure Lieutenant Peña has already told you how beautiful you look tonight."

"He may have." Jade drained half of her glass.

"I …" He cleared his throat, "I want you to know I will request a different agent for the Zihuatanejo task force so you can return home with Ezmé."

His offer took her by surprise. "So, you're reneging on your request that I be part of the task force?"

"I did not request you, my boss did. Without consulting me." Eladio stepped close to Jade and held her dark stare. "It was never my intention for you to feel as if you had no say."

"I doubt Benson will assign someone else," she finished her drink, "but thank you for the offer."

Eladio handed her another glass, then ran his fingertips along her collarbone. His eyes reflecting the memory of what she looked like under her dress.

"If you do come to Zihuat," he leaned closer, his breath warm on her cheek, "as hard as it might be, I promise to keep our relationship professional."

"Jade!" Ezmé rushed to her sister, Novio in tow. "Valéria is getting Novio's passport tomorrow so we can all fly home together." She waved Gwen over. "And Gwen is coming with us."

Jade exchanged a look with Eladio. "He's free to go?"

"*Sí.*" Eladio nodded and looked at Novio. "And I suggest you do not return to México."

Peña had joined them and looked annoyed that Eladio stood so close to her.

"Are we eating soon?" Peña asked. "I am starving."

"*Sí.* I believe dinner is ready." Eladio motioned toward a large table set for ten.

Sandrine had already claimed a seat and motioned for Jade to sit next to her. After everyone found a spot, Eladio sat in the last chair, which put him at the head of the table, with Jade on his left and Peña on his right.

Jade wanted to move to the other end of the table and sit next to Joy. She seemed to be enjoying herself as she watched Erica and Geovany flirt and laugh over which fork came first. She looked at Novio who quickly removed his arm from around Ezmé's shoulder. Jade smiled at him and saw a relief wash over his face. After her time with Raptor, Ezmé was probably more than capable of handling the enamored young man.

Jesús and another server placed platters of *Filete Ranchero* and *Pollo Margarita* at each end of the table.

"Where do you want the *verduras asadas*?" A young woman holding dishes of roasted veggies asked Jesús.

"In the middle," he smiled at her, *"Gracias."*

She set the plates down, gave him a coy look, and headed back to the kitchen. Jesús placed drinks in front of his guests.

When he put a flute in front of Peña, the lieutenant grumbled, "Can I trade for a *Pacifico*?"

As soon as Peña had his beer, Eladio stood and raised his flute. "I appreciate you all joining me tonight so I can publicly thank Lieutenant Amado Peña, DEA Agents Jade Mendoza and Sandrine Mortieau, FBI Agent Valéria Carrizo, and Officer Geovany Herrera for their bravery and determination in bringing down a human trafficking organization." He tapped Peña's beer bottle, then clinked Jade's flute. *"¡Salud!"*

Pings rang out as everyone clinked their glasses. They shouted, *"¡Salud!"*, and took their drinks. A cacophony of chatter ensued as dishes were passed. Once everyone had eaten their fill of the delicious food, Jesús and his employee cleared the dinner dishes. The young woman returned with a tray of desserts. When it was their turn, Jade and Sandrine did as they always had, picking two different desserts to share.

"Jade," Joy knelt by her chair, "would it be okay if I take the others back to the hotel?"

"Of course," Jade stood, "but I think we're all ready to go back."

"Right," Sandrine exchanged her caramel flan for Jade's chocolate cake, "but we won't all fit into a van."

"Got it." Jade laughed. "You guys go, and Sandrine and I will follow shortly."

"Perfect." Joy turned to the others. "Okay, gang. Let's go."

As the crew headed for the exit, Eladio stood, and Joy hugged him. "Thanks for a wonderful evening."

"De nada," he replied.

Joy smiled at Jade and Sandrine. "See you two soon." Then she walked toward the door.

Heading for the bathroom, Sandrine said, "I need to use the loo."

Peña's phoned dinged. As before, he scowled at the screen.

"Everything okay?" Jade asked. Though he nodded, she could tell something was bothering him.

"Would you all like a night cap?" Eladio moved toward the bar. "Jesús has prepared *carajillos* for us."

"What is a *carajillo*?" Jade followed him. Peña stood next to her at the bar.

"It is a coffee drink," Peña said. "And if we are drinking them this late, I hope Jesús brewed decaf."

Sandrine joined them. "I think the drink sounds delicious."

Eladio turned, eyebrows drawn together. "I am sorry," he said and took a couple of steps toward a man standing at the entrance. "But the restaurant is closed for a private event."

"Eladio Ortiz?" the man asked.

"*Sí*, but—"

Jade saw the gun at the same time Peña yelled, "*¡Pistola!*"

She saw Peña jump in front of Eladio as the shot echoed off the walls of the restaurant. Both men went down, and Sandrine rushed the shooter, tackling him. Jade hurried to Peña's side and could see a red stain blooming on his white shirt.

"*¡Jesús!*" Eladio shouted. "*¡Llame una ambulancia!*"

Peña's eyes were closed and Eladio eased out from underneath him. He checked for a pulse, then looked at Jade. "He is alive."

Jesús appeared with a stack of towels and Eladio pressed two against Peña's chest. "Hold these tight against the wound." Eladio took her hands and placed them on the towel.

"The ambulance is coming." Jesús put a rolled towel under Peña's head and two under his legs.

Jade watched as Eladio crossed the distance to Sandrine who'd managed to restrain the gunman with an electrical cord she'd yanked from a lamp. She handed Eladio a twenty-two revolver. "That's all I found on him."

"Who are you?" Eladio set the gun onto a table.

"I'm Mark Roberts." He glared at Eladio. "I believe you know my wife, Sienna."

CHAPTER FIFTY-SIX

Eladio watched Jade sleep. She sat with her head propped on her forearm, which lay on Peña's hospital bed, her hand holding his. The orange lily had wilted, and the petals stuck to the side of her face. He wanted to be jealous, but how could he justify being envious of the man who'd probably saved his life?

The doctor stepped into the room, a trail of antiseptic air, mixed with scents from a hospital food cart, following him inside. Jade stirred awake and pushed off the bed.

"Surgery went well." The doctor consulted a tablet, scrolling down a screen. "The lieutenant suffered injury to his spleen, but the bullet missed his left kidney. We have repaired the spleen, and he will be able to go home in a few days."

"What type of care will he need at home?" Jade asked.

"That is a very good question." A petite female stepped into the room. "Socorro Cortés." She held her hand out to Eladio, then Jade.

"He will need rest, and must stick to a liquid diet for a week," the doctor replied.

"Lots of *Pacifico* and tequila then," Peña rasped, and all eyes turned to him.

"When you are discharged, a nurse will send you home with a list of approved foods." The doctor set the tablet down on a counter and exited the room.

Cortés stepped to the end of the bed. "Glad you did not die, Lieutenant."

"Why are you here, Detective Cortés?" Pena's narrowed eyes and annoyed tone suggested he'd rather the dark haired beauty was not standing in his hospital room.

Eladio exchanged a look with Jade. He could tell she was wondering the same thing.

"Because you are ignoring my requests to come to Cabo," she looked at Jade, then back at Peña, "and because your niece, Bella, is missing."

"Detective Cortés," Eladio began.

"Coco." She smiled at him. "I would ask for your help, Agent Ortiz, but I heard you are being sent to Zihuat."

"*Sí.*" Eladio nodded and looked at Jade. "But Agent Mendoza and I have a few days before we leave, if you would like assistance."

"I—*mierda*!" Peña grimaced as he tried to sit up.

Jade raised his bed and added another pillow behind his head. "Better?"

He nodded, then continued, "I left Isabella a message. She is probably off with that *pendejo* I told her to stay away from, and will come home when she finally gets bored."

"Lieutenant," Coco began, "the *pendejo* is missing too."

"*¡Maldita sea!*" Peña tried to move his legs to the side of the bed. "You should have led with that, Coco."

"Amado," Jade touched his chest. "You need to stay in bed."

"You need to help me up." Peña shook his head. "And find my clothes."

"*Teniente.*" Eladio's tone was sterner than he intended. "Jade and I will see what we can do to assist Coco while you recover. *¿Entender?*"

"Bien." Peña glared at Eladio but settled back against the pillows. He took Jade's hand in his. "I have not forgotten our dinner date."

"I will bring some flan, and we'll celebrate you not dying." Jade bussed his lips.

"I do not like flan. It is too sweet." Peña smiled at her. "Just bring yourself and a bottle of *Hornitos.*"

Coco raised an eyebrow and looked at Eladio. He managed a smile, despite his discomfort.

"Jade," Eladio cleared his throat, "would you and Coco mind giving me a few minutes alone with Lieutenant Peña?"

"Detective Cortés," the look on Jade's face suggested she didn't appreciate being sent from Peña's room, "can I buy you a cup of shitty hospital coffee?"

"Sí." Coco headed for the door. *"Por favor*, call me Coco."

Jade shot Eladio another look, then smiled at Peña before marching from the room.

"When do you leave for Zihuat?" Peña asked, drawing Eladio's attention.

"I have asked for a delay, but my boss wants me there by the end of the week." Eladio stepped closer to the bed.

"I will be sorry to see her go." Peña closed his eyes.

"Ask her to stay." Eladio met Peña's questioning stare when he opened his eyes. "I told Jade I have requested a replacement, so she does not have to go with me."

"I would like her to stay." Peña shook his head. "But as soon as I can, I need to go to Cabo to find my niece."

"Maybe they will find Isabella before you are discharged," Eladio said. "And you can ask Jade to stay."

"Quizás, but you know how *terco* Agent Mendoza can be." Peña smiled.

"Stubborn indeed," Eladio nodded, "and she might go to Zihuat just to prove a point."

"I would appreciate it though," Peña began and looked down, then back at Eladio, "If you can delay your departure until I am released from here."

"Let me see what I can do." Eladio headed for the door. *"Muchas gracias por salvar mi vida."*

"De nada." Peña gave Eladio a salute as he exited the room.

As much as he wanted Jade to willingly choose to go with him to Zihuatanejo, Eladio felt he owed it to Peña to either persuade her to stay or to at least delay their report date. Besides, he still had to deal with Mark Roberts, who was cooling his heels in a holding cell at the station.

Eladio knew he should feel guilty for his encounter with Sienna, but she hadn't told him she was married. A memory of their time between his sheets flashed in his mind. He knew even if she'd been honest, it wouldn't have made a difference. But Eladio would have been more aware of his surroundings, and might have noticed Mark Roberts following them.

As he rode the elevator to the lobby of the hospital, questions bombarded his brain. *Where was Sienna, and was she safe? Could he and Jade help locate Peña's niece before they had to leave? And, would he be able to go without Jade if she chose to stay with Peña?*

Bright sunshine shown through a window near the exit and striped the floor in front of Jade and Coco. Even though Jade didn't smile when she saw him approaching, Eladio still felt drawn to her—emphasizing how hard it would be to leave her behind.

CHAPTER FIFTY-SEVEN

After a short nap, Jade set up a tracking app on Ezmé's new phone, pleased when the mirror app on her phone showed Ezmé was theoretically sitting right next to Jade. She guessed her baby sister would not be thrilled about Jade always knowing her whereabouts, but after what they'd been through, she didn't think Ezmé would resist too much. Jade also added the WhatsApp to both of their phones as an alternative to texting and using cell service for messaging or calling.

When she'd left the hospital earlier, Jade had headed for *Galerías Mall*. She bought Ezmé's new phone and an iPad for herself since it didn't appear she'd be home anytime soon. Part of her wanted to take Eladio up on his offer to request someone else for the fentanyl task force, but Jade could hit the ground running with what she already knew about the serial killer poisoning *turistas*. Besides, she'd never been to Zihuatanejo. And once her anger dissipated, being there with the handsome *Federale* might have its perks.

She searched social media for mention of Socorro Cortés and Isabella Fuentes. Isabella, who seemed to change her hair color once a week, had a Facebook page and quite the social life: parties, exotic vacations, and plenty of handsome men on her arm. Like Jade and Sandrine, Coco had no social media presence. That was common for people who worked in law enforcement or for a government agency. Coco also seemed more reserved than the effervescent Bella. Both women came from money. For Jade that always triggered the suspicion that family wealth came from nefarious businesses. When Jade signed into the DEA platform, though, it appeared neither woman had a connection to the drug world. She made a mental note to ask Valéria to check the FBI database. If the young agent didn't find anything, Jade would recruit Christopher to do a more in-depth background check.

"I thought you'd be at the hospital." Sandrine headed for the coffee pot. She added a splash of Baileys, then joined Jade.

"When I texted Peña, he asked me to wait until he was through with *hygiene hell*." Jade grinned at her friend.

Sandrine laughed. "I'm surprised he didn't insist you come give him his sponge bath."

Jade's phone chimed and she read the text from Eladio. "Ortiz says he's still searching for Sienna Roberts."

"How bizarre was last night?" Sandrine set her cup down, refilled Jade's, and set a plate of *orejas* on the table. "And who the hell is Sienna? Did you know Ortiz was dating someone?"

"I think *dating* might be a stretch." Jade sipped some coffee. "He called and woke me up to see if I'd go check on Peña. Said he had tried to question Mark Roberts, but the guy asked for a lawyer. In México, that can be a challenge."

"Did he say where his wife is?" Sandrine blew across her cup.

"No, not a word." Jade leaned against her chair back.

"Do you think Eladio knew his, uh, friend, was married?"

Shrugging, Jade said, "I'm not sure it's my place to ask him too many questions."

"Bullshit!" Sandrine wagged her finger at Jade. "That cuckolded husband could have shot all of us last night."

"All right." Jade held up her hands. "I'll ask Eladio more questions when I see him."

"When is Ezmé planning to fly home?"

"I asked her to wait until I know my departure date for Zihuat."

"So you decided to go?" Sandrine raised an eyebrow.

"I don't think Benson will let me out of the assignment and …" Jade began, studying the coffee in her cup.

"And maybe you're not as mad at the fine-looking *Federale* as you thought you were?" Sandrine grinned at her.

"Maybe I'm a little worried about being grilled by my parents as to why both Ezmé and I have been radio silent for a week." Jade plucked a pastry from the plate and took a bite.

"Come on." Sandrine did a circle with her finger. "Tell me the lie you've been practicing for your folks."

Jade took another bite, then sipped some coffee. "I plan to tell them Ezmé lost her phone, and I was on an assignment that didn't allow me to make contact."

"It will do." Sandrine tilted her hand side-to-side. "As long as Ezmé doesn't cave and tell them about being kidnapped by the mysterious Raptor."

"Why do you think she doesn't seem traumatized?" Jade sipped some coffee.

"You," Sandrine covered Jade's hand with hers, "were raped, and you didn't let the experience traumatize you or stop you from living your life." Sandrine squeezed her hand. "Maybe if you tell Ezmé what happened to you, she'll open up about Raptor."

"And she sees the good in people, despite their evilness." Jade swallowed the last of her *orejas*.

"Evil like your *mum*?" Sandrine's eyes twinkled and Jade glared at her. "What? She can't be all bad. She gave birth to you."

Jade's phone chimed and she looked at the text.

Ezmé: *We are going to the marina to say goodbye to Kyla at the bookstore. Want to come?*

Jade: *Is Joy or Valéria going?*

Ezmé: *Valéria*

Jade ended the text thread saying she was needed at the hospital but would see everyone for dinner. She added a kissy-face emoji, to which Ezmé replied with a thumbs-up emoji.

"Ezmé and the rest of the gang are going to Vallarta Beach Books to say goodbye to Kyla." Jade stood and took her dishes to the kitchen. "I'm heading to the hospital, want to join me?"

"Can't." Sandrine cleared her dishes too. "I have a phone date with Oliver in fifteen minutes, and then I'm going to start packing."

"Did you book your flight?"

"No." Sandrine dried her hands on a tea towel. "Kind of want to see how the dance with Peña and Eladio plays out, find out what happened to Ortiz's mystery woman, and make sure you actually get on a plane to Zihuat." Sandrine gave a finger wave and headed for her room.

"Ha ha," Jade called after her, then grabbed her purse and the Kia keys.

The sunny day and warm tropical air made her wish she was headed to the beach, or lying by a pool with a trashy novel, or planning what to wear on her dinner date with Peña. She made good time to the hospital, parked, and took the elevator to the tenth floor. When she approached Peña's room, she could hear him arguing with someone. She peered through the open door.

"Señor Peña," a nurse tied a band around his arm, "if you hold still, your blood draw will go much smoother."

"I do not like needles." He grabbed her wrist to keep her from sticking him.

Jade walked to the bedside and wrapped her hand around his. "Let her do her job, Amado."

"She is using me as a pincushion." He looked at Jade and she almost cried at the pain etched on his face.

"Tell me where we are going on our date." Jade held his hand when he released the nurse's wrist.

"I would prefer to talk about something more stimulating." He smirked.

The nurse neared the vein in his arm. Peña tried to resist, but Jade leaned in and kissed him.

He mumbled, *"Mierda,"* against her lips when the nurse inserted the needle, then settled into their kiss.

"Todo listo." The nurse taped a cotton ball over the prick site and bent Peña's arm at the elbow. "Ring the bell if you need anything." She winked at Jade before making her exit, closing the door behind her.

"She does not have anything I need." Peña drew Jade's lips back to his.

When he tried to reach for a breast, he spasmed in pain and fell back into a stack of pillows.

Jade touched his cheek. "Let's wait to finish," she said and pointed to him, then herself, "this when you're released."

"I know you are," Peña began, kissing the top of her hand, "going to Zihuatanejo with Ortiz." He raised his eyes to hers.

"Hopefully, not before you're home." Jade slid her hand under the sheet.

Peña tried to move toward her, and she placed a hand on his chest. "You could lock the door," he murmured.

"Is this a bad time?" Socorro Cortés asked from the doorway, her face clouded by a frown.

"He had an itch." Jade stood, stifling a giggle.

"Your timing sucks, Cortés," Peña growled. "What is it now?"

"I want to tell you why I am concerned about Bella." She set a carryout tray with four coffees onto the bedside table.

Peña struggled to sit up again, and Jade offered her arm as leverage. He grimaced and she noticed beads of perspiration on his forehead.

"Bien." Peña motioned for a coffee and Jade removed the lid before handing him a cup.

"When she started dating Carlos, I looked into him." Coco took a coffee too. "He's a podcaster who has been investigating a crew pretending to be US Custom Border Patrol agents." She took a sip. "And—"

"Buenos tardes." Eladio stepped into the room.

"Glad you could join the party," Peña quipped.

Eladio raised an eyebrow. "Sorry I am late." He lifted a cup from the tray.

"I was just telling them about Bella's boyfriend," Coco said.

"As I told Detective Cortés last night, most of these scams are run from the US." Eladio sipped coffee and exchanged a glance with Cortés. "But I heard there may be a boiler room operating in Cabo."

When Coco smiled at Eladio, a twinge of jealousy colored Jade's cheeks with the thought of them spending time together.

"Are these the fake CBP Agents who call people, telling them they've intercepted a package mailed to their home address containing cash and drugs?" Jade asked.

"Yes, and then they try to get the mark to reveal personal information like bank account locations, their social security number, and date of birth. But," Coco began and tapped her temple with a finger, "Bella's connection, besides going on a few dates with Carlos, is puzzling me."

"The *pendejo* probably put her in a dangerous situation." Peña tried to get out of bed again.
"I need to find her."

"Amado." Jade placed a hand on his chest. "You know you're not ready to be released."

"As much as I could use your help, lieutenant," Coco said as she cast a look at Jade. "It will not be good if you die." She smiled at Peña, then looked at Eladio. "Can you recommend any agents from your office in Cabo to work as UCs?"

When Eladio hesitated, Jade said. "What about Officer Vázquez from Mazatlán?"

"And if you can use more than one man," Peña added. "I can arrange for Geovany to be transferred."

"Two men would be great." Coco smiled. "I can clear their undercover status with my captain."

"They are both good police officers." Eladio looked at Jade. "Do you want to call Torres and ask about Vasquez?"

Jade felt like the air had been sucked from the room. How could she call Captain Marco Torres and ask for a favor without telling him she now knew he was her biological father?

Eladio's narrowed-eyed stare told Jade he'd misunderstood her hesitation. He probably thought it was because she was still angry at him. "Sure." She smiled. "I'll give him a call."

"Ortiz." Peña said, drawing Eladio's attention. "Has the *cabrón* who shot me said anything?"

"No." Eladio shook his head. "He has only asked for an *abogado*."

"Have you been able to reach his wife?" Jade asked, then wished she hadn't.

Without looking at her, Eladio gave Peña another head shake. "I called the police station in Punta Mita, and they said they will try to locate her."

Jade knew finding a woman in a tourist destination would be daunting. For Eladio's sake, she hoped Sienna Roberts was found soon—and alive.

"I need to make some phone calls." Coco looked at her phone. "It was nice to see you again, Jade. And Lieutenant, let me know when you are released." She headed for the door.

"I will walk you out." Eladio followed her, leaving without a goodbye.

Jade jumped to her feet and touched his arm. Eladio turned and met her questioning stare. "I'll let you know what Torres says about Vázquez."

"*Bien.*" A frown creased his brow and his lips parted as if he planned to say something more.

"Ortiz," Coco called from the elevators. "Coming?"

Eladio gave Jade a head nod and walked away.

When Jade turned back into the room, she found Peña breathing hard, sitting on the edge of the bed, his feet planted on the floor.

"Amado!" Jade rushed to his side. "Damn it!"

"I need to get out of here," he rasped.

"You need to stay in bed." Jade helped him ease back onto the pillows, then lifted his legs onto the bed. "I know you want to find Bella, but you're going to have to trust Eladio, Coco, and me," Jade brushed his bangs from his forehead, "to do what we can to find her."

"Isabella is my older sister's daughter." He shook his head. "My sister died a year ago from cancer and her *pendejo* husband ran off with some floozy." He grasped Jade's hand. "I am all the family Bella has left."

"What is her relationship with Coco Cortés?"

"They have been *amigas* since they were little." Peña smiled. "Their moms grew up together and raised the girls like sisters."

"I Googled them earlier, and it looks like they both come from money," Jade said.

"And not from illegal means." Peña laughed. "My sister's husband's family made their fortune in real estate, and Coco's family owns a fleet of charter fishing boats."

A knock announced Sandrine's arrival and she stepped into the room. "Bloody hell, LT," she exclaimed. She cut her eyes to Jade, then looked at Peña. "You look terrible."

Peña glared at her as she put a brown bag onto the hospital table, next to the discarded coffee cups.

"You're early." Jade stood and hugged Sandrine. "But thanks for bringing dinner."

"I know you didn't eat any lunch so when I had mine, I picked up your food." Sandrine winked at Peña. "And I brought a little present for our wounded partner." She pulled a pint of *Hornitos* from the bag and unscrewed the top. "You should take the first swig."

Peña grinned, tipped the bottle to his lips, then closed his eyes and took a large drink. Jade reached for the bottle, and he opened his eyes, leering at her.

"One thing at a time." Jade sipped tequila, then handed the bottle to Sandrine.

"Hope you're out of here soon." Sandrine raised the bottle, then took her turn. "Okay, kids." She headed for the door. "Have fun."

"Hey," Jade said, halting Sandrine's exit. "How's everyone else doing?"

"Joy's arranging a little dinner party." Sandrine looked at her phone. "And Valéria just texted to let me know she and the others are headed back to the hotel."

"Okay." Jade hugged her again.

"You spending the night here?" Mischief danced in Sandrine's eyes.

"I'm not sure." Jade shrugged.

"I won't wait up." Sandrine flashed a thumbs-up.

Peña's eyes were closed when she stepped back into the room. Jade pulled her phone from her purse and texted Ezmé, telling her she was sorry she'd miss dinner at Joy's. Ezmé's reply was *K* with the heart-eyed emoji. Jade hated missing time with Ezmé, but her little sister was obviously enjoying being with Novio.

"Do you have to leave?" Peña asked.

"No." Jade returned to her seat and took his hand in hers. "Are you hungry?"

"Only if there is a *carnitas de cerdo burrito* in that sack."

"Your doctor said soft food." Jade smiled at him.

Guessing, he said, "Flan?"

Jade shook her head, then lowered the bag to the bed and pulled a to-go container with a foil lid and two plastic spoons from inside. She lifted half of the foil from the top, loaded a spoon and smiled as Peña wrapped his lips around the bite.

He opened his eyes, and swallowed. *"Frijoles refritos con crema agria, queso y salsa picante."*

Jade spooned up a taste for herself. "Joy said you would like it." She finished her bite, the creamy refried bean concoction melting on her tongue.

"And what are you surprising me with for dessert?" Peña grinned at her as she offered him another spoonful.

"I'm not sure you're up for anything more than the chocolate pudding Sandrine brought." Jade reached inside the bag again, grabbing a small container.

Peña wrinkled his nose and Jade laughed.

"It was very nice of you to bring me dinner." Peña waved at the food. "But this is not the date I had planned."

"I know." Jade leaned in and kissed him. "But I wanted to thank you for the flowers and lovely note."

Peña tilted his head. "I wish I had thought to send you flowers." His forehead creased in a frown. "What did the note say?"

Jade blushed. If Peña hadn't sent the flowers and note, then it had to have been Eladio. She wasn't sure she wanted to share what he had written on the card.

"Está bien." Peña touched her cheek. "You do not have to tell me."

Jade reached for the pint of tequila, took a pull from the bottle, then handed it to Peña. He held her stare as he took a few sips.

"Do you know when you leave for Zihuatanejo?" He set the bottle on the table.

"No." Jade shook her head.

"But probably before this," he joked and pointed to her, then himself, "can happen again."

"Probably." Tears sprang to her eyes.

"Jade." Peña shook his head. "Please do not cry."

"I-I—" Jade couldn't stop the tears from flowing.

"Eladio is a good man." Peña pulled her to him, and Jade stretched out next to him on the bed. "But I am hoping you will come see me in Cabo after you capture the fentanyl killer."

Jade turned her face to him, and he kissed her. She wanted to promise she'd take the first flight to Cabo once the serial killer was either arrested or dead. She wanted to ask Amado Peña to wait for her until she was ready, but ready for what? She also wanted to know what waited for her and Eladio Ortiz in Zihuatanejo.

CHAPTER FIFTY-EIGHT

Cup of coffee in hand, Raptor stood on the wide deck and looked out across the Gulf of Honduras toward the sparkling Caribbean Sea. They had landed in Guatemala City safely and spent the night in a luxurious hotel. The next morning, he'd rented a car and they'd arrived in Puerto Barrios late in the day on Wednesday.

He had visited the seaport town with Belen when they were teenagers and had never forgotten the villa she'd pointed at during one of their walks through town. The vivid memory played in his mind as a breeze ruffled the curtains on the open double-slider behind him.

"Mateo." Belen shaded her eyes and pointed. "Do you see that beautiful home up on the cliff?"

"Sí, mi amor." He glanced at the large house, then smiled at her.

"We will live in that house someday." Belen wrapped her arms around his neck and kissed him. "And we will have many kids."

"If we hurry through dinner." He nuzzled her neck. "We could practice our baby-making skills."

"When you marry me." Belen squealed as she wiggled from his arms and ran down the street laughing.

The precious vision evaporated when a seagull screeched somewhere above him. He and Belen hadn't waited until they were married to consummate their love because they planned to marry that summer. But before a wedding could happen, the poor economy in their country had caused them to lose their jobs, so they left Guatemala and set out on the fateful trip to Arizona.

His mind jumped to thoughts of how he would find Belen and young Mateo. He hoped to bring them home to her dream house. He hadn't decided what to do about Blake. He knew she was in love with him. While he was fond of her, he didn't think he'd have room in his life for her once he was reunited with Belen. He also knew the process of finding Belen and his son could take a very long time. And he knew Ezmé was gone forever, but he still yearned for her and sometimes wondered if he could have her in his life too.

His phone pinged and he pulled it from his shorts pocket, smiling at the text from his *sicario*.

Toro: *All quiet in town. No sign of cartel's men.*

Raptor: *Bueno. See you tomorrow for lunch.*

Toro: *Sí*

Raptor had been surprised to find Toro waiting for him at the airport. He had assumed the *sicario* had died in the raid on his compound in *La Pedrera*. Toro had managed to escape. Knowing Raptor and Milo would have headed for the car hidden at the end of the trail through the jungle, he created a diversion and led the *policía* in a different direction.

After he'd learned everything he could from Julio, Toro had made sure the *cocodrilos* feasted on his corpse, then had taken a flight to Guatemala. Once he'd arrived, Toro staked out the airport daily hoping to see his boss. When Raptor and Blake arrived, the *sicario* made eye contact at baggage claim. Toro had bumped into Raptor, handing off a locker key, then exited the airport.

Inside the locker, Raptor found a new iPhone and a note from Toro saying: *Bienvenido a casa.*

Blake interrupted his musing when she wrapped her arms around his bare waist and kissed him between the shoulder blades. She moved to stand beside him, and he put his arm across her shoulders, drawing her close.

"Did you sleep okay?" Blake looked up at him.

"Yes." He smiled at her. "And you?"

"Very well, thanks to you." She stood on tiptoe and kissed him.

"How is your leg?" He brushed her jawline with his thumb.

"Much better." Blake kissed the palm of his hand. "Have you had breakfast?"

"No," he sipped from his cup, "would you like for me to fix something?"

"I'm thinking maybe we have brunch," Blake let her ivory silk nightgown slide to the floor, "after we work up an appetite."

Heat flooded Raptor's loins as he stared at Blake's lovely body. He scooped her up and carried her to the bedroom. When he laid her on the bed, she reached for the top of his shorts. He stepped closer and she pulled them down, then cupped his package in her hand.

Raptor climbed onto the bed next to her and covered a nipple with his mouth. Blake twined her fingers into his hair and held him to her. She arched her back when he moved to her other breast and dropped her hand to his crotch.

He rolled onto his back, bringing her with him until she straddled his groin. Blake lowered herself onto him and they found their rhythm. She bent down and kissed him, rising until he was barely inside of her. He liked when she teased him. Raptor moved his hands to her hips, pulling her back down.

Their sexual encounters were never the same and definitely not boring. Blake leaned back and matched his pace until they were both sated. She snuggled against him, and he stroked her hair for a few minutes.

"I'm thinking shrimp omelets." Blake stood and headed to the bathroom. When she emerged, she wore a pink cotton shirt dress. "Want to eat in bed, or on the deck?"

"Deck." Raptor climbed from the bed. "Showering first." He kissed her as she walked past him on her way to the kitchen.

Standing under the hot spray, Raptor thought back to when he'd bought Belen's villa. Once he'd dispensed with his boss and taken over the human trafficking ring, Raptor realized he was making more money than he could spend. He increased the salaries of his men and began sending money to a cryptocurrency account. Despite successfully restructuring the trafficking business into a matchmaking service, he knew he would eventually walk away from his operation. Looking for a place to escape to, Raptor paid a realtor to keep him apprised of properties for sale near Guatemala City. When the real estate agent emailed him a picture of the villa, rundown and in disrepair, Raptor had bought the property and hired the agent to oversee the renovations.

After toweling off, he dressed in shorts and a linen shirt, then made his way to the kitchen. Blake was fussing with a vase of flowers the wind kept trying to blow over.

"Maybe it is too windy to eat out here." Raptor caught the vase before it crashed to the deck's tile floor. "Come, we will eat by the bay window."

She followed him back inside, padded to the kitchen island and picked up plates and table settings. He pulled a bottle of champagne from an ice bucket, then popped the cork and carried the bubbly and two flutes to the table.

Blake passed him, grabbed a covered serving dish and met him at the small table. She took her seat as he poured champagne into the glasses.

"The omelets smell delicious." Raptor lifted the lid on the dish and served her first. When Blake didn't respond to his compliment, he looked at her and saw her face had crumpled into a wave of tears.

"What is wrong?" He replaced the lid and waited. "Blake?"

"I-I." She lifted her tear-filled eyes to meet his. "I'm pregnant."

Raptor's brain immediately rejected the idea. He knew he couldn't have caused the pregnancy—a fact Blake was unaware of. But now her recent behavior made sense. She'd stopped drinking alcohol and had been cooking healthier meals.

"And …" she whimpered and covered her face with her hands.

"Whatever it is, you can tell me." Raptor pulled her hands down and thumbed away a tear.

"I'm not sure it's your baby." Blake sobbed. "One of the soldiers … he raped me before my first time with you."

Raptor's jaw muscle tightened as he asked, "Do you know his name?"

"Julio." She looked at Raptor. "I didn't think I'd ever need to tell you." She closed her eyes as another round of sobs wracked her shoulders.

"Blake," Raptor waited for her to look at him, "tell me what you need."

"I-I think I'd like to keep the baby, no matter who the father is." She dried her face with a cloth napkin.

"Would you like to go home to your family?" Raptor asked.

"What?" Fear registered in Blake's green eyes. "No. I mean if you want to send me away, I'll understand. But I don't want to go home." More tears wet her cheeks. "Maybe we can wait until I can have a paternity test. Then if you still want me to leave, I will."

Unless his vasectomy from long ago had magically reversed itself, Raptor knew paternity was irrelevant. But since Toro had killed Julio for his betrayal, didn't he owe this baby a future? Though circumstances had caused Blake to allow herself to be captured, should an innocent baby pay the price for their mistakes?

Raptor took Blake's hand and pulled her to her feet. "There is no need for a paternity test." He touched her still-flat stomach and smiled. "We have survived so much." Raptor kissed her. "I am confident we can survive being parents."

CHAPTER FIFTY-NINE

The witness paperwork for Nacho lay in the middle of Eladio's desk. He had texted Geovany asking him to attend a meeting at noon with him and Detective Cortés. Peña's suggestion to send Geovany to Cabo to assist Cortés in her investigation of the crew posing as Custom Border Patrol Agents, and their telephone scam, made sense. And Cabo would be the perfect place to stash Nacho until Raptor's men were brought to trial.

He'd spent the morning packing his minimal belongings and giving notice to his landlord. He knew he should have negotiated to get a partial refund for May's rent since he would be gone before the first, but he hated the idea of taking money out of the man's pocket due to his employer's poor planning.

Eladio looked at the text from Salas again and resisted the urge to reply with the middle finger emoji. His boss wanted Eladio and Jade in Zihuatanejo by Friday for a meeting with Captain Valdez, who had another poisoning death on his hands.

Dread mingled with his anger at the thought of telling Jade their departure date. After seeing her with Peña at the hospital, Eladio wouldn't be surprised if she decided to take him up on his offer to request a different agent for the task force. He still didn't understand what Jade saw in Peña, but since the lieutenant had saved his life, he felt the right thing to do was to step aside. It would be interesting, though, to see if Jade and Peña could continue their relationship from separate cities.

Eladio had planned to ask Jade when they had their nightcap *carajillos* at Captain Jack's if she liked the flowers he'd sent, hoping she would see the poem as a romantic request for her to spend the night with him. But Mark Roberts had shown up at the bar, intent on killing Eladio. After Peña took the bullet meant for him, mentioning the flowers was the last thing on Eladio's mind.

He thought back to his initial musings that his attraction to Jade was because of his time with Sarita. But the more he learned about Jade Mendoza, the more he wanted to know about her. Personal things like her favorite color. What kind of music did she listen to? What were her plans for the future? Jade's naked body flashed in his mind and a shiver raced down his spine, sparking desire in his loins. It reminded him how much he liked making love to her.

"Dios ayúdame." Eladio said to his empty office. "How am I going to work with her every day and remain professional?" He was pretty sure God didn't plan to weigh in on his dilemma.

To distract himself from thoughts of Jade, Eladio dialed the police station in Punta Mita.

"Bueno." A male voice boomed in his ear.

"¿Puedo hablar con el Oficial Romero?"

"Un momento." The voice replied, then placed him on hold.

"Romero," he said.

"Hola, Oficial Romero." Eladio touched the speaker button on his phone. "This is Agent Ortiz, and I am calling to see if you have had any luck locating *Señora* Roberts."

"Glad you called, Ortiz." Eladio heard Romero flipping through a notebook. "I located the house your friend was staying in and spoke with her *amigas*." Another pause. "Her *amiga* Brittany said *Señora* Roberts left the house with her husband on Tuesday morning." Romero coughed, then continued, "Damn cold. Brittany didn't think her friend planned to return. She assumed *Señora* Roberts went back to Miami with her husband."

Eladio's stomach flipped, and his *huevos rancheros* breakfast rose into the back of his throat.

"Ortiz?" Romero said.

"*Sí.*" Eladio swallowed to clear the bile. "*Gracias*. This information is very helpful."

"*De nada.*" Romero coughed again. "Let me know if I can do anything else." Then he disconnected.

Eladio didn't have any proof Sienna was dead. But he felt if she was alive, she would have contacted him. He stood, grabbed his gun from the top drawer, slid his phone into a pocket, and picked up the Jeep keys from the desktop. He turned toward the door and found Detective Cortés watching him.

"Did I get the time wrong?" She looked at her phone.

"No." Eladio returned his gun to the drawer. "*Por favor*, come in." He pulled his phone free and placed it on the desk with his keys, then sat down.

"You might as well tell me what is going on." Coco took a seat.

"I just learned Mark Roberts picked up his wife Tuesday morning from the house she was staying in with friends in Punta Mita."

"And your frown tells me you are worried about her." Coco studied him. "We can talk to him together if you would like."

"Agent Ortiz," Geovany said from the doorway. "Are you ready for me?"

"*Sí.*" Eladio nodded and pointed to the vacant chair next to Cortés. "This is Detective Cortés from Cabo San Lucas."

Coco stood and extended her hand. "Nice to meet you."

Geovany gave her an admiring smile and shook her hand, then they took their seats.

Eladio looked at them. For a second, he couldn't remember why they were in his office.

"Officer Herrera." Coco took the lead. "Would you be interested in coming to Cabo to help with an investigation? We are looking into a crew posing as CBP agents, running a telephone scam."

Geovany looked at Eladio, then back at Cortés. "*Sí*. I would be very interested."

"*¡Bueno!*" Coco slapped Geovany on the shoulder. "Now, I need to tell you both something I would rather Peña does not know just yet."

"*Continua.*" His interest piqued, Eladio refocused.

"We believe this crew is being led by a female, and she is killing men in Cabo."

"Because?" Eladio asked.

"Not sure." Coco shrugged. "She manages to have sex with them first, so she could be driven by power or anger. Or she is just a demented serial killer."

"So more than one body?" Geovany asked.

"Three so far." Coco's phone chimed and she looked at the screen. "Thank God." She smiled at Eladio. "Isabella is home safe."

"Did she say where she has been?" Eladio reached for his phone.

"No." Coco shook her head. "Her text says: *Long story*."

"I will call Peña—" Eladio tapped his phone alive.

"Ortiz." Coco stood. "I would like to tell him, if that is okay."

"*Bien.*" Eladio raised an eyebrow and nodded. "Geovany and I will go over the details of his transfer, and we can meet later."

"*Bueno.*" Coco headed for the door. "But do not worry about meeting with me, go see *Señor* Roberts."

Eladio came to his feet as soon as Coco left, retrieving his gun, phone, and keys from the top desk drawer. "Geovany, I need you to speak with Captain Rivera and make arrangements for your transfer." He reached the door, turned, and added, "Also talk to the prosecutor's office and request that Nacho and his family be transferred with you. I think he would be a good asset for you in Cabo."

As he headed down the hallway, he heard Geovany say, "*Copia.*"

The afternoon sun held the temperature at eighty-two, so Eladio lowered the windows as he cranked the Jeep's engine. The fresh sea air, albeit a touch too warm, was a welcome replacement for the stuffiness of his office. His phone buzzed and he looked at a text from Jade.

Jade: *Benson called. We leave on Friday.*

Eladio: *Correcto*

Jade: *Can we meet for a drink?*

Eladio hesitated. He wasn't sure what mood he'd be in after interrogating Mark Roberts. But he knew he couldn't avoid meeting with Jade, since they'd soon be on a plane together headed for Zihuatanejo.

Eladio: *Captain Jack's at 7.*

Jade: *Copy*

Traffic slowed and Eladio honked his horn. He ran a hand through his hair and thought about how he planned to approach Mark Roberts. His logical ideas always morphed into him pulling his gun and shooting Roberts between the eyes.

He whipped around a stopped car and cut into the next lane. Maybe he should have had Cortés come with him to make sure he remained professional. Another break in traffic gave him an opportunity to shoot through a yellow light and break free of the bottleneck.

Eladio parked and headed for the entrance, the late afternoon sun raising a film of sweat on his skin. He stepped to the booking desk and waited for the officer to acknowledge him.

"*Buenos tardes.*" He looked at Eladio. "Who are you seeing?"

Eladio placed his credentials on the counter. "Mark Roberts."

"*Sala cuatro.*"

"*Gracias.*" Eladio handed his gun to the guard at the door and waited to be buzzed through.

"Roberts is on his way," the guard said as Eladio passed by.

Eladio opened the door to room four and stepped inside. He chose a spot at the back of the room and leaned against the wall. Another guard ushered Mark Roberts into the room and pointed to a chair. Roberts stared at Eladio as the guard secured his handcuffs to the metal ring on the table.

"I can stay," the guard said.

"We will be fine." Eladio glanced at the guard, then back at Roberts.

The guard nodded and left the room, pulling the door closed.

"I know you took Sienna from the vacation house in Punta Mita." Eladio focused on staying calm.

Roberts didn't react, just continued to stare at Eladio, his light gray eyes revealing nothing.

"Why did you kill her?"

A slight grin curved Roberts' lips.

"Where is her body?"

Roberts moved slightly, and his eyes widened.

"Her family deserves to give her a proper burial."

Mark Roberts looked down for a beat, then raised his eyes. Eladio saw pure evil staring back at him.

"You will be charged with the murder of your wife, Mr. Roberts." Eladio headed for the door. "And I plan to make sure you rot in one of our *fine* prisons."

Roberts didn't flinch, and Eladio reached for the knob.

"She wasn't dead," Roberts said.

Eladio turned to face him. "Where is she?"

"You should have heard her scream when the crocodiles had their way with her."

Eladio crossed the room and placed his hands around Roberts' neck. As he squeezed, Roberts laughed in his face, the sound driving Eladio's anger.

The guard was back with reinforcements, and they pulled Eladio off Roberts. One guard shoved Eladio toward the door, and another stood between him and Roberts.

As the guard dragged Eladio from the room, Mark Roberts yelled, "You should have heard her scream!"

CHAPTER SIXTY

It had been a whirlwind morning and Jade was exhausted. After breakfast with everyone in the Dragonfly Lounge, Jade had repacked her suitcase and left a voice mail for Marco Torres regarding Tomas Vázquez. The day had begun its ascent toward the estimated high temperature of ninety when she'd dashed out to buy a thank you gift for Joy and journals for Ezmé, Erica, and Gwen. She'd also found something for Peña.

Now, she stood in front of the bathroom mirror assessing her outfit. Jade turned and looked at the crisscross straps stretching across her bare back. Though the silver crepe top made her a little uncomfortable, Jade like the way it looked with her violet skirt. She picked up the bottle of perfume she'd splurged on, Dirty Coconut. Besides loving the name, she also like the earthy scent with just a hint of coconut. She stepped into a pair of dark gray slides, added a spritz of perfume, and headed back to the kitchen.

Sandrine walked into the suite with an armload of shopping bags. "Bloody hell it's hot out there." She placed her items on the dinette table.

"Did you get the pens?" Jade asked.

"Yes, mum." Sandrine handed Jade three blue boxes.

"Perfect." She added them to gift bags. "Okay, I think I'm ready." Jade looked at Sandrine. "You?"

"Yes, but I don't look as stunning as you." Sandrine whistled. "Got a date later?"

"You always look beautiful, and with minimal effort." Jade pointed at Sandrine who wore a turquoise wrap tank top and tan linen capris.

"Thanks, Love," Sandrine smiled, "now stop avoiding my question."

"I'm going to the hospital to see Peña," Jade fussed with the gift bags, "then meeting Eladio for a drink at Captain Jack's."

"So, two dates in one night," Sandrine teased.

"One goodbye, and one 'what's the plan.'" Jade countered.

"When do you and Ortiz leave for Zihuat?" Sandrine poured the last of the coffee into a mug.

"The bosses want us there tomorrow, but I'm hoping Eladio can delay until everyone else has left." Jade added their signed card to Joy's gift bag. "What time is your flight?"

"Three-thirty." Sandrine hugged Jade. "I'm going to miss you." She held Jade at arm's length, tears shining in her brown eyes. "And I seriously wish I could stay to see how things end with the lovesick lieutenant and the brooding *Federale*."

Jade laughed and wiped away her own tears. "Things will end with a goodbye kiss for Peña and a—" Jade's phone chimed. "It's Joy. She says everything's ready in her suite if we'd like to come up."

"Your failure to share how things end with Eladio did not escape me." Sandrine picked up Joy's gift. "Are you nervous about talking to Ezmé?"

"Yes," Jade gathered the other three bags and they headed from their suite, "but I'll feel better once I talk to her since I'm not going home too."

The elevator doors whooshed open, and they stepped inside. Jade pushed the button for the PENTHOUSE and the car shot upward.

Joy stood at the open doorway to her suite and smiled when they stepped from the elevator.

"I can't believe it's only been a week since you both arrived." Joy headed inside. "It feels like our ordeal lasted much longer."

"We're glad it's over too," Sandrine said.

"Jade," Ezmé crossed to her sister, "we just booked our flights home."

"Great." Jade hugged Ezmé. "When do you leave?"

"Tomorrow at three." Ezmé took Jade's hand and led her to a seating area. Large windows looked out on picturesque Banderas Bay. "I called mom, and she and dad are picking Gwen and me up." Ezmé sat on a couch next to Novio, who looked like he was ready to run if Jade made a move toward him.

"I'm sure our folks will be glad to see you." Jade smiled at Novio, and he relaxed slightly.

"Our parents are picking us up too," Valéria said. "We're very grateful to you and Agent Ortiz for allowing Novio to leave Puerto Vallarta."

"Given his intent was to rescue my sister," Jade looked at Ezmé, who now held Novio's hand. "I think he deserves a second chance." She drilled Novio with a dark stare. "Don't blow the opportunity."

"*Sí.*" Novio stuttered. "I mean no, I will not be in trouble again."

"Good." Jade nodded, then said, "Ezmé, can I talk to you alone?"

"Sure," Ezmé popped up from the couch, "about what?"

Without responding, Jade plucked Ezmé's gift bag from the bar counter and led the way to the large dining room. She set the bag on the gleaming *parota* table and pulled out two chairs.

"This seems serious." Ezmé faced Jade, hands on hips. "Is this about Novio?"

"No. Please sit down." Jade sat.

Ezmé took her seat and crossed her arms. Jade slid the gift bag toward her and Ezmé looked inside. She lifted out a journal with a cover featuring a purple dragonfly and then the blue pen box.

"It's beautiful, Jade." Ezmé smiled. "Thank you."

"You're welcome." Jade rubbed her palms on her skirt. "You don't have to tell me about your time with Raptor," she took a deep breath, "but I wanted to tell you I was raped a long time ago, so I know what you've been through." She pointed at the journal. "I tried seeing a counselor, which I encourage you to do, but I found journaling thoughts about my experience helped me put the trauma behind me."

"Mateo," Ezmé looked down, then back at Jade, tears pooling in her eyes, "didn't rape me."

Jade nodded and waited for Ezmé to continue.

"I-I." She swiped away tears. "I met Mateo for coffee several times before all of this happened. Although I didn't know who he really was until Novio took me." Ezmé held Jade's hands in hers. "I don't want you to think badly of me, but I was attracted to Mateo and wanted to be with him." She tilted her head, a look of sadness clouding her eyes. "My only regret is that Novio will not be marrying the girl he fell in love with."

"Are you in love with Novio?" Jade asked.

"Yes." Ezmé smiled. "I want to be married to Novio, to be a wife and a mother." She swiped away a tear. "But I have—had feelings for Mateo. And despite how it came to be, I'm not sorry for my time with him."

Ezmé held her stare. Jade had feared her sister had been traumatized by a monster, but now saw only a mature young woman. She also admired her little sister for admitting she wanted something exciting before she settled into an existence where she might lose herself for a time.

"I'm proud of you, and though I'm confused about your relationship with—Mateo, I understand how you feel about him more than you know." Jade stood and pulled Ezmé into her arms. "Also, you should know that if Novio hurts you, I will kill him." Jade held her sister away from her and smiled.

"A fact he is well aware of." Ezmé laughed. "Thank you for the journal." She placed the notebook and pen box back in the sack. "I will put it to good use."

"And you told mom our little white lie?" Jade hated asking Ezmé to fib, but it seemed better than their mother knowing the truth.

"I started to tell her. She said she wasn't worried about us, so I didn't push the issue."

"Sounds like mom." Jade smiled.

The sisters were joined by the others as lunch arrived. After everyone had taken a seat, Jade and Sandrine handed out the remaining gifts. Joy smiled at the blue dragonfly light they had bought for the hotel's lounge.

"It's perfect." She hugged Jade, then Sandrine. "But I should be giving you gifts for rescuing my Erica."

"We just did our jobs." Sandrine said.

"The journal is perfect." Erica held hers up for them to see the pair of dolphins gracing the cover.

"I love mine too," Gwen said, fingering the mermaid on her cover.

"I ..." Jade said, then pointed to herself and Sandrine, "we ... encourage you to write about your experience with Raptor and his crew."

"We were blessed no one was ..." Sandrine added, "well, let's just say we're glad everyone's okay. But if the memory of your ordeal becomes too much to handle, get some counseling too."

"Now," Joy clapped her hands, "let's eat before these beef *barbacoa* tacos grow cold and the sunset margaritas get warm."

Valéria came to Jade and Sandrine's seats, and the two agents stood.

"I can't thank you both enough for everything you've done." Valéria offered her hand to Jade, who wrapped her in a hug instead.

"It was a pleasure working with you too." Sandrine also hugged the young FBI agent.

"What's next for you?" Jade asked.

"I requested a few months of desk work at the Phoenix field office." Valéria glanced at her brother. "I want to make sure Novio settles in before I take another assignment."

"I'd—" Jade began.

"You'd like me to keep an eye on Ezmé and Gwen too," Valéria said.

"Yes." Jade smiled at her.

"I plan to watch all of them like a mother hen—for both of us." Valéria laughed. "We'd better eat, or Joy will just order another round of hot food."

"Good plan, cause I'm starving." Sandrine took her seat.

Jade looked at the time on her phone. She didn't have to hurry to the hospital, so she sat down and served herself a couple of tacos. She sipped some margarita, the tang of orange dancing on her tongue, and looked at her tablemates. Joy had been right. Jade agreed their time together felt longer than a week. As she chewed a bit of spicy taco, she realized everyone but Joy, Erica and herself would be on their way home tomorrow.

"Thinking about your impending dates?" Sandrine grinned.

"I'm thinking how lucky we are everyone is safe and able to go on with their lives." Jade sipped more margarita.

Sandrine lifted her glass and touched Jade's. "Do you feel better about Ezmé's ordeal?"

"Yes." Jade took another drink. "My little sister is a stronger woman than me."

"No." Sandrine smiled at Jade. "She's strong because of *you*."

Jade snuck out while the others were enjoying a second round of margaritas. She stopped in her suite and picked up the wrapped gift for Peña, then hopped into the Kia and headed for the hospital. Even though the temperature had warmed to near ninety, Jade had the windows rolled down to welcome the swirling salty sea air.

She'd been awake from one AM to three AM, comparing her connection with Peña to her interactions with Eladio. Sandrine had been right when she said Jade needed some stress relief. Peña had been the perfect distraction. He made her feel sexy and desirable, but she couldn't see herself in a long-term relationship with the handsome lieutenant. When she thought about her time with Eladio, Jade felt something different than an intense sexual need. And as boring as it sounded in her mind, she couldn't deny he made her feel safe. What had Sarita said? *"You should pick Eladio. He is a good man."*

Of course, if she was being honest, Jade wasn't sure she was ready for any type of relationship. Her mom's wise words from long ago flitted through her mind: *True love is not what the body desires, but what the heart knows to be true.* The idea of working with Eladio Ortiz in Zihuatanejo, without the attention of Amado Peña, washed away any second thoughts she had about her next assignment.

Jade stepped from the elevator and headed to Peña's room. When she entered, she found Detective Cortés sitting in the chair Jade usually occupied, holding his hand. The two of them were laughing. As ridiculous as it was, a twinge of jealousy colored Jade's cheeks as she knocked on the doorjamb.

"It's good to hear you laugh." Jade stood at the end of the bed.

"Coco just told me the good news." Peña withdrew his hand from hers and she came to her feet. "Isabella is home safe."

"That's great." Jade smiled at him. "Does this mean you won't have to go to Cabo after all?"

"Yes." Peña flashed a wide grin. "And I'm being released tomorrow."

"I should be going." Coco headed for the door. "I told Bella you will be home tomorrow."

"Bueno." Peña gave Coco a thumbs-up. "Thank you for the good news."

"De nada," she smiled at him. "I will check in with you *mañana.*"

Before she left, Coco looked back, and Jade thought she saw an envious stare. She maintained her position at the end of the bed, and Peña gave her a questioning look.

"Is that for me?" He pointed at the gift she'd laid on the bed.

Jade picked up the present, handed it to him, and sat down. Peña turned the package over in his hands, then ripped away the paper. He smiled at the framed picture of him touching the lily in her hair, both of them smiling, then ran a finger across the etched message at the bottom of the frame.

THIS ~ WAS FUN

"You look so …" Peña raised his eyes to hers and grinned.

"Sandrine took the picture." Jade returned his smile.

"I love *this*, but I do not have a gift for you." Peña took her hand in his. "When do you leave?"

"I'm not sure." Jade shrugged. "As soon as tomorrow, or maybe not until Saturday."

"Saturday would give me time to take you to dinner tomorrow night." He raised her hand to his lips. "But I may not be able to give you a proper send-off."

"Dinner would be lovely." Jade stood and kissed him.

Peña placed a hand at the back of her head and held her lips to his, kissing her as if it could be the last time.

When he released her lips, Jade said, "I'm glad Isabella is safe."

"*Sí.*" Peña nodded. "Is your sister headed home yet?"

"She and the others leave tomorrow." Jade crumpled the wrapping paper into a ball and set it on the hospital table, along with the photo.

"Eladio texted. He is arranging for Geovany to be transferred to Cabo to assist Coco in her CBP telephone scam."

"He's a good officer, and this type of assignment will give him more experience."

"Jade." Peña took her hand again. "I know *this*," he pointed to her then himself, "may be over once you leave for Zihuat. But I will always just be a plane ride away."

"Same for me." Jade smiled. "Have you ever thought about how hard it is to have a lasting relationship, given our jobs?"

"Not until I met you." Peña pulled her to him for another kiss.

Jade's phone chimed, and he touched his forehead to hers before letting her go. She looked at the screen and was surprised to see a text from Jesús Medina.

Jesús: *Can you come to CJs ASAP?*

Jade: *Yes. What's up?*

Jesús: *Ortiz is here in bad shape.*

Jade: *On my way.*

"I have to go." Jade stood.

"Someone in trouble?" Peña sat up and grabbed her hand.

"It's Ortiz." Jade placed a hand on his chest. "Jesús says he's at the bar and not doing well." She leaned down and kissed him.

"You will let me know when you are leaving?" he asked.

"Yes." Jade walked toward the door. "And you keep me posted about your release from here."

Peña's *"Sí,"* echoed behind her as she headed down the hallway.

When Jade reached the lobby, she hurried to the Kia and raced toward Captain Jack's. She tried to imagine what would send Eladio on a bender. For a few minutes she worried it had been her behavior, something he'd seen between her and Peña, or her hesitation to call Torres. Of course, it could also have nothing to do with her.

Jade pulled up next to the curb in front of the bar, climbed from the Kia, and headed inside toward whatever waited for her.

CHAPTER SIXTY-ONE

Eladio waved at Jesús and pointed to his empty shot glass. When his friend looked past him, he turned to see Jade Mendoza headed toward him.

"*¡Maldita sea!*" Eladio slapped the bar and glared at Jesús. "Why did you call her?"

Jade sat on the barstool next to Eladio. "Because you've obviously had too much to drink."

"No." He shook his head. "Just getting started." He raised his glass. "*¡Uno más!*"

Jade nodded at Jesús and held up two fingers. He brought another glass and filled both with *Herradura* tequila. Eladio narrowed his eyes at her when she picked up both glasses.

"I'll give you your shot as soon as you tell me what the hell is going on." Jade sipped from her glass.

Eladio scowled at her, then ran a hand over his face. When he looked at her again, he knew he hadn't hidden his pain because she covered his hand with hers.

"Sienna Roberts is dead."

Jade handed him the shot and downed hers as he emptied his glass. Eladio turned the shot glass upside down on the bar and slid off his barstool, almost falling to the floor. Jesús caught him under the arms and held him steady.

"Let go of me." Eladio tried to extract himself. "I am going home where I can drink in peace." He pointed at Jade. "And you are—"

"Driving. I'm parked in front," Jade said and looked at Jesús. "Can you help me get him in my car?"

Jesús nodded and guided Eladio outside. Jade opened the passenger door and Eladio fell onto the seat.

"Thanks," she said to Jesús before climbing behind the wheel. He gave her a nod, then looked at Eladio through the window. Eladio flipped him off and Jesús headed back inside.

"You can drop me in front of the building." Eladio stared out the window.

Jade didn't respond, and he sat in silence as they drove the short distance to his apartment. She pulled into the small parking lot and found a spot near the entrance. Eladio opened the door and stumbled out of the car. By the time Jade reached his side, he had his keys in hand and was almost to the building. He punched a code into the keypad on a wall next to the entrance and the doors swung open.

Eladio stepped inside. "You do not have to escort me any further." He walked toward the elevators.

Jade silently followed him, and he didn't try to stop her when she entered the car. Without a word, he unlocked the door to his apartment and walked straight to the kitchen. He opened his fridge, pulled out two beers and popped off the tops.

"I do not have *Corona*." He handed her a *Pacifico,* then crossed to a couch and sat down.

Jade took a seat in a battered armchair and tipped the beer to her lips. Eladio picked at the label on his bottle, then finally took a sip.

"Do you want to talk about it?" Jade asked.

Eladio drank half of his beer. "Her husband killed her." He emptied the bottle and headed back to the kitchen.

Jade followed him and when he reached for a bottle of *Hornitos*, she touched his arm. "I'll make us some coffee."

Eladio ignored her and took the fifth back to the couch. He could hear Jade searching the cupboards. Then the sound of coffee brewing echoed from the kitchen. Jade resumed her seat and raised an eyebrow. He wasn't bothering with a shot glass and drank straight from the bottle.

"The bastard fed her alive," Eladio tipped the fifth to his lips, then took a long pull, "to the *cocodrilos*."

He noticed a flicker of revulsion cross Jade's face. A vision of Lexi's mutilated body lying on the beach flashed in his mind. She reached for the *Hornitos*, and he passed the bottle to her. Jade took a gulp, then set the fifth onto the coffee table.

"I-I'm sorry." Jade looked at him and he saw his pain reflected in her eyes.

"It is my fault she is dead." Eladio closed his eyes for a few minutes, opening them when he felt her sit next to him on the couch.

"Did you know she was married?" Jade handed him a cup of coffee.

"No." He shook his head, then set the cup next to the *Hornitos* bottle.

"Eladio," Jade placed her hand on his thigh, "you know her death isn't your fault."

He covered his face with his hands and tried to believe Jade's declaration, but the fact remained. He'd had a one-night stand with a married woman, and now she was dead. Jade shifted and he grabbed her hand before she could leave his side.

"I—" Eladio looked down at his hand holding hers. "I do not want to be alone."

"Okay." Jade settled into the couch, and her warm body felt comforting.

"I delayed our flights to Zihuat until Monday." Eladio picked up his cup and sipped some coffee. "Salas was not happy, but I told him I could not leave until murder charges are filed against Mark Roberts."

"And you think that will happen before we leave?" Jade's tone was skeptical.

"Yes." He set his cup back down. "I spoke with the prosecutor's office after Roberts confessed." Eladio flinched as Roberts' words echoed in his mind, *You should've heard her scream.*

"What?" Jade turned his face to hers.

Eladio kissed her, then backed away. *"Lo siento."* He stood and ran a hand through his hair. "I will understand if you need to go."

Jade walked to him and kissed him. "I don't want to leave."

"I can order some takeout then, and we can just talk." Eladio reached for his phone.

"Eladio." Jade took his hand in hers and led him toward the bedroom. "We can eat later and talk all night if you'd like, but—"

He stopped and pulled her to him, covering her lips with his. As badly as he wanted to make love to her, Eladio knew he couldn't do so in his bed, where Sienna's scent still lingered.

Jade tugged at his shirt, and he helped her pull the polo over his head. Eladio ran his hands under her crepe blouse and found her breasts, then returned his lips to hers as they stumbled backwards until they hit a wall. He stripped off her top and covered a nipple with his mouth. Jade moaned and reached for the button of his chinos. Eladio stepped back from her and headed for the guest bedroom, Jade following him. If she understood why he chose the guest room, she didn't say so. He removed his shoes and stepped out of his pants as Jade moved to him.

She kissed his chest and lowered her hand to his crotch, where his desire for her was revealed. He took a deep breath to curtail his need for release. Jade raised her face to his and he kissed her, twining his fingers into her dark hair. She stepped away and let her skirt float to the floor, then walked past him in nothing but a lacy white thong. Jade laid on the bed and crooked her finger at him.

Eladio joined her on the bed and hooked the thong with his fingers, kissing her flat torso as he slid her panties off. When he moved his mouth to her breast and kissed her dragonfly tattoo, she clawed at his back. He lowered himself to meet her rising hips and kissed her as their rhythms fell in sync.

"Despite my earlier promise," Eladio looked into Jade's eyes, "I would like for us to be more than partners."

"Bueno, Señor Moon," Jade twined her hands around his neck, "because I have no intention of letting the sun walk me home in the morning."

Eladio smiled and kissed her, thankful this would not be his last time in Jade Mendoza's arms.

CHAPTER SIXTY-TWO

Jade woke to find Eladio missing from the bed. When she shuffled into the kitchen wearing a shirt she'd plucked from his suitcase, she saw he'd showered and donned a pair of jeans.

He greeted her with a kiss and a cup of coffee. She sat at the dinette table, taking advantage of his focus on whipping eggs in a bowl to ogle his bare chest and washboard stomach. Despite their lovemaking until the wee hours of the morning, a flutter of desire suggested she hadn't had enough of the handsome *Federale*.

"If you do not stop watching me with your bedroom eyes," he grinned at her, "I will have to take you back to bed."

"I promise not to resist." Jade crossed her legs and loved that he took in the sight. Her phone chimed and she looked at a text from Ezmé.

Ezmé: *Are you coming to the hotel or meeting us at the airport?*

"Everything okay?" Eladio added the eggs to a skillet of browned chorizo.

"Ezmé wants to know if I'm coming back to the hotel or meeting her at the airport."

He pointed at her. "I think you may want to wear something other than my shirt or yesterday's clothes." He grinned and stirred the eggs.

"Do you want to come to the airport?" Jade thumbed her response: *Hotel. See you soon.*

"*Sí*. I would like to come with you." Eladio plated their breakfast and served her first. After refilling their cups, he took his seat.

"This smells wonderful." Jade smiled at him, then forked in a bite of the spicy sausage scramble.

Eladio watched her eat. "Would you like to leave the hotel and stay here until we leave for Zihuat?"

"I ..." When she hesitated, a slight crease etched his brow.

"You have plans with Peña?" He studied his plate and took a bite.

"Eladio," she touched his arm and waited until he looked at her, "it's just a good-bye dinner."

They ate in silence for a few minutes, then he stood and so did Jade. She put her arms around his waist and drew him close. Eladio tilted her head up and kissed her, and Jade was tempted to lead him back to bed.

"I do not believe I have a right—yet," he said, and tucked a strand of hair behind her ear, "to ask you not to—"

"I Googled spleen surgery recovery." Jade stood on tiptoes and bussed his lips. "If he's actually released from the hospital, all he'll be able to manage is dinner." She pulled his shirt over her head and headed down the hall. "A quick shower and I'll be ready to go."

Jade squealed when Eladio grabbed her from behind and carried her back to the guest bedroom.

"We don't have time," she giggled.

"We will be quick." Eladio laid her down.

Jade didn't want to be quick, but when he entered her, she was swept up in their intense passion and enjoyed the fast track to another glorious orgasm.

Eladio had cleaned the kitchen while Jade showered and dressed in her clothes from yesterday. They took the Kia back to the hotel, and Jade kissed him goodbye before he headed to the station. When she walked into the hotel, Joy was standing at the check-in desk and rushed to greet her.

"Girl," she grinned at Jade, "I'd like to demand the details that go with your luminous smile, but everyone's waiting for us upstairs."

"What time do we need to leave for the airport?" Jade asked as they stepped into the elevator.

"Half hour." Joy pushed the PENTHOUSE button. "All the bags are downstairs with the bellmen, so we'll just need a van when we're ready to go."

"Eladio is picking me up and we're going to the hospital after all the flights leave." Jade held the door for Joy when the elevator arrived at her floor.

"Okay." Joy opened the suite door. "So, are you and …?"

"And?" Jade raised an eyebrow.

"I know one of those handsome cops landed your heart." Joy faced her palms up. "I just don't know which one?"

"What's the question?" Jade smiled at her friend.

"Would you … and whoever, like to use the suite you're in until you have to leave for Zihuat?"

"Yes." Jade hugged Joy. "That would be great."

"You're finally here." Sandrine handed Jade a glass of champagne. "Nice outfit." She took a sip of bubbly. "Looks similar to what you were wearing yesterday."

"Come on." Joy headed for the seating area with the stunning view. "We wanted to have a last group toast."

Jade's phone chimed and she looked at the screen.

Eladio: *Can you catch a ride to the airport, and I will meet you there.*

Jade: *Yes. What's up?*

Eladio: *Explain when I see you.*

Jade: *Okay*

"All good?" Sandrine asked over her shoulder.

"Yes. I'd like to make a toast," Jade held her glass aloft, "here's to each of you, and to all of your new beginnings."

Clinks rang out as they touched each other's flutes, followed by loud slurps and lots of laughter. Jade took in each smiling face. Even Gwen seemed more relaxed. Jade was grateful to have played a part in their happy endings.

"I'm going to change," Jade said to Sandrine. "I'll be right back."

"You have fifteen minutes," Joy called after her. When she arrived at her floor, her phone rang. She took a deep breath at the sight of Marco Torres' name on the screen.

"Captain Torres." Jade steadied her voice and entered her suite. "Thanks for calling me back."

"It was good to hear from you."

Jade heard something different in Marco's usually professional tone as she set the phone down on the dresser and hit the speaker button.

"I, um." He cleared his throat. "Sarita sent me a letter and indicated she has already told you I am your—"

"Bio-dad." Jade stripped and selected a seafoam green sundress from her suitcase.

"*Sí.*"

"I wanted to talk to you in person, but it's so like Sarita to …" She dropped the dress over her head, adjusting the spaghetti straps.

"Control the delivery of this information." Marco's voice held an edge.

"I'm glad I got to meet you in Mazatlán, even though we didn't know about our relationship at the time."

"*Sí*, me too." Jade heard him shuffling paper. "I spoke with Officer Vázquez, and he is interested in the undercover assignment in Cabo."

"Oh." She was surprised by the shift in topics. "Great. I can let Detective Cortés know and have her call you to work out the details."

"*Bueno.*" Marco hesitated. "I would like to see you soon so we can—"

"Learn more about each other." Jade finished his sentence.

"*Sí.*" Another pause, then, "Jade, I am very proud of you."

"Thanks, Marco." Jade pinched the bridge of her nose to keep the tears from flowing. "Maybe I can come to Mazatlán for a visit after my assignment in Zihuatanejo."

"That would be *perfecto*," Marco said. "Be safe, and we will talk soon."

Before Jade could respond, the line went dead. She blew out a breath, stepped into her flip flops, and exited the suite. As she headed back to the penthouse, Jade thought about how bizarre learning about her biological parents had been. But now she had answers to questions that had been created by Benson's revelation about her adoption.

"As much as I hate to be the task master," Joy said, clapping her hands as Jade joined the melee. "You need to gather your things, and I'll call for the van."

Jade and Sandrine stood and watched the flurry of activity.

"We did good." Sandrine bumped Jade's shoulder.

"Best team ever." Jade held her hand out and Sandrine slapped her palm.

"Remember that when you're slogging through your next assignment with …" Sandrine laughed and made a circle motion at her, "or should I say *shagging*?"

The partners laughed, but quieted when Novio approached.

"Agent Mendoza," he wiped his hands on his tan shorts, "may I have a word with you?"

"Sure." Jade looked at Sandrine as she walked away.

"I …" Novio squared his shoulders, "I would like your permission to ask Ezmé to marry me."

Jade held Novio's nervous stare for a beat, then said, "You need to ask our dad for Ezmé's hand."

"*Sí,*" Novio nodded, "but I would like your blessing also."

"Here are my conditions." Jade looked across the room at her little sister, smiling and laughing as she shouldered a carry-on bag. "You get and hold a legitimate job for six months, then you can ask her. If she says yes," Jade almost laughed at the fear that flashed in his eyes, "you wait another six months before you get married. Longer, if Ezmé needs more time to plan her dream wedding."

Novio shifted from one foot to the other, waiting as if there were more conditions to come.

"One more thing." Jade stepped close and whispered in his ear. "If you hurt my sister, I will kill you. *¿Entiendes?*"

Novio nodded, then walked away as fast as he could.

"Van's here." Joy said. "Let's go!"

The van driver rubbed the stubble on his chin, then began the daunting task of playing luggage Jenga as he loaded the cargo area. They piled into the van. The four young women sat together, with Novio sitting in between Ezmé and Valéria. They promised they'd stay in touch with Erica via social media, texting, and maybe an annual vacation somewhere other than Puerto Vallarta.

When the airport came into view, Erica began to cry, and Joy handed everyone tissues. The driver found a spot at the curb and began deconstructing his expertly-packed cargo. The Phoenix flight was first, so they gathered in front of the check-in counter.

Jade searched the crowd for Eladio and was shocked when she saw Amado Peña walking toward her.

"What are you doing here?" Jade asked, then saw Detective Cortés following closely on his heels.

"On my way to Cabo." Peña took her hand and led her away from the group. "Isabella has been arrested for killing her boyfriend."

"Oh my God." Jade said. "I'm sure it's a mistake."

"*Sí,*" Peña nodded, "but I must go and help her."

"And you're okay to travel?" Jade could see pain in his eyes.

Dropping his carry-on, Peña whispered, "If I did not have to go," he pulled her into his arms, "I would show you just how okay I am." He kissed her as if they were the only two people in the airport, then studied her face until Jade blushed. "Remember," he touched his lips to her forehead, "I am just a plane ride away."

Before Jade could say goodbye, Peña picked up his bag and strode toward Coco Cortés. As they walked away, Coco turned and looked at Jade as if she were sizing up her competition. Then a swarm of people closed in on Jade and she lost sight of Peña in the crowd. She cast a glance at the check-in counter and saw Ezmé waving at her. Jade rushed to the line as Ezmé ducked under the switchback barriers.

"I'm going to miss you terribly." Jade hugged her little sister.

"I'll miss you too." Ezmé said. "Thank you for coming to my rescue and for—understanding." She searched Jade's eyes.

"You're welcome, sweetie." Jade hugged her again.

Ezmé stepped back to the barrier, but the line had dissipated, so she hurried to the counter. As they headed for their gate, Ezmé, Gwen, and Valéria waved and blew kisses, while Novio just tried to keep up.

"That boy has his work cut out for him." Sandrine hitched her bag higher onto her shoulder. "It's my turn to go, and don't you bloody cry." Tears loomed in the corners of Sandrine's eyes as she hugged Jade.

Jade gave her friend a mock salute as she walked away. Once again, Jade found herself scanning the crowd. She spotted Joy and Erica talking with someone. When she approached, Eladio stepped around her friends and walked toward her.

"How are you holding up?" He put his arm around her shoulder.

Before she could reply, Joy and Erica joined them. "It looks like you have a ride, so we're catching a cab and doing some shopping therapy." Joy took Erica's hand. "We'll see you two back at the hotel."

"Joy." Jade called after them. "Thanks for everything you did today."

Joy gave her a thumbs-up as they headed for the exit.

"Back at the hotel?" Eladio asked.

"Since we have a few days before we leave," Jade began, "I thought you might like a change of scenery."

Eladio responded by kissing her. He took her hand and led the way outside.

"Did you hear about Peña?" she asked as they stepped into bright sunshine.

"I brought him and Detective Cortés to the airport."

Jade stopped, bringing him to a halt. "You?" she searched his eyes, "You were here then?"

"I know you care about each other," Eladio touched her cheek, "and he had a right to tell you goodbye."

Jade nodded and swallowed to clear the lump in her throat. "I don't think Coco Cortés likes me." Jade took Eladio's hand and started toward the parking lot.

It was Eladio's turn to bring them to a stop. "Peña did not tell you?"

"Tell me what?" Jade cocked her head.

"That he, Isabella, and Coco grew up together?"

"No. He said Bella and Coco were like sisters." Confusion muddled her brain at first, then Coco's behavior began to make sense. "Coco's in love with him?"

"I am not sure." Eladio grinned. "But she and Peña were engaged before he moved to Puerto Vallarta."

"Well damn," Jade said. "So, for Coco Cortés, there's more at stake than helping her friend."

"Yes. And the ex-lovers will have their work cut out for them," Eladio slid his sunglasses into place, "since Isabella Fuentes' boyfriend's body was discovered in one of her suitcases."

~THE END ~ 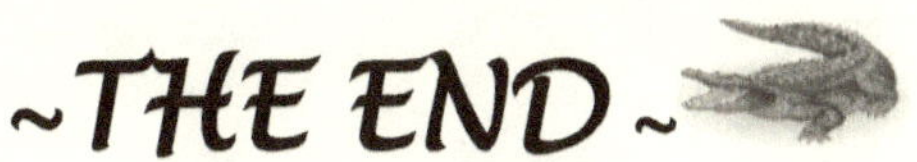

ACKNOWLEDGEMENTS

Though heartfelt, my simple "thank you" seems lacking when acknowledging my team of editors: Sharon North, Story Editor and Joyce Wise, Editor. These women dedicated endless hours helping **VANISHED IN VALLARTA** become a masterful piece of fiction. Every mistake they find or suggestion they offer, help make me a better writer. I'd also like to thank my Beta Readers, Stacy Robinson and Cindy Schmid, who bolstered my confidence with kind words of praise.

DISCLOSURES

My team of editors and readers, including myself, made every effort to ensure this novel is error free. But we're human, so please accept our apologies for any mistakes you may find. Should you uncover errors while enjoying **VANISHED IN VALLARTA**, please feel free to email me at: author.kimilakay.com

ABOUT THE AUTHOR

Kimila Kay lives in Donald, Oregon with her husband, Randy, and a feisty black cat, Halle.

She is currently a member of Northwest Independent Writers Association (NIWA), Ladies of Mystery, Sisters in Crime, Willamette Writers, and Windtree Press.

Vanished in Vallarta is the third book in her cross-cultural series, Mexico Mayhem. The series also includes Peril in Paradise and Malice in Mazatlán. Still planned for the series are Chaos in Cabo (2024), Lost in Loreto, and Fiasco in Peñasco.

Kimila's Stoneybrook Mysteries series currently offers Redneck Ranch, Book One, and Five Golden Rings, Novella/Book Two. Both novels are available on Amazon. Whispering Willows, Novella/Book Three and Willows Woods, Book Four, will both be available in 2024.

You can learn more about Kimila through her blog posts on her website, Ladies of Mystery, and Windtree Press.

CHAOS IN CABO

MÉXICO MAYHEM – BOOK FOUR

CHAPTER ONE

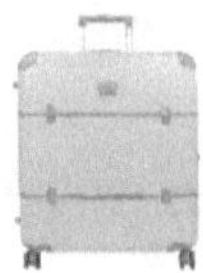

Alida Burton looked at Carlos Morales and a flicker of concern snaked through her gut. This was the first time she'd killed a man who hadn't been a sadistic bastard. He had, however, yelled at his girlfriend, crushed her phone on the sidewalk, and left her crying in front of Los Cabos International Airport, begging him to stay.

But that wasn't her main reason for killing Morales. "He shouldn't have stuck his busy-body nose where it didn't belong."

Alida guzzled some water and contemplated the incompetence of men. The mistakes they made were mind boggling. Of course, if not for one man's stupidity, she might not be alive. She donned a pair of nitrile gloves. The smell of rotten eggs when the gloves touched the hydrogen peroxide cleaner, made her nose twitch. Her mind wandered down memory lane as she wiped down the inside of the suitcase.

Fresh out of business school, Alida tried working a regular job, putting her typing and organizational skills to good use. But there was always one man who thought she needed to be graced with his male prowess. It didn't matter if she declined, the lusty lothario would persist, driving her to quit. She'd move to the next job, where the dreaded dance repeated itself. To ward off unwanted advances, Alida wore ill-fitting clothes, used little makeup, and rarely smiled at anyone. Her efforts only seemed to make her a more desirable target.

Deciding working for herself was the best solution, she set up a home office inside her small Palmdale apartment and offered her services as a bookkeeper. After a year, she'd built a nice clientele. Always looking to make more money, Alida agreed to meet a new customer at his home in the hills north of Los Angeles. It was the worst mistake of her life. A bad decision that sent her down a rabbit hole of anonymity looking for revenge.

What had the first doctor called it after she'd been rescued from her kidnapper—Rape Trauma Syndrome? The next said she suffered from Post Traumatic Stress Disorder, and a third declared she'd had a psychotic break affecting her mental well-being.

After six months in the psychiatric facility, Alida had been deemed fit to return to society. The first thing she did was track down her kidnapper. He woke, naked and standing with his ankles tied to metal stakes protruding from the cement floor of an abandoned warehouse and his hands tied to a beam above his head. He'd spewed vile threats and Alida had done as he had when she'd pleaded with him, she ignored everything he said.

Now, men were intrigued by her stark white hair and what she'd been told was a pretty face. But when they saw the various scars marring her porcelain skin, they recoiled as if she had a disease. She'd lost count of how many abusive, evil men she'd removed from this earth. She had a sixth sense for when it was time to move to a new place, hence how she'd ended up in Cabo San Lucas, México.

"All I'm trying to do is make a living," Alida told Carlos' corpse as she folded his right arm. She grinned at the cracking sound of his bones when she forced the limb to lay above his head at the bottom of the luggage. "But see what you made me do?" She repeated the process with his legs, a slightly more daunting task.

Standing and smiling at her handy work, Alida zipped the metallic pink Gucci suitcase closed, and headed for the door of the vacant building.

CHAPTER TWO

Socorro Cortés watched Amado Peña mop his brow with a paper towel for the third time. Their trip from Puerto Vallarta to Cabo had been uneventful and he'd slept most of the way. They'd stayed at her house last night. Peña had fallen asleep on the bed in one of her guestrooms before she could get him an extra pillow.

Coco had removed his shoes and eased off his pants. She blushed at the familiar sight of his package. Then she'd checked his bandage, the sight of his toned physique raising gooseflesh on her arms. He didn't appear to be bleeding so she covered him with a light blanket, kissed him on the forehead and closed the door.

Now, dressed in clean clothes, he sat at the nook table sipping coffee and staring out at the *Sea of Cortés*.

¿Qué? " He glared at her.

"Should I take you to the hospital?"

"No. You need some decent coffee," he pointed to his mug, "this is too weak."

Coco pulled a pound of dark roast from a cupboard and made a fresh pot. Even though she knew she didn't have a right, she wanted to ask him questions. *Are you in love with Jade Mendoza. Are you in a committed relationship with her? Are you still mad at me for not coming with you to Puerto Vallarta?*

While the coffee brewed, she took a bowl of diced fruit and yogurt from the refrigerator, then plated a buttery *banderilla* for herself.

"When can I see Isabella?" Peña asked from behind her.

His closeness lit a flicker of desire. Coco blew out a breath, then turned. "We are meeting her and her attorney at one." She searched his face. If he felt the same longing she did, he didn't let it show.

"Bien." Peña removed the coffee carafe and sniffed the coffee. "Much better." He carried a fresh cup back to the table and Coco followed.

She took a seat across from him and they sat in silence for a few minutes.

"You have a beautiful home." He reached for her croissant. "Only you live here?"

"The yogurt is for you." Coco took the pastry from him before he could have a bite. "And you can add banana and mango."

"I am not hungry."

"Amado." He raised an eyebrow, but she continued, "Please eat something."

He picked a hunk of mango from the bowl with his fingers and popped it into his mouth.

"Either you have done well for yourself." He looked around the large kitchen, his gaze drifting back through the bay window. "Or you married for money instead of love."

"Can we talk about—"

"No." Peña held up a hand, then plucked another piece of mango from the bowl. "Tell me more about Isabella's boyfriend."

Coco picked up the croissant, slathered it with butter, then took a large bite. She held his dark stare as she chewed. *Fine,* she thought, *he doesn't want to talk about their past. His decision to leave for Puerto Vallarta. Her choice to stay in Cabo. And subsequently, the end of— everything.* Well, obviously he was still angry and thought she was a bitch so she might as well act the part.

"His limbs were broken and twisted until he fit into the suitcase. The case was large, but whoever crammed him inside has strength."

"How was he killed?" Peña took a sip of coffee.

Coco pulled apart the pastry, then laid a piece on her tongue and licked her fingers. "The tox screen is not back yet. He was probably drugged, then his neck was broken."

"And he was investigating the US Customs Border Patrol scam crew?" Peña popped a slice of banana into his mouth.

"*Sí.*" Coco walked to the counter and grabbed the coffee carafe. She refilled her cup, topped off Pena's and sat the glass pot onto a trivet. "What puzzles me is why someone would kill him, then stuff him into Isabella's suitcase?"

"He discovered something that could bring down the fake CBP crew and they are sending a message?" Pena frowned. "Is it possible Isabella is in danger."

"I requested she be placed in a holding cell by herself, so she is fine for now."

"Do you think whoever killed Carlos is the same person committing the other murders?" He drank some coffee.

"Maybe." Coco shrugged. "I have only been working the scam investigation for a few weeks." She finished her croissant. "The murders belong to another detective." Coco tipped her mug to her lips. "We do not have a good working relationship." She didn't see any point in mentioning she'd dated Javier Perez and things hadn't ended well.

Peña raised an eyebrow. "Do you think he will talk to me?"

"I can ask." Coco looked at her phone. "I should take a shower." She stood and carried her cup to the sink. "Do you need anything?" She leaned across him, picking up the bowl of fruit and yogurt container. Her breasts brushed his shoulder.

"No." Peña came to his feet. "I will check in with Officers Herrera and Vázquez to see if they have made their travel plans."

He held her stare. She thought a whisp of her young Amado flashed in his dark eyes. Coco stepped close to him and gathered the carafe. She set the pot back into the coffee maker. Placing the end of a second croissant into her mouth, she headed from the kitchen.

When she turned to see if he watched her, she was pleased to see Amado Peña standing, hands on hips, staring at her. Coco knew she'd broken his heart. Now that he was back in her life, though, she hoped she could rekindle their love and make him forget Jade Mendoza.

CHAPTER THREE

Amado Peña wanted to be anywhere but in Socorro Cortés' mansion. *How does the girl from his younger days become an accomplished detective, own a home big enough for a family of five, and be more beautiful than the day he left?*

He poured out his coffee and opened a cupboard looking for something stronger. When he tried to reach the top shelf, he felt his stitches pull.

He cringed with a wave of pain. *"Maldita sea!"*

Peña lifted his linen shirt and looked at the bandage over the surgery wound, thankful there was no blood. He aborted his hunt and decided to explore Coco's ridiculously big house.

As he took himself on a self-guided tour, he texted Geovany.

Pena: *When do you arrive?*

Geovany: *Monday*

Pena: *¿Vázquez too?*

Geovany: *Sí*

Pena: *Bueno. Text your arrival time.*

Geovany: *Copia*

Pina wandered from the kitchen, into a formal dining room with entrances at each end of a wall decorated with pictures of Cabo. He stepped close and recognized a black and white shot of a young couple. The couple waded into the surf, with the man holding the woman in his arms. It was one of the last pictures Isabella had taken of him and Coco.

He could almost taste Coco's salty lips from the ocean as the memory of that day on Lover's Beach washed over him.

"Come sit with me." Amado had taken Coco's hand and pulled her down onto their blanket lying on the sand. He'd kissed her and swept her damp hair from her face.

"Are you done surfing for the day?" Coco reached into the cooler, plucking two *Pacíficos* from their icy bath. She popped the tops off with a Bic lighter, then handed him one.

"*Sí.*" He took a long pull, then stuck the bottle in the sand and came to his knees. Amado ran a hand through his wet hair and smiled at Coco.

"Are you okay?" she tilted her head.

"Socorro Cortés." He took both of her hands in his. "I would—"

She rose onto her knees too. "Amado?"

He took a small box from under the blanket. "*¿Te quieres casar conmigo?*" A small diamond in a simple setting winked at them when he opened the box.

"*¡Sí!*" Coco threw her arms around his neck and they both fell back onto the beach. She kissed him then said, "Yes, I will marry you."

When she'd let him up off the sand, Amado had placed the ring on her finger and helped her stand.

"Thank God." Isabella laughed. "My uncle was sure you would say no."

"She said yes!" Amado wrapped his arms around his fiancée and kissed her. He swept her up into his arms and carried her toward the bay.

He hadn't known until he was at the airport ready to board his plane for Puerto Vallarta that Isabella had taken the picture. She'd tried to give him the framed photo as a goodbye gift.

Peña touched the photo on Coco's wall of the two young lovers, then marched from the dining room. When he stepped into the next room, he spotted a bar and made a beeline for a well-stocked liquor counter.

Searching the selection until he found a bottle of *Hornitos*, Amado hadn't noticed that the bar top was his old surfboard. He placed a crystal shot glass on top of the scarred, shellacked board and poured tequila to the rim. He tossed down the shot, poured another, then ran a hand across the board. When he reached the tail, he looked underneath and touched the fin where Coco had signed her name as, *La Futura Señora Peña*.

Amado rounded the bar and took in the stools, each one featuring a round seat cut from an old board. He sat on a stool and lifted his glass in toast. "You can take the surfer girl and make her a detective, but you cannot take the surf out of the girl."

"I knew you would find the tequila on your own," Coco said behind him.

Amado tipped his glass and took a sip. She walked around the bar and stood in front of him. Coco looked beautiful in a white blouse and black pants. She had pulled her dark hair into a bun at the nape of her neck.

Coco opened a bottle of water and took a drink. "I know you are to stick to a soft diet for a few more days, but I do not think tequila is the sustenance you need."

"Are you ready to leave?" Amado finished the shot, then headed toward the bedroom he'd stayed in.

"Amado." Coco followed him. "We might as well be civil since you are staying here, and we will both need to help Bella."

He grabbed his phone off the nightstand where he'd put the framed picture Jade had given him. "I will find somewhere else to stay after we meet with Bella."

Amado Pena might have to work his niece's case with his ex-fiancée, but he didn't have to stay in her house. Stay close enough to smell her citrusy perfume. Stay within arm's length and not be able to touch her.

CHAPTER FOUR

Alida balanced a shopping bag on top of a box of pastries. She punched in the security code at her new call center. Cameras had picked up an image of Carlos Morales trying to break into the rundown building. Alida knew she'd not only have to dispatch with the podcaster, but she'd also need to move her enterprise to a new facility.

The house she'd rented was perfect since it was owned by a woman who was almost as paranoid as Alida. Cameras rimmed the outside roofline. A security system had been installed and the front door featured a ring doorbell. The cream-colored stucco home also sat at the end of a dead end street next to a collection of cell towers. Another bonus was a large master suite on the top floor, which Alida had claimed for herself.

"Buenos días," Antonio Ruiz greeted her.

"Morning." Despite living in Mexico for almost six months, Alida hadn't bothered to learn Spanish.

"I have new workers coming in an hour." Antonio turned his attention back to a laptop.

"And they all speak English?" Alida set the bag of supplies on the credenza that served as a coffee bar. She placed the box next to the pot and lifted the lid.

"Yes." Antonio replied and she was pleased he did so in English.

Alida looked around what should be a living room at the small desks and chairs. Each station had a stack of notepads, cup with pens, and three burner phones. When she'd opened her first call center, Alida had done all the heavy lifting required to spoof the numbers she used to call individuals, but that task now fell to Antonio. He was also responsible for training staff and purchasing the necessary equipment and software to run the office.

"Jefa." Antonio stood and walked toward her, a look of chagrin on his face when she glared at him.

"Antonio." Alida faced him, hands on hips. "I don't mind if you call me Boss, as long as you use English."

"My apologies, Boss." Antonio nodded. "I receive new list from dark web for workers to start calling today."

"Good." Alida perused the assortment of pastries, selecting a chocolate *concha* roll. "And you have the script ready?"

"Yes." Antonio glanced at the donuts. "And I will have them practice before they make calls."

"All right." Alida poured coffee into her favorite mug, grabbed a napkin, and headed for the dining room. "I'm going to go over the budget."

She pushed through the swinging door she'd had Antonio install to separate the two rooms. Alida was pleased she'd hired Antonio and glad they'd met when she first arrived. She set her cup and roll onto her desk. The memory of their initial encounter ran through her mind as she opened her laptop.

"What can I serve you?" Antonio had asked from behind the bar at *Bebidas de Playa.* The quaint taco restaurant sat on the sand near the surf.

"What's your best whiskey?" Alida asked.

"No whiskey." Antonio cocked an eyebrow. He held up a finger and ducked inside the small restaurant. "Try this." He poured her a shot.

Alida held the small glass to her nose, inhaling a hint of oak and vanilla, then took a sip. "Very nice." She smiled at him.

He returned her smile. "Eating?" He held a menu.

"Yes." Alida took the menu. As she looked at the variety of tacos, a surly looking man appeared next to Antonio. The young man shrank away as if he expected to be hit.

"I'd like the pork tacos," Alida said, and the man glanced at her. "Also, can I try another good tequila."

Despite the man's original intent, Alida recognized the look of someone who would rather make money, than berate staff in front of a customer.

"Nos vemos después del trabajo." The man smiled at Alida, and a familiar sense of revulsion raised the hair at the nape of her neck.

Antonio set another shot in front of her, but his jovial demeanor was gone. He set to the task of washing dishes and Alida sipped the tequila.

"What does your boss want?" Alida met Antonio's wary stare.

"To talk after work." He rinsed a sink full of clean glasses and stacked them onto a towel.

"What's your name?" Alida asked as her tacos were delivered by a young woman in a dirty apron.

"Antonio." He placed silverware and a napkin next to her plate.

"Nice to meet you, Antonio." She extended her hand. "What time are you off?"

Antonio hesitated, then grasped her hand with a quick shake. "Seven."

Alida noticed a scar between his thumb and forefinger. Though she couldn't know for sure, she assumed he'd had a gang or cartel tattoo removed from his hand.

She ate the delicious tacos, watching Antonio as he waited on an already drunk young couple who ordered margaritas. Though she didn't care for the second tequila, she drank the shot anyway, then waved at Antonio.

"Would you like more?" He pointed to her empty shot glasses.

"No." She pushed her plate forward. "Everything was very good. What is the name of the first tequila?"

"Patrón Anjeo." He showed her the bottle and laid a bill on the bar.

Alida looked at the paltry amount she owed for her meal and drinks. She placed a twenty dollar bill next to the empty plate. When Antonio reached to pick up the cash, she touched his hand and he looked at her.

She handed him another twenty. "Meet me at the Monkey Cave Bar after your shift."

The ringing doorbell evaporated the memory. Alida focused on the chatter coming from the living room. Antonio greeted everyone by their first name. He offered them coffee and pastries, then instructed them to take a seat until it was time to begin.

When you're someone constantly on the run, it's easy to recognize the same flight instinct in others. Alida had offered Antonio a job and never asked what he was trying to escape because it didn't matter. What mattered was that her office manager had his own demons, which would keep him from being concerned about hers.

CHAPTER FIVE

Coco's cheeks burned hot as she led the way to the garage. Amado followed while he texted someone. She knew she was the reason their relationship ended. Still, she'd hoped once they were brought together due to Isabella's predicament, maybe they could start over. When an image of Amado and Jade Mendoza frolicking between the sheets flashed in her mind, her cheeks warmed further.

She almost swore out loud as she punched a code into the alarm panel, opened the door, and stepped into the garage. Amado walked past her to stand between her two vehicles.

"I am guessing you are no better driver now than you were three years ago." He pointed at the dark blue Porsche 911. "So, I am not riding in that death trap."

Coco opened the driver's door of her gray Jeep Rubicon and climbed behind the wheel without replying. She pushed the garage door button on the panel above her head and pulled her black sunglasses from their compartment. Amado sat in the passenger seat and secured his seatbelt. Placing the shades on top of her head, she backed out of the garage. Another push of the button lowered the door and she headed for the side street that led from the *Pedregal* district toward the ocean.

Coco lowered the sunglasses and glanced at Amado. She remembered the taste of coconut on his lips from his favorite ChapStick the last time he kissed her.

He stared out his open window, the sweet scent of oleander flowing into the Jeep. *Did memories of their childhood roaming the cobblestone streets fill his mind? Did he think about picnicking in the open fields while enjoying the spectacular views of the bay? Did he remember their first time making love close to a cliff with the pounding surf serenading them from below?*

"Do you know this *abogado*?" He looked at her.

"I have worked with him before." She slowed for a sharp corner. "He is a very good defense attorney."

"Is the suitcase the only evidence linking Bella to the body?" Amado's phone dinged and he checked the screen.

"One of the officers coming to Cabo?" Coco asked to avoid answering his question.

Isabella hadn't said she was sleeping with Carlos. But Coco assumed she'd had sex with him before he was killed, leaving behind biologicals.

"They will be here Monday night." He finished his text and looked at her. "You did not answer my question."

"You have been *policía* for six years, so I know you have already been through the list of possible evidence in your mind." Coco cut her eyes to him and thought she saw another glimpse of the boy she'd fallen in love with.

They reached the highway that would take them to the station and Amado had turned his attention to the scenery beyond the window.

"I can recommend a hotel near the marina." Coco jumped on the breaks when traffic came to an abrupt halt.

"*¡Mierda!*" Amado braced himself against the dashboard. "I knew your driving did not improve."

"There is nothing wrong with my driving!" Coco hit the horn. "You are what is wrong! I should have never told you about your niece and helped Bella myself."

"I am what is wrong?" Amado yelled. "That is rich coming from you!"

Coco yanked the steering wheel and ran the Jeep up onto a sidewalk. She cut across a side street, stopping in a dirt lot. She jammed the gear lever into park and climbed out. Amado had exited on his side and raced around the back of the Jeep.

Coco slapped him across the face, and he stumbled back a step.

"*¡Perra!*"

"Bitch?" Coco reloaded for another slap, but he caught her wrist before she could make contact.

"Do not hit me again." Amado glared at her.

"I have been nothing but polite since I stepped into your hospital room." Coco headed back to the driver's door. "You are just pissed because you had to give up a piece of ass to come to the aid of your niece!"

"Do not." Amado grabbed her arm and spun her around. "Speak about Jade that way."

Coco jerked her arm free and jammed her hands onto her hips. "How about if we do not speak to each other at all?"

She wrenched the door open, climbed in and fired up the engine. The Jeep spewed dirt and gravel as she sped away, leaving Amado Peña watching her through a cloud of dust.

CHAPTER SIX

Peña took a cab to the station and by the time he arrived his anger had dissipated; an old wound had been reopened. Even though three years had passed since Socorro Cortés let him board a plane to Puerto Vallarta alone, he still felt the pain of her abandonment as if it were yesterday.

He'd lied to Coco about the text he received. Jade's text said Ortiz had been successful in having Mark Roberts charged with his wife's murder despite being unable to find her body. She'd ended with the news that she and Ortiz were headed to Zihuatanejo on Monday. He wondered what might have happened between himself and Jade if they'd been able to stay in Puerto Vallarta.

The cab stopped at the curb in front of the station and Peña hopped out. He paid the driver the fare, plus a generous tip since he'd given him a bottle of water. Peña walked through a plain lobby to a counter and pressed a buzzer.

"Lieutenant Peña?" a voice said behind him.

He turned and nodded at a young officer. *"Sí."*

"Por favor, sígueme." He headed for a door, held it open for Peña, then continued down the hallway.

Peña followed him until he stopped at a closed door and knocked. The door opened and the officer motioned for Peña to enter. He stepped inside and Isabella ran into his arms, her familiar jasmine perfume wafting over him.

"*Tío*, thank you for coming to save me!" She looked at him and he could tell she'd been crying.

A tall, Hispanic man stood and extended his hand. "Alejandro Ortega."

"Amado Peña." He shook the attorney's hand.

Coco sat at the table for four with her arms crossed and a scowl on her face. Isabella sat next to Coco and Alejandro resumed his seat across from her. Peña sat opposite Coco.

"I was just telling Detective Cortés and *Señorita* Fuentes I believe a judge will release Isabella on bail given the limited evidence the *policía* have."

"Is all they have the suitcase?" Peña asked.

"For now." Alejandro checked his notes. "At first glance, the suitcase appears to have been wiped clean. Other than the victim's, there has been no other discernible DNA. The only thing linking the suitcase to Isabella, is the name plate attached inside."

"And I was not even in Cabo." Isabella began to cry, and Coco put her arm around her shoulders. "*Tío*, please speak with someone and ask if I can go home with you." She reached across the table, which caused Coco to meet his eyes.

Peña held Coco's stare for a beat, then looked at Bella. "I believe Detective Cortés would be the better person to ask about your release."

"Detective Cortés," Alejandro said. "Do you think you can get approval for Isabella to be released into your custody?"

"Maybe," Coco continued, "Captain Rivera will let her stay with me if she wears an ankle monitor?"

"I know bond has not been set," Alejandro said. "But you could also offer something as collateral."

"I can sign over my villa if that helps," Bella added.

"I will," Coco stood, and Peña came to his feet too, "go alone to see if Captain Rivera is here and if he will come and entertain our proposal."

Peña frowned at Coco but didn't attempt to follow her from the room. He rounded the table and sat down next to his niece. "Bella where were you that Coco could not find you?"

"As I told her." Bella started to cry. "Carlos and I had a fight." Alejandro handed her a white handkerchief. "He-he said I could not go with him. That I should go home." She shook her head. "I told him I would call Coco to see if she could help him with his investigation." A wave a sobs stole her words and Peña drew her into his arms.

"You do not have to tell me anymore." He smoothed her wavy dark hair with a hand.

"I want to." Bella sat taller. "He took my phone and smashed it so I could not call anyone." She blew her nose and mopped tears from her face. "I took a cab and checked into the San Jose del Cabo Hilton." A small sob, then she continued, "It is our hotel and I thought he would come looking for me there."

The door opened and Coco walked in followed by an older man. He wore blue pants and a white, long sleeved shirt. Badges of his rank had been sewn on the shirt.

"Captain Rivera, this is my friend, Isabella Fuentes." Coco looked at the *abogado*. "Her attorney, Alejandro Ortega and uncle, Lieutenant Amado Peña from Puerto Vallarta."

"Buenas tardes," Captain Rivera said. "Detective Cortés has explained your situation, *Señorita* Fuentes. I am comfortable releasing you into hers and your uncle's custody." He waved forward an officer who'd been standing in the hall. "You will need to wear an ankle monitor until you can be arraigned on Monday." He looked from Coco to Peña and continued, "And I expect one of you to be with her at all times. *¿Entender?*

"Sí, Capitán." Coco and Peña chimed.

"Once the monitor is in place you can sign for your belongings and leave." Captain Rivera headed for the door, then turned. "Do not make me regret this decision." He gave a slight nod and exited the room.

As the ankle monitor was secured around Bella's ankle, Alejandro said, "It is encouraging that the captain has released you." He gathered his notes and stuffed them into a briefcase. "It may mean he does not think you should have been arrested in the first place."

Peña waited as Bella collected her things. Coco thanked Alejandro, then the trio made their way to Coco's Jeep.

"The ankle bracelet is heavy," Bella whined.

"Isabella Fuentes, I swear if you complain about the damn monitor, I am going to return you to jail." Coco beeped the door locks open.

"Do not be cross with Bella because you are angry at me," Peña barked.

"Did you find a hotel?" Coco sat behind the wheel.

"You heard Captain Rivera …" Peña opened the back passenger door for his niece and helped her into her seat. "We are to be with her at all times." He glared at her as he climbed inside.

"You two want to tell me what the hell is going on?" Bella leaned between their seats.

"No!" The ex-lovers said in unison.

Coco pulled out of the parking lot and merged into heavy afternoon traffic. His phone dinged and he smiled at a text from Jade.

Jade: *Nacho and his family arrive Tuesday.*

Peña: *Copia*

Jade: *Hope things are going well with Bella … and Coco.*

Peña wanted to frown at the text but smiled instead. He hadn't realized Coco had told Ortiz about their past, which meant Jade also knew their story. Peña tell her he and Socorro Cortés were just old friends, but he knew Jade wouldn't believe him.

"Text from your young lover?" Coco swerved around a city bus.

"*Sí.*" Peña resisted the urge to palm the dash.

"Lover?" Bella tapped him on the shoulder. "You did not tell me you were seeing someone."

Coco tailgated a cab and then darted around the car almost colliding with a van. "Your *tío* is *dating* someone younger than you."

"Jesus, Coco!" Peña finally grabbed the support bar above his window. "I am only three years older than Bella and two years older than you."

"How much younger?" Bella asked.

"Enough!" Peña yelled. "My love life is not either of your business."

"Sorry, *Tío*." Bella leaned back in her seat.

Peña waited for an apology from Coco even though he knew one wasn't coming. She hadn't apologized when she decided to stay in Cabo. She didn't say she was sorry for not joining him in Puerto Vallarta. And there'd been no note expressing her regret when she'd mailed him her engagement ring.

CHAOS IN CABO WILL BE AVAILABLE FALL OF 2024